THE
SECRET
AT
No. 4

T0050063

THE SECRET AT No.4

S. L. McMANUS

HarperCollins*Publishers*

HarperNorth
Windmill Green
24 Mount Street
Manchester M2 3NX

A division of
HarperCollins*Publishers*
1 London Bridge Street
London SE1 9GF

www.harpercollins.co.uk

HarperCollinsPublishers
Macken House
39/40 Mayor Street Upper
Dublin 1
D01 C9W8

First published by HarperNorth in 2023

1 3 5 7 9 10 8 6 4 2

Copyright © S.L. McManus 2023

S. L. McManus asserts the moral right to
be identified as the author of this work

A catalogue record for this book
is available from the British Library

ISBN: 978-0-00-855385-2

Printed and bound in Great Britain by
CPI Group (UK) Ltd, Croydon

This novel is entirely a work of fiction.
The names, characters and incidents portrayed in it are
the work of the author's imagination. Any resemblance to
actual persons, living or dead, events or localities is
entirely coincidental.

All rights reserved. No part of this publication may be
reproduced, stored in a retrieval system, or transmitted,
in any form or by any means, electronic, mechanical,
photocopying, recording or otherwise, without the prior
permission of the publishers.

This book is produced from independently certified FSC™ paper
to ensure responsible forest management.

For more information visit: www.harpercollins.co.uk/green

For all the women who inspired me

DAY ONE

Prologue
Ruth

Flashing lights swirl into the black.

There is a body on the pavement.

A mother is screaming.

My phone vibrates in my back pocket and I turn away from the scene. Reluctantly, slowly, because it is hard to tear my eyes away. I take a step back from the crowd pressing up against the police tape and tuck my notebook underneath my arm.

I look at the screen, my heart sinking.

It's Tom. My boss.

'Hello?' I yell over the sound of more approaching sirens, blue lights dancing in the puddles, one finger plugged in my ear. I'm hoping he won't realise I'm out chasing crime leads, exactly as he's told me I shouldn't.

'Ruth, you're from Manchester, right?'

'Yes?'

'You ever hear of someone called Henry Carr? Bloke went missing fifteen years ago; no one's seen or heard from him since.'

I pause. I feel my body respond to the name and I walk further away from the chaos behind me, squeezing between bustling shoulders.

'I know the case,' I say carefully.

'Great. Big chance of a development in it – I've got a contact in the force over there who says they've got a new lead. And it's all over social media right now because of some cold case podcast digging into it. I figure, since you've got a connection, maybe you can head down to Manchester and start turning over rocks. It's the kind of story you've always wanted, isn't it?'

I step into an alleyway to shelter from the crowds that are continuing to gather and turn the idea over in my mind. I think of Manchester, of home, and my mouth turns dry. I don't know if I can go back, especially if it's to look into the Henry Carr case.

It's too close to home. Far closer than Tom can ever know.

I swallow but my throat is sticking.

'You'd have five days to get a story together, just in time for the anniversary of his disappearance. I want to go live with it then, so you'd be on a tight deadline, Ruth. This could be a big break for you,' Tom says, sensing my hesitation.

I watch a group of drunk men stumble by, and consider this for a moment.

It *could* be a big break.

Reporting on crime is the dream for me; up to now, Tom's mainly left me to cover missing cats and fly-tipping.

I feel a lurch of something: excitement, anxiety? Could I actually do it? Go back to Manchester? Interview people about Henry Carr? Five days seems no time at all to uncover fifteen years of mystery.

'I really feel you're the best man for the job,' Tom says, his voice wheedling. 'Well, woman.'

I smile, let it fall again. The thing is, I *am* the best woman for the job. He doesn't even know it – no one knows it, because I never talk about it.

I can't.

But yes, I know the Carr case. Because I knew Henry Carr.

I grew up across the street from his house.

The house he vanished from fifteen years ago.

DAY TWO

1
Ruth

It's Sunday morning and the sky leading to Manchester has split itself in two. The carriage groans and sways, lulling its passengers into quiet. I take a mouthful of cold coffee and grimace, pushing my earphones in. After the phone call with Tom, I went straight back to my flat and was up all night, tossing and turning. Dreams of Henry Carr punctured holes in my sleep and by 4 a.m. I had given up entirely and trudged into the living room, spending the rest of the early morning trawling the internet for more information about the disappearance. It made me feel connected to something I hadn't for a long time.

Home.

The train is crammed full, and despite an autumn chill clinging to the air outside, inside the carriage is humid and heavy. I glance down at my duffel bag, my only commitment to coming back. It was as small as I could manage, a symbol of my reluctance to stay for too long. I feel in my jacket pocket for the plastic key chain. Running my thumb over the picture I feel comforted, knowing I have Mum close. I wonder what she'd think of this, what she would have said. She hated gossip, hated rumours, and I know she would tell me to tread gently, to think twice before making judgements on the people she called friends.

I will, I think. *I'll try.*

Picking my phone up from the table, I type into the search bar: #HenryCarrDisappearance. Thousands of results emerge. I sit up straighter in my seat, untangling my legs. It feels important to find out from an objective perspective exactly what has gone on, what people know. Or *think* they know. Not just what I remember from living in the house opposite.

I pause.

I grew up opposite the home of a man who disappeared and never returned. I consider this for a moment. Of course, I knew about it at the time; I knew him, and for a while the whole street had whispered of little else. Children had gathered, attempted their own searches, and had come up with their own explanations. The man who vanished.

Then, it was just part of the life I knew. It all seems so sinister now.

The thing that interests me most is the renewed obsession over it on social media. It isn't just the UK, *it's global*. It looks like a true-crime podcast started it all off. I can't help but smile at the idea of our tiny insignificant Crow Street making headlines around the world. The podcaster has clearly been researching unsolved crimes in the UK and somehow found the Henry Carr case. I click on the podcast with 1.2 million views and turn up the volume. The podcaster's voice is low and urgent. Her accent is thick New Jersey.

'Morning you guys! It's Rosa here, back with another episode of *True Crime Revisited*. There's a case that has been perplexing me for weeks, and it took place in a city in the north-west of England: Manchester.'

I feel myself tense at the dramatisation; it makes it all seem fictional and cheap. Especially the description of Manchester. She makes it sound like a war zone, poverty stricken, grim. It's the description of the north made by everyone who never bothers to visit it. I take another sip of coffee and observe the man sitting opposite me. He's wearing a sharp suit and is holding a newspaper sturdily in front of him.

I catch sight of an article, just beside the main headline.

Henry Carr disappearance case reopened as fifteen-year anniversary approaches

I feel a twist of anxiety in my gut. Someone has picked up on the story already. It was naïve of me to think I'd be the first to report on it, but I can't help feeling a sense of pressure. Like we are all clambering to get a snippet before one another. That's how cut-throat the industry is. You have to fight for the story.

I exhale slowly. It's probably just a vague description of the case and a lingering question about why it has been reopened. They won't have found anything out – the street does not talk. I genuinely believe that only someone from the inside can find the answers, can make the residents talk about what they've seen and heard. The bolded name of Henry Carr stirs a discomfort in me, seeing it there in print with a picture of the street I haven't seen for almost seven years. My breath catches a little in my throat. I still remember like it was yesterday. The chaos when Henry vanished. The police, the media. Now here I am, the press myself. I try to ignore the newspaper and instead focus back on the podcast. In a way it's easier to hear it from someone so far away, someone detached and objective. I turn the volume up and settle in.

'Now, the case centres around the disappearance of 34-year-old Henry Carr. Henry was an office worker from a suburb on the outskirts of Manchester. By all accounts, he was a pretty solitary figure, only one known conviction for theft in his teenage years, but generally someone who kept his head down. He had fallen onto hard times and was living with his parents, Patrick and Marianne Carr. You'll need to remember those names, since theory number one puts them right in the frame.'

I clench my jaw at the accusation. I still remember Patrick and Marianne, Henry's doting parents, now frail and elderly.

They are grieving parents, not murderers. Aren't they? I anxiously bite down on the Polo between my teeth as the woman continues to talk.

'Henry Carr disappeared fifteen years ago and has never been seen since. He didn't show up to work on the day of the disappearance. Reports state he left pretty much everything behind, almost as if he never planned to go anywhere at all. The last confirmed earwitness places Henry outside his own house on the afternoon he vanished. This neighbour overheard an argument in the street, and then no one saw him again. The police checked CCTV around the area, but nobody came or left in that time, except for those already living on Crow Street. This led police to suspect that whatever happened to Henry happened right there, and was perpetrated by someone close by. Murder? That seems obvious here. The question of motive is a harder one to answer, and the whereabouts of a body even more so. Despite lengthy investigations, no one has ever been charged with any crime in relation to Henry's disappearance. Yet the important thing here is that while Patrick and Marianne Carr have always appeared to be grieving and distraught parents, Patrick himself was initially arrested as a suspect.'

I inhale the cold sludgy remains of my coffee and cough until tears stream down my face. The man opposite lowers his newspaper.

'You all right?' he asks, concerned.

I nod fervently and wipe the tears with the cuff of my jumper.

Patrick as the main suspect?

I definitely don't remember that.

'Patrick Carr was questioned overnight, though without enough physical evidence to charge him, the police were forced to let him go. So why arrest him in the first place? This is where it gets weird. A preliminary search of the house found nothing untoward. Yet a second search was called after some suspicious behaviour was exhibited by Patrick and his wife Marianne, who has mental health problems. Marianne reportedly spent hours screaming about 'a body in the house' and that the 'killer was among them' – completely horror-movie stuff. The second search found a sweater belonging to Patrick, suspiciously placed in the attic. But why was it hidden? Because it was stained with Henry's blood. However, the forensics team only found minimal stains, barely enough to lead anyone to speculate where it might have come from. There was no evidence that Patrick wore those clothes on the day of the disappearance, and Patrick reportedly explained it by saying Henry had suffered a nose bleed as "he often did". Sounding convincing yet? Nope. Thought not.'

I hit pause and pull out the earphones. That isn't what I remember at all. Patrick was the patriarch of the street, the stoic father, the loyal neighbour. Henry was his only son, his pride and joy: why would he want to harm him? I slouch back into my seat and push my knuckles into my eyes, colours exploding. Could I have romanticised my memory of the Carrs? But out of what? Sympathy? Forgetfulness? My mind flickers through snippets of memories, words and smiles and moments that build up a picture. I can't remember any friction between them, no uncomfortable expressions or stern words. Henry himself had been a presence in my life since I could walk and talk. He was like an uncle, lifting me on his shoulders, slipping me pocket money, making jokes that made me roll my eyes, only for him to stick his tongue out and laugh. Then just like that, he was gone.

I agreed to this story for a reason. It's not just because of the reporting opportunity, or because I'm a local that people might trust, I realise. It's to resolve something in myself, about Henry, about the street. But I have a sinking feeling in the pit of my stomach at the thought of the deadline. Five days. I open my eyes and adjust to the light, blinking slowly before putting my earphones back in and hitting play.

'But that's not the only strange thing about this case. It gets more mysterious. So just for context, the street Henry lived on is secluded, pretty tight-knit you might say. You'd expect such a street, where Henry was born and grew up, to have an outpouring of emotion at his disappearance, to give statements, to plead to the public for help and tell the police anything at all that might help their investigation. Right? Wrong. After the initial interviews, not one resident of the street said a word. There was a complete media blackout, no interviews, no statements, nothing. For fifteen years, there's been a conspiracy of silence. We're talking about a small, intimate street where a man vanished outside his own front door, and all that remains is a big, silent question mark. Surely if an outsider came to your street and killed a man, made him vanish without a trace, you'd be concerned. So concerned, in fact, that you'd raise a public outcry for the case to be solved – if only to protect your own family, to protect yourself. Yet *silence*. Someone must know something, but no one's talking. So, my true-crime fans, that leads us to ask the why? What are they covering up? Who are they protecting? What do they know?'

There are thousands of comments beneath the episode link, filled with theories, wild claims, even abuse directed towards those who live on the street. I can't help scrolling through them, shaking my head or gritting my teeth at the particularly vicious ones. I feel fiercely protective of Crow Street, even if it doesn't feel quite like home any longer. At age 10 I hadn't noticed a deliberate silence, only an unnatural heaviness. I can still remember watching from the upstairs window as the police hovered around like wasps, their fluorescent jackets stark against the grey skies. They went door to door, extracted what they could while understanding little about the people they got it from.

Something in the podcast struck a point that has never made any sense to me.

The last witness to hear Henry alive.

There were claims of an argument, but no details of who was arguing, or what it may have been about. I pull up the internet on my phone and try to find an answer as to who the argument might have been with, but to no avail. Either the witness didn't know, or the police didn't want to reveal that information. Either way, it's a blank for now. I let my head fall back against the seat, my thoughts pressing themselves into a headache. It isn't just the complexity of the case that weighs heavy on me, but how personal it all feels. As though I am by association being branded a conspirator.

I'm glad Tom has given me the case, I really am. No one else can do this right. No one else can end fifteen years of silence, except for someone on the inside, someone who was part of it. But the ever-present blend of guilt and anxiety rises in my throat. I left Dad alone, vanished as soon as school ended, and I never looked back. Even now, I type out a message three times before deleting it. I can't bring myself to tell him I'm coming back. Partly because I need coming home to be about *me*, dealing with the wounds I left gaping open; I don't think I can deal with his emotions too, and I feel selfish just thinking it. And partly because there's a distance between us that we have never been able to bridge, not since Mum died. It has meant fleeting Christmas cards, brief voicemails, promises of visits and conversations that have no substance. Sometimes I think about him, home alone, drinking himself into oblivion. I wonder how often he thinks of us, the two members of his family he's lost.

* * *

I rifle through the duffel bag by my feet, pulling out my reporter's notebook and pen. I know how clichéd I must look and laugh at myself as I flip over the cover. I sort of hate the traditionalist in me, but I start a list anyway.

My first priority is finding out what has led to the reopening of the case. Tom had been vague about the tip-off, but he had a hunch something big was going to be revealed. I make a note to interview the Carrs first. I want to ask Patrick about the arrest, to gauge his reaction. It feels wrong to me that he's a suspect, much less the only suspect, but I feel a duty to be honest about the history of the case. I need to get talking to someone involved in the investigation, and scribble a reminder to call Tom for the contacts of the officer he knows on the inside. I need to find out what fresh evidence they have to reopen the case, who their suspects might be, and who the last person to hear Henry alive was. That all feels easy. The difficult bit will be getting the rest of the street to talk. I can imagine it now, doors slammed in my face, scowls in the corner shop. It makes my throat constrict to think about it. It's one aspect of the job I'm still working on – the thick skin. It's overwhelming, scarily so, and I'm glad to lose myself in the grey and endless sky for half an hour longer.

It takes a long time to get from Newcastle to Manchester: that is one benefit of the awful northern train system. Time to think. It's nine o'clock in the morning when the train pulls up alongside the city, the rain becoming slanted lines that hang on everyone and everything. On the platform, I stand momentarily, watching the crowds disperse and the overhead boards flicker. I inhale, exhale, in an effort to compose myself, to settle the flutter of my heart as I recognise the land and the accents around me. Home and yet home no longer.

The walk to Crow Street is twenty minutes, though I drag it out. The roads home linger in my memory and in my feet as I cut through alleyways and fields without thinking. I see the Victorian brick of my old comprehensive and the steamed-up windows of the café where I worked weekends. I follow the canal and cut off early to take the longer way around. This part of town looks stranded, almost as if it's been left to rot. Like a plaster peeling away, the ugly wound beneath exposed. The majority of homes here are council houses, lined up together in a square block. I keep my head down as I pass the corner shop I'd run to as a child on hot summer days. The sign is cracked with age and some of the lettering has flaked off.

My eyes drift to the Beehive opposite. The pub looks decrepit now, faded St George bunting slung across its front. I remember the street parties hosted there, the call of songs in the early hours, the feeling of family as we all crammed together into stained booths, clinking glasses and laughing until our throats were raw. It is the hub of this place, the beating heart. The buildings alongside the Beehive and the corner shop lie mostly empty and boarded up; only the laundrette has survived. From what I remember, having your own washing machine was a rare luxury that few could afford. I come to a stop at the top of the street, hovering on the corner. I'm here. Home.

I look over Crow Street. The place it all happened. We only ever called it *the street*. Maybe because it is the *only* street to its residents, where they socialise, where they were born and raised and never left. Once you were here you were bound to it, tied to the place forever whether you liked it or not. Just as I am.

The street used to be twenty-four terraced houses, twelve on each side. Now, 'To Let' signs stand crooked, and at least two are boarded up to protect their fragile insides from further ransacks and squatters. Sometimes residents of near-by streets appear, cutting through quickly to the wasteland, their dogs tugging at the lead. Here, only ten of the houses are inhabited even less than I remember. There was a time when the locals were hounded by a company hoping to pull them all down and build an industrial site here. There was such backlash from the likes of Mrs Montgomery and Patrick that they soon realised it was too much hassle.

I stare at the empty houses, their black gates like prison bars as they stand desolate. They are small and narrow, built as some late-Victorian council estate for local workmen. The area is working-class, a remnant of the factory workers who left their blood, sweat and tears in the roots of the place. The doors of each house had been painted an array of colours some years ago, an attempt to add life to an otherwise dreary place. Now the paint is flaking and so too the façade. The houses are all identical inside, two bedrooms upstairs, a reception room and a kitchen downstairs, and a cellar beneath it all. Behind each row of houses runs an alley, dark and narrow, where people keep their bins, and the stray cats roam and judge those dwelling there. To the east, the spires of Manchester's empty factories loom. They stand brooding like lonely watchmen, displeased with what they see. To the north and west, however, is nothing but wasteland: the same Victorians who'd built the street hadn't intended for it to be only a single street; they'd envisioned a whole neighbourhood. But for some reason, the rest of the houses never materialised. Perhaps they realised the darkness this place harbours, or perhaps the people fled rather than submitting to living here.

The wasteland is a wild and scrubby grassland, cut through with paths made by dog walkers. Flattened calf-length grass and wildflowers curl up together sleepily. In the distance I spot a small structure – a summer house, built fifteen years earlier by everyone on the street. It was a community effort, perhaps, I think now, an effort to pull together after Henry's disappearance. I smile at the sight of it, at the memories bundled up in the ramshackle building. Of Eoin, the teenage romance and closest thing to home I ever had on this street since Mum died, of us curled up on its battered sofa, safe from whatever lay outside it. It's weatherworn and fragile now. A sadness creeps up on me; the place has aged in my absence.

I lift my gaze up and over to beyond the summer house, to the railroad bridge and the canal. Despite being at the edge of a town near one of the country's largest cities, the street is isolated, and alone. It's overlooked and forgotten, pushed out of sight and mind like a blemish on the Manchester landscape. Yet people live their entire lives here, and then their children, and their children's children. The street is a bloodline, a fortress that can't be accessed by the outside unless they're pulled in and become a part of it. No wonder no one here ever talks about Henry Carr's disappearance. On Crow Street, if you're not a resident, you're an outsider. This street takes care of its own.

I remember the street cramped with police cars, men in white suits swarming in and out of number four, police tape fluttering in the wind. The whole street had been standing opposite, watching. They stood from morning until night, arms crossed, whispers stirring. The case stuck to them all like a stain when Henry wasn't found, something physical that lingered.

The disappearance is engrained in my mind, though I was only 10 when it happened. I could see Henry Carr's house from my bedroom window, the shadow of it. I shiver and nestle my chin into my jacket. The rain is starting to let up and the smell of it is sticking to my clothes and my skin. I look over at my childhood home, swallowing down the bile as it rises. I just need to remember why I'm here: for Henry, the paper, for me – no one else. I take my phone from my back pocket and photograph the street for the article. It looks different through a lens. Smaller. Yet, through my eyes, my childhood home looks unchanged as I stare it in the face. It all seems innocent enough, the whole street does. But I know what lies behind the peeling paint and the potted plants, the false static smiles and nods in the street. I know of the secret that clings here. I edge closer and feel the crackle of peeling paint against my palm as I push the gate open. With the path ahead open I hesitate, unable to shake the feeling that someone is there watching me. But the street is quiet, so I shake off the paranoia and continue forwards. At the front door, I lodge the duffel bag between my ankles and rummage for the loose key I haven't used since the day I left. My fingers are closing around the unfamiliar sharpness of it when I hear the scream.

It is piercing, guttural.

There is a flurry of activity on the road.

It's an elderly woman, covered in blood.

The woman falls to her knees and looks up at the man looming over her. She's screaming.

'He's dead. You've killed him.'

2
Patrick

I SIT AND OBSERVE the street from my window seat in number four. I fear my body has morphed into the fabric, and, inevitably, me and the chair are one.

Adjusting my position, I push my reading glasses on top of my head and place the *Daily Express* flat onto the coffee table. Outside I notice a woman walking by and lean forward to gain a better view of her. Some spark of familiarity ignites itself in my memory and I feel myself frown. I like to know the movements of the street, who comes and who goes. Everyone knows everyone here, that is the way it has always been. Newcomers are not often welcomed: this is a street with a history, an identity.

I squint and watch.

She is faltering outside number five. Rainwater dripping from the ends of her hair. She opens the gate and places a bag by the door. An 'ah' sound escapes my lips and I nod.

Peter Cavanagh's estranged daughter. Gone what, six years now? Seven?

'How interesting,' I murmur, settling back into the chair.

New arrivals always unsettle me, they prey on my mind. I can't quite regain focus to pick up the newspaper and continue with the morning crossword. The microwave beeps from the kitchen. The porridge will be steaming and ready. It is all part of my morning routine, carefully planned and perfected over the years. I've got it just as I like it. It is also taped to the fridge, there in black and white, though that is for Marianne's benefit rather than my own. I make a mental note to go up and check how she is doing, see if she needs help dressing after breakfast. Each day is different with Marianne. Entirely dependent on what she remembers, her mood, her dreams the night before. It is exhausting, not knowing what I am going to wake up to. Turning the radio up, I'm happy to distract myself by muttering furiously at the state of politics and the state of pretty much everything. That is the old man in me. Settling down at the table I scald my mouth on the first spoonful of porridge.

'So it's going to be that kind of morning, is it?' I sigh, push the bowl away and pad upstairs to check on Marianne.

My knees creak as I rise, the sound of my bones and groans echo in the stairwell. I did once enquire about a stairlift. I saw one on TV, the shopping channel to be exact. But the prices were extortionate. No. I'm not quite ready for a stairlift yet. I will go back to the doctor about the possibility of a knee replacement; that would suit me just fine. Although the thought of having to get someone in to care for Marianne while I'm gone sets my jaw sharp; I cannot do that. What if she said something she shouldn't? She gets so confused, remembers things from the past. I shake my head.

I can't leave her, not ever, not until the end.

Our secrets will die with us.

I pause on the landing, sucking in air until I feel inflated again. I hear her gasp as I knock on her bedroom door, separate to mine since the dementia set in. She often wakes with night terrors, screaming, fighting. She also forgets who I am, tries to attack me, accuses me of unthinkable things. I can't deny that I miss sleeping with her, the feel of her head on my chest, a stray hand on my back in the night. I feel my lip tremble.

'Keep it together, Patrick,' I whisper firmly to myself, straightening my cardigan and nodding.

I push my way into the room at her silence and find her at the dressing table, staring at her reflection.

'You all right, dear?'

She nods wordlessly, still staring.

'I'm going to head over to the allotment in a minute. I'll run your bath before I go. Don't forget to check the temperature with the thermometer before you get in. I'll have done so already, but just to be sure.'

I shift awkwardly at her continued silence.

'Are you sure you're feeling all right?' I ask, inching forward.

She nods, grey curls bouncing. I smile sadly and retreat, leaving her alone with her thoughts. Walking past the third bedroom, I kiss my fingers and press them to the wood as I always do. Henry's room. My boy. Emotion catches in my throat and I take a jagged breath. The shrill ringing of the house phone echoes off the walls. I freeze solid.

'Bugger!'

I know who it is.

The detective won't give up easily. He has already left three voicemails and doesn't seem to be respecting my wish for privacy. It makes me feel faint, digging up the past. Makes sleep difficult, life difficult, at the thought of Marianne remembering things that are better left forgotten. Things that are better left in the dark.

3

Marianne

THE TELEVISION FLICKERS STATIC, the voices jarring.

Outside the street simmers in the rain, and despite it, Patrick walks steadily to his allotment, his stick in hand. Silence has filled the house, and in the safety of it, Marianne has ventured downstairs. She sits on the floor, her knees drawn up to her chest like a child. Above the drum of the rain against the glass, the news correspondent continues, shuffling papers on his desk.

'Next this morning, this coming week marks the fifteenth anniversary of the disappearance of Henry Carr from Crow Street in North Manchester. The case has recently been reopened by the police, a fresh investigation prompted by renewed interest thanks to a popular American podcast. The 34-year-old man vanished from his parents' home in September 2008 and has not been seen since. Henry Carr's case has gained global attention after trending on social media due to the podcast *True Crime Revisited*. Phone-ins relating to the case are reported to have risen sharply in recent months. Here's Sophia Flinton with more.'

Marianne switches the television off. Henry's name has stirred something in her, though she doesn't recognise him as her son. The blank space frightens her and she studies the remote for a moment, running her fingernail over the buttons, observing the symbols. They are familiar.

She smiles.

Scattered around her on the floor are her thoughts. They are scrawled onto scrap pieces of paper, old letters, blank envelopes. The cabinet that held them looks as though it has been ransacked, its guts exposed and spilt out. She will be in trouble for that, she thinks.

She bites down on the mint she is chewing and hears the crack as it splits between her dentures. The taste of mint on her tongue settles her a little, and takes her back to a beachfront she can't quite remember the name of. This often happens, small things that bring her back to a time or a place or a person she no longer recognises. It frightens her, this big world full of people she should know but doesn't.

Her shaking hands are balled together in the lap of her skirt, twisting the lilac material into a knot. She chews fervently on the inside of her cheek until she feels the skin pucker, and after a slow exhale she looks down at the paper in her fist.

'I followed him inside,' she whispers.

Her eyes search the ceiling, memories flickering a silhouette onto the white. Still she can't connect the words to a memory. She reads the paper again.

'I followed him inside.'

Inside where? she wonders.

It feels important to find out. She gets angry, then upset. Emotion churning and dragging her on a wave.

She can't find the scrap that answers that yet. She fumbles with various pieces, reads the words scrawled on them. None of them match, like they all belong to another story, someone else's. She can feel her skin sagging with tiredness, weighing her down. She feels like she is drowning in her own memories, scraps of them everywhere.

She cut her diary up, all those years ago. Tore it into shreds before they could find it. Fifteen years ago.

She had been filled with panic, terror, that they would come for her too, and she had hidden her words around the house piece by piece. The illness had already begun to creep in, slow and cruel. Now she has forgotten who and what she is afraid of. How can she hide when she can't see the danger coming? She must treat everyone as the enemy, she thinks. Be on her guard. This is all she can do, week in week out, in the few moments she is left alone. She finds parts of her diary and tries to reassemble it. Tries to remember. The scraps of paper are what she has seen, what she heard that night. They are things only she knows.

Just her and the killer.

4
Ruth

THE ELDERLY WOMAN'S HANDS are marked with red, blood embedded deep into the grooves of her skin. She is shaking, violent vibrations that make her body shudder. Her hair is grey and matted, hanging limp around her face.

I am running before I realise, an instinctive response.

I know the woman, can remember her from my childhood. Mrs Montgomery from number nine. A solemn figure, lonely. I've only ever seen her standing inside at the window, cats sitting and purring against the glass. I glance up to number nine and see the door ajar.

What caused her to venture outside?

I look around, but the road is empty. Mrs Montgomery looks just as old and frail as when I left, and must be almost 80 at a guess. She is folded in on herself, the thin frame of her shoulders caved.

I fall down to my knees beside her, following her eyeline to the corpse lying in the middle of the road. The body is broken, distorted limbs and unblinking eyes. The mouth is ajar, a permanent scream. I look from the woman, to the man, to the body. We are all looking for someone to act, for someone to fix what has been broken. The man's car is still running. I don't recognise him and it unsettles me. Edging forward on my knees, rainwater and grit soaking my jeans, I scoop the body up into my arms. The cat's head lolls on its neck, its green eyes staring up at the sky. Mrs Montgomery watches blankly, the tears drying into white lines against the leather of her skin. She is murmuring something indecipherable, repeating it until her voice breaks down the middle. I extend my arms, the cat spread across two palms. I expect the elderly woman to take it, to hug it to her chest, but she just stares. Maybe it's the shock, the grief, but she remains rooted to the spot, unblinking. The cat is still warm in my hands. The man remains hovering, a hand on the back of his neck. He looks mortified, pale, and the exhaust of his car rattles behind him.

'We can handle this,' I say to him. 'Thanks.'

He looks at me, his mouth still ajar.

'It was an accident. It ran out in front of me. I didn't have time to stop,' he stammers.

'It's all right. I'll sort it,' I say softly.

I smile at him, hoping it will ease his guilt. Though I don't know how it can be sorted; the cat is definitely dead. Mrs Montgomery lets out a small sob, a strangled sound that catches in her throat. I smile sympathetically at the man as he slowly backs away, his eyes still rooted on the crooked corpse in my arms.

'Mrs Montgomery. You might not remember me but I'm Ruth, Ruth Cavanagh from number five. Can I get you a drink? You're in shock.'

The elderly woman looks up slowly, the watery blue of her eyes showing a sign of recognition. Her gaze falls back to the body in my arms. Carefully cradling the cat with one arm, I help Mrs Montgomery up with my other and together we venture to number five. I hesitate slightly at the gate, running a finger along the peeling paint that clings to the iron. I remember when I used to swing on it as a child, my feet gripping the thin strips of metal like it was made of ice. The flaking paint is like skin, shedding itself of my memory. It feels as if the whole street is watching, willing me to take a step and then another. I look into the face of the house I fled from, remember the rushed and blunted last conversation with Dad, trying to find anything left of Mum's to take with me.

I fumble around in my pocket for the key, balancing the cat in the nook of my other arm. The key is stiff in the lock as I push it in. Instinctively I kick against the bottom of the door and push my shoulder into the wood to prise it open.

Muscle memory.

The door groans and splutters forward. It is as though the house doesn't want any visitors, which is what I am now, I suppose. The hallway is cloaked in darkness, sheltered from the outside by the drawn curtains in the lounge. When I was here I would pull them open every morning, will the street to come in, to fix what Dad and I couldn't. Post has piled up in the entrance, scattered towards the stairs. An advertisement for the local Chinese takeaway is stuck to the wetness of my heel. I bend awkwardly and peel it off, the ink bleeding onto my fingers. The air feels heavy and stale, as though it has been a long time since a window has been opened. I swallow the lump that sits firm in my throat, pushing the silver key back into my jacket pocket. I'm aware of Mrs Montgomery, lingering behind me. I feel her eyes boring into my back and I shiver. Moving aside to let her in, I push the door closed behind us.

It still smells like home and I inhale the old wood and lingering cigarette smoke that clings to the walls. I would smell snatches of home on old jumpers or bedding when I left. It broke and mended me all at once.

I look at Mum's sofa, the one that for so long still held the imprint of her body. Where she would read long into the night and I would sneak down, clamber up and find safety in her. Always in her. I shake my head, try to dislodge the painful nostalgia of it all because it is mixed up too in misery, in grief.

I usher Mrs Montgomery to the lounge, sitting her on the sofa. The heating isn't on and the room feels damp. Dad stopped putting the heating on, even in the winter, after Mum died. He told me to layer up and so I did; even now, heating feels like a luxury. I lay the cat down gently on the rug and shrug off my damp coat, balancing it on the bottom of the banister. It hangs and covers the etchings in the side that followed me as I grew. The lines stop abruptly at 7, when mum was no longer here to mark them. Tracing the ages down, I stare for a moment at the droplets of rainwater that fall from my hair to the floor. The wooden boards are chipped and worn; they've lived a life. I wonder which marks I caused, through running and jumping and living as I had. Before it all went wrong.

I glance back at Mrs Montgomery, follow her transfixed eyes to the body of her friend. I give her a moment in silence, to grieve in whatever way she can. I'll admit that I need a minute too to ground myself, to be immersed back in this version of myself that I left behind. I step into the lounge when I feel the silence has stretched out for long enough. The room feels cramped, littered with charity-shop furniture and resurfacing memories. Magazines spill out of the innards of newspapers, and empty mugs dot the coffee table. Rings of coffee are etched like a geometric pattern. Something feels disjointed. Everything looks almost the same, but something is just a little off kilter, at an angle that I can't pinpoint. It all looks smaller than I remember, more fragile almost. I move to the window and pull open the curtains, allowing light to spill into hidden corners. Mrs Montgomery doesn't seem to notice; her eyes are still firmly on the animal. Silence hovers around and between us, floating. What if this is all she has? I feel a pang in my chest and gently take the cat from its place on the lounge rug and put it slowly across her lap. I watch the liver-spotted hands bury themselves into its black fur, unafraid of the brokenness of its body. It's hard not to cry, watching her grief. I push away a tear with the back of my hand and clear my throat.

'Let me get you a drink – tea?' I offer.

The woman says nothing. She is as still as the cat.

I edge away, glancing over my shoulder as if both might just get up and leave. Moving around the kitchen, my feet land on something and the crunch of aluminium hits my ears. I hope I haven't startled Mrs Montgomery. Easing my foot from the beer can, I watch the remnants of amber liquid trickle into the cracks of the floorboards. The weight of being back is starting to press on me, heavy on my chest. My phone vibrates in my back pocket and I pull it out. Tom. He's asking for an update, to check I have arrived safely and if I've spoken to anyone yet. I push the phone back into my pocket and run my fingers tenderly along my neck as I think. Tom doesn't know what I'm coming back to, he can't. I keep my old life hidden, push it into the furthest corners of my mind. Yet here I am. The kitchen looks frozen in time. This house is both the place I loved and hated. A place where I grew close to Mum and became fractured from Dad, healing and bleeding all at once. I still remember the long Sunday mornings spent out here, sitting at the table with feet resting on the chair opposite while Dad was still unconscious in the living room. I would balance a book on my knee, sleep still clinging to my eyes as I scanned the words and hoped to absorb them. I was used to being on my own for hours, climbing up onto the counters to reach the cupboards while Mum worked two jobs. If Dad hadn't spent all of our weekly allowance at the Beehive, then there would be bread ready for Sunday toast. It was those slow and tired mornings that I loved, the small hours that, when she was home, I could steal alone with Mum before Dad awoke. I was six when the cancer started and I noticed then for the first time how thin she'd become, how skeletal the frame of her arm seemed as it wrapped its way around me. Later, it had been hard to ignore that her eyes seemed a little more sunken, and that her cheekbones were sharp under paper-thin skin. Her lungs sounded like a bottle being squeezed in an iron fist as she breathed, in and out. She was the string that tied us all together. We unravelled without her. Looking around I can see the scars left behind, things she did that we never questioned, that we never really learnt how to do without her. The damp above the window she could get rid of, how to remove the glass of the oven door to clean it, simple things, real things that I should have learnt from her. She didn't have time for any of it. In the final months it took all of Mum's strength to keep living, to keep smiling through cracked lips, her gums red and raw. Still, I had wanted to believe that she would live forever. We would fall asleep together, dreaming of better endings than the one we had been given. The memories feel so real, even now, that it's cruel. The house is different yet the same. Still the clock keeps ticking, the fridge continues to hum. Except now the evidence of grief lives here in the small things, in the overflowing bin, in the crumbs lingering on the table. Grief gnaws at me, as it always does in small moments. When I think about a future without her in it, when I remember how fragile the ties are now that bind me to this place. They become more frayed every day.

The stench from the bin is stuck to everything. I stare out of the window into the yard, at the curling weeds, at Dad's battered tool shed. How many times did I try to sneak in there as a child? Just wanting a glimpse of the things he treasured, the things I saw him care for. I just wanted to share something with him, but it was always locked away. I wonder what it is going to be like to see him again. It's hard to admit but I yearn to be close to him, to be connected to my blood in a way I haven't for so long. Yet there is also a deep fear that it will dislodge all the parts of myself I have put back together since I left. I'm a new person now. There is no room for the old me.

I look away and something catches my eye: a newspaper is lying open and gaping on the table. Henry's face stares into the room, the black and white image of him looking straight back at me. I need to focus, to remember why I'm back. For Henry Carr. Looking down at him, it feels as though he's here again, sitting around the kitchen table, his face cracking into a grin. I pick the newspaper up slowly, the soft noise of it filling the air. It's different to the one from the station and I'm eager to see if it contains anything new. I read hungrily, anything to distract me from the house. I lose track of time, too embroiled in the mystery of Henry, in the mystery of this street. I focus on any snippet of information that hints of the lead that has caused the police to reopen the case. I don't hear Mrs Montgomery approach. A bony hand reaches over my shoulder and snatches the newspaper from me.

'Enough of that. Best to let sleeping dogs lie.'

Mrs Montgomery scrunches the newspaper between the claws of her fingers, her face contorts and her eyes are wild.

'I don't understand—'

The sound of a car pulling up outside the front window interrupts us. Its rumble filters through the glass. And then a door slams, keys jingle in a palm. Is that Dad back? It can't be, not yet. I know his routine, memorised it as a child, know what minute he would likely be home, know the sound of his footsteps dragging themselves to the door. I try to stop myself panicking. What did she mean, *best to let sleeping dogs lie*? What is she concerned about me finding out? And *why*? She must have been at home on the day Henry disappeared; the woman hardly ever left her house. She must know something. I step into the living room and hover by the window, my lips whispering a prayer. It can't be Dad yet. I'm not ready. I exhale at the sight of the delivery man approaching next door, a parcel wedged under his arm, and take a breath.

'Mrs Montgomery, would it be okay to ask you a few questions?' I say, still staring at the delivery man.

A slam.

I whip around.

Mrs Montgomery has fled.

The cat remains.

5
Peter

I TURN THE ENGINE off and sit in the van for a moment.

The radio fades out and the sound of stillness fills my ears.

It only takes a minute for it to get too much. I have to move, have to disturb it.

I wipe my rough, muddy palms against my work trousers and stifle a yawn before climbing out onto the pavement.

It isn't often I come home for lunch now. There's nothing to come home to except more space, more emptiness. I like solitude like any other man my age, but sometimes it starts to fill me and that's when I know I've got to get out. I usually head over to the local café, chat with Lynsey for a while, practise my best chat-up lines that she bats away with a roar of laughter and flick of her long nails. Every time is the same: I grab a brew, a bacon barm, let the noise of the lunchtime rush play like background music. We're critical, I think, of sameness. Yet sometimes it's the sameness that keeps me going. The reliability that things are going to be exactly as I expect them to be. Today, though, seeing the headlines, seeing his face. It was too much. Too much on top of everything else.

I slam the van door, a finger up to the neighbours who have been complaining about it and stretch my back until I hear the click. The street is mostly empty, just a solitary pensioner wandering back from the local shop. I nod at them in greeting and stop abruptly at the gate. It's hanging open.

It's not that unusual really, except the postman always closes it behind him. It's just what happens, day in and day out. It's the sameness of this street.

I close it and feel better at the normality of it. Opening the front door, I immediately know something has changed. There is a shift in the air, a fullness that wasn't there before. I follow the scattered post and water droplets on the floor reaching the banister, to a coat. I stare and stare but I don't recognise it.

I reach into my pocket for my keys, sliding one between my knuckles. I train my ear to the noise of the house but hear nothing. I try to calm my breathing, the sound of my heart thundering is taking over. I lower my shoulders and edge slowly, my senses razor sharp now. I sense movement from the next room and ready myself. I round the door to the lounge and lunge, my arm extended and knuckle out in front of me, ready to strike.

What the fuck is that?

I stop.

Is that a dead cat?

I am genuinely dumbstruck.

My arm falls to my side.

There's a dead cat on the rug.

I lean a bit closer, look at its mangled face.

'Well, shit.'

I look away. I'd take my cap off if I had one on. Edging around it, I respect the space it's using. I feel for the key again, the coolness of it against my skin, and run my thumb along the jagged edge. One, two, three, I kick the kitchen door open with the sole of my boot.

Mud splatters and the door groans as it swings.

I hear the key hit the lino before I realise I've dropped it.

My voice gets lost somewhere and I feel myself stuttering before I can get anything out.

'Oh.'

It isn't profound, in fact it's stupid, but I can't physically say anything else. I lean on the door frame to stop myself falling. She spins in the chair, her face pale.

'Oh.'

She says it too and stands.

I wonder if she can't find her words yet either. Maybe we are more similar than I remember.

She places the newspaper on the table and tangles her hands together. An old habit. I feel a spark of anxiety. We look at each other, not a normal look but something prolonged, as if trying to reconcile old memories with the new people we are now confronted with. The jigsaw pieces don't quite seem to match up. She is still Ruth but also something other, something I had no part in. I'm aware, suddenly, of everything she has seen.

Can she smell the alcohol on my breath? I look down at my hands to make sure they're not trembling with the effects of the night before and force them into my pockets. I feel exposed, as though a layer of myself has been peeled back without my permission. My face is hot, burning even, and I can do nothing but move things out of the way, kicking things into the corners, and avoid catching her eye for fear of being seen further. I grab a fistful of plates haphazardly and throw them in the sink; one chips as it hits the edge of the counter and I see Ruth flinch out of the corner of my eye. I've messed this up already, this reunion I have thought about over and over. I pick up takeaway containers and try to force them into the already overflowing bin.

Why? Why today?

I kick a container and it splatters sauce up the fridge door. I lean on the counter, try to suck in air, try to forget she's standing behind me.

Watching.

'Dad, it's fine.'

I wince. It's been so long since she's called me that.

35

'It's not fine.'

It's all I can manage through gritted teeth.

She has seen this before, seen it every day since Katie died, but it is different now.

She is a woman who has seen the world, she has seen this isn't what home is supposed to be like. It's why she never came back. Is she expecting me to fly off the handle? She's probably coiled like a spring, waiting for me to explode. I lift my head from over the sink, releasing my grip from the counter.

'I didn't think I'd see you again.'

I don't know where the words come from. I am not one to talk about feelings, I'm not capable of it. The words must have been sitting there, ready.

She looks startled.

Guilty?

I hope not.

She sits back down and pushes a stray strand of hair behind her ears and nods, as if the comment was fair enough.

'I should have called to say I would be coming back for a little while. I'm sorry.'

I nod. *It's okay.*

'I haven't heard from you in ages. I tried to forward some post on to you but it got returned to sender. I guess you moved or something.'

She nods again and stares at a stain on the table.

'So you're staying a little while?' I sound casual, almost disinterested.

'I've been sent down to report on the Henry Carr disappearance. You must have heard already, but they've reopened the case. They want a local to write a story on it, to speak to the neighbours.'

I fall into the chair beside her. It rocks under my weight.

She looks at it cautiously, as if trying to steady it. The care in her gaze makes the lump in my throat thicken. She glances back down at the newspaper, at the headline. I have been trying to ignore the police presence, the outsiders lingering on the corner, trying to get a glimpse of us. The Carrs have practically buried themselves away.

I can't blame them.

My own daughter reporting on my best friend's disappearance? It sounds like a twisted fucking crime story. I run a hand through the coarseness of my stubble and try to process what she has told me. I can't, so I stand up again. I pace a little, my boots spraying mud around the lino. My eyes fall to the newspaper. To Henry's grinning face. How many times did I see that face growing up? How many times did he sit around this table with us and let the walls absorb his booming laugh? He saw Ruth grow up. What would he think of her now? What would he think of me? The man I have become.

I turn the paper over without thinking. I can't stand to look at the best friend I lost, can't stand to have old grief stirred back up.

I'm angry.

Angry at Henry, at Ruth, at the police for digging around fifteen years later when all it will do is cause more damage.

'Sorry if I startled you.' She smiles, tentatively.

I puff my cheeks, allow myself to laugh.

'I thought someone had . . . Did you know there's a dead cat in the lounge?' I ask, pointing back over my shoulder.

She laughs, an outburst that she immediately grimaces at. Leaving the kitchen, I follow her through the hall.

'I do. Oh God, sorry. Mrs Montgomery's cat got ran over. I brought them over here to check she was okay. She wasn't and she left and now . . . well, there's a dead cat in the lounge.'

We both turn and look at it.

Fuck.

'I'll get a shovel.'

* * *

'I should say a few words.'

The wind has picked up and I can barely hear her over the howl of it. The grass of the wasteland shivers. I wipe the sweat off my forehead with the back of my hand and rest for a minute on the shovel. Ruth has taken a piece of old wood she found at the back of the summer house and crafted it into a makeshift cross. Do cats conform to a religion? Aren't they a symbol of witchcraft?

I'm overthinking.

I bow my head obediently as Ruth murmurs something compassionate and pats the raised mound of soil. The grave isn't as deep as it should be – what with the threat of more heavy rainfall, we did the job and we did it quick. Ruth had knocked on Mrs Montgomery's door for what felt like an age; she believed it was important for her to be here, but there was no answer. I tried telling her. This street isn't what it used to be. Everyone is hiding away, hiding something. Even her.

We stand in silence, let the cold air and the smell of the earth simmer around us. I feel the urge to take her hand, to feel more connected to her than I do right now, but I don't.

I can't. I wonder how I look to her now. Whether she has noticed my yellowing skin, the purple under my eyes, the brittleness of my bones.

Am I a paper man to her now?

She looks over at me as if she can read my thoughts, and there is both anxiety and something yearning in her expression. I don't understand what it means. She blinks and looks away. Perhaps this is the only way we can coexist now, given all that has come before. Silently and peacefully, without understanding too much. There's a selfish part of me that doesn't want her here. That doesn't want her to see me again for who I am. That doesn't want her digging around Henry's case. The street is not a safe place to be. She isn't safe while she's here, not snooping where she doesn't belong.

I can't lose her all over again.

6
Ruth

As a journalist I've come to expect the unusual.

You can be sent out to report on one thing and find something completely ridiculous and wonderful instead. It's a part of the job I like, finding the stories that wouldn't otherwise be heard. There's a charm to them, the small local stories. I have never, however, been to investigate a murder and ended up leading a funeral for a cat. It's one I plan to keep out of the *Chronicle*. I laugh as I imagine Tom's face.

I sit on the low wall outside the house and gulp down the energy drink in my hand until my heart is beating out of my chest. The sugar sticks like a film to my tongue, and I close my eyes with the pleasure of it. I can give myself this today, this of all days. I'm back in my childhood home for a start. I'm investigating a fifteen-year-old disappearance on a street that is filled with rather eccentric characters and I did just bury a dead cat that had been left sprawled on the living room rug. I had decided to brave the corner shop. It seems silly really, to worry about bumping into people who have known you all of your life. It's just that it feels different, I'm different.

I didn't need to worry. When I arrived it felt like I'd never left, like these people have been standing beside me the whole time.

I think back to my exchange with Dad and shake my head, wiping my palms on my jeans, leaving streaks of mud. Since Mrs Montgomery vanished and refused to answer the door, it was a more intimate funeral than I might have liked. I said a few words and a prayer with the help of Dad, which did make me question our sanity. Still, the cat now has a nice view out over the wasteland. I didn't want it to face the street.

I feel like maybe Dad is watching me, but when I look over my shoulder at the house, he is nowhere to be seen. I think back over our reactions to seeing each other again. He has changed. I can't yet figure out in what way. Family relationships – they're made of such fragile and complex pieces that I've never quite been able to slot into place.

Despite the rain starting to drizzle again I sit and watch the comings and goings for a little while longer, pulling up my hood for protection against the elements.

There's something about this street, something about the faded paint on household doors and the sagging charity-shop furniture. The darkness that lingers, even now. I can't help but think back to Henry and to what the podcast said. How could no one know what happened to him, when it all must have taken place right here? And, if anyone really does know anything, how can they not say it? The street is interconnected, not just by the walls that link one house to another, but by the flickering curtains, the chain of whispers and the eyes that seem to see everything but know nothing.

I kick my heels against the low brick wall as I think back to the clearest memory I have of Henry Carr. I must have only been 7, bent over a book of fables I had read and read until the cover was curling and scuffed. There was an explosion of laughter from the kitchen, so loud it felt the walls were vibrating with the joy of it. It startled me, the alienness of it. I had grown up learning to squeeze myself between tense whispers, roaring arguments, heavy silence. So the laughter, the carefree lilt of it, had my book tumbling from my hands, had me bounding down the stairs barefoot and spilling into the kitchen to find its source. There was Henry, a bottle of beer in his hand, a knowing smirk on his lips, my parents either side of him, all of them laughing. I was transfixed, toes scrunched up against the lino, searching and eager for a place in the moment. Desperate to be a part of it. I'm not sure if it really ever came, but one thing did: a wink from Henry, a nod that confirmed he knew what this meant to me, that he would ensure he would bring laughter with him every time he visited. This man from across the road, a mystery, still a question mark fifteen years later, and yet, he means something to me. A family friend, yes, but also a light in the darkest moments.

Everything seemed to disintegrate around us at the same time, first Mum dying, then Henry vanishing, leaving just me and Dad. The father that could never quite hold the weight of that title. He had been forced to grieve for his best friend and wife almost simultaneously. The man who didn't know how to deal with his emotions began to drown, leaving me watching from the sidelines. When I hit 18, escaping the street and its weight felt like the most freeing thing possible. Like flexing wings I never knew I had. Now, being back alongside him, they feel clipped in a way I hadn't expected. There is love in this street, but also something much darker. I think back to the reception I received in the corner shop while picking up my snacks. It felt like a place of safety. I smile at the thought of Mr Chandra's hug. I'm both shocked and delighted that the corner shop is still in his hands. How many times did he scoop me up onto the counter as a girl, letting me scan items and pack them away into rustling shopping bags that I would take home when my father eventually reappeared from the pub? Too many. I stifle a smile. I fear I'm becoming too nostalgic.

I glance across the street at number four, at Patrick and Marianne's. It's exactly as I remember it, potted flowers covering the front, lace curtains in the window. I think for a moment that I can see a figure, movement, maybe even a wave, from behind the curtain. I stand up and take a step forward, squinting. The figure is ghost-like, haunting. The energy drink drops from my fingers, it's sticky liquid oozing into the drain. I ignore it, desperate to identify the face in the window. The light against the glass obscures my view. I pull my jacket around myself and step into the road. It is definitely someone, their hand is on the glass now.

'Ruth? Shit, is that really you?'

I spin around and then look back to the window of number four again, but the figure is gone.

I gasp. 'Eoin.'

That voice. I would know it anywhere.

My lips part but no words come out. I turn my back on number four to face him. Time has not changed the familiar ring of his voice. It's the kind you feel in your bones, settling in your feet.

He sounds nervous, excited. Maybe something else; I'm not sure.

I've tried to push the possibility of seeing him again to the back of my mind. A teenage fling, my first love – I have tried my best to forget. My body floods with heat; I feel sick. It makes sense that he has stayed here. He had always said he was made of the place. Despite the excitement of what life could be else-where, of different people, different experiences, he couldn't leave the street. In the end, he hadn't followed me to university; he said it was a betrayal of his roots, and wasn't for someone like him. He feels he belongs here.

And here he is. He's never left.

He hesitates, as though afraid to come closer in case he spooks me and I leave again. He exhales slowly. His face curves upwards into a smile and he walks closer, surer. As he nears, I can see the puckered skin that tugs at his lips when he is unsure how to respond. He's dressed in his overalls and I wonder if he still works at the same building site. If he has finally raised enough to buy his mum a new car, or visit his grandfather's house in Galway – all the dreams he shared with me once.

We both speak at the same time.

'It's been so long.'

'I didn't know you were back.'

We laugh at the overlap, both crossing our arms against our chests in an act of self-preservation. I unfold them only to smooth the ends of my hair with my fingers, aware suddenly that I have no makeup on, that my hair is limp and still damp with rainwater. I push my hair back, take a step towards him to meet him halfway.

'I can't believe you're here.' He grins. 'I thought you were still in the North East?'

'I was until this morning. I'm here for work, actually. It's complicated,' I say.

'Work? For the newspaper you mean.' He grins again at my nod. 'That's amazing. It was always your dream. I'm really happy for you.'

Silence slides between us. He clears his throat. 'So you're living back at home while you're here?' His eyes flicker to number five, concern in his voice.

'It's just for a few days, a week at the most. I need to be on the street.' I avoid the intensity of his gaze.

'On the street,' he repeats, frowning. 'Hang on. You're here to report on the anniversary?'

I nod, aware of how it must look for me to come back only to intrude. Only to bring up unwanted history. He shifts on his feet, rubbing the shaving rash along his jaw.

'People won't be happy about that. They don't like the press snooping round. There have been enough people sneaking onto the street and trying to pester us all since that podcast was released. We're like a tourist attraction for them. Everyone is putting their foot down. They're protective, you know that. Protective of the Carrs.'

His mouth is a straight line, his lips pulled taut. He's frowning, a loose dark curl falling into his eyes. He doesn't shake it away; he doesn't look anywhere but at me.

'If it's not me it'll be someone else. At least I'll do it properly, with respect. I'm part of this street too,' I say, hating the defensiveness in my voice.

He nods at that, considering what the alternative would look like. We stare at each other's feet, a thousand unspoken questions between us. There is so much I want to say; so much has happened in the years we've been apart. Too much. I swallow the lump that had formed in the base of my throat. The autumn wind picks up around us, pushing us towards one another. My ringtone cuts through the air, shrill and mechanical. The caller ID reads Tom, again. I grimace.

'I'd better go,' I say, almost drowned out by the slamming of a car door.

'Of course,' Eoin replies, disappointment concealed in a smile. 'It really is nice to see you.'

I turn around before he can say anything else. I uncurl my fingers, leaving crescent moons in my palms. How is it still possible to feel like this around him after all this time? I'm surprised by it, the deep velvet of his voice, the broadness of his shoulders, and yet the eyes, always the eyes, remain the same. I concentrate on putting one foot in front of the other until I'm almost home. I wipe the smears of rainwater from the phone and answer.

'Tom, hey. Sorry, I was going to reply to your messages but there was an old woman in the road and a dead cat. It's a bit complicated. Everything all right?'

A pause. 'Sorry, say that again. A dead what?'

'It doesn't matter. Well, it does. It was in my living room. Dead. I had to bury it. Do you know what you're supposed to do with dead cats? Should I have taken it to the vets?'

'No.' He sounds unsure.

'Hmm.'

I glance over my shoulder at Eoin walking away, observe the curve of his shoulders, the downward tilt of his head.

I spin again to number four.

No one.

'Listen, can you put me in touch with your guy on the inside? There're so many blanks in this case. I need a bit more to work with.'

'No can-do, Ruth. Sorry pal. He made it very clear he wanted contact to stay between me and him. If you let me know what you need, I can do a bit of digging.'

'The new evidence. I've seen the uproar on social media, and read about the supposed hundreds of new leads coming in, but I haven't managed to find out what new evidence caused the investigation to be reopened. I also need to know if they have any suspects in mind, anyone on the street that I can get close to.' I push the hair back from my face, thinking.

'Well, one of those I can help you with.' A pause, a shuffle of papers. 'Ah, here we go. The main reason for the reopening was an anonymous phone-in from a local dog walker. Said she found an old wallet in the wasteland behind Crow Street and when she looked inside, the bank cards had the name H. Carr on them. She remembered the case and phoned it straight in. They're running it for fingerprints but doubt they'll find much if it's been exposed to the elements. Still, weird if it has just been lying there all this time.'

'Do they think someone planted it?' I ask.

'I don't know. We'd have to consider why someone would bother planting a wallet after fifteen years.'

'Maybe they're worried about the anniversary coming up. They could have planted it to deflect attention, push the police in the wrong direction. Keep them off the scent,' I suggest.

I know all too well how many times the wasteland was searched after Henry vanished, sniffer dogs pulling taut on their leads and officers kicking up undergrowth for hours. Every inch of the wasteland was searched, even all the way back to the perimeter of the abandoned substation and its chain-link fence. That was always out of bounds to us. The dominating grey structure and the sight of fluorescent jackets out in the bleakness of it was scarily illuminating. As though exposing a part of the street that was not supposed to be seen. Though he wasn't there, he was never anywhere. Eoin and I had watched them as children, knees drawn up to our chins, fear and excitement like electricity between us even then.

'I don't know. This is a really weird case. I'll get onto him and find out the answer to the rest of your questions. You doing all right, Ruth? I know you don't like talking about your past but if you ever need anything or you want me to pull you out of there, I can. I can send Rosie or Greg or any of the others. You hear? Don't let your pride get in the way.' Tom doesn't often show emotion, but the concern in his tone makes my breath catch in my throat.

'I'm fine, honestly. I've got this. Thanks, Tom. I'll update you when I can, and I'll meet the deadline for the anniversary. No problem.'

I hang up before he can protest, push the phone into my back pocket and exhale. My mind is filled with theories about the wallet. Is it possible that Henry dropped the wallet there and no one ever found it? I don't think so. I reach into my pocket for the key, still thinking. And then a police car pulls up in front of number four. Marianne Carr is standing at the window once more, looking out.

7

Marianne

MARIANNE WATCHES THE WOMAN watching her.

She feels a flicker of recognition, like smelling a familiar scent or tasting something from somewhere you can't quite place. It raises a frustration in her, and she squeezes her hand around the crucial piece of paper cupped in her palm. She turns again towards the window streaked with rain. She sees the fluorescence of their jackets first. The authority with which they walk scares her. It brings back a memory she can feel the edges of, sharp and cold. She is shaking before the knock comes, though it is gentle and that surprises her more. When she pictured them finally coming for her, she had imagined a hammering, a breaking down of the door from its hinges. This feels worse, she thinks. Her breathing grows shallow, panic setting in. One of them steps off the gravel path and heads towards the window. She turns and runs, stumbling into the hallway. The sound of their muffled voices carries through the glass and falls around her. Using the wall as a guide, she is on her hands and knees going up the stairs as one of them opens the letterbox to speak.

'Mrs Carr. Mrs Carr? It's the police. There's no need to be frightened, we're just here to talk about your son. Henry.'

She hears the metal click shut as she strips off her clothes and jumps into the bath. The water splashes and surges around her, lapping over the sides and covering the floor tiles in suds. The water is cold. Patrick had run it before heading out to the allotment.

Marianne doesn't remember this, though she does remember promising she would use the thermometer before getting in. She hasn't done that and worries that she will be in trouble when he returns. There are goosebumps along her flesh. She sits up quickly, the water swirling around her in tidal waves. She waits a moment before pulling herself up with great difficulty and stumbles out of the bath. Water droplets fall from her, drumming onto the mat beneath her feet. She curls her toes against it and pulls a hand towel to cover herself, wondering at its disproportion. She pulls the bathroom door open and gasps at the cold.

'Hello?'

She doesn't recognise her voice.

It is thin and haunted and old. Still, there's no response. She titters and walks slowly to the landing, leaning over the banister for a better view of the hallway below.

Nothing.

She feels a swell of childlike glee at the freedom of being alone. She is never allowed to be alone. She pauses, towel clutched to her chest. She is alone.

She chews her lip in thought and lets out a nervous laugh. Taking the stairs one at a time, she's careful not to rush and ruin everything. The thin line of goosebumps nibble at the loose flesh on her arms and she stops, momentarily, to warm herself against the hallway radiator that blows hot air onto her fragile skin. She inches towards the kitchen, the floor cool against her feet. Pulling the cupboards open, she drops biscuits and medications onto the counter. She can't decide at first, but eventually settles for digestives, she forces multiple into her mouth. Chocolate fuses with the skin on her fingers and lips. She licks the mess from her hands vigorously and laughs, looking around quickly for any witnesses. Closing her eyes, she takes a moment to relish in the sweet treat.

'If you say a word, I'll kill you.'

Her eyes snap open.

'Who said that?'

She cranes her neck around the kitchen door. There's no one there. She doesn't recognise the memory, or the voice. Why would someone want to kill her? She thinks carefully for a moment.

'What have I done?'

She feels drawn to the living room, to the wooden cabinet in particular, and returns to the stack of papers from earlier, fumbling with them, watching as they tumble.

'Oh, for *feck's sake*!'

There is the panic, bubbling away. She struggles to keep the towel tight around herself, her flesh exposed to the draught. All she can hear is the chattering of her own teeth, her breaths fluctuating as she cries and tries not to. In her growing desperation she lets the towel fall to the floor.

'I know you're there,' she says. 'I saw you there. You won't listen. No one does. Not to silly Marianne. The mad woman.'

She speaks through gritted teeth as she digs against the splintered wood of the cabinet for papers, envelopes, memories, until her fingers are scratched and sore. The living room is strewn with old diary entries again. The memories she can no longer remember. She is on the ground before she realises it. She is clothed in her own writing, the carpet covered in a sea of words.

She feels as though she is drowning. Like she is being chased and hunted and all she can do is hide beneath the waves. She screams and shouts and digs and flails until her searching hands find the smallest piece of paper. She stops. Stands. Unfolds the paper and walks with it to the window. Her nakedness irrelevant. She reads the paper then looks out at the street, searching the houses trying to find the right one. The killer's house.

Then turns around and looks at her own house. She can't see them but she can sense them, the person who killed her son.

8

Ruth

I WATCH THE POLICE car drive away, taking a right turn towards the town.

Marianne had been at the window. Why didn't she answer the door when the police knocked? Surely if there is new information then the Carrs would want to know about it? Or maybe they already know.

I shake away the thought. I shouldn't think like that, condemning them like everyone does. I consider knocking on the door myself and asking them some questions, but I falter. If Marianne didn't answer for the police, she surely wouldn't answer for me either. I type a note into my phone, detailing the time and date and what just happened for the article. I stare down the road, casting my mind back to who lived where, and who might know anything worth knowing.

After a moment's deliberation I leave the house, walk to number two and knock on the door.

Nothing.

No one answers.

This is exactly what I had been worried about: closed doors, stares from behind twitching curtains. It's how the street always was. Everyone who lives here is insular, secretive, wary. There was a reason this side of town had been abandoned, a reason this was the last street on the edge of the wasteland. Everyone here is stranded by their own choice, fused to this place and its past. I squeeze my hands into a fist, my mind flittering between Henry

Carr and Eoin. Both making it a little harder to breathe. I look up and down the street, wondering which door would open for me. Who would even talk to me. I decide to start somewhere easy, somewhere I know will welcome me. In the joy of seeing Mr Chandra again earlier, I'd forgotten to ask him what he knows. I turn the corner of the street, walk past the laundrette and push my way into the shop. A bell jingles.

Mr Chandra is serving a young woman I don't recognise, a child attached to her leg. The little one is screaming, her face crimson. I smile sympathetically, standing back out of the way. When he's finished serving and the child is being dragged down the street, I approach, grabbing the first thing I see. Putting the mints on the counter, my eyes flash to the display of lottery tickets in their clear casing.

'Can I have one of the scratch cards as well?'

Mr Chandra smiles. 'For your father?'

I smile in return at the narrative we both remember. Of course, it wasn't always scratch cards, but there was almost always something my dad needed or something that I felt would please him. My childhood had been spent wandering to and from the shop, happiest when I had a purpose. I push Henry Carr to the front of my mind, where he should be.

'Actually, Mr Chandra, would I be able to ask you a few questions?'

He raises his eyebrows, handing me my change as he nods.

'It's about Henry Carr,' I say tentatively.

His face falls, his cheeks growing pale. Henry's name is almost taboo on the street, I know that. I can feel the shop stop around us, the other customers freezing at the name.

They are all listening, waiting.

I lower my voice.

'I work for a newspaper in Newcastle. Nothing major, but we want to run the story of Henry's case, respectfully, to coincide

with the anniversary. They're going to run the story regardless.'
I gulp. 'As someone from the street, I just want to make sure it's
done right,' I say, almost apologetically.

He sighs.

'So that is why you're back? I thought you said you were just
visiting.' He adjusts his tie, uncomfortable.

'I am but . . . Well, it's both, I suppose. I'm sorry to ask, I
know it's hard to talk about.'

A tut echoes around the shop. I glance over my shoulder to
see an elderly woman shaking her head. With that, the shoppers
carry on about their business.

'I see dear, I see,' Mr Chandra says gently. 'What is it you
want to know?'

I smile at his tone, feeling heartened. He has always been
kind. I ignore the ring of the bell as people come and go.

'There are reports that some new information has come to
light. I know news spreads pretty fast on the street, and was
wondering whether you had heard anything.'

He looks down at his cracked palms, his almond-coloured
eyes full of something I don't understand.

I continue. 'Is there anything that's happened, anything anyone
has mentioned?'

I'm sounding desperate, I know it. I want so badly to get the
story quickly and leave again. To escape back to Newcastle, to
its people, to my flat, to a city with thousands of people: not one
street, not one secret.

'I do hear some things, what with people coming in and out,'
he finally says before swallowing audibly. 'Rumour would have
it that a dog walker found Henry's wallet in the wasteland behind
the street. Buried underneath a piece of wood her dog tried to
drag up. She took it to the police. They haven't confirmed anything
but it had his bank cards and a picture of his parents in it.'

He shakes his head sadly.

'Anything else?'

He looks from left to right quickly, to see who else might be listening, then lowers his voice.

'Apparently someone called the station, saying they reckon they know who put it there.'

'They think it was planted?'

Mr Chandra shrugs, his eyes wide.

'From what I've heard, they think it was Patrick. They think the person who planted the wallet was Henry's father.'

* * *

It takes me twenty minutes to get out of the shop. Once the conversation with Mr Chandra was over, a swarm seemed to gather. Locals questioning my return, my intentions, frowns and pursed lips at my explanation. Sam, the landlord of the Beehive, saved me. He wrestled me into a hug, familiar with me from the times I'd followed my father to the pub so that he could drink himself into oblivion. Sam would hoist me up onto a stool and tell me stories of the strange and wonderful characters that filtered through his doors. It was hard to remember an evening I hadn't spent in the Beehive after Mum died. It had become our only link to the outside world. It was our anchor in the storm, though it felt like we had both drowned anyway. It would be then, in the quiet corners of the night when Dad was swaying, his eyes clouded with thoughts I couldn't reach, that Sam would nod stiffly at Henry. Sitting in the corner, Henry would swallow the dregs of his drink and pull me under one arm as he lifted Dad with the other to walk us both home. He steered us to safety. He'd do that every night, any night we needed him to. Until he was no longer there, and it was me braving the storm to get Dad home.

I look at the Beehive sitting proudly amid the old red-brick factories that rise high in the distance behind it. The people here are as gritty as their past, doing what they have to do to survive. I had made friends across generations at the Beehive; men that would pull me up onto the creased knee of their trousers and growl stories of the war and things to come. Life had all seemed so exciting then.

I pull my gaze away and look through the window of the laundrette instead. I catch sight of Mrs Montgomery, the wild nest of her hair taking on a life of its own. I wonder if I should go in, talk about the cat, ask if she is okay. I falter. Mrs Montgomery is the oddity of the street. She's eccentric, lives alone. A million stories about her have always spilt from the lips of frightened neighbourhood children. She is the bogeyman, the witch, the woman in black. Yet all I feel is sadness at the sight of her. She is older and frailer. Lonely. She'd been so distraught by her cat's death. She'll be more alone now than ever. She catches my eye and mouths something, indistinguishable. I smile and put a hand up in greeting. She looks away. Says something else. I leave her to her thoughts and survey the boarded-up shops and vacant buildings, broken glass in the gutter and the wasteland behind the houses that harbours rubbish and people's secrets.

I catch sight of the summer house we had all helped build. Even my father. I leave the street and walk towards it.

The summer house has a view of the city beyond from one window and the street from the other; even though now it's all flaking paint and leaking windows, there's still a crumbling magic to it. It still contains a tattered sofa and a coffee table of old books and magazines, a stained rug and brown curtains. We had hidden in it as children, building adventures out of the summer. Later it had given us privacy, solitude, where we hid even then, until the world tugged us back to reality. When I broke up with Eoin the summer before university, I would flee, away from my father, away from the street, and seek solitude in hardback books and the lonely figure of the summer house. I feel a pang for it then, for the place it had been for me. Though it seems tainted now, with the knowledge of Henry's wallet having been found somewhere nearby. I can't wrap my head around the idea of Patrick planting it. He had spent all the years after the disappearance protecting his wife, shielding her from police and press, neighbours and strangers. He wouldn't want to cause her pain by forcing the case to reopen. Would he? I shake the questions from my mind. Standing here isn't answering any questions. I turn and head home.

It is only once I'm on the street that I see the commotion. A small crowd has gathered around what looks like a person on the ground. As I get closer I recognise Patrick Carr and my heart sinks.

There he is, the man whose son vanished and never returned. The one whose wife is wild and mad, who screams of death. Patrick is lying motionless, his limbs at odd angles. The whole street is holding its breath as they stand around him. I rush to join them but there's nothing I can do to help. I look down at the splayed ends of his coat, the arch of his legs. An elderly couple, who I remember as Frank and Margo, are knelt by Patrick's head, talking slowly to him as if to rouse him. They are good friends, and I can see the quiver of Margo's lips as she speaks. They both look so much frailer than I remember. Their clothes hang loosely from them, their eyes sunken and backs arched with age. I overhear someone on the phone calling for an ambulance, their voice fast and frantic. I stand back from the swell of the crowd, aware that there are already too many people gathered around.

Eoin and his mother, Laura, are running towards us. She is a nurse, and as she races towards Patrick with a first-aid kit slung over her shoulder, a calmness settles the anxiety in the air. The older residents are shouting her name, as though she is a hero they have been waiting for. Laura doesn't react, her eyes are focused on Patrick. I edge a little closer, worry stirring in my chest.

Laura squeezes his shoulder and he stirs, groaning. She rests her finger on his wrist, searching for the throb of a pulse.

'Will he be okay?' Margo asks her quietly, her hand on Patrick's arm.

'He's got quite a nasty bump on his head there. He didn't have much to break his fall by the looks of it. Lucky he fell so close to home, really. Has someone called an ambulance?'

She smiles at Margo's nod and takes off her cardigan, pushing it under Patrick's head.

'Shouldn't someone tell Marianne?' Eoin asks, looking up at the house, tracing the windows for any sign of movement.

There is none.

Eoin's mother shoots him a look I try and fail to read. Something passes between them and Eoin gives a curt nod. The crowd seems bigger, a swell of protection encasing him. I feel people closing in around me, walls that threaten to hold me here. I look around, trying to find an easy way out but there isn't one. Shoulders are like boulders keeping me encased. My heart quickens, my breath trapped in my throat, my surroundings beginning to spin. A hand touches my elbow, the smell of Eoin's aftershave behind me. He guides me out and sits me on the low wall behind the crowd.

I can breathe again.

I smile a thanks, and he nods.

The sky hangs low, adding a tension to the air that even the breeze can't shift. I pick at a loose thread in my jacket, unsure what to say.

'He'll be all right.'

I'm not sure if he's saying it for my benefit or his own. He doesn't look at me as he speaks. He is clenching and unclenching his jaw. We both breathe in at the same time, still in sync. His hand hovers over my knee before settling back on his own. It's easy to forget that things have changed.

'This is the last thing the family need, especially with the anniversary coming up . . .' He speaks gently, meditatively. 'You remember when we used to think the summer house was haunted with Henry's ghost? That his body was scattered in the wasteland? I never realised how grim that all was until now.'

I do remember, it's hard not to.

Rumours had circulated that Mrs Montgomery had performed some sort of witchcraft on him, or that Henry had grown tired of the dullness of life on the street and had changed his identity and walked off into the distance. Eoin kicks his heel against the brick.

'You don't have to hang around,' he says. 'I know stuff like this makes you anxious. Though I suspect it might be good for your story.'

He hadn't meant the comment to sting, though it does. He eyes the crowd with mild disapproval before looking back to me. I stare at our feet, side by side. We sit there in a comfortable silence, something we had become well-adjusted to. We sit on the wall until Eoin nudges my ankle; the ambulance arrives and the crowd bulges outwards, creating enough room for the paramedics to get through. Patrick is still in the same position. His corduroys are covered in the wet grit of the street and his hands are skinned and bleeding. The paramedics get to work and it's some time before they bundle him into the back of the ambulance, a blanket draped over his shoulders. The bleep of radios disturbs the quiet. Eoin's mother walks towards us as the ambulance turns off its lights.

'Is someone going with him?' I ask.

'Ruth. Gosh how you've grown!' Laura embraces me. She has a way of making you feel welcome, even when others don't. 'I'll go with him. His wife isn't well enough and I know the staff at the hospital. Might be able to get answers a bit quicker. If you two want to help, you can go in and keep an eye on Marianne. She shouldn't be alone. I'll call when there's news.'

Eoin must notice my reluctance and squeezes my arm in reassurance. It isn't that sitting with Marianne is a problem; I want to help however I can, but I don't want my urge to interview her to get in the way of what she needs right now. It feels like a conflict of interest.

Of course, I can't deny a burning curiosity to speak with her. However guilty that makes me feel. I remember the animalistic wails of her grief night after night when Henry failed to return home. There is so much mystery shrouding them both, the idea of going into number four makes my palms tingle. I probably won't get another chance with Marianne alone, let alone in the house Henry vanished from. It feels wrong. As though I'm taking advantage of someone's tragedy. I pause again to think of an excuse, but can't find one. I hesitate and then nod.

'Of course, anything that'll help.'

I walk alongside Eoin tentatively, our footsteps mismatched like a dance that's out of practice. The engine of the ambulance drums up to its movement and it drives to the dead end at the bottom of the road before turning around and driving away.

'I know where the spare key is kept,' Eoin says over his shoulder. He bends down near a row of plant pants that frame the Carrs' doorway and stands back up with a gold key.

'You coming, Ruth?' he asks.

I say nothing but join him at the door to number four, which is now ajar and waiting. Suddenly I'm aware of the prickling feeling at the back of my neck again. I glance over my shoulder, expecting to meet someone's gaze but there is nobody behind me – watching. I turn back to Eoin and we give each other a sidewards look before pushing our way into the unknown.

The house is a time capsule, even the wallpaper tells a story. It smells of dark wood and worn furnishings. I take everything in – each ornament, the pattern on the carpet, the smouldering warmth from the radiator that makes my throat prick instantly with dry heat. Neither of us says anything, but we hover by the stairs. Eoin clears his throat, a deep furrow in his brow.

'Hello?' he calls.

Nothing.

There is a painting in the hallway, a seaside town depicted with such life it seems out of place in a house as solitary as this. I can't take my eyes from it, the white froth of the waves breaking, the laughter in the painted faces. There are little beach huts, vibrant against the pale sand. It churns up a nostalgia in me that won't subside. Eoin nudges me gently and we move through the house like shadows. The walls are covered in paintings, each with the same signature beneath, a scrawl that is impossible to read. It's as though the walls are trying to speak to us, but it feels intrusive to look at it. We stop by a picture of Henry, the only one of him in the hallway. He's younger than the Henry I knew. It looks like a college photograph. I've never seen him look so smart. His eyes are creased by his slanted smile and his dark hair is slicked back with too much gel. He looks so much like how I remember Marianne, the same eyes, the same slender nose. Patrick must see him every time he looks at her now. We hold our breath at the sight of him, at the ghost of him.

'There's no one down here, Ruth; we're going to have to look upstairs.'

Eoin is already moving towards the stairs, sure footed and firm, when a sound erupts from upstairs, a single wail that is more animal than human. There are footsteps above me and a murmuring that is unintelligible. I follow the sound until I reach a bedroom, lilac carpeted and filled with light. It smells like baby powder and washing detergent. Eoin is standing by the window, his face etched with worry. I follow his eyes to a woman on the bed, cowering and exposed beside a small towel that she clutches to her chest. She is shaking, the duvet around her like ripples on a pond.

It's Marianne. The woman the street still whispers about, the one who has turned mad, the one who shrieks and sees things no one else can. Her eyes flicker between us, desperate and afraid.

Eoin crouches, his gaze never falling from her face.

'Marianne, it's me, Eoin. Marianne, please don't be frightened. You used to give me sweets in the summer whenever I was playing out the front, do you remember? No? Don't worry, it has been a while. I'm a bit big for all that now.'

His face breaks into a smile that she does not reciprocate. His voice only makes her tremble more. She is a shell of the woman who would sit on the wall at the front of her house, laughing as children ran around her, throwing sweets for them to catch as they tumbled at her feet.

Eoin looks up at me, prompting me to try. I shake my head but he nods in encouragement. Her childlike need reminds me of Mum in those last weeks, the fleeting images that I can remember. I kneel beside her, my jeans digging into my skin.

'Marianne, your husband had a fall. We're certain he will be fine but they just want to check him over at the hospital. We're just here to make sure that you're all right, and that you don't need anything.'

I rest my hand beside hers, resisting the urge to hold them. I don't want to startle her. I know I should do more but I am scared to be too close, to say too much in case she breaks.

Still there is no response. The only sign of life is the vibration of terror that rocks Marianne's slight frame. Her mouth is opening and closing, as if the words might tumble out of her. I kneel a little closer and decide to take one of her hands in mine. It's warm and creased with age and I wonder how long it has been since Marianne has felt any physical touch at all. There is a raw emotion in the room that sneaks up on all three of us. Marianne stills, looking down at her hand as if it is disconnected from her body. She stops moving. The atmosphere is balanced on a knife's edge. We stay like that, connected, hand in hand. Until, all at once, she collapses forward into my arms like a child and sobs until there are no tears left.

* * *

Marianne cradles the cup of tea between her hands and smiles like it's warming her bones. She's staring down at the mug like it's her favourite: it's ceramic and painted the colour of a sunset. She smiles again at no one in particular and sips the milky tea. She lets out a long sigh, so long that her frame crumples like an empty bag. I observe her silently, considering every movement, every flicker of emotion. She isn't at all what I expected, vulnerable yes, and distressed too at first, but she also radiates strength. As though she's the one comforting us. Eoin is smiling at her, and they share a giggle as they catch eyes. I wish I was just here as a neighbour, not as a journalist with a motive. The need for information is nibbling away at me, my phone burning a hole in my pocket. Guilt sits in my chest, guilt for constantly looking around for a glimpse of the truth. Marianne seems peaceful now, settles back into her chair like it is an old friend. One hand stroking the arm of it. After she had stopped crying, she had fallen into a deep sleep. We had wrapped her in a dressing gown from the back of the door and left her to rest, though it was only half an hour before she eventually wandered down the stairs and joined us in the kitchen. Her eyes were red and swollen, her face puffy. Despite it all, beneath the red, her eyes now are bright hazel. She has a songlike voice, and a light Irish accent. It isn't unusual for Irish families to live on the street – the area has long been home to those who moved to Manchester for work generations ago. Eoin tells her that her accent reminds him of his own family. She looks like a child, sitting within the huge fabric of the dressing gown.

'Are you feeling better, Marianne?' Eoin's voice fills the kitchen and we all relax against the noise of it. She looks at him, her eyes full of curiosity.

'Have I not been well?' She stares at Eoin, concerned.

'Not that I know of, but you were a little upset before when you first saw us.'

She nods at this, though her expression remains blank. She finishes the rest of her tea and gets up to place the cup in the sink, humming a tune as she does so. Eoin spots a radio on the worktop and switches it on; music tumbles out. Marianne cocks her head to the side, like she's waiting to see if she recognises the tune. She doesn't seem to, her words don't match it, but it doesn't stop her from shuffling along to it, spinning in circles and laughing hysterically when she trips into Eoin's arms. They dance together like that, laughing and bumping into almost everything. Marianne has a contagious laugh, a kind of whooping that echoes off the walls and hangs around us. It is surprising how fluidly she moves, her feet remembering what her mind cannot.

I cheer them on from the table, singing along with the music now I recognise it, clapping. From outside we might have looked like a family, might have seemed genuinely happy. I catch sight of a picture on the far wall, concealed mostly by a calendar that hangs above it. I wander closer to it, still distractedly singing. The picture is framed, faded in colour and not as clear as it might have been. It is easy to tell who the three of them are: two parents, Henry sandwiched in between. He is holding the handlebars of a bike, a blue bow tied around it. A present, it seems. Marianne is beaming, her eyes on Henry. But I recoil at the look on Patrick's face, his jaw clenched, his mouth closed tight. His arm is hovering above Henry's shoulder, barely touching it. As though they've had an argument before the picture was taken. As though he can barely stand the sight of him.

Eoin lets out a howl of laughter as a chair topples over and Marianne does a spin. I drag my eyes from the picture, but not before slipping out my phone and capturing it for later. Eoin catches my eye and stops, a question on his lips. Marianne stomps her feet impatiently and grabs Eoin by the arm. I hear another explosion of laughter as I slip away into another room.

* * *

I find myself in the living room, a small and homely space. It is filled with dark wood and cream furniture. A window looks out onto the street, allowing puddles of light to fall in and settle on the beige carpet. There is an armchair, angled towards the window, its seat worn and fraying probably from the hours spent there. The side tables are filled with trinkets and memories, sticky-notes on them with explanations of what they mean and where they are from. An effort from Patrick for Marianne? Or perhaps her own writing from when she knew what the illness would do to her, what it would take. I wander around, hands rooted in my pockets for fear of knocking something over. It is then I see the cabinet half open, paper hanging over the edges of the shelves. My hands leave my pockets of their own volition, my fingers tracing the scraps of paper and envelopes. One of the drawers in the cabinet is pulled out, paper spilling onto the floor in scattered piles. Someone has been through it in a hurry. Most are letters, addressed but seemingly never sent. I pick up a scrap of paper, my blood turning cold at the words.

We watched him die.

I panic.

I try to close the drawer, suddenly more desperate to conceal its insides. It won't move, it's sticky and reluctant, as if it wants its contents to be read. My force on it increases until it jolts forwards, not back, exposing more of its innards. My heart is hammering. Who watched who die? Marianne watched Henry die? Patrick did? I put a hand to my chest, try to settle myself. The sets of letters inside the drawer are tidier, formed into a tall pile. They seem different altogether. The paper is less yellowed, the ink sharper than the others. Sunlight hasn't danced on these pages. I don't dare handle anything. The journalist in me, however, stirs. I exhale. A letter on top is not addressed to anyone, it is simply an open letter. I hover over the top of it, trace the lines of writing with my finger in the air.

I could not sleep again tonight. Every time I closed my eyes I could see Henry looking back at me. Patrick says that I must get some sleep. It is as though I am there again, standing at the abyss, ready to throw myself into it. I have tried tablets and natural remedies, even talking through this diary though still, I find it difficult. Some things cannot be put into words. I am treated now as though I am mad. I know what people say about me. That I am a mother driven to madness by grief. But it isn't just that. It is the truth that haunts me, even worse, that no one believes me. Who would listen to a mad woman? They say Henry simply wanted nothing more to do with us. That he is living a grand life, somewhere south. Yet every time I go to sleep, everything is the colour of blood. I am haunted by the noise of it. I saw them together that day. The day he never came home. I shouldn't have followed them, maybe then I wouldn't have seen what I did. My poor boy. Tell me, how do you forget the smell of death?

I stand up sharply, my back aching from crouching over the paper. Guilt washes over me. It had been easy to accept what people said about Marianne after Henry disappeared – that she was insane. It's what everyone said, even my dad would make cruel remarks about her. He always warned me to stay away, and I did. Even when other children gathered beside her for the sweets she gave out or the jokes she offered. I would stand back, edge away. It is the same story for every other woman who has ever dared to grieve openly: raw emotion leads to judgement. Yet here is a letter that suggests Marianne knows something. Marianne has the answers that have been kept hidden for fifteen years.

Who did Marianne follow? Is there a murderer still on the street? I turn away from the letters strewn across the carpet, my finger running across my lip in thought. It is intrusive, to read what I have. These are someone's most private thoughts, someone's experience that I have no right to be a part of. It is Marianne's voice in the letters, a person desperate to be heard. It seems something so haunting had to be contained to paper. I turn back to search for a date on the paper but find nothing.

The mess seems out of place with the rest of the house, and I wonder if Marianne had been searching for something before we found her. We both paid little attention to the papers when we first looked around but now they seem to hold answers that Marianne could never give us. Poor Marianne. She has been shouting into a void. The age-old paradigm, trying to tell people you aren't mad only convinces them further that you are.

I rub my eyes with the back of my hand.

I fumble around the cabinet for other letters that might detail Henry's disappearance, my hands becoming more clammy with nerves as if my body knows it's doing something it shouldn't. But what I find makes no sense at all. Most of the letters and notes are ramblings, addressed to no one, scrawled and shoved into the pile. I all but give up when I see the edge of a piece of paper sticking out the back of the cabinet. I pinch the edges, trying to pull it free. After a moment I become frustrated, thumping the back of the cabinet with my closed fist. Doing so releases a spring, the back of the cabinet opening into a hidden space. It's small, only big enough to hold an A5 notebook. I pick it up tentatively, glancing over my shoulder cautiously. It's brown leather, bound together by a thin piece of string. Whoever stored it inside the cabinet wanted it to remain hidden. My hands are shaking, adrenaline pumping.

The outside gives no clues to what might be inside. I peel back the fabric carefully, aware of how fragile the book feels in my hands. I can barely believe what I'm reading. I flick through the pages, scanning names and addresses and scribblings I can barely decipher. One of the names has been circled several times, frantically, messily.

Initials and an address.

R. K.

Who is R. K.?

Why is the name, the place so important?

I look up as I hear the living room door being pushed open. Panicking, I fling the book into the cabinet and close it with my foot. Eoin looks at me quizzically, his eyes going to the cabinet – he must have heard it snapping shut. He must be able to see the whiteness of my face, the wide circles of my eyes. He hasn't noticed the phone in my hand, the camera still open on the screen from the picture I took. He opens his mouth as if to enquire when we hear the sound of something being dropped in the kitchen. He clenches his jaw, his hands lingering on the door knob.

'We'd best go in and see if she's all right,' I whisper, getting up and walking to him, my mind still elsewhere. The name of the person whose handwriting is scrawled on the inside cover like a tombstone. The person to whom the notebook had belonged.

Henry James Carr.

9

Patrick

My leg is jittering as the car pulls into the street.

I press my forehead against the cool of the glass, and it stems some of the throbbing in my skull. My fingers are clenched tight around a leaflet on concussion and I swallow down a wave of nausea as we hit a pothole. Laura smiles as I murmur under my breath to ring the council about it. They know me instantly now when I phone them, I've called that many times. I frown at Laura. I am not sure how potholes are amusing – they cause untold damage and injury. I let it slide; I am too tired to question her response.

Her smile wavers as she watches me out of the corner of her eye. Our time in A & E had been spent stuck to the plastic fabric of the chairs and listening to the alcohol-induced ramblings of those around us, though it was more than this that had put me on edge. I had paced up and down the corridors, my hands knotted together. I couldn't stop repeating myself, over and over, about the need to get to Marianne. Before she did something, *before she said something*, that would get us into trouble. Laura pulls up outside the house, scuffing her wheel on the curb as she comes to a stop. That'll scratch her alloys, but I bite my tongue to keep from telling her. I reach for the door handle, wincing as I stretch.

'Patrick, before you get out,' Laura begins. 'There's something I've been meaning to ask you.'

I pause. I feel weary, half defeated, but I wait.

'I read about the police reopening the case,' she says tentatively.

There it is, that secret simmering below my surface. I swallow audibly and heave myself up out of the seat. I am out of the car and leaning against it before Laura can run around to catch me. She has been so good to us over the years. I never knew if it was out of loyalty to Henry or to us, but either way she has been a godsend. Right now, I can't see the love in what she has said. Instead, I focus on getting my legs to work. Stubborn as they are. She attempts to support my arm, a gesture of care I throw off. It feels loaded now. Now she's mentioned *that*.

'I was waiting for you to bring that up,' I say.

I can feel myself getting hotter, my heart beating hard. A chill in the air ripples around us and I pull down the bottom of my cardigan, my body swaying in the cold.

'You're all the same, you people,' I declare, my hand gesturing to the street.

She looks crestfallen. She tucks a strand of blonde hair behind her ear, the purple shadows under her eyes darkening. 'Sorry. Sorry, no, I didn't want to intrude. We care; that's all, we all care. You have both been so withdrawn since Henry left, and we used to be so close. We're worried. It's been hard not to notice the police cars, the press. You don't have to say anything, just know that we're all here for you. We stick together, you know that.'

'Oh, believe me, I know that.'

There is something hanging in my tone, like a loose thread dangling in plain sight. I know Laura wants to pull it, to reveal all the hidden meanings, to really know what happened all those years ago.

She nods instead, palms up like a white flag. I respect her for that.

I nod, an end to the conversation. She watches me shuffle to the door, the leaflet still clenched in one fist.

* * *

I fumble for my keys with shaking hands. I can feel Laura's eyes on my back. Before I am even through the door, I can hear voices: foreign, alien, and then Marianne speaking. Panic crawls its way up my throat, choking me, making it harder to push forward to reach her. She could have told them anything, shown them anything, and I haven't been here to protect her. That is my only job, the only real job I have had as a husband since we lost our Henry. I just hope I haven't failed her. There is silence as I push myself inside, as if the house is holding its breath and waiting. I stop for a moment in the hallway, not sure exactly what I am disturbing. I see movement from the kitchen, hear the music as I creep closer in small, measured steps. There hasn't been music to fill the house in a long time. I try not to listen to any at all for fear of the memories. There is a rainfall of laughter.

I push the door more fully with a knock of my fist and it swings open to reveal a sight I will never forget. Marianne in her dressing gown, spiralling in circles around young Eoin. Her face is split open in joy, her bare feet bouncing in a quickstep rhythm. They stop dancing when they see me walk in and Eoin leans over to turn the radio down. He is watching Marianne's reaction with care. He looks up and smiles at me.

'Mr Carr, it's good to see you,' Eoin declares with a smile in his voice.

There's someone else here too: Ruth Cavanagh. Peter's daughter. She's a reporter. That's what Laura said. My eyes come to rest on Marianne, and she seems to recognise me instantly – she holds one hand over her heart and reaches out for mine with the other while looking to the dressing covering the cut on my head. The room has grown heavy suddenly.

Then I wonder why these two young people – strangers, really – came here. How they seem to care for Marianne. After watching Eoin dance with her, I am grateful. Ruth seems about to say something, when I take a step forward. I wobble, a wave waiting to crash. I don't fall, but walk into Marianne's arms. The radio calls out louder, a song that lifts us off our feet. We are one now, husband and wife. My hand is on her waist so gently, afraid that she might break. Her hands are on me: one on my shoulder, the other cradling my face. The room around us fades away. We could be anywhere, it wouldn't matter. This is what I cling to, the remembering, when she comes back to me with open arms. It is like falling in love all over again, better even. I could stay like this forever.

'Marie,' I whisper delicately into her hair.

She closes her eyes as if she is far away from the kitchen. Under her breath, she is humming along to the tune, her body responding to the notes. The song draws to a close, abruptly. The adverts cut in like barbed wire. She stops then, plants her feet firmly. Her hands do not move from my face. She opens her eyes and takes me in like a landscape, her gaze lingering on the tears on my cheek.

'I'm here, Patrick.' Her voice is clear, her eyes watering.

I nod, for there is nothing more to be said. I know.

I know.

10
Ruth

NIGHT HAS FALLEN ON the street in a thick smear, not clear enough for stars.

The cold air is a relief after the smothering warmth of Patrick and Marianne's home and I swallow as much of it as I can. I glance across the road and see the living room light on. I wonder what my father is doing, if he is lonely or drunk. Does he feel different now that I'm in the house too? Have I upset some hidden balance?

It isn't just this thought that sparks anxiety in me, but the book I found in the Carrs' cabinet. I don't understand why it has been hidden or who it has been hidden from.

Patrick? Marianne? The police?

'That was weird,' Eoin notes.

I glance back to Marianne's bedroom window. The light is still on behind the net curtains. I can imagine Patrick sitting with Marianne, speaking to her softly until she drifts into sleep. She will probably have no recollection of today's events by tomorrow, and it makes me sad to think that she might see Eoin again and not laugh with joy at the memory of their impromptu dance.

'Do you think she'll remember us?' I whisper.

Eoin lifts his eyes to the window.

'I don't know. I hope so.'

My mind flickers back to the letter I found, to the torment that must have eaten away at Marianne for years. I wonder if that is why Marianne is how she is now, if the grief and exhaustion have chipped away at her.

'I'm going to go over tomorrow, check that they're both all right. I'll fill you in on how it goes.' Eoin's voice is matter-of-fact.

'Thank you. And Eoin?' I swallow hard, ignoring the doubt gnawing away at me. 'I found something, in the house.'

He turns to face me, his eyebrows drawn together.

'What, Ruth? What did you find?'

There is an edge to his voice, almost as though he already knows.

'When you and Marianne were in the kitchen, I went to look around. I just needed some air, I felt overwhelmed by it all: by being back at home, Patrick's accident, with Marianne being so upset. I was just looking around, admiring all the books and the artwork. I came across a cabinet that had piles of letters, scribblings, in it. I don't know. I read one of them, I know I shouldn't have. It was wrong of me.' I say it quickly, my eyes to the ground.

I don't have to look up at him to know he disapproves.

'Listen, Eoin. I know it was a shit thing to do and I had no right.'

I consider telling him about the contents of Marianne's letter, but can't ignore the part of myself that whispers to keep it hidden, just for now.

'Henry Carr has a notebook in the cabinet. It was in a hidden compartment and I don't know what's inside, but if you go back into that house tomorrow to see them, I need you to get it.'

I think about telling him about the picture I took of the address inside the book which was circled over and over, before deciding against it. The deadline from Tom is looming over me and I already feel on the back foot. It is all so much more complicated than I could have imagined. Eoin's eyes are wild with the things he wants to say. He shakes his head.

'That would be completely betraying their trust.' His voice is sad.

I feel acid rise in my chest.

'I know. But what if it was kept from the police? What if could help find Henry? Eoin, you saw how torn up Marianne is about it all. It's destroying her.'

'It's not your place, Ruth,' he says, his voice hard. 'Marianne has problems beyond that. You don't even know them. You're a journalist, not a detective. You don't live here any more. You left. Ask your questions, but don't get involved in something you have no right to be a part of.'

He turns away. I feel stung. There is a sharpness to Eoin's voice I didn't expect, a confirmation of what I already felt – I am a stranger here now. It doesn't seem so long ago that we had argued endlessly about the street, about how trapped we felt.

'I'm sorry.'

He nods, then looks up at the black sky. 'It's impossible for people not to talk about it at the minute,' he finally says. 'The police, the press, it's all over social media. It usually feels like we live at the edge of the world, forgotten about, and now this. They've tried interviewing everyone but there's been resistance, you know what it's like. People want to be left alone.'

I smile wryly. I know all too well what it is like.

'Goodnight, Ruth,' he whispers as he turns and walks away.

I watch him as he goes, thinking of the story I need to write. Tom will want whatever I can get, but I know my work will feel like a betrayal to the street if it's nothing more than the gossip they're so used to hearing. I exhale and start walking. The terraces crowd together and press inwards, trapping me between them. I'm not ready to face home yet. Spending time with Marianne has struck something in me, like a nick on the skin. Reading in the newspaper and hearing things about her through the podcast seemed informative, almost objective. Yet seeing her in person, frail and grieving, makes questioning Patrick's involvement all the more difficult. I think back to what Eoin had said about the whole street being interviewed, about the resistance. Is everyone in on Henry's disappearance? It certainly feels that way.

* * *

I'm not sure why I've walked to the pub. It seems ironic that *it* is the home my feet remembered, not number five.

I push open the door of the Beehive with more force than necessary, plunging myself into the centre of the room. I feel eyes turn to me. It's largely quiet, the music still audible over mumbled conversations from corners of the room. The bar is empty and I smile at the vividly patterned carpet as I walk across it and slide myself onto a tall bar stool, pulling my purse from my jacket pocket. The smell of ale and wood and the age-old carpet mingle together into a memory that makes me half smile; the sound of darts and old music, the clink of glasses and deep hearty laughter seem the album of my childhood. Sam catches my eye from his corner of the bar. His face creases into a grin, and he sweeps a hand through the thick grey curls of his hair to see me better.

'Fuck! Ruth! I didn't think I'd be seeing you sat at my bar again. Let alone getting a drink!'

He places his enormous arms on the bar, the barrel of his chest hanging over it.

I laugh. 'Me neither, to be honest.'

He leans forward.

'I want to know everything. How was university? How's the job? How have you been? Any men I should know about? Any women?' His eyebrows shoot up, his mouth flickering upward. The northern roll to his voice booms across the space between us. Sam was one of the only people in my life, before I left the street, to really ask and want to know the answer. He listened to my hopes and dreams and fears, he held them all for me and helped me try to make sense of them when no one else could. He knows more of the darkness in my life than anyone else, and he still wanted to know, *really* know me. Sam has always been generous with free drinks to troubled souls. I have no idea how the place stays open.

'I think I'll need a drink before I tell that story, Sam. I'll have a cider, thanks.' I smile and offer my card, which he pushes away with a flick of his wrist.

'Don't be daft. This one's on me. We've a lot of missed years to catch up on.'

He plunges a hand into the fridge beneath the bar, slamming the cap off a cider bottle in a swift motion. I let the cool of the glass rest against my wrist, turning the veins to ice. The tension eases out of me as I unravel the past six years, laughing and whispering and unloading in a way I didn't realise I needed to. We reminisce about every famous fight in the pub, about the people – both savoury and not – who have passed through here. We speak about the street, about things that have changed and things that haven't.

'I was worried about coming back. Mostly coming home to Dad and admitting that I feel guilty about leaving him.' I sigh.

My dad has always needed someone to prop him up, as though some integral part of his skeleton is missing.

Sam nods, knowingly.

I continue, 'But also, I guess I worried I had turned my back on the street and that I wouldn't be seen as one of their own any more.'

'So why come back?' Sam asks, pouring a pint for an elderly gentleman at the end of the bar.

'Truthfully? At first for my career. To get onto a big story. Now? It feels like there's more to it for me. I don't know how to explain it but I want to represent the street fairly and truthfully in the media. To help work out what happened to Henry Carr,' I say, downing the rest of my drink and wiping my mouth with the back of my hand.

Sam frowns, concern in his expression. I wonder if there's something about Henry he wants to say, but a woman stumbles up to the bar and he's pulled away. I close my eyes, take the opportunity to go over what I've found out today. It isn't enough. Not enough for an article. I pull out my phone, ignoring the missed messages, and type Crow Street into the search engine. No new episodes of the podcast. Nothing new at all. I had expected as much. I set my phone down on the bar and push my palms into my eyes. Colour explodes, yet still I see nothing. The jigsaw pieces that might build a picture are out of my reach. I need to talk to Marianne again but know I can't ask her outright. She's too fragile, unpredictable. I also can't admit I read her diary. What had her writing meant? What exactly had she seen? It's possible that Marianne doesn't remember anything about it now, and maybe that's best for everyone. I scroll through older articles online while I wait for Sam, now encircled by two other women. I tap a link to an article. The heading seems to shout itself into bold.

Man still missing from Crow Street. Police reach dead end.

The article is old, published by a local newspaper. I read it ferociously, before starting from the beginning more slowly. I hover over the second paragraph.

> The family of the 34-year-old say his disappearance is out of character. They have called on locals to come forward with any information as to his whereabouts.

Reports suggest that detectives believe Henry Carr never left the street, as all CCTV of surrounding areas has been thoroughly analysed. A Mrs Montgomery of Crow Street, the last person to hear Henry before his disappearance, refused to comment. The missing man's father, Patrick Carr, stated: 'We are aware that people have been talking, suggesting he's run away somewhere. Let me be clear, he left absolutely everything behind. If he had decided to leave, he'd have taken it all with him. Something serious has happened here. The last sighting of him describes him in a distressed state. If anyone knows anything, please do the right thing and tell the police. We need everyone's help. He's our only son.' A search of the house and surrounding area brought some flurry of activity after a leaked source stated police had found blood on an item of clothing in the Carr household. There is no explanation so far as to how or when the blood appeared. The police investigation is ongoing.

I put the phone on the bar.

'Mrs Montgomery.' The name comes out as a whisper.

She's the key witness the reports refer to, the last one to hear him – alive. I wonder how the podcast and newspapers could have missed this, and realise the article is from a much smaller local press. One the other media outlets probably hadn't bothered to pick up. Would she have spoken to them anyway? I groan, regretting not asking Mrs Montgomery what she knows when I saw her today. Though asking something so insensitive with the poor woman's dead cat stretched out in front of her would have been cruel. What *had* she seen that day? Had he been with anyone? I read the article again, absorbing it. The word *blood* simmers in my vision, lingering. The article mentions nothing about suspects, though Henry's so called 'distressed state' and the blood all point to something far more sinister than a man leaving for a new life as some of the podcast theories suggested. I think back to Marianne's letter: about the mention of blood, the smell of death. The answer has been buried by the street, locked away behind muffled whispers and averted gazes. Mrs Montgomery might just have the key. I can speak to her. I can find this out, I know I can. I notice Sam watching me as he wipes down the bar in slow strokes.

'You all right over there, Ruth?' His voice cuts across the quiet now the women have left.

'Actually, Sam, I need to ask you something.'

He smiles hesitantly, cautious at the edge to my tone.

'I was with Marianne earlier, Sam,' I say. 'Eoin and I made sure she was all right while Patrick was being checked over after his fall. I found something that I think was about Henry's disappearance. Do you think you could tell me a bit more about him? I remember he used to come over to see Dad, and he was always really nice. But I was so young, I can't really remember much more.'

Sam's face falls, the colour draining from his cheeks. He puts his hands to use and arranges the bottles on the back of the bar.

'I should have stopped you earlier in the conversation, Ruth. I know you've a job to do but the truth is we don't say that name around here any more.' His voice is firm.

'Why? He was never found; doesn't that make people wonder?'

'It isn't fair on the Carrs to keep whispering about what might have been. We haven't allowed talk of him on this street since the day he disappeared. Not to the media, not to the Carrs, not to each other. Not a word. He's gone and that's the end of it. Best for everyone that they move on with their lives.' He turns away, his shoulders tense. I can see him breathing heavily.

I sit forward in my seat.

'Sam.'

He looks up, the sweat on his upper lip glistening. 'Listen, I'm gutted for the Carrs, I really am. But you need to let this go. Don't get involved. It's for your own good.' He rubs a calloused hand over his face, sees my expression, sighs.

'Please, Sam. The sooner I get a bit of information, the sooner I can leave. I won't bother anyone.' The lie lodges in my throat.

He considers me for a minute before leaning across the bar and whispering, 'The thing is, I can't pretend to really miss Henry. He was a nice kid who turned into a troubled guy, and he got himself into some dodgy stuff by the end. My bet? Someone finished him off. He pissed off a lot of people, maybe the wrong one.'

I try to read his expression, gauging how much he really knows. This is new.

'From what I've read,' I say carefully, 'he was well liked?'

Sam scoffs. 'Who told you that? His parents, probably. They're proud people, I get it. But in those later years, the street couldn't stand Henry Carr. He had a lot of friends on this street and lost a lot of them through his own doing. Borrowing, lending, scrapping. He was a mess by the end. Old friends don't forget being screwed over. They're not going to come running to his aid when he goes missing, are they? They still live on the street, they see what goes on, but they keep quiet because he's not their business no more. He got into a lot of trouble as a youngster too. Wouldn't surprise me if some of that trouble finally caught up with him.'

I digest the information slowly. Could that explain why the street has seemingly taken a vow of silence about Henry Carr? What did he do that was so bad? It doesn't sound like the Henry I knew, though I was so young I guess I couldn't have known what went on behind closed doors. I wonder, besides my parents, who was friends with Henry – and the truth is, I just can't remember.

'How did he upset everyone so much they'd wish a man dead?' I ask, tapping the record button on my iPhone.

'Let's just say he brought some unsavoury characters to the street. Drug dealers, loan sharks. The street was never perfect, don't get me wrong. We have our fair share of petty crime, but nothing like what he turned it into. They used to come in here sometimes, reserve that table.' He indicates a small round table in the corner, out of the way.

I chew the skin around my nail, rubbing my bottom lip against the puckered skin.

'He was a criminal,' I summarise, staring at the carpet.

Sam seems uncomfortable suddenly. As though he's said too much. 'I don't know the ins and outs of it, but he was involved in some dodgy stuff. Let's just say the street wasn't as surprised by his disappearance as you've been led to believe.'

'I read the news reports online. There was no mention of any of this. Just that Mrs Montgomery was the last person to hear him. I'm surprised the press didn't do more digging.'

Sam turns white for a moment, a memory clearly flickering in his vision. It passes and he gives his characteristic wry smile, tapping the side of his nose with his finger, his face solemn.

'It has long been a rule around here. What happens on the street, stays on the street.'

I sit forward, covering my phone with my sleeve. 'Surely his parents would have told the police all this. Even if it got him into trouble. They'd have wanted them to know everything if it helped find their son!' I can feel myself growing hot, exasperation rising in my chest. This information, it doesn't fit. None of the story is making any sense. In fifteen years, no one has ever dug up any information about his criminal connections. Why?

'I just don't get it, Sam. If I had a child, no matter how old, I'd do anything to help find him. Regardless of what it would do to my reputation.' My voice rises, and I sense that people are turning in their seats. 'Why didn't the street stand by him? Why wasn't the street honest when the Carrs were struggling? Why didn't they help them?'

Sam laughs, cold. 'Who do you think instructed us all to keep quiet from the off?'

* * *

I stumble out into the night, heart pounding. I keep my eyes down. I can see the street approaching, menacing in my peripheral vision. I wonder if I should keep walking and walking until I reach the edge of the world. I have my phone to my ear before I realise what I'm doing.

'Hello?'

'You kept the same number.' I smile.

Eoin's voice.

Thank God. His familiar burr soothes me. I don't say anything for a moment, I just revel in it.

'Ruth, is that you?'

I stop by the laundrette, catching my breath. 'I'm sorry about what I asked you to do. I know you can't take the book,' I say.

Silence.

I panic at his lack of response. 'I am sorry. Truly. I'm embarrassed at asking you, for not knowing you better. I've been in the Beehive, talking to Sam.' I wet my bottom lip. 'He told me stuff that's got me thinking. About people still on the street that had it in for Henry. Eoin, when you see Marianne tomorrow, can you ask her what she remembers? Just about Henry's friends? Who he knew before he disappeared? If anyone was upset with him?'

There's a pause.

'Ruth, where are you? Are you drunk?'

I shake my head. 'No. Marianne knows something. She genuinely knows something and no one will listen to her. Everyone thinks she's mad because she's a woman grieving.' I hear my voice cracking.

Eoin sighs. 'Ruth, she's struggled with her mental health for years. She's said a lot of things over the years that aren't true. I'm not going to ask her about something that will upset her – you saw how she was today.'

'I really think she has the answers to the whole case, Eoin,' I say desperately. 'The man deserves to be found. If you speak to Marianne, I can talk to Mrs Montgomery. She was the last person to hear Henry that day.' My voice rises a little, an echo in the emptiness of the street.

'Ruth, I appreciate what you're trying to do and I get it, you're a journalist. But you really need to leave this alone. There's a lot more to this story than we'll ever know. A lot more than Mrs Montgomery or the police probably even know.'

My blood runs cold. He knows something. He's kept something from me.

'What do you mean? Eoin, what do you know? Is this about the drug dealing? Do you know something about who wanted Henry dead?' I whisper frantically, conscious of someone overhearing my line of questions.

'Ruth, you need to know when to back off. Or you're going to have the whole street incriminated. Leave Marianne alone.' He says it softly but it stings. 'Goodnight, Ruth.'

The line cuts out.

The whole street incriminated? What does that even mean? I stand still and look down the street feeling a cocktail of fascination and revulsion. I make a note to ask Tom's police contact about Henry's criminal record and if it involved anyone on the street. I walk to number five, trying to ignore the impulse to glance over at Patrick and Marianne's. I fumble with my keys in the door. My father is on the sofa, the television blaring out into the room, colouring the walls in shadows. He's asleep with his head tilted upwards, his mouth slightly open, spluttering the sound of sleep into the room. He looks ill in the dim light and I consider stirring him awake and guiding him to bed, something my instincts tell me to do and my experience tells me to ignore. I pull a blanket from the chair and drape it over him, watching the rise and fall of his chest.

He opens his eyes a fraction and he sees me standing over him. Something flickers across his face: a loneliness? A need?

'Ruth,' he whispers.

He sits up and pulls on my arm, his own extending round me into a hug. The familiarity of him haunts me and I hug him back, moulded together into our mismatched family. His hand lingers on my face, his eyes swimming.

He is a man still grieving.

Maybe it's the alcohol, maybe it's just all the things he has always wanted to say but doesn't know how.

'I'm glad you're back.' And with that he lets go and walks off into the kitchen.

I nod, smile. Am I glad? I'm not so sure.

11
Peter

SHE LAYS THE NEWSPAPER out flat, crumbs sticking to the paper.

My eyes are still blurry from sleep and I rub at them viciously to force myself awake.

I stand, sweep my hand underneath, collect the remnants of another meal eaten alone with the radio blaring. She looks at me questioningly, tries to find meaning in the action.

I nod – I'm not sure why – and feel heat rise up my neck.

I clear my throat, throw the crumbs into the overflowing bin and pace a little before opening the fridge and removing a beer.

'You want one?'

'I've had one tonight already. That'll do me. I don't really drink,' she says, with a small smile.

We both know why.

I sit heavily back in the chair and it sways on unsteady legs.

My phone vibrates in the pocket of my jeans and I fish it out clumsily, glancing at the screen.

'Just a work mate seeing if I fancy a pint,' I explain.

'You should go, I'm all good here.' She smiles, settling in to read the newspaper.

I shake my head, push the phone back into my pocket. 'Nah, it's all right. Bit late now. I'll sit this one out.'

Ruth raises her eyebrows, unable to hide her surprise. Is she replaying all those childhood moments when I'd be out of the door without a thought? Countless nights into the early hours when I would wake her as I stumbled home? I feel sick at the thought of it, of who I was then. I wipe my mouth with the back of my hand, try to push the thoughts back where I've been keeping them.

She is reading now, squinting with concentration. Her dark hair falls around her face and conceals any emotion I might have been able to decipher. I want to tell her that I'm glad she's here, that it feels right to have her home, but I say nothing.

She makes a noise, a grunt of exasperation, and I lean forward in my chair, craning my neck to see the article.

'More of the same, is it?' I ask.

It usually is, dodgy reporters exaggerating, stretching the truth so thin it is barely recognisable. No one will have answered their questions, not here. They know they're not wanted, foreigners on our land. They don't care about us, about our safety. They want a story, want to demonise the working class as they always do. I feel a stab of worry for Ruth, about what kind of reporter she will be.

Will she talk about us as they do?

I take a swig of beer; it warms my chest and settles my nerves a little.

She is one of us, after all. The street is in our blood.

'There's no interviews, no sources. It makes it difficult to know if what they're saying is speculation or fact.' She's annoyed. She sweeps her hair back in an erratic gesture and leans back in her seat.

'You sure you want this story? There's a million other crimes out there.'

She looks at me, and I don't understand the look in her eye. She unclenches her jaw, tries to relax.

'I'm sure. If I don't do it, they won't get any answers. No one will talk, Patrick and Marianne will get no peace and this street will continue to be something swept under the rug. You're invisible to them, Dad. The whole street is. Don't you want a voice? To be heard?' She rubs at her eyes; they flare red and she closes them momentarily.

It isn't like her to be so vocal, to show her anger. I bite my tongue, accept that this is her now, that she isn't the Ruth who left all those years ago. I admire the fight in her, even if I wish it was for something else, about another street. The fridge hums and the clock ticks and we allow a silence to further the distance between us. I glance down at the trail of mud my work boots have left behind, something her mother would have told me off for. The memory tugs at a nostalgia deep in my gut and I drink another mouthful to dislodge it.

Ruth pulls a notebook from her bag and rifles through the pages. Her fingers scan the lines, and she chews her lip in thought.

'There's something I still don't understand,' she says, shaking her head. 'I was speaking to Sam and he mentioned Henry's past, about the people he associated himself with. It makes it seem like he had it coming to him – the disappearance, I mean.'

I shift in my chair, uneasy at the thought he deserved anything like it. I let her continue without interrupting, as I might once have.

'Except, that isn't the Henry I remember. It doesn't fit with the person I knew growing up or the friend I thought he was to you.' She pauses and I open my mouth to speak. 'It's not just that.' She closes the notebook, her hand guarding the cover. 'There's nothing about any of this in the news reports, no spec-ulation about it on social media. If he really was as dodgy as Sam says, why is no one talking about it?'

She turns to face me. This isn't rhetorical, she wants answers.

My mouth is now dry. For the first time in a long time, I'm useful to her. I can give her something she wants, something she needs. But doing it feels like a betrayal, to the street, to Henry. I don't quite meet her eye; I focus instead on the hardened parts of my palm. The life they've lived. I don't want to ask her how much Sam has said, just in case he hasn't said it all. No one wants to talk badly about someone who can't defend themselves, least of all someone who was your close friend. Christ, none of us were perfect. We were all idiots, in fact; we actively sought out trouble at times. Except, when the rest of us tried to grow up, tried to keep our heads down, Henry just couldn't. It was like it kept him going, the only thing that made him feel alive. He'd burst into the Beehive, desperate to tell us all the sordid details. He wanted us to feel the tug of it, the appeal of a life where every day was a risk, every job might be your last. I couldn't live like that any longer and nor could Sam.

I don't say this to her, can't say this.

'His parents weren't aware of a lot of it, still aren't as far as I'm concerned. They've suffered enough, suffered every day he has been gone. What good would it do to smear his name in the papers? What good would it do to tell them the shit he was up to? If the police had found anything worth saying, they'd have said it. It's not for us to get involved.' My voice is stern, final, and I pray that she accepts what I'm saying and moves the conversation on. She doesn't.

She is glaring in frustration. She sits up straighter, shakes her head a fraction. Enough for me to notice.

'I'm sorry that it isn't what you want to hear,' I say.

Her frown deepens.

'You think you're all being kind, that you're doing what's right, but you're not. Yes, maybe knowing about Henry's other life might upset them, but it can't be worse than never finding out what happened to him. They need closure, Dad. The whole street does.'

'How do *you* know what *we* all need?' I hear the flare of anger in my voice, try to settle it before I lose sight altogether. This isn't her fault, I remind myself. 'We were the ones who kept this street standing, kept it unified. We wiped the crime away, we kept it clean. We haven't lied to anyone, Ruth. We've just let the police do their job, let them investigate. What we know? It's better left unsaid.' I stand, crumple the beer can in my hands and toss it onto the side.

I try to hide my annoyance, my worry. This is bigger than she can understand, goes deeper than she can know, a ribbon so close to fraying. I turn my back to her. I don't want to see her expression as she watches me. I have seen so much disappointment when she looks at me that I have tried to stop seeing.

I look at the flickering overhead light, the stained lino, the clogged sink, and I want to burn it all down. Rebuild something for her from the rubble. Except I can't. This is what I have to offer. It was never enough.

I hear her chair scrape back, hear her footfall behind me as she hovers. I can see the reflection of her in the kitchen window, the silhouette of her arm as it reaches out and then drops back by her side. I dig my hands into my pockets, unsure of what to do with my own arms. This is new territory for me, showing emotion, being vulnerable – but it's the only thing that will keep her here. Even if it means opening old wounds, making new ones. I know what she needs, what she craves from me, and if I don't give it then she'll only get it from somewhere else, somewhere far more dangerous. I swallow, clear the lump in my throat. Half turn to face her.

'I can help you. Not with everything – there's too much even I don't know. But I'll share what I do, and I'll try and get some of the others to speak with you if it'll help. I can't make any promises, Ruth. These people are proud, they're protective of the Carrs. That's all I can offer.'

It's then that I feel her, her small hand on my shoulder. It is momentary, so fleeting that I begin to think I have imagined it. But it's in her face, the remnants of it, and I feel as though I'm finally a dad to her.

DAY THREE

12

Patrick

THE SOUND OF PERSISTENT birdsong stirs me from sleep. It's still early, and my glasses tumble from my chest. It seems I've fallen asleep reading again. I allow myself a minute to wake fully and stare at the bumps in the ceiling. The closeness of the anniversary is creeping up on me like a disease: it is reaching, threatening to consume me. It's only two days away, too near for me to ignore. I'm grateful Marianne won't remember. It isn't a date I mark on the calendar, nor one we speak of over the dinner table. Her memory loss seems like a blessing in that respect, and I feel sick admitting it. I sit up slowly. My head feels like it is split open, pain extending around the thickest part of my skull. I groan and squeeze two tablets from the packet beside the bed and throw them down with stagnant water from the glass I left there last night. I get up and wash, have a shave, dress, put in my dentures. Marianne's door is closed and I press my ear against it on the way past. I can't hear anything.

I make a quick to-do list on the jotter pad from the drawer: get the papers from Mr Chandra, collect Marianne's prescription. It is a dose of something for her blood pressure; she can get herself worked up so easily. It feels a mammoth task to care of her in the way she needs. I read something once about professional carers for elderly people, but I could never let strangers care for her, seeing her at her most vulnerable. It is *my* job, *my* duty. I remember a phone call from the previous week, about Marianne needing a check-up before the doctor will prescribe further medication. That is an obstacle I can't overcome; I'll have to book that in later today. I add it to my list.

I cook porridge on the stove and listen to the radio. As much as I try to stick to normalcy, I can't help feeling different. The house is different. Everything is different. It feels that we have both been exposed to the whole street now that Ruth and Eoin have seen Marianne. No one knows much about the dementia, and I have tried to keep it that way. I'm not ashamed, not at all. But I worry about what Marianne might say, the trouble it might get us into. I can't face her being taken away. She isn't able to keep secrets any more – whatever she remembers comes out.

It is only a matter of time before she says something that will destroy us both.

I've read numerous leaflets on dementia, about how to calm those with it, how to answer the questions they drag up from an earlier stage of their lives. It isn't lying, not really. It's about keeping up an act, not scaring her, not upsetting her. Though that is getting harder to avoid. I can't stand the look in her eyes when she is searching for something she will never find, some past that is beyond her grasp. It had all started with small things, losing her purse, putting her house keys in the cutlery drawer. We laughed about it then, convinced that it was the stress she was under. It had gone on that way for a while; we ignored jumbled sentences and forgotten names. It was only when she went into town one Saturday for some shopping but didn't come home that we realised what was really happening. She had walked for hours, tried at least three buses, and however much she tried she could not remember where she lived.

She was shaking when she eventually got back to Crow Street. Someone had been kind enough to drive her home, circling streets for an hour until she thought she recognised the right one. She walked through the door defeated, her shoulders shrinking in on themselves. I had lost her then.

'I need help.' She said it to herself rather than to me.

She was unblinking.

'No, you got confused. It happens in old age. I lose things all the time.' I tried to pacify her.

'This is different, you know it's different.' Her voice was soft, scared.

'Marianne,' I whispered.

She blinked, and a tear fell. I reached for a hand she didn't give to me.

'I know what this is, we all know what this is,' she said, firm.

'We don't know anything.'

'Denial won't change it.' She closed her eyes.

She looked scared to death, as if standing on a cliff edge knowing where she would end up.

'So we'll go to the doctors, then. They have all sorts of medications nowadays,' I said, forcing a lightness into my tone.

'They can't cure what I've got. I know it. It's just getting worse, and worse.'

She clasped her hands behind her back to stop the tremble in them. The tap dripped; we both turned to look at it.

'We will sort this. I'll do some research. We will manage, Marie; you can't give up yet.'

We both knew it wasn't about giving up, but that we had to find some form of acceptance.

'I don't want to forget you. I don't want to forget Henry.' Her voice broke as she spoke. She was gasping for air then, suffocating under the thought of it. I rummaged in the drawer, pulling out a paper and pen. I wrote down everything, everything she had forgotten so far, and how often it happened. I then pinned it to the fridge. We would take it to the doctors, together. It seemed heavier than paper. It was the black and white evidence of her mind's failings, held up to the world.

'There are some things I won't mind forgetting,' she admitted.

I knew what she meant then, the *day* she meant. I turned away as though I didn't. I leant over the sink, my breath condensing the window.

I relented. 'I'll call the doctor's tomorrow morning. You're right, its better we know what we're dealing with.'

'All right, then.' I could hear the fight in her disintegrating. It was what she wanted to hear, though it brought its own worries. I pulled my sleeves back and began the washing up as though it was something urgent. She sat down, quietly. We stayed like that, the knowledge of that new beast between us. It was then that Marianne thought of a diary, of writing down everything. Not what she had forgotten, but what she could remember. It seemed like the only way she could reliably remember, to try reading it back when she needed to. Though it wasn't just that. There was a look in her eyes sometimes, flashbacks to a memory that still stung, the one we had silently agreed to bury. Someone had to know, even if she wasn't there to tell them herself.

* * *

Our lives have moved beyond notebooks now. Marianne's ability to write coherently has dissolved day by day. They are still stored, as far as I know, somewhat haphazardly in the locked cabinet. It was my idea to lock it, to let her have the key. It had been her only way of having control over herself, of her own thoughts. I head into the lounge at the thought of them and notice the cabinet is open. My breath catches thick in my throat. It is never left open. Never. Panic rises in me. What did Ruth and Eoin see? What might they have read? My hand is on the brass knob, ready to turn it and collect the contents inside. A pang hits my chest, aware of how intrusive it is to read them without Marianne's consent, when she can't give it. I instruct myself to leave it well alone. It's gone seven o'clock when I return upstairs to check on her. I hear something fall over on the dressing table. I let myself in. Marianne is sitting and brushing her hair, her arms struggling to coordinate. She has showered, her hair releasing tiny droplets onto the carpet behind her. The room smells of her and I let it fill my lungs before offering to help. She accepts gratefully as she watches her reflection in the mirror. It feels like a good morning: she knows me instantly. I gently towel-dry her hair a little more. She's holding a piece of paper, sodden and bleeding ink in her open palm. The letters are indecipherable, a sea of black on white. What does it say? I squint to see better but the ink has run. Why would she take it in the shower? Then I remember most of her actions now make little sense to me. I feel relieved: it must have been Marianne who opened up the cabinet. I study her closely and watch as she nibbles the edge of her lip.

'That woman who was here last night, she reminds me of someone. I had a dream, I just couldn't work it out,' she whispers.

Frustration works its way into her face, her lips pursed. I feel myself sag, dreading another confused dream and the emotions it might bring.

'Everyone looks like someone, love. Don't fret over it.'

I try to conceal the anxiety in my voice; I can't bear watching her torture herself as she tries to remember. I pray she doesn't speak of Henry.

'I'm going to get changed now,' she says.

'I'll be at the shop. I won't be long,' I reply.

I linger a moment over the picture frame beside her bed: Henry as a young boy on a bicycle. His grin is stretched wide, his face a cluster of freckles. If I only close my eyes I'm back there, pushing my son to get him going, laughing as he wobbled along the grass of the wasteland. What I would do to have it all back, to change the day that changed everything else. I close the door behind me, placing my hand over the uneasy feeling in my chest. She seems distracted this morning, and not in the way the illness often makes her. Her mind is still on them, trying to remember something she has long since buried away. I knew it was a bad idea to leave her with them, that new faces often have a strange way of helping her remember old ones.

Ones she is safer to forget.

13

Ruth

I TRAWL THROUGH THE wildflowers, their petals brushing the bottom of my thighs. I slept well but woke early, plagued with dreams about Henry Carr. I got up and dressed before Dad had a chance to rise and walked to the wasteland. Breathing in the morning air, my lungs are filled with the scent of dew and wild heather. I look around. This is the first time I've felt respite from the eyes of the street. The constant feeling of someone watching my every move - I'm getting paranoid. The sight of this place, the smell of it, brings me back and I smile. I stop at the spot the police search has centred around. A dog walker from the street sees me lingering and we get talking. She tells me they had sniffer dogs all over the wasteland earlier in the week. She said this was the exact spot where the wallet was found. I stare down at the trampled grass; the small spot is almost opposite the summer house, and I know there is no way it would have been there for fifteen years untouched. This is a place people walk through to reach the canal, where animals roam, where youths gather and drink until the threat of their parents drags them home again. So why plant a wallet here?

'Because they knew it would be found,' I whisper.

It's the only answer that makes any sense. Someone snuck onto the wasteland, planted the wallet and waited for someone to find it. They must be a local to know how well-used this part of the wasteland is, which suggests it's someone from the street. I look over my shoulder, swallow. I duck down to the grass, feel the length of it through my fingers, and think. Whoever it was wants the case reopened. *Or do they?* Maybe the public interest and the anniversary panicked someone, and in an effort to sway the attention away from themselves they planted the wallet. Maybe they wanted to throw the police off the scent. *Was the person who phoned in the wallet and said they saw Patrick plant it the same person who killed Henry? Or are they protecting someone else? Was it even just one person, or more? A whole street? Why did Patrick tell everyone not to talk about the case? Why did they listen?*

I rub my eyes and groan. I don't feel much closer to the truth than when I got here. I stand up and stretch, feeling the burn in my muscles. I have the sudden sensation I'm being watched. The hairs on my arms and the back of my neck prickle against the air. Everything has gone quiet, no birdsong, or breeze in the grass. I spin, squint against the grey. No one. I exhale.

'Ruth.'

I jump. There's a hand on my shoulder. Fingers pressing into flesh. I turn. It's Laura. She looks different to yesterday. Her eyes are so shadowed they're almost purple, her hair is swept back and unwashed, her eyes wide.

'Sorry,' she says, pulling her coat tighter around herself. 'Didn't mean to make you jump.'

I smile, take a step back. I'm always glad to see her. She's the person you know will ask how you are and really mean it. She cares about people, it's just in her nature.

'It's all right. I think I'm just a little on edge.' I laugh. 'How are you? How's Patrick today?'

I look behind her at the back of the street, avoiding eye contact. There is something in her expression, her manner, that's suddenly setting me on edge. She looks at me for a moment, studying me before smiling and pushing her blonde hair behind her ear.

'A little tired. I was on night shifts last week, and it's hard to get your body to adjust. I find myself wandering sometimes in the early hours. I like the quiet of being alone.'

'That sounds like bliss,' I say. 'Except the nightshifts.'

She laughs.

We stand in an awkward silence for a moment, listening to the world around us waking up. She glances at the ruins of the substation, something sad in her expression, and then at the summer house behind her.

'You sure you're okay, Laura?' I ask.

'Sorry?'

'You just don't seem yourself. Is there something bothering you?'

She swallows audibly, folds her arms and looks at her feet. She reacts like someone who is not often asked, as though she is normally the one doing the asking. I have caught her off guard; she blinks tears away, her jaw tightening.

'Just the anniversary, I suppose. It's coming around so fast. Anyway, enough about me. When's the story due in?'

I'm unsure what to say.

'Eoin says that's why you're back. A story on the disappearance.'

I shift my weight. 'Oh, yeah. I have to produce something for tomorrow. That's why I'm out here so early, actually. Just getting my thoughts in order. It's hard to write something when no one will talk.'

'People here don't forget, Ruth. That day is engrained in all of us. It's a day we don't want to put into words.'

'What do you mean?' I ask, hoping for something – anything – I can use.

There is something she isn't saying. She opens her mouth to respond when the slam of a car back over on the street makes her head snap around. She shakes her head, exhales shakily. The moment has gone.

She smiles. 'I love you like a daughter, Ruth, we all do. You know that. But we can't be part of this story.' She looks around, lowers her voice to a whisper. Her hand is on my arm, her grip firm but her eyes warm. She used to be like a second mother to me and I see a fondness in her expression as she observes me. She looks sad suddenly and her grip tightens.

'My advice? Just take what you've got and go.'

* * *

I sit on the window ledge and sip my coffee, watching Laura as she walks down the road and into the distance. I can't shift the feeling she left me with. Like Sam, I'm positive she's hiding something. I just don't know *what* that something is.

I pull up the internet and search. The next episode of the crime podcast has been released. It has already been downloaded half a million times and I settle in to listen to it. The episode and comments take me a full two hours to work through. The episode just covers more conspiracy theories, all based on hearsay or fabrication. There's nothing concrete to work with. Most of the people commenting aren't even from the country, never mind the street. I keep hoping that someone with genuine information will have their memory stirred, something they may have seen and thought nothing of at the time, something that would tell us more about where Henry went that day. The most popular comment speculates that Henry was killed in his parent's attic, dragged up there by Patrick in a fit of rage. Their only theory as to why his body wasn't found in the initial search of the house is that the officers were incompetent and didn't check the attic. It's not impossible, I suppose, though the claim seems to be based entirely on Patrick's initial arrest and the rumours that had circulated in the press of Marianne's continual wailing. I imagine Henry, lying above the warm room where Marianne and Eoin had danced last night, his fingers claw-like and reaching out, his decomposing mouth an eternal scream. There is still no conclusive evidence that Henry is even dead, and while it is unlikely that he is abroad somewhere, sunbathing, it isn't impossible. Maybe Henry himself orchestrated someone to dump the wallet to further push the narrative he was killed because he doesn't want anyone to come looking for him. The hope that Marianne might see her son again comforts me.

But it is a hope that has been quashed by Marianne's own hand.

Her note. Her admission of what she saw. I sigh. I feel too invested in it all. A maze with no exit. I push myself upright and take in my childhood bedroom. There are still fairy lights half falling down, a stain on the carpet from makeup I had tried to remove, and posters of bands I had loved and still do. I smile at the haven I had made for myself. Most of the pictures are of Mum before she passed away, or of Eoin grinning and looking at me in that way he always did. Everything and nothing has changed. I hear my father shout goodbye as he leaves for work and I say it back, smiling. He's the one thing that feels a little different. Our interaction last night moved me in a way I hadn't expected. I felt more love from him than I ever have. I watch him on the street below, loading his van, his movements slow, the alcohol still sitting heavy in his system. He isn't perfect but he seems to be trying, and that's all I've ever wanted.

It had been easy to forget this life. Newcastle is different. It is loud and bright and so distracting I can forget almost everything. When I moved up there, I had known no one and that was exactly what I wanted. To be anonymous. It isn't like that on the street: everyone knows everything; no matter how small or insignificant it is, they still have claim over it. After Mum passed away when I was 10, I had decided firmly I would be free of the place at the first chance I got. Nothing could be warm or whole or home without my mother in it. Tears prick at my eyes and I press them away. I can't deny the guilt I felt at leaving dad behind, despite the alcohol and the shouting, despite the bruises: I knew there was love buried somewhere beneath.

I am lost in my thoughts when two police officers approach my dad. I press myself to the window and open the latch to hear what they're saying. The window creaks as it opens, stubborn until I force it with my elbow. Their conversation filters up in odd words, questions with the endings cut out. I can tell my father is being hostile – his body language is defensive, aggressive. He won't like them sniffing around. He's made of this street, his ancestors were made of this street, and he'll defend Henry the only way he knows how. The officers aren't giving up – they seem determined to speak to all the residents. I am peering down at them when my phone rings, shrill.

'Hello?'

'Ruth, it's Tom.'

I see my father climb into the van and drive away. The officers watch him leave. I pick at a flake of peeling paint, the sharp tip of it embedding itself under my fingernail.

'Hi Tom. Sorry, I meant to call again. It's just all been a bit hectic since we last spoke.'

'Don't worry. How are you? How is it all going?' He sounds eager.

'I haven't put any of it into words yet, but I plan to get on that later today. I've met a few members of the street. The parents. It affected me more than I thought it would, their grief. Their frailty.'

'Sounds like the makings of a good story. Remember, you're on a tight deadline. The anniversary is only a couple of days away so I need to you to send me something I can print as soon as. I've just sent you over the number for my officer. He'll be furious I've passed it on but he'll get over it. I know you have questions only he can answer. Tread easy, though; he really is edgy about speaking to journalists.'

This is it. This is what I need.

'Amazing, yes. I'm going to get on that now and I'll call you back, is that okay?' I ask.

A laugh.

'Sure it is. You look after yourself, okay?'

There's that concern again. I reassure him and hang up, relieved at having something concrete to do. I click on the text message he has sent with the officer's details. They have been sent with a lengthy warning to keep him anonymous, and to not share his details with anyone. I take a deep breath as I decide what questions to ask. I'm an insider, with my own insight into the case. I can bargain with him. I exhale and press dial. The ringtone buzzes with no answer, and my chest deflates. I check the number again and redial. No luck.

'Shit.'

I throw the phone on the bed and drag my hair into a bun. I look back down at the street, at Frank and Margo walking hand in hand, at Laura carrying items from the corner shop. It all seems so normal. I look across at Patrick and Marianne's house, at the heavy silence of it. I wonder what Marianne is doing, what she remembers today.

I pull my laptop from my desk and begin writing, typing without thinking, about a mother who has lost her son and is losing herself. I write about the street, about its hostility, about its secrets, about the façade it has built to protect itself. I'm almost a thousand words in when the phone rings.

'Oscar Fields. I had a missed call from this number?'

It's him. The informant Tom has spoken of.

'Hi, this is Ruth. I got your number from Tom at the *Chronicle*. He said you had information relating to the Henry Carr investigation.'

A pause. Heavy breathing.

'I didn't agree to this. Now isn't the best time to talk.' He is abrupt, panicked.

'Sorry, I understand this is sensitive. It's just, I'm a journalist, and I've been given the Henry Carr anniversary to write about. I need information and I'm guessing you do too. I might know something that could help you. I grew up here, I know everyone. Henry was my parents' friend so I have a perspective others won't. I can be the eyes on the inside, so to speak. I think we could be pretty useful to each other.'

A cough. Another pause. Muffled sounds as a palm covers the speaker, voices and polite excuses.

'All right. Listen, because this is all you're getting. No one knows this yet, and it didn't come from me. You hear?'

'Yes. Yes, absolutely.'

'Items belonging to Henry were found in the wasteland behind the street he disappeared from. Forensics haven't found a lead on any items so far, there's no DNA on them that tells us anything. After excluding the prints of the dogwalker, we couldn't lift anything from it. The wallet wasn't as weathered as you might expect. I mean, it's clear it's been outside for a period of time, but fifteen years? Definitely not. One last thing, the best thing we have. There's been more anonymous phone calls stating that there is more evidence around the street. It's like following bread-crumbs at this point. We're chasing it all up.'

'More evidence? Like what?' I sit bolt upright.

'That's all they've said so far. They're volunteering information but it's unclear what their motive is – whether it's genuinely to help us, or if it's to send us in the wrong direction. They were right about the wallet but there's a lot of questions around that. They've got in touch with us a couple of times now.'

I remember Tom's advice, the training he has drilled into me.

'Anything to suggest what actually happened to Henry? If he's alive or . . .?' I let the sentence fade out.

A sigh.

'I can't say much more but we reckon the tip-off is genuine. Officers are on the ground as we speak. We have reason to believe this is about to become a murder enquiry.'

I swallow a gasp. This is more than I'd hoped he'd give me and I don't want to mess it up. I balance the phone between my shoulder and my ear and begin typing on my laptop. My mind is racing.

'Can you tell me what the caller has said? What kind of evidence there might be?'

Teeth grinding, an exhale. He's getting irritated. Tom was right, he doesn't really want to be telling me anything. So why talk at all? Money? Corruption?

'Look, if I tell you this detail you have to promise to wait to publish it. You can be the exclusive but it can't be yet. We need more time. Promise me, or this is over and Tom can have his cash back.'

I put my feet flat on the floor. 'Of course. I promise.'

'Whoever is phoning in has been watching us. They know our movements, our leads. Only calling when they see us reach a dead end. We believe they must live on the street. What they told us this morning has blown the case wide open. There's no going back for us now.' He falls silent.

'What? What did they tell you this morning?'

A growl of frustration, a shaky breath down the phone. 'They said the body is on Crow Street. It's been there all along.'

14
Ruth

THE STREET IS SIMMERING in the rain. The terraces seem to nudge up closer to one another, huddling against the incoming storm. There is little movement to be seen, just cats sheltering under cars and the odd shopper braving the rain for a carton of milk. All houses remain silent. Their windows smeared with rainwater, distorting the view out and in. I stoop beneath my hood, still baffled that I managed to forget to pack an umbrella for what is the rainiest place on earth. Nerves flutter and I press my hand to my middle to settle them. It feels silly to be anxious over something so simple. I ring the doorbell and wait, observing the trinkets and flower pots that line the front of number four. I pick up a small gnome that has fallen over and the door creaks open. I see Patrick's tartan slippers before I see him and I smile to myself.

'Thanks for coming. The hairdresser has never cancelled before, but she said it was a family emergency. Margo's nowhere to be seen and I tried calling Laura this morning but had to leave a voicemail. She still hasn't got back to me. She usually helps with things like this but I thought you could maybe handle it after settling Marianne while I was gone. Her hair gets tangled if it's not done properly. I've tried combing it, but . . . well, she won't really let me at it.' He grimaces an apology.

I put a hand on his arm as I step into the hallway. 'It's a pleasure, honestly.'

My voice sounds more certain than I actually am. Squeezing my hands into a fist, I swallow down the nervous energy that's rising in my chest. It doesn't really feel right, being here, seeing them like this. There's an understanding in journalism that to get too close, to see behind the story, can be as much of a hindrance as it can be a help. It's getting hard to view them as I need to.

I find Marianne standing on the landing, a towel clutched to her chest. She puts a hand up in greeting as she sees me and I feel a spark of warmth that she remembers me. I shrug my coat off and hang it on the banister, pulling myself upstairs slowly towards her.

'Hello again, Marianne. Is it okay with you if I wash that beautiful hair?'

She twists her feet inwards, shy suddenly at the attention. A meek nod comes and I let her lead me into the bathroom. The smell of soap and talc hangs in the air and I help her sit down with her back to the tub. I pull her hair free and place it on the side of the bath, then adjust the temperature of the shower until I feel it is gentle enough for her.

Her bright blue eyes look up at me, studying my face, as I begin to wash her hair. I use my fingers gently, taking care with the fragile skin of her scalp. I stroke the area around her face lightly, watching the flicker of her smile. I rub the shampoo in gently, cautious to avoid getting it in her eyes. We don't speak at all; just the sound of the running water fills the room. I place the shampoo bottle securely on the side and turn back, noticing the tears brimming in her eyes. She blinks them away before they spill over. I reach down for her hand, and she grips mine tight. She shakes her head, laughs, kisses the top of my hand and beckons me to continue.

I laugh too. There is a fondness deep in my bones for Marianne now. I dry her hair carefully in the towel, then she leads me to her room. Marianne tugs me close beside her and proudly points out items of importance. We take our time this way, existing purely in the moment, and I can't help but feel she may be fond of me too.

* * *

I wave goodbye to Patrick and step back out into the street, squinting against the brightness of the grey. The stillness is disrupted as a police van pulls in. There is a flurry of activity, and Oscar Fields steps out of his vehicle. It isn't difficult to spot him after completing a quick search online earlier. He's shorter than I imagined, younger. He must only be in his thirties. He keeps his eyes to the ground as he approaches a group of officers and begins talking hurriedly with them. I pull out my phone and take a picture of the scene. The team seem to come to a decision and Oscar leads the officers and a canine unit away, towards the wasteland. If they're going to search the whole area, it will take them days; the wasteland goes on for at least two miles before reaching the canal beyond. A body could be anywhere. Following them, I keep my hood low over my brow. I walk quickly, splashing through the puddles. As I turn the corner I stop, seeing someone's shoes, their legs, their stillness in front of me. I don't look up at first but attempt to sidestep them, and they mirror my movement. I pause, and as I reach up to pull back my hood, they seize my hand, gripping it in theirs.

'No you don't.'

It's a man. I don't recognise the voice.

'They know you're here, girl. Glad to see you return too up until hearing exactly why you're back. That changes things. You may have forgotten, since you've been gone so long, but there are certain rules here. Crow Street looks out for its own.'

I nod. My hands are shaking. Is this who I've felt watching me over the past days? I'm not sure.

'I understand, I really do. I'm not trying to cause any trouble. I'm trying to help the Carrs.' I stutter, angling my wrist to slip it free of the man's grasp.

It isn't Patrick or Frank. I'd recognise their voices anywhere. *So who?*

My mind works through the possibilities as he leans so close I can smell his breath.

'The Carrs don't want your help. They want you as far away from this as possible. You'll thank them one day. Trust me. Listen when you're told to go. Don't speak a word of this place to anyone.'

There is tobacco on his breath, smoky and strong. He smells of ground in dirt and sweat. I don't say anything, just breathe and stare at his feet and legs. He lets go and I'm frozen in panic. By the time I bring myself to look up and turn, he's gone.

* * *

I wait several moments before continuing, paranoid about who is watching me or following me. I'm shivering by the time I start to move again, rainwater soaking through my clothes. My skin is slick and covered in goosebumps. I walk faster, making a shortcut through the alleyway, and sidestep an old fridge-freezer someone has dumped there. I stop momentarily. It seems an odd thing to do. Not in general, but here, in this spot. It's an unspoken rule that the alleyways are a place for bins and bins alone, with food for the stray cats the only exception. I can't remember any fly-tipping here, not ever. It's hard to say which house it has come from, lying as it is in the middle of the path. I lean closer and study it. It's the cheapest model of a popular brand, half the houses on the street have this fridge or similar from what I can remember. Yet, something unsettles me and I step back at the sight of it. *What if there is something in it?* I look up at the windows above the alleyway, though I know all too well how good the residents are at concealing themselves when required. I bend a little closer to the fridge-freezer. I look down at my bare hands, at the white cold numbness of them and contemplate whether I am brave enough to open the fridge door.

I decide I am not.

I retrieve my phone and call the number in my recent list.

'Oscar, it's me. Ruth. There's something you need to see in the alleyway off Crow Street, by the wasteland. It could be nothing and probably is, but I think you should check anyway.'

He hangs up without saying anything. Has he heard me?

I balance my phone in my palm, wondering if I should call back. I decide against it. He is my only contact on the inside, and I can't afford to piss him off. I'll steer clear of the wasteland for now. If I encroach too much, Oscar might just cut me off altogether. Especially after that phone call. Instead, I cut down through the alley and come out by Eoin's. I smile at the memory of his house and text him to see if he's home. The front door is ajar and a trickle of music pours from the gap. He hasn't replied and I haven't spoken to him properly since last night. I can't shift the nagging unease that he might still be angry with me. I inch closer. The house has always been a magnet to me. It was the place I had learnt what a real home looks like, where arguments and laughter and silences were all knitted together with love. I knock delicately on the wood and the door slides open an inch further. The music grows louder.

'Eoin?' I call.

I step into the hall tentatively. The smell of him hangs in the entrance like a coat hung on a hook. I edge forward, following the music. It is a song I don't recognise, something that sounds vaguely from the Eighties. I stop before the living room, realising that whoever is home might not be Eoin. I freeze, then look back towards the door, still open. An easy exit. I retreat slowly, sneaking backwards like an animal caught in the headlights. I am almost there: my foot is kicking up the edge of the welcome matt.

'Hello?'

Laura stands by the living room door, a book in her hands. She sees me and her eyes widen, then she pulls the book behind her back.

'Laura. Sorry.' I slick my hair back, mortified. 'I was just seeing if Eoin was here. I called out but you mustn't have heard me. I'm really sorry to intrude.'

'No.' She smiles and pushes the fallen strands from her ponytail behind her ears. 'No, don't be silly. Come in. Sorry if I look a little weathered; after my walk this morning I fell asleep on the couch – that's what happens when you work nights, eh? I've only just started moving again. Thought I'd do a bit of spring cleaning. Do you want tea or anything? Eoin's still at work, but he'll reappear soon I'd imagine.'

Despite the weird vibe I got from her this morning, it feels normal in a way to be here with her. I get the distinct feeling that Laura is lonely, hurting, and even without my desire to get a scoop for the paper, I want to check she's all right.

'Of course. That would be lovely, thank you.'

Laura ushers me into the living room, turning down the radio. She doesn't make me feel like I'm intruding, and I find myself liking her as much as I always did. Neither of us makes any mention of this morning's encounter and I'm glad. I choose the chair nearest the window, a solitary turquoise armchair where Eoin and I had often snuggled up for hours.

'Ah, that always was your favourite spot.' Laura smiles wistfully before pottering into the kitchen. The sound of the kettle clicking and the low rumble of it heating fills the house. I smile gratefully as Laura returns, her hands cupped around a scalding mug. She has remembered how I like my tea and my heart swells at the thoughtfulness.

'How are you? Gosh it just feels like so long since I've properly spoken to you. Sorry about this morning, tiredness got the best of me. You look well, you really do,' Laura says, kindness in her tone.

'Thank you, Laura. I'm good. Great actually, though it's difficult being back. It's nice to see familiar faces. Newcastle can be a bit lonely sometimes.'

'I can imagine. This must be a strange place to return to, with all the good and bad that's happened to you here. Newcastle sounds amazing. I've never been of course, but heard about it. Full of busyness and noise, but that doesn't always equal company.'

'I'm sorry if me being back on the street is upsetting. I understand why people aren't happy. It's my job, but to be honest, I feel strongly about getting the story right. For Patrick and Marianne but for Henry too.'

Laura sips from her mug and perches on the sofa opposite. At the mention of Henry's name her eyes wander to the piles of paperwork on the floor. There is a book, the one Laura had tried to conceal behind her back, peeking out from the paper she has forced it under. It seems odd, to make such an effort to hide it. She must have done it as I walked to the chair.

'Do you mind me asking what that is?' I say, nodding at the book.

Laura hesitates before nodding, sets her tea on the coffee table.

'Of course. I was just tidying, like I said, trying to declutter. Though I doubt that will ever happen. The whole house is still filled with Eoin's stuff. I don't think I'm getting rid of him anytime soon.' She smiles fondly. 'I came across my old yearbook from when I left school. I was just doing a little reminiscing, hence the music.' She laughs, embarrassed.

'Do you mind if I have a look? You and my dad were in the same year, weren't you?'

'We were. All feels a long time ago now,' she says wistfully.

I set my mug down beside hers and pick up the yearbook. Balancing it across my knee, I flick through the pictures and run my fingers across the glossy pages. There are faces I recognise, residents of the street, and people I have seen in local coffee shops and the town centre. The community is small and it's hard to avoid being recognised, even despite the age difference. It takes me a couple of minutes to find my father's picture, the broad shoulders, the sweep of dark hair, the set jaw. It's hard to see how he has changed at all. He hasn't included a quote beneath his photo, like some of the others have, and I smile sadly to see he'd been an outsider even then. I scan the other photos. I laugh when I find Laura and we both joke at the hairstyles of the Eighties.

It isn't until I begin to close the book that I spot him. I gasp.

'Wait, Henry Carr was in your year? I always thought he was younger than Dad – they used to joke about it. It's kind of why Dad was like a big brother to him.'

There is an uncomfortable silence, the shifting of body weight and thoughts collecting themselves.

'Just about,' Laura finally says. 'The way the birthdays fell for the school year meant he was the youngest in the class. He didn't always fit in too well, he needed us.'

'Was that something he always felt, do you think? That he didn't fit in?' I enquire.

Laura looks at her hands, at the cracks and the lines of life embedded in them. She looks weary.

'I think so, though his personality changed as we got older. We stayed friends for a while after school, the group of us from the street, but in those last few years he just seemed to lose himself a little. He was distant, stressed. Like the weight of the whole world was on his shoulders. He'd been brought up not to speak of his feelings much . . . like most of us of that generation, I suppose.'

'Do you have any idea what might have changed to make him feel that way? Who might have made him feel that way?' I lean forward.

Laura looks up, a crease forming in her brow. 'Ruth. Please.' She hesitates. 'Like I said, we weren't really close in those last few years.'

I sense something else, something heavy and unsaid.

'Did something happen, Laura? Between you and Henry? Or between the group as a whole?'

She grips the arm of the chair and adjusts herself, caught off guard. She licks her lips anxiously. I can tell I'm onto something, so lean forward a little more urgently.

'If something happened, it's never too late to come forward. However insignificant you feel it may be.'

She shakes her head, tears welling in her eyes. 'I can't talk about this. Not now. I told you this morning.'

There is something torturing her. Whether it is Henry or something else, I can't tell.

I feel that this confirms what I have started to suspect: that there is something more sinister, some deeper secret between the people of this street.

'Sorry,' I say, smiling weakly. I can feel her retreating. 'I'm just trying to find out if there was anyone who might have wanted to harm him or if he'd fallen out with someone in some way.'

There is something there, something she is waiting to share, waiting to be asked about. Maybe it's because I'm part of the street, maybe it was the affection Laura had once felt for me, but something pushes her to let it fall out and it lands in the space between us.

'Martin,' she says.

'Martin?'

'From number ten. He used to hang around with us. Me, Henry, a couple of other lads, your dad. We were all about the same age, all lived here; I guess it was inevitable that we'd all sort of be friends.'

I nod, willing Laura to continue.

'He and Henry had a falling out over money. Seemed that Henry had to borrow a pretty big sum from Martin, some left-overs inherited from his parents. We were all tied together, the lot of us, we'd been through a lot together, so when Henry asked, Martin couldn't really say no. Except, time went by and Henry never paid him back. That was a couple of years before Henry disappeared. I really doubt it's related,' she says, her eyes flittering between mine anxiously. She seems conflicted, between her loyalty to the street and her old loyalty to Henry. I sense that this isn't exactly what is bothering her, there's something bigger that she is hiding from both me and the police.

'Would Martin not just have taken a legal route? He could have gone to the small claims court or whatever. Anything else seems a bit extreme for two childhood friends.' I can tell I am pressing her too far, but something isn't adding up. This friend-ship, these group of friends, there's something sharp and dangerous beneath the surface of it.

'Like I say, we'd been through a lot together. Grassing each other up wasn't an option. I can't shed any more light on it, Ruth. If you want anything else answering, you'll have to speak to Martin.' She looks at me, pleading with me not to ask her any more and mutters a 'good luck' under her breath

What had happened between them that was so significant it bound them together this way? I think of Dad's friendship with Henry, which never seemed taut at all. Except, I think back to what Sam said about Henry, his tone, the anger in his eyes. I scribble some notes down and smile at Laura. It's as good as I'll get from her right now until I figure out what she has hanging over her. I take one last drink from my tea and pull my coat back on.

'Number ten, right? Thank you, Laura. That's really helpful.'

I want to say more, to thank her for being like a mother to me all those years, to say how much it meant to be welcomed in as I had. Instead, I stop as I pass, squeeze her arm, and when we look at one another, I know that Laura understands.

* * *

The rain has grown heavy, drumming on the cars and dancing in the potholes. I spot a new police car parked at the end of the road and wonder if Oscar has sent them to check out the fridge-freezer in the alleyway. I hope so.

I look down at number ten and realise how little I know about the occupant. It always seemed derelict. The front gate is rusted and hanging off, the vegetation growing up and over it. The windows are black with grime and the curtains are stuck to the glass like skin. It looks abandoned, left to rot and decompose back into the earth. Some of the roof tiles are loose, and leaves are clogging up the guttering. Without thinking, I rummage in my pocket for a Polo and place it between my teeth, just as Eoin approaches.

'You're getting drenched out here. You all right?' he asks.

I laugh. His hair is plastered to his forehead. His eyelashes are heavy with water droplets and his lips are shining. I feel an urge to draw him closer, to shelter him, but I smile and turn back to number ten.

'I'm all right, honestly. You just seem to always catch me when I'm staring at people's houses,' I say, grinning.

'I suppose I do. You won't see much from this one. Martin's a recluse. Never comes outside. Mum sometimes drops shopping round. He never opens the door, but the next day the shopping is always gone and there's money left with the receipt.'

'Ah. Your mum said he was friends with Henry Carr. That they had a falling out over money?' I ask, gauging his response.

Eoin shrugs. 'I didn't know that.'

Something in his expression strikes me. His eyes are on his feet. *Is he lying?*

'I need to speak to him. See what he knows about the disappearance. If he never gave a statement in the original investigation, he could have the answers they're missing.'

Eoin looks dubious. He steps up onto the pavement to let a car pass by.

'He won't answer, Ruth. I'm telling you,' he says firmly. He pushes his hands into his work trousers, orange clay staining the black.

'I have to try. Marianne deserves answers.'

I glance back at number four, a sadness settling in me. I think back to Henry Carr's notebook and can't help wishing I had it. To know all the answers it might hold.

I feel Eoin behind me as I approach the house, the bulkiness of him like a shadow. I feel soothed by it and it gives me the courage to push through the vegetation to the front door. I press the bell tentatively, unsure if it will work at all. I hear nothing and knock just for good measure. A heavy silence follows. I step towards the window, my face to the glass.

'It's impossible to see anything. Are you sure he still lives here?'

'Mum seems pretty sure he's still there. Who else would be accepting the shopping and leaving money?'

I step back and look up at the front bedroom window. The curtains are drawn. I push past Eoin before he can ask where I'm going, my arms above my head to hold off some of the rain. I run down the alleyway that will lead to the back of his house. I count down the houses as I reach the back gate of number ten.

'Ruth?'

Eoin is behind me, slipping on the sodden cobblestones. He has little time to stop me as I unlatch the gate. I had expected a padlock, barbed wire, something that would keep me out. The street continues to surprise me in how trusting it is. There is some resistance behind the gate and I have to shove it with my shoulder to push through. I am met by tangles of thorns that claw at my hair. The yard is filled with broken furniture: tables, a mattress, a wardrobe. There is a narrow path to the back door between the foliage and rubbish, and I crouch beneath the canopy of branches in order to reach it. The stench of rot hangs in the air, mixing with the damp. Eoin clambers through behind me, his foot catching a pile of rubbish that tumbles down around him.

'Shit. Ruth, what are you doing? This is trespassing!' The panic in his voice is muffled by his efforts to whisper and I put my hand against the back door.

'It's open,' I mouth, rain dripping from the ends of my hair as I look up towards him.

I can feel mascara running down my cheeks and Eoin sighs as he wipes it with his thumb.

'I know you're trying to do what's right, but we need to leave now.' His voice is shaking, his eyes pleading.

'You know something, don't you?' I ask forcefully.

'Ruth, please. Look, people aren't happy you're back. They know you're a journalist now. They don't want you snooping around asking questions that have already been asked. Henry Carr is gone and none of this will bring him back.'

'Who are you protecting—'

The sound of glass smashing inside the house interrupts me. We both hold our breath, our chests bursting.

'Keep watch for me? Please,' I beg.

He throws me a look I can't decipher and turns away.

I edge through the back door, hit by such a physical warmth and stench that I almost gag. It stinks of decomposing food, faeces, mould. I cup my nose in the bend of my elbow, smelling the wet fabric of my jacket. The room is filled with every kind of rubbish imaginable, empty boxes, empty packets, cat litter, plastic bags. It towers over me like some great beast. I can just about see the small patch of empty space the glass had fallen onto, its shards scattered over the black of the floor.

'Shit!'

It is then I see the cat, the green glow of its eyes, the white tip of its tail. It looks like a stray that roams the street. I force my breathing to slow. I have to move my arm away from my nose to steady myself as I climb up and over the piles of rubbish. It doesn't seem feasible for anyone to actually live here. I am through to what looks like the living room, though it is hard to distinguish one room from the next. It is dim, barely any light able to creep through the curtains that are clinging to the bay window. I notice a desk, the only surface cleared of rubbish. It's the only sign of life in this place and it startles me. Working my way towards the deep mahogany, I find there is a piece of paper on top and a fountain pen with the lid off. I pick it up, to read what has been written, when I hear his footsteps coming from the opposite direction. I gasp. Drop the paper.

'Are you—'

I spin around at the voice.

The figure is dishevelled. His clothes hang from him like bandages and his hair is wild and matted. He has a long beard that completely obscures his mouth and his eyes are misty.

'What are you doing in my house?' His voice is hoarse, like someone who hasn't said a word in years.

'I'm sorry, I rang the door bell and knocked but you didn't answer. I heard you were living here and I was worried. I'm Ruth, I live at number five.'

'I know who you are,' he says, matter-of-fact.

I blink.

'Oh, well it's nice to meet you, Martin. Are you all right?'

I feel an intense pang of sympathy for him, for the hell he is living in. He raises his eyebrows at the question, clearly unsure how to respond. More boxes tumble in the kitchen, an aftershock. I swallow, clear my throat. I feel like I'm choking on dust and dirt. I wipe the grease from my hands on my jeans and smile.

'Thank you for letting me be here. I know you didn't let me in, but thank you for not throwing me out all the same.'

He nods, perplexed.

'How long is it since you've left the house? If you don't mind me asking.' I keep my voice low and quiet.

He shrugs, itches his stomach. 'Fifteen years.'

That can't be a coincidence.

I smile again, nod.

'That's a long time. Is there something keeping you here?'

He seems to sense the kindness in my tone and relaxes his stance a fraction.

'It's what's out there I'm afraid of,' he mumbles, gesturing to the front door.

'Like what?'

He shakes his head. I nod again.

'There are people who can help you, if you'll accept it. People care about you; they'd love to see you.' I step an inch closer.

He narrows his eyes. 'Oh yeah, who's that?'

'Laura.'

His lip quivers. 'She leaves me food still. Even after all this time.'

'I know. It's because she cares about you.'

'Guilt, more like.' He spits out the words.

'What does that mean?' I ask.

He looks anxiously about the room. He runs his tongue across his bottom lip.

'Nothing. We have a lot of history, let's just say that.'

'Did something happen?' I ask, thinking back to Laura's earlier reaction.

He jolts forward, just enough for me to gasp.

'What has she said? She should have kept her mouth shut. We promised, we all promised not to say anything.'

I inch backwards, feeling something crunch underneath my boot.

'Nothing. Just that you all weren't particularly friendly with Henry near the end. I just wondered if something had happened. That's all.' I raise my palms in surrender. I don't want to prod him any further. Not while he's this volatile.

He seems reassured by this somewhat and slumps his shoulders. 'Right. I see. Friends are complicated things, let's just say that. The whole group are tied together, for better or for worse.'

Before I have the chance to push it further he moves sharply on. 'In fact, with Laura and me it was more than that.'

I can't tell if he is throwing this in to steer me away from his previous comment. My instinct is tugging me towards the friendship group and their friction, but I take the bait anyway.

'Oh really?'

He nods, inhales sharply. 'Left me, didn't she. I always thought it was for Henry – they always seemed to have something between them. Had a fling of sorts when we were younger. I reckon it was unfinished business.'

'Laura was dating Henry Carr?' I ask, shocked.

'Once upon a time.' His voice has cleared a little, as though he has settled into the sound of it filling the room.

Why hadn't Laura told me that? When had they dated? Did she think it made her look guilty? That she was involved, some sort of lovers' tiff? I check quickly for Eoin but remember he is keeping watch outside, and I feel marginally safer.

'I know this might sound forward,' I say gently, 'and I'm sorry if it seems that way. Henry Carr's disappearance – the case has been reopened.' I sense no surprise from him and wonder if he still gets newspapers delivered. I continue. 'Someone mentioned that you had fallen out with Henry over money. Though I suppose him going off with Laura added to that?'

Martin's lip curls again. His fists close in on themselves.

'The fucker owed everyone money. Why do you think I'm like this now? It's because of him. That bastard. Take, take, take. That's all he knew how to do. He thought he could hang what happened with the group over us. We were traumatised. He used it for his own benefit. I reckon that's what killed him in the end.' His voice is rising and spit is flying from his mouth as he vents his rage.

I command myself to relax my muscles. I find myself feeling oddly defensive over Henry. He meant a lot to my family. Anyway, this resentment doesn't mean it was Martin who killed Henry. The anger doesn't mean he is dangerous. I need to wait for the rest of the answers.

'What happened, Martin? What was he holding over you all?'

He is trying to calm down, pacing the room, murmuring. His shadow floats up the walls in the dingy light. 'I've said too much already.'

My heart is skipping in my chest, I'm desperate not to lose this momentum.

'Martin, do you know of anyone who may have wanted to harm Henry?'

'List's too bloody long,' he snarls, a laugh escaping his throat.

'Anyone specific?' I ask, almost pleading.

He stops. My hand hovers over the phone in my pocket.

'You could always try the loan shark. Rob Knight. You didn't get that name from me, though, you hear? I've done my running from him. Spent years trying to convince him I was dead, that the house is derelict. He stopped coming around here years ago but I still wouldn't dare go outside. He's ruthless. He'd kill me.' His voice raises an octave, his eyes wide and white.

'Robert Knight?' I repeat the name, my mind ticking over.

R. K.

Underlined and circled.

The initials and address I photographed at the Carrs' house, the ones I found in Henry's notebook.

'Thank you, Martin.'

I turn and scramble back over the rubbish. I know exactly where I need to go next.

15
Peter

I STRETCH UP AND unscrew the bulb.

The ladder shakes and tilts beneath me and I grunt to keep myself balanced.

Autumn light falls through the cracked window of the shed and I can feel the warmth of it on my skin. I feel both heavier and lighter with Ruth home, and I haven't found a way to understand it yet.

Keeping busy is all I know. It has filled the loneliness for years, though it doesn't seem to work today. I pull the new light bulb from my pocket and screw it in. I've found that the thing I most value is my utility – fixing a leaking tap for Laura when Eoin was busy, weeding for Margot and Frank, getting one of Mrs Montgomery's wild cats out of the tree for the sixth time this year. There isn't a resident on the street that I haven't helped, young or old. Those are the things that make me feel like someone, someone worth having around. Maybe it's my attempt to work off my sins, a way of making up for the poor husband and father I was once. Either way, this tool shed, these tasks, they make up who I am. I'm still working out whether that's something to be depressed about or not. Maybe everyone feels the same. I can hear the muffled song on the radio through the kitchen door and hum it half-heartedly under my breath.

I hear the back door open and close before I see her. My heart thunders in my ribcage – I'm still not used to her being around. The sound of another person in the house, knowing which squeaking floorboard to avoid, running the shower for too long, closing her bedroom door softly so as not to wake me. The everyday, normal sounds of another human both comfort me and put me on edge.

'Hiya,' I call behind me.

She pushes through the door, sets a cup of coffee on the work bench.

'I forgot how you take it so I just added a bit of milk,' she admits awkwardly.

I don't tell her I take my coffee black. I just smile over my shoulder, nod.

'I was wondering if I could ask you about something? If you're not too busy, that is.' She's talking quickly, nerves pricking her tone.

I finish tightening the bulb and step carefully down from the ladder.

I wonder if it is my fault that she is anxious to ask me, or if it is the nature of the question.

'Go on.' I pick up the cup, slurp boiling water and try not to yelp.

Tastes like shit. I smile, make the obligatory sound.

'I was just speaking to Laura.'

I struggle to hold my composed expression. My heart drops, and it takes me too long to pick it back up. She's noticed. I let the cup scald my palms, let it wake me up, feel the danger that is present.

'Speaking to Laura about what?' I ask, treading carefully.

Ruth shifts on her feet, unsure where to place her weight. She has always been too afraid of taking up space, as if just her body alone is a burden. That's my fault, and I'm winded by this realisation.

'I don't think she wanted me to notice but I saw some photographs, articles lying around. I didn't know she knew Henry quite so well – Eoin never mentioned it either. I should have guessed, I suppose. This isn't a big street; they were bound to be involved in some way,' she says, hands twisting together.

I say nothing because there is no question. I simply wait.

'There was something there, though, a deeper emotion that I couldn't place. Almost like she was guarding herself, like she didn't want to admit how she felt, or what happened between them.'

I take another mouthful of burning liquid, feel my tongue swell in response.

'You'll have hit a raw nerve there, Ruth. Some wounds take a lifetime to heal.'

She frowns, leans against the work bench.

I sigh. 'They were in a relationship, though I'm not sure Henry would have called it that if truth be told. She was . . . infatuated with him. It wouldn't matter what he did, if he blew her off, ignored her calls, forgot to show up – she worshiped the ground he walked on. There was nothing she wouldn't have done for him. I think he liked her, don't get me wrong. But not in the way she liked him. He was still young, he didn't want to commit to anything or anyone, that's just how he was. He left a lot of destruction in his path, did Henry. He'd just climb from the wreckage and carry on, dust himself off, start over.' I stop, my mouth dry. I think of Laura, of our friendship, and it becomes harder to speak.

'So, what happened?' she prompts.

'He did the worst thing possible. He just broke it off. No explanation, no other person, no excuse. I think she could have coped with that, if he'd fallen in love with someone else or he was too busy, or anything really. But to break it off just because he'd rather be alone than be with her. That cut her deep. Cut her beyond repair, I think. He was the love of her life. Four years, on and off, and God knows how long before that really, over with just like that. They were young, like I say. But she's never got over it. Even when she married Eoin's father you could tell it wasn't genuine, it was just the only option she had left. Rumour has it that's why Laura and Eoin's father got divorced. She had a lot of demons still circling. Henry, still circling.' I shrug. It doesn't feel like my story to tell.

'She must have been distraught when he went missing, then? If she still loved him?' Ruth asks, curiosity in her tone.

'She was. She shut herself away, wouldn't talk to anyone. She couldn't even look after herself at that point. We rallied around her as much as we could.'

'Who is "we"?' Ruth asks, frowning.

'Well, me, Sam, a couple of others. We grew up together, you know? We look out for each other, even now,' I admit.

She doesn't look surprised. She looks like she wants to say something else. I wait.

'Dad, did something happen? Something between you all?'

I take another drink of shit coffee and let the question hang between us. How much does she know? It is a difficult thing to balance, both the truth and a lie mixed together.

'Life happens, Ruth. We were childhood friends that drifted apart, as does everyone. We're still loyal to each other, despite that, of course. I think you're looking into this a bit too much, if you don't mind me saying.'

She tilts her chin in that way she does.

'Dad, do the initials R. K. mean anything to you?'

I turn away before she sees the blood drain from my face. I pretend to look for something beneath the bench, my fingers refusing to work. I clear my throat, try to regain my composure. *Where the fuck had she got that from?*

'R. K.? Don't think so. Why?'

'No reason,' she says, her eyes narrowed a little. 'So there's nothing else you remember about Laura? Nothing that could help the case?'

I shake my head and smile. 'Sorry, nothing to report. Just what I've said already and that's probably too much. A failed relationship, a broken heart, old friendships, but that's life. Nothing that the rest of us haven't done or been through.'

I hold back on saying anything else, have to bite the tip of my tongue to fall into silence. I taste blood and swallow it. There are some things I shouldn't share. If she finds out, then I don't want it brought back to me. I think of the day that binds all of us together: me, Sam, Laura, Martin, Henry and Robert. I think of the secrets we have tried to bury and I pray that Ruth doesn't find more than she needs.

* * *

I tug my collar up and pull open the gate, wincing as it squeaks.

I look left and right, checking for peering eyes behind curtains or movement behind the bins. You can't go anywhere on this street without people watching you.

The air has grown bitter and I keep my head down against the wind. There is a movement opposite, a figure at the window. I pause momentarily before holding my hand up in a wave. Patrick nods in response and I sense his eyes following me as I carry on walking. I feel my heart lurch at the thought of him stood there, still waiting for his son to come home. The anniversary is looming, a storm heading for all of us. It doesn't get easier, grief, no matter what people say. You just learn to live with it. The other person in the room.

I make a mental note to go over and see him later, make sure Ruth hasn't been bothering them too much with her questions. Maybe I'm being harsh, but she can't fully know what it was like that day, what it has been like ever since. She was too young to remember the chaos of it, the panic. It isn't just her, though. I try and pop around to Patrick's when I can. Even if it's to check in, touch up some paintwork outside, to show I'm still there even though Henry isn't. I spent my childhood with the Carrs, waiting for Henry to come out on his bike, hours sitting in the kitchen shovelling Marianne's warming Irish cooking into my mouth, summers spent watching Patrick's black and white TV and laughing until we were hoarse. I have memories bound up in that place too, and I want them to know just because Henry's gone it doesn't mean we have too. They can have some of him back, even if it's just through the rest of us.

I march on, praying that Ruth has occupied herself with something else and bought my excuse of heading to the corner shop for cigarettes. There has always been a slight mistrust between us – I'm aware we both have secrets we can't share.

The sky is getting darker now, clouds gathering in great swoops. I pick up my pace and turn into the house at the top of the road. I rap my knuckles sharply twice and throw another glance over my shoulder, just to check Ruth isn't following me. I hear muffled footfall from behind the door, a figure outlined through the glass pane. There is the jingle of keys before a pause.

'Who is it?' she calls. I can hear the tremble in her voice.

Her door is almost always open, members of the street frequently in and out visiting. In fact, I don't think I ever remember her locking her door. It's something we joke about, her place being open 24/7. I can't help wondering if the conversation with Ruth has made her paranoid.

'It's me, Laur. Peter. Can you get a move on, I'm freezing my arse off out here.'

I hear a nervous laugh and the key in the door.

She smiles, but it doesn't quite meet her eyes. She is paler than I remember. How long has it been since I've seen her properly?

I wait for her to invite me in, but she doesn't. She is blocking the doorway. I falter – this isn't like her and I don't know how to respond without seeming rude. I don't usually bother about what other people think of me, but me and Laura go way back. We've told each other things no one else knows.

'You busy?' I ask.

She itches her arm and glances over her shoulder. She shakes her head reluctantly and ushers me in, though I see her linger at the door, her eyes sweeping the street.

The house smells like bleach and I stifle a cough in the crook of my arm. Laura takes my coat and puts it over the banister. Her hair is swept back neat, but the lines of worry in her face and the shadows beneath her eyes are hard to conceal. She's had a difficult life and I can see it now. She lost the love of her life twice, only to move on and be reminded every day that it isn't the person she dreamt of waking up next to. She's spent the rest of her time trying to raise Eoin. Everything she did and does is for him. There's something so selfless about a mother's love, something unique and ineffable. It both scares and fascinates me. I look at her now and feel a stab of pity. There is a sourness in the air between us that I fear isn't just the bleach.

She moves in front of the door to the lounge. Blocking it she spreads her arms a little so I can't see through. I crane my neck to get a better view and pray that isn't what I think it is. All I can make out is paper splayed out across the floor and . . . is that . . . ? It can't be. Newspaper articles, clippings with Henry's name in bold letters. *Shit*, she's spiralling.

'Laura, is that—'

'Come on, I'll put the kettle on.' Her voice is firm, final. Her blue eyes are impenetrable, impossible to gauge.

I relent and head through first. I'm not used to this coldness from her and I wonder if she thinks that I'm egging Ruth on, telling her who to speak to. I clench my jaw at the thought, that she might think I'm a traitor. She busies herself making tea. I remain in the doorway, unsure how to broach the topic. From the look on her face, she knows why I'm here. I lean against the door frame, try to clean a stain from my T-shirt.

'Is the lad in?' I ask, nonchalant.

'No, at work I think,' she says, tossing teabags into two mugs. 'Can't say it's what I wanted for him, mind you.'

'Nothing wrong with having a trade, Laura. He'll be on decent money and never be out of work.' I try to keep the hurt from my voice, try to ignore the irritation creeping into my throat. This has been a constant friction between us, what we see as right for our kids, what success really looks like.

'I wanted more for him than that. Than being stuck here forever. As much as *we* belong here, for them, it is not all there is. Ruth's proof of that,' she says, collecting the milk from the fridge.

There it is again, that catch in her voice. That fear.

'Is everything all right?' I ask.

It is more direct than I am used to, talking to her like this. Except I don't know how else to come out with it. I'm a loyal friend. I'd never doubt her. There's still something off, though. She clearly needs to speak to someone, someone who won't go off and write about it or gossip in the corner shop. I know that person right now is me. She leans on the kitchen counter, catching her breath.

'It's just that time of year, you know. The anniversary coming up. It's always difficult, for everyone.' She hands me a mug.

I nod a thanks and warm my hands around it. 'Of course. Of course.' We share a look, knowing. She realises what the look means, what I'm asking. She gives a stiff shake of her head and we offer each other a small smile for the continuation of our loyalty.

I look at my feet, at the ceiling, anywhere but at her as I continue. 'Ruth mentioned she popped round. She was really happy to see you. I think she's missed you, you know, with her and Eoin not being an item any more.'

She tightens her jaw, smooths down a stray hair with her fingers.

'She's always welcome here. I hope she knows that.'

I smile. It's not why I mentioned it and she knows it. She sits down at the table with a sigh, crossing her ankles and clasping her hands together. An empty silence fills the room and I hope she'll be the first to break it.

She looks up at me, her mouth slack. 'I didn't say anything about that night. Christ, it was before she was born, before all this mess with Henry disappearing. There's no reason to drag it up now. But she was asking me, about Henry. She suspected something had happened between us all, some falling out.' She sweeps a crumb off the table and we both watch it tumble to the lino. 'I think I . . . I wasn't expecting it, the questions, what it might bring up. I'm not sure I said it how I wanted to. You know I would never say anything. I realise she's a journalist, but I'd hope she wouldn't twist things, make it seem like . . .'

I nod. I understand. I join her at the table, try to meet her eyes.

'I know, I know. It's just . . .' I pause, wet my lip. I feel my heart miss a beat and the wave of nausea that comes with it. 'She asked about R. K. She asked me who it was.'

I see a jolt of realisation go through Laura, an awareness of exactly what that means.

'Peter, please. We can't go there. If she digs too deep, it'll ruin us all.'

'I know. Don't worry, I've got your back, Laura. I've spoken to her about that and about your conversation earlier. I've put it to bed. We'll make sure that whatever goes into her piece is fair, that it doesn't paint you in any light other than a woman who once loved him. Our secret is safe, Laura. That stupid pact we all made as teenagers, it's still with us. It was just a mistake.'

'I know, thank you. You're right about loving Henry. About still loving him,' she whispers.

I let it sit, ignoring it just as I have ignored the truth for fifteen years.

16

Patrick

I PACE THE ROOM.

My hands are behind my back, my face feels red-raw and no doubt the veins in my temple are raised. The room is like a furnace, the radiators and anger adding to the heat. The young officer shifts uncomfortably, watching the female detective with his peripheral vision. They think I don't notice these things, but I do. I'm not stupid. The woman is watching Marianne carefully, at the way she sits with her arms wrapped around herself.

'I can't believe you forced your way into our house,' I snarl.

'As I've said, Mr Carr, we knocked and Mrs Carr answered and invited us in,' the officer says.

'She's vulnerable! She doesn't know what she's doing,' I shout, exasperated.

The officers wait and we all listen to my heavy breathing until it slows.

'We're just here to update you on the investigation, Mr Carr. We assumed you would want to know of any developments in the case,' the woman says calmly.

I rub a hand over my face, the stubble prickly. I feel cornered, trapped. They're saying things to get a reaction, I need to remember that.

I nod, smooth down my cardigan.

'Right. So what is it then? What have you found?' I ask.

The woman sits forward, opening the case file balanced across her knee.

'As you know, we found Henry's wallet in the wasteland.'

I roll my eyes. 'I told you already, I didn't bloody put it there. Haven't been over to that wasteland in I don't know how long. My knees can't take that uneven ground.'

She nods curtly. 'After conducting a further search, we found a photograph we believe to have fallen from the wallet. We've sent it to the lab for restoration and should know more shortly. We just wanted to ask, do you know of any photographs Henry used to keep in his wallet? Maybe family photographs?'

I feel a ripple of recognition. I push my tongue onto the line of my dentures. I glance once at Marianne before looking back to the officers.

'No.'

'Are you sure?' the man asks.

'Yes, I'm sure. I've no idea what he kept in his wallet. He was a grown man.'

I hold my hands up, case closed.

'Was?' the man asks cautiously.

'Is. Was. I don't know,' I say, exasperated.

Bastards.

They're trying to trip me up any chance they get. I'm old, my memory is shot. Surely they've dealt with old people before.

'Mrs Carr invited us into the kitchen before you arrived. On my way through I noticed a family photograph, Henry as a young boy. It's quite an intriguing picture.'

'Is it?' I ask, my eyes on the floor.

'You look angry in it. Were you?'

'What does this matter? He was a boy then. Are fathers not allowed to get angry at their sons?'

'Did you get angry often?'

'When I needed to,' I reply through gritted teeth.

The story behind the photo is mundane; it tells only of a boy who misbehaved, whose mother loved him too much and couldn't wait to give him his bike as a present, despite our agreement of discipline first. I disagreed, and my face shows as much.

The woman scribbles something in her notebook, the pen scratching the paper. That only agitates me further and I try to make out what she has written.

'Well, is that it then? Are you going now?' I demand.

Marianne laughs.

We all stare. It is so light-hearted, so childlike that no one seems to know quite what to say. My jaw clenches, the skin of my jowls tightening.

'Are you all right, Mrs Carr?' the man asks, watching her carefully.

Her eyes fall to him. She is still smiling. Her hands sit contentedly in her lap.

'Oh yes. I'm quite all right, dear. I was just thinking of Henry and that wallet. It was a present, you know. The wallet with a little picture in it.'

'Picture? What picture was that, Mrs Carr? Can you remember what might have been in it? It might help us identify if it was his when we get hold of the lab.' The man leans forward, resting his elbows on his knees.

I step forward.

'That's quite enough. I've told you already, she's not well!' I try to block her from them, protect her.

My arm is outstretched, a barrier. Marianne doesn't seem to notice – she is laughing again, her head tipped back to the ceiling.

'Mrs Carr?' the woman presses, her fingers tight around the pen.

'It was of a girl. I used to tease him about it, you know how mothers can be about things like that. He was so secretive with it, always tucking it in so no one could see. I was desperate to take a look at her, this person that had captured Henry's heart. Although, I never did,' Marianne replies.

Enough. 'Right. That's quite enough. Out. Out, both of you. Should be bloody ashamed, you should. Taking advantage of her illness like that. Shame on you.'

I pull both of them up, my grip firm on their shoulders.

'Mr Carr, I would advise you not to assault two police officers,' the man says.

He looks so smug I nearly thump him.

I want to wrestle him to the ground, take out fifteen years' worth of anger and hurt out on him. See how he copes. But I let go and hold my hands firmly at my sides. Marianne is beginning to whimper, the laughter melting from her face. She is getting more agitated at the mood in the room, her whimpers growing into a wail.

The woman gives the other officer a nod and they walk to the hallway.

'We still have more to tell you and more to ask, Mr Carr. It's for the benefit of the investigation. We just want answers for you both, so you can have some closure.'

The woman has softened her tone but it is drowned out by the hysteria from the front room. I nod and open the front door, ushering them out. I check there's no one around, try to save whatever dignity we have left.

'Don't come back here again,' I growl.

I slam the door in their faces and watch through the keyhole as they stand, perplexed, in the pouring rain.

17
Ruth

THE STREET IS BUSTLING with officers, both plain-clothes and uniformed. It has generated a crowd of residents on the far corner and the mood seems to be turning hostile. They have grouped together into a circle, watching, whispering. The rain is falling in sheets and the mass has blended into the watery grey. They stand unblinking, unmoving. I feel my phone ring.

'Hello?'

'We're getting specialists to look at the fridge-freezer you reported earlier. They're just running tests to check if there are any traces of blood or anything else, and if so, how long it may have been there.'

'Thanks, Oscar. I appreciate you keeping me updated.' I look up, turn my back to the crowd. I try to find Oscar in the mix of officers but can't. I dip my head in case anyone tries to read my lips. 'It seems odd, doesn't it, for all this potential evidence to be falling at your feet?' I ask.

'For a street that hates the police, we sure have had a fair few tip-offs. It isn't making a lot of sense to me either right now. Just that someone is either keen to have this off their conscience, or else keen to pin it on someone else before we find them.'

'Sure. Well, thanks.' I hang up.

My head is spinning.

Before I try to deal with what Martin told me, there's something else I need to do. If anyone knows the personalities of the street, who might be behind the new evidence, it's those who have been here the longest.

And in order, after the Carrs, it has to be Frank and Margo.

* * *

Like the Carrs, Frank and Margo have seen pretty much everyone come and go, or come and stay, more accurately. I sidestep the ornaments that line the short path to their front door, and the bell releases a shrill ring behind the glass as I press it. Rushing footsteps approach the door and it creaks open a fraction, a pair of watery blue eyes peering out.

'Can I help you?'

'Hi there. Frank, isn't it? I'm Ruth Cavanagh from number five, Peter's daughter. Sorry to just show up like this. I'm sure you've probably heard why I'm back, to do a report for the anniversary. Do you mind if I ask you a few questions?'

The door opens a fraction further and an elderly man stares back at me. Frank is dressed smart, a shirt, tie, and jumper with a pair of beige trousers. He looks past me at the crowd and clicks his tongue against the roof of his mouth.

'You shouldn't be here.'

'I've been hearing that a lot. Listen, Frank, you're very close to the Carrs. I'm honestly just trying to help, to write respectfully and accurately, and to get some closure for the Carr family.'

'Is that what they want? Closure?' His eyes are narrowed.

I hesitate.

It seems whatever I say won't be the right answer.

'You'd better come in,' he finally says. 'You'll catch your death out there.'

Frank looks over my shoulder and I wonder if he feels them too, the unknown eyes always watching. He shuffles into the house and beckons me to follow.

The house smells of lilies and every room is pristine. The layout is identical to the Carrs, the decor just as dated.

'I can't tell you much, I'm afraid. I didn't see him the day he disappeared, neither of us did.' He nods towards his wife who is sitting in the corner, observing.

'Hello Margo.' I smile. She looks at me wearily. 'I'm just trying to gather as much as I can for my story. Anything would be really helpful. Anything about what Henry was like, what either of you remember about that day or after. Anything at all.'

Frank sits down, his body weight falling to the back of his chair, his feet not quite reaching the floor.

'We're firm friends of the Carrs. Henry is our godson,' he says, his eyes to the carpet.

'I see. I'm sorry. It must be very hard to talk about.'

He smiles, clasps his hands together. 'He was a good lad, but quiet. Kept himself to himself mostly. He was very private, took after his father.'

I nod. Glance over at Margo. 'So you're not aware of anyone he might have had problems with?'

The air in the room grows heavier, and Frank shares a look with his wife that seems to contain a question. Her lips are pursed; she blinks slowly.

'He had an office job, but he hated it. Wanted to find new work elsewhere. Difficult in a place like this. Saying that, he seemed to get along with everyone at the office, I thought. Used to get a pint at the Beehive with some of them every Friday after work.' He laughs.

'I love the Beehive.' I smile. 'Hard not to with Sam running it.'

I feel like I need to prove my belonging here, that I know people too, that I am part of this narrative like the rest of them.

'That's right, our Sam. Not ours exactly, but you get my meaning. Yes, they went way back, Sam and Henry. Used to go to school together. A group of them on this street did, actually. A few were a little older and have moved away but there's still some here – Laura Finch, Martin Banks, Sam, Henry.' He pauses. 'There were others I can't quite remember the names of now. Oh, and your dad.'

I try not to flinch at the names. The weight they carry.

'Did they stay friends, do you know?' I ask lightly, trying not to let what Laura told me interfere.

Frank glances to the left, at nothing. I can sense the reluctance in his response.

'Some of them, I suppose.' He shrugs, picks at a loose thread.

'Are any of them still friends now?'

'Well, I'm not really sure. Perhaps not,' he mumbles, pushing his feet together.

Margo coughs, a subtle sound but one that feels like a warning.

'Why is that?' I ask, intrigued suddenly by the change of energy in the room.

Margo intervenes. 'You'd have to ask them.'

Frank heaves himself out of his seat, wobbling on his legs when he eventually stands. 'Shall I show you out?' he asks. His tone is polite but he is clearly agitated, his eyes flittering between Margo and me.

'Of course. Sorry to intrude like this. It's really helpful to hear from you and I appreciate you letting me in. Thanks to both of you, I really appreciate the community's support.'

He nods, curt.

'Actually, Frank. Just one more thing. Do the initials R. K. mean anything to you?'

His face falls and he grips my arm as he steers me out.

'We don't speak of that name in this house. Now, I'd appreciate it if you took your questions and left us in peace.'

I step out of the front door and just as it begins to close, the last thing I hear is Margo as she hisses to Frank.

'You fool.'

* * *

I have barely left Frank and Margo's when he calls.

I panic to swipe it in time when I see Patrick's name on the caller ID. As soon as I put the phone to my ear, I can hear the urgency in his tone, and I have to will my heart rate to slow so I can focus on exactly what he is saying.

'Ruth. I'm sorry. I know you were only here earlier, but it's the police, their questioning, their prodding. It's bringing up too many emotions in her, she can't process them all in her condition. I can't get her to come out, Ruth. You and Eoin, you have to help me. We need you.'

My heart drops. I'm surprised that he thought to call me. I'm suddenly strangely emotional – Patrick has actually considered me as a part of their life, an ally.

I call for Eoin and he comes straight away. We run to number four. Patrick pulls open the door, panting.

His face is white and droplets of sweat bead his forehead. He looks as though he may collapse and I step forward instinctively, hold out my hand to steady him. He shakes his head, soundless, and glances quickly over his shoulder. The silence behind him is concerning. Where is Marianne?

He opens and closes his mouth; no sound escapes but he looks so frail I feel like crying. This isn't like him. He runs his shaking hands through his hair and makes no attempt to flatten it again. I cast Eoin an anxious glance and we both usher him inside. He couldn't explain on the phone why he needed us here, what was so urgent, how Marianne was in trouble. He just called, we answered and we came. That is what you do on this street. You show up for those who need you. Eoin takes him into the kitchen, tries to sit him carefully at the table, but he stands almost immediately, shaking his head, leading Eoin upstairs. His slippers scuff and judder up each step and Eoin hovers behind him, anticipating a fall.

The house is stifling, heat blaring from the radiator in the hallway. I turn it down, sling my coat over the banister and rush upstairs. I pause on the landing, looking to each door to detect movement, strain my ears to hear voices.

There is nothing.

I inch my way to Marianne's bedroom, smell the sweetness of her perfume, expect to hear her singsong Irish voice, but instead find Patrick and Eoin by her bed.

They are speaking in whispers, quick and frantic, and I hover by the door until Eoin beckons me over. Outside the clouds have formed a blanket now, and thin slices of rain dash against the window. It makes Eoin raise his voice a little, a deep whisper in my ear.

'It's Marianne. She won't come out.'

I feel his breath on my neck, glance up to see the concern in his eyes.

I follow Patrick's stare to the wardrobe.

No one says a word. I can hear the other two breathing, heavy, strained.

'I've tried everything,' Patrick whispers, tears welling in his eyes, threatening to spill over. I feel sick. I have never seen him like this, so vulnerable.

'We'll sort this, Patrick. Please don't worry,' Eoin says, giving a squeeze of reassurance to his frail shoulder. Patrick doesn't respond, can't respond, as his chin crumples in the way it does when you're doing all you can to stop yourself from falling apart.

Patrick wipes his eyes roughly with the back of his hand. He groans as he kneels on the floor, bats away any help from Eoin, and leans unsteadily to pull the wardrobe door open. It creaks as it swings and it's impossible to see anything at first, except the back-to-back clothes that are hanging. I start to doubt that she is really in there at all until he pushes the clothes back and I see her curled up in the foetal position. We bend down, Eoin and I, bury our palms into the rough carpet in some effort to be close to her. She isn't moving at all, and I focus on her chest, willing it to rise and fall.

'Marianne, love. Please.'

She does not respond and Patrick looks at us, pleading.

This is why he called. There isn't anything he can do. He has become used to weathering these storms himself, bracing himself for every wave. But today, he needs us. Eoin responds first. He leans into the wardrobe, blocking all the light with the width of his shoulders. He whispers something to her and at first there is nothing, just the rain on the window, just our breathing. Another minute goes by and she stirs, her fingers move a little, she says something he asks her to repeat.

Patrick glances over at me, a question mark in his expression.

I shrug and we both turn back to Eoin, waiting for him to translate.

'She wants you, Ruth. Just you.'

I feel their eyes on me and heat travels up my neck. I don't really understand what I can offer; I don't have Patrick's intense knowledge of her, or Eoin's easy compassion. I'm usually clumsy or awkward in these fragile moments. Eoin moves out of the way, helps Patrick to the bed and encourages him to sit.

I'm not sure what makes me do it, but I clamber into the small space left in the wardrobe, half in and half out. It is dark with me blocking the door like this and there is just a snippet of light keeping her visible. I can't see her face very well but I do see her reach out, feel her hand as she finds me and interlaces her fingers with mine. They're cold and so I blow on them, instinctively, to warm them up. Just as you would a child. A small noise escapes from her throat and I'm unsure if it is a laugh or an exhale. She tugs me a little closer until I am lying beside her, my legs sticking out of the doors. The base of the wardrobe digs into my hip and I wince as I find a position that is bearable. I rest my head as close to her as I can, want her to sense someone beside her. Her breath is hot on my face, the smell of toothpaste in short bursts. She does not let go of my hand but grips it tighter, keeping it close to her chest. I feel the soar and dip of her breathing, alongside the flutter of her heartbeat. She is crying now, short sniffles that become sobs. Her body rocks and I hear the bedroom door close behind me and realise that Eoin has taken Patrick away. It is too much for him. I find myself crying too, silent tears that cling to my eyelashes and make it hard to see her. But I feel her. More than maybe I've ever felt anyone, I can feel her soul in ways that I didn't think were possible. I understand Marianne even when she doesn't make sense because that feeling is all too familiar to me. Feeling something inside of you tug with a yearning you can never subdue, a desperation for someone who isn't ever coming back. It's like a weight, dragging you down, keeping you from the surface and from ever truly being able to catch your breath. Sometimes I walk past someone wearing Mum's perfume and it takes me back to an exact moment, an exact conversation, and my body nearly gives out from the longing. So I recognise how desperate it can feel to want to be loved. Even at our worst. Even at our lowest. She doesn't understand where her son has gone and nothing anyone says will help it to make sense in her mind. She is reliving it every day. A mother without a child. I don't know what it's like to have a child, but I know what it is like to lose the one you hold most dear. Marianne is more than a jigsaw piece to my looming deadline. She's a person who deserves respect and dignity and love.

I lift my free hand, finding her damp cheek in the dark. I stroke her cheek so gently I wonder if she can feel it at all. It's what Mum used to do for me, in the nights when Dad was shouting or missed another one of my concerts, when I was inconsolable and words only made things worse. It was the only thing that grounded me, that constant, unending rhythm. So I keep going. I stay present for her. I don't know if it's ten minutes or an hour but I carry on until her breathing slows, until the crying stops and she slips away into sleep.

DAY FOUR

18
Ruth

THE TRAIN PLATFORM IS singing by the time I arrive. I stifle a yawn, and think of the note Dad left for me this morning. It just said *If you're in tonight, we can have takeout together?* It was a hurried scrawl, but I think it's the only thing he's ever written to me. Of course there were birthday cards and parental signatures on school trip notes, but this time he's writing it because he wants to. I smile.

A fog has settled over the train tracks, low and thick, concealing any sign of an oncoming train. The station sits a mile from the street, run-down and rusting against the backdrop of the town.

It is a twenty-minute journey into the city, fast enough to be connected to it and far enough away to be forgotten. I stand beneath the clock, aware of the weight of it above me. I know myself this is a terrible idea. Tracking down an address from the book of a man presumed dead. Still, there's no questioning the impact Robert Knight had on Martin and potentially on Henry. Frank and Margot clearly weren't his biggest fans. I need to find out whatever I can before I send the article to Tom later. The reactions of everyone I have spoken with confirm that R. K. is worth pursuing. *How does a man generate a reaction like that after all this time?*

It's gone 10 a.m. by the time I reach Manchester. I grab a coffee from a café on Oxford Road in an attempt to calm my nerves (caffeine will do that for a journalist). I stare at my phone screen as I sip, looking at the address I photographed from Henry

Carr's notebook. I give myself ten minutes: to finish the black scalding coffee and to appreciate the bustling of life in town away from the cold insularity of the street. I type up some more of Marianne's story into a document on my phone, teasing out the right wording, being careful not to say too much or too little. I call Tom with an update, tell him about the search of the wasteland, about the fridge-freezer, about the anonymous caller and the hints of a body. He seems pleased, and I avoid sharing any information about the loan shark.

'If they find a body, that'll be it. This is our big break. This will be headline news.'

I agree but can't help feeling that the story is about much more than what we'll be telling people. It's someone's life, someone's identity. It's Marianne's son. It is the street itself. Someone knows something. Perhaps everyone does. I know they think they're helping, but they're hurting her instead. I take another sip of coffee and sigh. It's becoming clear to me that all I really have begun to care about is giving Marianne a voice. I want to support her and confirm that someone is actually listening, someone believes her. I wish Marianne knew how much the community really cares for her. Yet I can't help remembering what Sam had said about Henry, about everyone's disdain for him, about the list of suspects the street could hold. *Who was Henry Carr?* A devoted son? A loyal friend? Or else a man in debt, a drug dealer, a person his parents thought they knew but didn't? It's like he's lost form to me now, the man I once knew. He is shape-shifting, changing before my eyes. I don't want to become embroiled in something dark, though it feels too late for that now. Crow Street is under my skin and in my bones. If this is the last time I will ever be on the street, then I'm at least going to bring down its demons before leaving.

* * *

The heavy, low sky over Manchester presses into my temples as I walk. My feet move through the streets with a familiarity that soothes me. I feel lighter away from the street, like I can breathe a little better, see things more clearly. The city is brooding, Victorian brick against dark skies, a pulse of activity beating like the heart of it all. I let my mind clear as I cut down by the canal near Deansgate. I pull up the photo of the address from Henry's notebook below the initials R. K. It still isn't clear to me why the address has been written down, what it means, or how it might be connected to Henry's disappearance, but it's all I have to work with. Maybe whoever lives there now will know a bit more about him. It's unlikely he'll still be there, but if it's even a possibility then this is probably a dangerous move. After typing and deleting a message a number of times, I finally decide to send my text to Eoin to let him know where I am. He'll probably be angry about it, especially after his reaction outside Martin's house. Still, he'd want to know. I google the address, balancing myself against a bollard to avoid the swell of office workers walking by. The address pings up a result a twenty-minute walk away. My fingers have a slight tremble in them, adrenalin and anxiety blended. This person could have the answer to Henry's disappearance. I know it is stupid to be here alone, but with the story due and the police milling around, this is my last chance to find out the truth. I close my eyes and inhale the muggy air, before turning around and heading, sure-footed, to find out who R. K. really is.

I stand outside the building with my heart in my mouth, and wish I'd walked more slowly. I check the address for what must be the tenth time. I forgot to charge my phone last night, and only have ten per cent battery left. Though I don't really want to admit it, I know I might need to call for help if things go south with R. K. I stand still and focus on my surroundings. The address looks like an office sat above a vacant lower floor. The empty shop below has graffiti scrawled across its shutters, gang names and obscene words in fluorescent colours. It all looks run-down and empty. I wonder who would want to live in a place like this, if not to avoid detection. I consider for a moment that the person may have moved on – fifteen years is a long time to stay on premises like this. The thought reassures me, relief that it might all amount to nothing. I crane my neck to see the building better: it hangs on the corner of a derelict street, framed by large windows and a balcony that overshadows the pavement below. There's no one else around, hidden as the maze of streets are from the lines of bars and restaurants five minutes away. There is a buzzer in the doorway, its numbers eroded by the elements. I press my thumb firmly into each, hearing the distant rings. I look up for any signs of movement, the twitch of a blind, or the glow of a light. Nothing. I wait for several minutes before stepping back from the doorway and looking up. It's hard to see anything with the sky reflecting against the glass. I blink and look harder. I see something, the blinds stirring in the upstairs window, just a fraction. There is no face to be seen, no great reveal or opening of the door, but between the slats: a pair of eyes watching. I feel the heaviness of resignation as I turn to walk around the side of the building, to find a way in. I have almost turned the corner when I hear the voice, a woman sheltering in the hollow of a doorway. Her sleeping bag is pulled up to her chin, her eyes glowing in the dim light.

'If it's Rob you want, he's not been round here for years.' The woman flashes a toothless grin. 'You're not the first, and you won't be the last,' she continues. 'He's a man that's found only when he wants to be.'

'I thought as much. Thank you for letting me know.'

'Give us twenty quid and I might just be able to help.'

I hesitate, my fingers floating at the edges of my jacket. This feels wrong, but it looks like my only option. I pull the note from my purse before I can stop myself. The woman plucks it with greedy fingers and lets out a howl of laughter.

'The women do be desperate to find him. Don't know why, he's a nasty son of a bitch. You'll find him at the corner of Victor Street. Good luck, love – you'll need it.'

* * *

Rainwater drips from the gutters and dances in the street below, liquid gold at the feet of the streetlamps. It's quiet, unnaturally so, and I find myself walking with more force just to fill the space. The alleyways are closer together here, as though conspiring. Bins overflow and leave a stench that hangs in the air like something physical, and I try to breathe through my mouth. I catch weary reflections of myself in smashed glass and the mirror of the water along the ground, snippets of how others might see me. I stand up a little straighter and tilt my chin, a front. What if the woman has given me a random address? She hardly seemed like someone I could trust. I can't shift the uneasiness I feel, but I know that Henry Carr – or someone – has circled the name for a reason. R. K. isn't just a contact or a friend, he is someone who matters, someone of importance. Whether he genuinely is the loan shark Martin mentioned or not, I feel sure that seeing him will answer some questions.

I resist the urge to call Eoin. Funny how quickly that urge has returned.

The alleyways are getting narrower, the walls closing in until I am holding my breath down each one. This is a different world altogether from the Manchester I know. I cross a narrow street, squeezing down a final alley to get to the pin on the map. I have almost reached the end when I hear yelling from a doorway, a one-sided conversation being spat with such ferocity that I halt, mid-step. I skirt the opposite wall to get by unnoticed. I can see a slice of the man's face. His eyes are wide and white even in the dim light, his beard wild and matted. Yet it is not the man's face that draws my attention, but his hands. The glint of silver is unmistakable. The blade is large and wide, and he is polishing it with the tatters of his coat. His eyes are flickering, paranoid, before they find me. They settle there, absorbing me. A smile wavers at the corners of his mouth.

'Hello.' The greeting hisses through decaying teeth.

He steps forward out of his shelter and lets the river of light wash over his face. Deep-set scars line his skin. I nod and hope it will be enough to satisfy him. I have learnt from experience that sometimes acknowledgement is enough to appease. But my nod only seems to intrigue him further. Nothing I can do will make him leave me alone now. He cocks his head to the side, moving forward in slow, deliberate steps. He never takes his eyes from me. His gaze feels as if it is burrowing underneath my skin. I try to remember the tips and advice that have been whispered to me from the mouths of fearful women over the course of my life. I am inhaling in staggers, breaths that catch in my throat on their way out. I make a decision. He is only five steps away from me and if I don't leave now, I might be trapped. I will my legs to move. They don't. Panic rises, great hot floods of it in my chest. I eye the end of the alley, beyond him, and his eyes follow. A grin spreads across his face.

'Leaving already?'

His accent is heavy, inner city.

I can only nod. That seems to please him, seeing I can no longer speak. Sweat is beading on the back of my neck, plastering my hair to my skin. His shadow blends into mine, sickening. I have to go. Now. I jolt and begin to run, but the heaviness of my boots and the terror that has paralysed my muscles slows me down.

He lunges, his one free hand grabbing the hood of my jacket and yanking me backwards. It tightens around my throat, closing off any air I might have gasped. My hands are outstretched, I'm falling. I have no option but to drop back into him, gravity forcing us together. I can smell the streets on him, marijuana and stale sweat.

There is no one around to witness what is happening, no bystander to help. I close my eyes, try to calm myself down and think of a way out. I poise my elbow, ready to strike back against him, when a voice shouts out.

'What the fuck are you doing?'

I am released in a flurry of movement. There are muffled noises, grunts and fists on bone. I stay still for a moment, my eyes adjusting. There are two figures wrestling. I recognise the man on the ground as my attacker. He has blood leaking from his nose and mouth. The man on top of him is much bigger, broad shouldered and long limbed. His hair is slicked back off his face, revealing jaunt features, sharp cheekbones. Fighting seems natural to him. There is no hesitation in his violence, and despite him saving me, I'm scared of him. I look behind me, deliberating whether I can slip through the gap between the bin and the wall. If I run, I might make it out of the alleyway. But then where? I feel for my phone slowly, my hands trembling, my eyes still on the fight. I feel the cool hard shape of it, solid in the base of my palm. Neither of the men look up at me as I unlock it and find Eoin in my contact list. I call him without thinking. It rings out for four beats before a shadow falls over me. I look up and see the man who saved me, his arm outstretched.

'Come on then, let's get you inside.'

19

Marianne

MARIANNE CLIMBS THE STAIRS before hesitating, her hand gripping the banister. There are three doors upstairs. She looks at each, giving them thorough consideration. She is already bathed and dressed. She feels clean and new. With firm fingers, she rubs at her temples. The harder she tries to think, the more her mind feels heavy and empty. She stays that way for several minutes, her slippers teetering on the edge of the top step. She came up for something, it had seemed important. She sits down slowly on the step, to wait until she can remember. She pushes her hands into the carpet, feeling the pile on her skin. It soothes her to do that, over and over again. It makes her feel grounded. Her stomach rumbles; she is not sure how long she has been there. There is clattering in the kitchen, shoes squeaking against the floor. Marianne swears at herself, frustrated at forgetting what has made her journey upstairs in the first place. She has several pieces of paper in her pocket that make no sense. She pulls them out, rips them into tiny pieces and watches them fall like confetti. She hums a tune but can't remember the name of it. Taking the stairs back down one at a time, she makes sure each foot is firmly planted before taking the next. Her brother fell down the stairs once when he was running down for supper; he tumbled all the way and broke two fingers. She remembers that her mother wasn't pleased.

'No, she was not. So now I walk down like this. One at a time.'

Marianne reaches the bottom and catches her breath before entering the kitchen. The smell greets her. Patrick smiles at the sight of her and places a slice of cheese onto the bread he has cut. He sets a plate down in front of Marianne and watches as she inspects it. She stands up suddenly as if burnt, horrified at the puddle on the floor. Her cutlery clatters to the floor, her hand is over her mouth. She pulls her skirt up to her knees, as the liquid zigzags down her legs. Patrick stares, his mouth slightly ajar.

'Don't worry, Marie, I'll get the mop out,' he eventually says, calmly.

'I don't understand,' Marianne whispers.

Her skirt is still in her hands, exposing her bare legs.

'It was just an accident. If you can't have an accident at our age, when can you?' Patrick asks. He forces a short laugh and gets a bottle of disinfectant from the cupboard under the sink. He works a mop around her, leaning on it when he wobbles. It is clear in a matter of moments, the floor gleaming. The scent of it catches in the back of Marianne's throat and she coughs.

'Are you the cleaner?' she asks.

Patrick gives a sad sort of smile but doesn't answer. Her hands are shaking now. She doesn't take her eyes from the patch of wet on the floor.

'Did I do that?' she asks.

Patrick doesn't respond.

'I'm sorry,' she says. 'I'm really sorry.'

He takes her shoulders.

'It's okay,' he whispers.

His words don't soothe her. She feels worse. Her face crumples and she begins to sob. She empties herself out, drawing in a staggered gasp of breath. Patrick pulls her into a hug, whispering gentle words into her hair. She is still for a moment, as though finding refuge in his arms. It lasts only a moment. In a heartbeat she pushes him away, a spark of fear in her eyes. He staggers, gripping the table.

'Get away from me,' she cries, throwing her hands to her side.

'Marie?'

'Stop calling me that! That's not my name.'

She takes a step back, feels the wetness on her legs again.

'I'm sorry, Marianne. Let me help you get cleaned up,' he pleads, eyes wide.

'I said, *stay away*!' She is screaming, backed up against the door.

He is a stranger to her, an enemy, trying to manipulate her. He looks distorted, as though the edges of his face are razor sharp. The floor moves beneath her, and she lets out a wail. Patrick tries to calm her, his hands around her shoulders. She looks around, desperate for something to defend herself with, something heavy or sharp. She thinks he is going to hurt her. She catches sight of the knife laid beside the loaf of bread. Patrick lunges for it as she does, and they wrestle with it over the sink.

'Let go! What are you doing?' He's twisting the knife to loosen her grip.

She digs her nails into skin, still screaming.

The man looks at the blood, shocked. She recognises him then.

'It was you!' She is panting, forcing something out of herself she has long buried under the rubble.

'It was all you! You did it, you did it!' she cries.

'Did what! What are you talking about?' He sounds scared.

'Henry!' She is almost on her knees. 'You killed my Henry!'

20

Patrick

I FREEZE, MY HANDS still around the handle of the knife she is also holding. There is nothing I can say; no explanation will stop the cycle of distorted remembering and forgetting again. I can't stand to hear Henry's name, to think about what might have happened to him. I close my eyes and try to regain my composure.

'You killed him. Where did you put the weapon? Tell me where?' She is screaming now, something primal in her voice. I know the neighbours will be able to hear, I know what they will think. I'm not sure I can do this again. I feel her loosen her grip on the knife as she wails, her head thrown back to the ceiling. I prise the knife from her hands. I set it down on the table, gasping for air. I am very used to being accused of being responsible for what happened to Henry by everyone, used to being seen as the enemy. But it still cuts me every time. Especially hearing it from Marianne. I feel faint; turning my back on her, I hold the counter for support. Marianne has stopped screaming. When I look back her hands are clutched together on her chest. She seems to catch her breath and looks at me quizzically. She looks at the sandwich on the table and sits down, picking her knife and fork from the floor.

'Aren't we going to have any lunch, then?'

* * *

Laura pauses on the other end of the phone.

'Patrick, is that you?'

'Yes. I'm sorry to be calling you, I know you're probably busy. I didn't know who else to reach out to. It's Marianne. She's getting worse. One minute she's tearful, afraid, the next she's violent then inconsolable. She turns against me. She talks about Henry.' I put my face in my palm, embarrassed by the tears in my voice.

'How long has this been going on?'

'She's been having memory problems. For a while. I think it started when Henry was still here, actually. She's grown more aggressive recently, though. It's a lot to manage.' It's hard to admit, hard to say aloud.

The doctor had said it was PTSD, all those years ago. After Henry. He prescribed some medication for her at the time, something to calm her down, help her sleep.

It worked for a while, but I couldn't bring her back. Not with what she started saying. Not with what it meant. I feel the sting of guilt – things have gone too far now.

'Oh, Patrick. I'm so sorry. We all noticed a change in her, especially when she stopped going outside. Thank you for calling me. Violent too, did you say?'

I close my eyes.

'Yes, she doesn't know what she's doing. She doesn't realise it's me.'

'I understand. I see a lot of patients like that at work, so I really do understand. It must be so difficult for you to see her like that. It's important you get support too, especially with the anniversary coming up. I'm on shift soon, but will you let me send Eoin round? He's off today and from what he said, Marianne seemed to really enjoy his company the other day. They got on like a house on fire the other night.'

I feel so tired, where I would usually fight, protect, shut the door on the world, I cannot. I relent and wince at the marks she has left on my arm.

'Yes, please.'

I place the receiver in its cradle. I didn't want it to come to this. I despise having to ask for help. I watch Marianne circle the living room, her hands full of loose sheets of paper. There is a paper trail behind her from the cabinet. She is muttering under her breath, reading them over and over, as though trying to make sense of them. I want the ground to swallow me up, to never have to face a day like this again. She has been rifling through the drawers in the living room since we ate lunch. When she has an idea in her head it is impossible to distract her. I simply watch from a distance. I look up at a painting in the hallway. It is Marianne's favourite. The landscape of the seaside is wild, a snap-shot of one of our daytrips. It is where I proposed, all that time ago. It is the place she seems to remember the most. I often find her here in the middle of the night, staring up at it. Now I just want to tear it down, to take it from the frame and burn it. I want to forget about Marianne too, the Marianne I married. She's gone now. I remember hearing once that loving someone with dementia is like losing them twice. They are wrong. I lose her every day.

* * *

It is late afternoon when the doorbell rings. The rain has finally stopped and the sun is beginning to creep its way through the clouds. It filters its way into the living room and settles like a film on Marianne's pale skin as she sleeps. She is on the sofa, curled up in a blanket, looking more peaceful than I have seen her for a long time. I pray the doorbell doesn't wake her and, thankfully, she is already far away. I open the front door slowly.

'Mr Carr.'

Eoin is looking down at me, his hair falling into his eyes. He has a kind face.

'Eoin. Thank you for coming over. It really is good of you.'

'No, don't worry. I just wanted to check in on you both, make sure you were doing all right.'

He smiles. I wave him in and head for the kitchen.

'Drink?' I ask.

'Tea, no sugar. Thank you.'

He hovers in the hallway, looking at the array of paintings. I make the cup of tea, being careful with the spoon as I stir, afraid of making any noise at all. I usher Eoin into the living room, away from the draught of the hallway. Marianne looks childlike as she lies on the sofa, small and fragile. I hand Eoin a tea-stained mug and see him glance down at my hands; blood has dried along my arm from Marianne's attack. He eyes me cautiously and I move instinctively away from view.

'How are you feeling? I know the anniversary is coming up. You don't have to talk about it but I just want you to know, we're all thinking of you. The whole street is,' he says quietly, looking straight at me.

I smile stiffly, nod my thanks.

'I try not to think about it, truthfully. Hurts too much. I need to keep going for Marianne.'

He says nothing but just looks at me, something unreadable in his expression. Marianne stirs before falling still again and we retreat into the kitchen, not wanting to wake her.

'Again, you can tell me to mind my own business . . .' Eoin begins tentatively, 'but have you considered getting an updated medical diagnosis for Marianne. The medications she would have access to now might really help her. And you, for that matter.'

I turn suddenly, my hands still resting on the sink. How does he know I haven't? Laura must have been talking.

'I don't want anyone near her. She's too sick for all that. She wouldn't cope.'

There is grit in my voice, a mixture of stubborn love and fear that grind together.

'What happened today?' Eoin's eyes return to the backs of my hands, covered as they are in red scratches.

I tug at my sleeves uncomfortably.

'It was a misunderstanding.'

'Patrick, did Marianne do that to you?' Eoin asks.

The concern in his voice makes me stumble, and I don't know how to respond. A stiff nod. It's all I can manage. I can feel that my face has fallen, like all the scaffolding has been removed. The fight has drained the life out of me, the months of battling suddenly too much. My shoulders cannot stand to carry the weight of it any more, the lying, the hiding, the loneliness. I know what I have become as a result of it, far from the man I had been.

'I do appreciate all of this,' I murmur.

'I know. It's hard to accept help when you're used to being the sole carer.' He says it matter-of-fact, taking a sip from his tea in the next breath.

I reel from the last word. I can't stand to hear it. It is too clinical, too detached from what I really am to Marianne. I often find myself tortured by the thought of it, that if I die first and leave Marianne, then they'll take her away. She'll be put in some home somewhere to rot. She is much too precious for all that. She needs love and care and protection. The steam from my mug fogs up my glasses. It is no fun getting old.

21
Marianne

MARIANNE WALKS SLOWLY TO the kitchen, stifling a yawn with the back of her hand. She doesn't quite recognise her surroundings but she does recognise a voice and so she follows it. There's late-afternoon sunlight streaming into the kitchen through the window and she can hear birds tweeting. She walks to the window, aware of them watching her as she goes. The young man observes her and she waves him over to the window to join her.

'Do you see them?' she asks him.

The young man smiles and leans on his elbows to get a better view. 'I do,' he says.

They watch the birds preen and ruffle their feathers.

'They're wood pigeons, you know,' she says, a bit smugly.

'I didn't know that. I'm a bit useless with wildlife, actually. You seem to know a lot, though?'

'I wouldn't say that. I used to paint in the countryside – I'd see lots of different things,' she recalls, her mind wandering. He looks back to the hallway, a smile on his lips.

'You're amazing.' He laughs softly.

She is confused by what he means. She doesn't ask, but just watches the birds hop and preen and shake their feathers. They stand there, side by side like kindred spirits. The birds strain their necks before flying away, soaring high before dipping low. She is jealous of them. That they can leave like that. That they don't have to ever come back. Her hands are shaking and she stares at them.

'Marianne, are you feeling all right?' the young man says. He sounds tentative, as though the subject is made of something delicate.

'Yes,' she whispers.

Patrick excuses himself to use the bathroom and they hear the door close upstairs. On hearing the noise, Marianne feels like a switch has been flicked. She grabs Eoin, her hands tight around his top. Her fingers are gnarled, arthritic, and they cling on as though he is her last chance at survival. She pushes her face close to his. She can smell his breath. His eyes are green and wide. He's searching hers for something and neither are sure if he finds it. Marianne can see things in her mind, little flashes, fragments of something that stick before falling away. It's a man, it's blood, it's Henry gasping for air. It's his face as he realises he's leaving this world, his hands clutching at his throat. She thinks she might be sick but she swallows hard. This is her chance.

'You have to listen to me, listen to me carefully. My son is missing. Did you know my son is missing? He took him, you know, on Wednesday. They got into a terrible fight – he just didn't agree with them being together. He lost his temper. I saw him drag him inside. He did it, he did it,' she insists, begging him to understand.

Eoin looks away, then back again. He doesn't try to move away from her. He's listening, thinking. Marianne thinks that he probably won't believe her. No one else ever has. She thinks she is old and mad and grieving and forgetful of who she is and what she is doing here. Eoin is frowning as though confused, his brow furrowed as he considers what she has said.

'It's him, you have to get her away from him!' she whispers ferociously, frustrated that he isn't understanding what she is telling him. She is struggling to breathe, small gasps escaping her throat. She thinks she might collapse, and his hands find their way underneath her elbows, propping her up. A tear balances on her eyelid before dropping, landing in the space between them. Something unspoken is shared then. He nods once, squeezes her arm.

'Okay,' he says.

He seems to be promising her that he is listening, that he won't mistake her warning for illness. It's all she has wanted, and she lets her hands relax their grip. He leaves her at the window; there is something determined in his expression as he leaves the room. Marianne watches him pause before entering the lounge. She stays very still, listening to the sound of the cabinet being opened, papers being rifled through. Something tells her not to move. She counts her own breaths and it is almost sixty before he reappears in the hallway. He almost bumps into Patrick, who has reached the bottom of the stairs. Patrick frowns at him, his hand lingering on the banister.

'What's going on?' he asks, his voice gruff.

'Sorry, Mr Carr. Marianne mentioned she wanted a particular cup and I couldn't find it. I went in here to look and, well, there's no sign.'

Patrick sighs and rubs his face.

'Don't worry, boy. I know the one she means. I'll find it for her.' He fumbles around in a cupboard and passes Marianne a cup. She stares down at it as though she doesn't recognise it at all.

'I need to get going now, Mr Carr. Unless there's anything else either of you need?'

Eoin keeps his eyes on Marianne as he speaks.

'We'll be just fine, thanks again,' Patrick murmurs.

The young man lingers, his hand pressed against his chest, almost as if he's concealing something.

'If it's all right with you, I'll call back over sometime. Maybe tomorrow?'

Patrick's face lights up. Though Marianne doesn't understand why. He doesn't like visitors.

'We'd like that, wouldn't we, Marie?' he says to her gently.

She smiles. There're wood pigeons back on the fence. Patrick leads Eoin out into the hallway. He waves as he goes, and Marianne sees something tucked into his trousers. A book. She points at it as he turns. They talk on the doorstep, hushed so she does not hear, but she can.

'She likes you, lad; she seems calm when you're around. I owe you one.'

'Anytime, Mr Carr. You know where we are.'

Patrick calls after him like an old friend. 'Listen, lad. Call me Patrick.'

22
Ruth

THE ATTACKER IS STILL on the ground, splayed at such a vulgar angle I can't bear to look. I keep my eyes to the pavement and edge around him. My defender takes me by the elbow, guides me down the alley, through a narrow door to the right and up a flight of stairs. It's concrete and cold and we soon arrive inside a flat, guarded from the elements and the people below. I don't know who this person is, or what his motives are. The four walls press inwards, sucking the air from my lungs. I watch the man cautiously as he shrugs off his jacket. He beckons me in and sits in an armchair. His dirty-blonde hair is slick with rain and streaks of silver, the only clue to his age, which I guess is around 50. He has a thin nose and straight lips, his features pointed. He's broad and agile and I know I would lose any fight against him. My pulse is drumming in my ears and I try to slow my breathing, looking around the flat for some clue as to who the man might be, and if he can be trusted.

His mouth lifts into a lopsided smile.

'Please, sit.' The voice is low and gritty. Along with the grin, it has a forced niceness which makes me flinch.

'I'm fine, thank you,' I say, my voice quivering.

I'm still unsure as to why he went to such lengths to defend me.

He looks up, eyes glinting.

'What happened to that man?' I ask.

I keep my eyes on his face, studying him. He waves a hand nonchalantly.

'Don't you be worrying about him. I've dealt with it. He won't be touching you again.'

Dealt with it?

I rub my forearm, urging myself to slow down and think. I ground myself by studying my surroundings. The flat didn't seem much from the outside, though in here it drips in expense.

'Aren't you going to thank me?'

I shift a little.

'Thank you,' I say.

He nods, appeased. He walks over to the bar that sits against the wall.

'Drink?' he asks.

He has a bottle of Southern Comfort in his hands and is pouring some slowly into a tumbler. I shake my head but his eyes are fixed on the river of gold trickling into the glass. He hands it to me and holds my gaze until I smile and thank him. It's hard not to notice his need for control. We drink in silence for a moment, as though he is daring me to speak. I catch sight of a letter on the coffee table. It's unopened atop a pile of magazines. I lean forward as if stretching, and take in the name. *R. Knight*.

I sit back rather sharply and let the air empty from my lungs. R. K.? How convenient, strangely so. Could *this* really be R. K.? My mind flickers back to what the woman outside the old flat had said, that he delivered himself rather than being found. I consider asking him who he is directly, though something holds me back. I watch him. He's studying me too.

'I'm a neighbour of the Carrs,' I finally say.

I say it with a false conviction. The man's face twitches, a miniscule spasm of his muscles. So he recognises the name. He says nothing, but sips again at the whiskey, letting it balance on his lips.

'Is that right? You came looking for me then, it seems.' He speaks calmly.

So he *is* the R. K. I'm looking for.

'What can I do for you, Ruth?' he says, smiling, breaking the silence.

I freeze as I hear my own name. I try to regain my composure. Someone has warned him I was coming, someone who knows who I am, obviously someone from the street. I have to play this smart.

'I found something. Something of Henry Carr's,' I say. 'I'm guessing you remember him? He mentioned you in a diary. He wrote down your address, circled it. Several times.'

The man's eyebrows rise.

'Several times? Wow, I am honoured. I'm sure I don't need an introduction then, but I'm Robert.' He outstretches a hand and stares at me, smiling thinly, until I shake it.

'Nice to meet you, Robert.' I swallow, clearing my throat. He's amused. 'Henry Carr disappeared fifteen years ago, and the police never found out what happened to him. His parents are devastated. I just want to help them find some closure. I came across Henry's notebook. It was hidden – I don't think the police ever found it. That makes me think they never questioned you either, asked you what you know. I'm a journalist . . .' he nods at this, as though he knows it already. If he knows my name, odds are he knows my profession already too. I try not to let that throw me off. I continue, as though rehearsing a script.

'I'm here as a neighbour, as a friend. I just want to get as much information about Henry as I can, about what might have happened to him that day.' I think about mentioning Martin, but I falter. Remembering how scared Martin had been for his life, I can't put him in danger again.

Robert's smile fades as I speak. The mention of the notebook seems to have agitated him. He must be wondering what else might be in there.

'A journalist? How interesting.' His tone is aggressive. My mouth dries up, and I place the whiskey on the counter beside me. I need to win him over.

'Like I said, I'm not here as a journalist. I'm not recording this conversation in any way, I swear. All I want to know is anything about Henry, anything at all, that might find him. I'm hoping you can help me.' I hold up my palms, try to stay calm.

He stands up quickly, the gold of his watch catching the light. 'Stand up,' he barks.

I hesitate. He's standing over me now, the heaviness of his build casting huge shadows. I stand slowly, one hand on the back of the chair. Is he going to hurt me? *I wouldn't be surprised after the violence I'd just witnessed.* He grabs my arms and holds them into a T before patting down my clothing with rough hands.

'Phone.' It isn't a question. His hand is extended, waiting.

I fish it from my pocket, looking at the screen before placing it on his palm. There is one message notification. Eoin.

He seems satisfied I don't have anything else on me, that our conversation is contained within the walls of this place. He nods at me to sit down. Pulling a packet of cigarettes from his back pocket, he places one between his teeth.

'You want one?' he mumbles, the cigarette dancing.

I shake my head. He lights and takes a drag before exhaling a silverly tendril.

'I might have some information.' He takes another drag and sits before continuing. 'How do I know you're not going to run to the police after this? The information I have is . . .' He considers his words for a moment. 'Sensitive.'

'The police did a pretty shit job the first time round,' I say. There is no reason not to be honest about that. It's pretty public news. 'Like I said, I'm doing this for his parents, not for them. You can choose what to tell me; I don't expect you to trust me. I just want to find out what happened to him. It's eating away at them, the not knowing.'

'Ah, the Carrs.' He lets out a laugh.

'You know of them?'

'Know of them? Oh, Ruth. I grew up on that shithole of a street. Of course I do.'

My heart stops. I shift in my chair. I feel stupid. So stupid. I should have known. I should have checked Laura's yearbook more carefully.

'That's how I knew Henry,' he continues. 'He was at the same school as me, year above. He was the baby of their group though, that made him a bit weak.' His lip curls at the memory of him. 'We weren't friends. Not really. I saw how the others used him, and when the time was right I did the same.'

I tilt my head, confused by his decision to share this declaration first. He holds a hand up in apology.

'You must forgive me,' he says amiably. 'In the end, we did not get along well.'

My eyes fall to a stack of cash on the table. If he wasn't friends with Henry, then why did Henry go to him for help? Surely there were other people to ask? People who would *want* to help him? There has to be more to this than a loan.

'Was Henry a dealer?' I ask. The words are out of my mouth before I can consider the implication of them.

Robert flashes me a look, withering judgement on his face.

'A what?'

'I'm sorry, I just assumed . . .'

'You just assumed what?' he asks, cocking his head. 'Drugs? Don't make me fucking laugh. He didn't have the balls for anything like that. Control a room, hold up a deal? No, you need something about you for that. Henry Carr, he had nothing about him. The police were knocking on the wrong doors, if you ask me.' He seems pleased by that as he stubs the butt of the cigarette in the ashtray on the table.

'Where should they have been knocking?'

He throws me a look.

'Henry wasn't a drug dealer. Sure, he liked to think he had his hand in the game but there was no way. Don't get me wrong, he wasn't as innocent as he seemed either. He got himself into trouble. Those friends of his made sure of that. Toxic lot. They turned to me when they needed to right their wrongs all those years ago. I fixed as much as I could but they were indebted to each other and to me for life. That's a long time ahead of you when you're only 17. The years passed and he got shitloads into debt. When he was swimming in red letters and calls from his bank, he remembered me, remembered who I was and what I could do. He tracked me down again all those years later. He was a shell of the man I knew, even more pathetic, more desperate. He brought one of his friends along with him, as if that would help.'

Friend. Could that have been Laura? Martin?

Robert stands and walks to the windows. They're tall and wide, opening onto the narrow streets below. I'm holding my breath, keeping it contained in a ball in my chest. He isn't lying. It's clear from what Sam had said at the Beehive that Henry had got himself backed into a financial corner. Why else would he get involved with such a dark figure from his past? Yet I still don't get why Robert is sharing so much information with me.

'So that's why you hated him so much?' I ask, sitting forward a little. 'He borrowed money from you? I'm guessing he didn't repay his debt?'

Robert starts pacing, his shoes clicking against the hardwood floor.

'People like him keep me in business. They borrow money they can't pay back, the interest rises, they realise it's just going to get worse and worse and they start to drown.'

'If you don't get paid, how do you make more money?' I sound naïve again and I guess I am, but the curiosity in me is burning.

He smiles. 'Desperate people will do desperate things. Whatever you ask in the end.' He stops again at the window. 'So no, I didn't hate him for borrowing money. I hated him for screwing me over.'

I sit forward, aching for answers.

'What did he do?'

'It's strange, really,' Robert says, almost philosophically. 'That a man can disappear without a trace. What's even stranger is that the very man who disappeared, the one who police claim they failed to find, worked for the coppers once himself.'

He turns from the window and his eyes find me, waiting for my reaction. I stay very still, assessing the information. I couldn't find anything online that stated exactly what Henry's job was, except that he worked in an office. Why wouldn't the police name him as one of their own?

'He was a policeman?' I finally venture.

'God, no.' Robert laughs. 'He couldn't cope with that. The problem with Henry was that he didn't know when to stay away. I told him and told him, I'll contact you. You wait for my word. I'll tell you when I have a job so you can pay me what you owe me. But he couldn't. It was getting to him, the tension, the pressure. He was being buried alive. No, he never went to the police himself. They found him.' He walks into the kitchen and leans on the counter. His sleeves are rolled up to the elbow, all veins and muscle.

'What happened then?' I press.

'What happened then is he let them get into his head. They promised him protection, immunity, if he grassed me up. He gave them everything. Contacts, addresses, history. They wired him up when I finally sent him on a job, to catch us in the act. You can see why I'm suspicious of wires now, can't you?' He smiles again, holds his hands up as though to say *who can blame me?*

I nod. Wait for him to continue.

'He should have known I'm wiser than that. That I make friends in high places. There was a bent copper in the force who gave me the heads-up. We ripped out the wire, beat the shit out of him. He got no evidence. The police had a night sat with him at the hospital.' He shrugs. 'Wasn't the greatest night for my source either once the coppers figured it out, but these things happen'.

I can't shake the feeling that Robert is very capable of killing a man. He hated Henry, and it makes him an obvious suspect. On paper. Yet hearing him speak about it all, something still doesn't make sense. Why, if Henry had been an informant against Robert, would the police not question Robert after his disappearance? Henry ran afoul of a criminal organisation and they killed him. The police just missed it.

But there are still too many gaping holes even in that theory. No CCTV, no clues, no body. I close my eyes and focus on why I wanted to find R. K. in the first place.

'Do you know what Henry needed the money for?'

'Listen, Henry might have grassed me up but I keep my word. Whatever happened with him stays with him. If you're that desperate, ask the friends.' He laughs; it sounds like a bark. 'You came here looking for answers. I don't pretend to have all of them. I see the way you're looking at me: you see danger, a threat. I'm not the man you're after, my dear; dead men don't pay. They don't do jobs and when they expose you, you stay as far away as possible. You want to know what I think happened to Henry Carr? Ask that father of his.'

* * *

Manchester has fallen into darkness. Its lights flicker, sleepy red dots against the black. I am sitting down by Deansgate Locks when Eoin finds me. He's out of breath, sweat glistening in his hair.

I'd managed to text him the two words of my location before my phone died and had been sitting here in a daze ever since, hoping he'd come and find me.

'Shit. Are you all right?'

His hands are at his sides, but move restlessly. I hadn't expected him to come. I left a rushed voicemail, talking without thinking, and the sight of him in front of me brings every emotion to my throat. I realise I'm crying. He's standing ten feet away, his face cast in shadows, but the bulky solidness of him visible, enough to make me feel safe even from a distance. He opens his arms and lets me fall into him. His hands meet in the small of my back.

'What the fuck happened?' His voice is rough.

He never has been good at hiding his emotions. I guide him to the steps and we sit down, shoulders pressing against one another. It takes half an hour to tell him everything. I keep pausing in the middle of sentences, rephrasing them in ways that better depict what happened. Eoin stays silent throughout, as he always does, just staring at me with heaviness in his eyes. His fists are in a ball on his lap. They are all I can see as I speak. I know that it's his way of showing his anger. I feel guilty for calling him. For getting him involved in something he wanted no part in.

'Eoin,' I finally say.

'You can't keep doing this.'

'I know.'

I look at my feet, our feet, inches apart.

'No. You can't. You can't keep doing this – you're putting too much of yourself into this investigation and you're going to get yourself killed.'

He's shouting, his voice echoing off the scaffolding around us. He isn't looking at me; his eyes are everywhere but on me. He paces, his emotion too big to sit with. His words don't sting; he's right and we both know it. I've always been too good, too skilled at detaching myself from danger and emotion, storing it somewhere far away. Eoin has seen the tears, the smashed glass, all the remnants of arguments half finished. He has seen my father swaying in the street, lying in the gutter outside the Beehive, drowning himself and pulling me down with him. He was a sinking ship but I couldn't abandon him. He might have been a drunk, a terrible father, but he was *my* father none the less. *Today* had been different. I had taken risks to help someone else, not to hurt myself.

'I have to do this, Eoin. I have to find out what happened to Henry. I have to keep trying.'

'I-I know.' His voice is defeated, his shoulders sunken. 'I don't want you to do it on your own. I don't want to lose you again. Not even as a friend.'

The last words sound strange from his lips.

He leans forward suddenly, as if remembering something, and removes a bulky square from his pocket. Henry Carr's notebook. He holds it carefully, like something dangerous. He's done it. He's taken it. His face displays a tortured expression, guilt etched into every pore. I take it slowly, gratefully, and hold it to my chest.

'Thank you, Eoin.'

I look through it, though none of it seems to make sense. I skip past R. K., to other names, to other clues. There are dates and numbers crossed out, birthdays, events, but nothing that sketches out the identity of his killer. Nothing even close. I try to swallow my disappointment. I shouldn't have expected it to be that easy.

'If Patrick doesn't tell me why Henry needed the money, what he might have been running from or towards, then I'll need to speak to someone else who might have some answers. Someone who will have known about Henry's sting operation gone wrong.'

Eoin frowns. 'Like who? I don't know if anyone on the street knew about that. If they do, I doubt they'll talk.'

'I've been thinking. If I can use my police source to get the original detective's details, the one originally assigned to the case fifteen years ago, they're bound to know something that can help me. Some things that were maybe never followed up, kept in the files, buried.' I'm talking quickly, excited by having a plan.

'What makes you think the original officer will even talk to you?' Eoin asks, rubbing his hands together to keep warm.

'I don't know. Things Robert said, things he didn't. Things I can use as a bargaining chip, that I can threaten to take to the press. It might not work. But I'm going to try.'

Eoin nods, like he knows there's no point talking me out of it. His phone rings slicing the moment in two, and he fumbles clumsily in his pocket for it. He looks concerned.

'Hello?'

There is such quiet around us and the sound on the call is so loud, I can hear everything. There's noise in the background, screams, shouting, footsteps. Eoin shakes his head and puts a finger into his ear.

'Mum, I can't hear you. Is everything all right?'

There is more commotion. I hear Laura's voice.

'You need to get home. To the street. Everyone's talking about it. They've found a weapon. It's – it's covered in dried blood. There's been an arrest. For Henry's killer. They're saying Henry's dead, Eoin.'

23
Peter

THE BEEHIVE IS FULL and bustling. Workers from the nearby factory and those filtering down from the train station have stopped by for a drink. People are standing shoulder to shoulder, pint glasses welded into their hands. The music from the jukebox is more upbeat than those attending and it makes the atmosphere awkward. One man is slamming the side of it, his coin stuck in the slot.

'This is bullshit!'

'Your taste in music is bullshit, more like.'

With that, he is pulled into a headlock, laughter erupting all round. The light inside the pub is dim and I speak to Sam hurriedly in hushed tones. I spot the officer first, the briskness of his walk as he uses his elbows to reach the bar, parting his way through a dense group playing darts. He gets a drink spilt on him in the process and I can't help letting out a laugh.

'Peter.' A whisper, a growl. I look back at Sam. 'Promise me?' he says.

I look into his face, at the deep lines of his eyes, the crease of his brow. When did we get so fucking old? I don't know what to say to him. I'm thinking about Ruth, about Laura.

He grabs my shirt, his breath hot in my ear.

'Promise me.'

I nod, trying not to cause a scene, aware of the eyes burning into us.

The officer sidles up behind us, nods to Sam and motions to the back for privacy. I try to hold back but he beckons me through too. It's polite conversation at first but I can see his notebook, can see the junior officer lingering in his fluorescent jacket.

'We appreciate the statement you gave us earlier in the week, Sam. Are you sure there's nothing you'd like to add to that?'

I feel him squirm beside me.

I don't understand why he wants me here too. Maybe he thinks I'll grass him up, let my conscience play me for a fool. I sit tight.

'No? Well that's a shame. We've had an anonymous phone tip, you see. The explosion on social media recently made the caller rethink a visit to the pub they took on the day of Henry's disappearance. Said their partner has been listening to the podcasts and happened to mention it. They claim that as they left the pub to head home, they saw *you* fighting with someone in the alleyway beside the pub. Said you grabbed the guy by the throat and then you both disappeared down the street. When an officer asked for a description of the gentleman you were fighting with, they said they couldn't see the other man too clearly. But from what they could describe, it fits a very decent description of Henry Carr.'

Sam says nothing but his breathing is heavier. I look up at him just a fraction, wondering. It isn't that I'm doubting him, not really, but Henry was my friend.

'Nothing to say to that, Sam?' the officer asks, a smirk on his lips.

'No comment,' he replies after I nudge him in the ribs. He knows the score.

The officer seems to expect this. He continues. 'I got the guys at the office to do some background checks on you, and it appears that you came into a substantial amount of money the day after Henry's disappearance. Almost twelve thousand, from the looks of the statement. You then transferred it all to an overseas account.

Given the rumours of Henry being in debt and using a loan shark, it makes it all the more interesting. Don't you think?'

I snap my head towards him, I can't help it.

'Twelve thousand pounds?' I whisper. What else has he not told me?

'Am I under arrest?' he asks, tilting his chin up. His pride is hurt.

I don't give a shit.

I can feel my blood bubbling. What has he done?

'I really need to get back to work,' Sam says, his voice glassy.

The officer is about to respond, his junior moving in, when his phone rings.

'Yeah, what is it?' He stands, moves away from us towards the fireplace.

I listen hard, trying to make out the response, my heart thumping in my ears. Christ. What has Sam got himself into?

I can just about hear a voice on the other end. The officer says he'll be down to the station as soon as.

He whispers to his junior, something about a fridge-freezer.

They look at both of us, their faces sombre.

'We'll be back.'

24
Oscar

I EXCUSE MYSELF, TUCKING my notebook and phone into my suit pocket. Someone had kept Henry's remains in a fridge-freezer. Or at least that's what the forensics team suspect so far.

The sentence rings through my head like a bell.

Where has the fridge-freezer been all this time? *And where the hell is the body?*

Why? Why keep it only to move it recently? Why not destroy the evidence straight away? Why leave it lying in the middle of an alleyway for anyone to find? Sure, it was empty, but they must have known that if it was investigated, tested, there would still be traces, regardless of how well it was cleaned. It isn't making any sense to me right now. *This street doesn't make any sense to me.*

I force myself to slow down; all we know is that the blood is a match. We don't have a body. We don't have anything concrete.

I remind myself to do what works, what my superiors have always advised: to get inside the minds of the people you're interviewing, you need to think like them. Act like them, to some extent. I nod, decision made, and stop at the bar. I lean over, checking out what they have. It'll have to be non-alcoholic since I'm driving. I accept my Coke and take a swig, looking around as I order my thoughts. The place is cluttered, not just with people but with things. It's worse than my grandparents' fridge-magnet collection. Tat everywhere. Every shelf is filled with weird and wonderful objects, busts of people I don't recognise, figures of eerie-looking animals, trophies from darts games.

I pause.

Blink twice.

Is that . . .? *No. It can't be.*

I edge closer, not taking my eyes off the object.

There is something on the furthest shelf, tucked beside two looming trophies. So obviously out of place. A wrench. I fumble for my phone and shine my torch up at it. The hairs on my arms stand on end: is that rust? Or blood?

Eyes around me are following the light to the wrench, and people begin to gather around. The earlier hubbub dies down and is replaced with hushed tones of disbelief as understanding dawns on them.

Then someone shouts for his friends to come and look, piercing the atmosphere, and soon the whole place erupts. I immediately radio for backup, and stumble against the wave of people either nudging in closer to get a good look or else trying to get as far away from the scene as they can. Some have sensed what might be happening, and no one wants to be around when the police arrive. I catch sight of Sam amid the chaos, perplexed by the reaction of the crowd, the glass knocked from his hand, beer spilling, glass spraying at his feet. He is standing completely still, surveying the scene in front of him. He finally looks up at what we have all seen. His face turns white.

Why would there be a bloodied wrench on the shelf? There can be no other explanation for it. That, along with the new information about him fighting a man matching Henry's description, the money moving to his account after Henry's disappearance. No. It doesn't add up. Sam stares at the shelf and then stares at us, frozen. I squeeze myself through the stampede, feeling for the handcuffs on my hip. I release them carefully and pull Sam's hands behind his back before he can register what is happening.

'Sam Carter, I am arresting you on suspicion of the murder of Henry Carr.'

'Someone's framing me,' he mumbles. He struggles half-heartedly against the cuffs. He's looking around dazedly. Then he seems to come to his senses and shouts 'Get off me! It wasn't me . . . I'm being framed . . . '

There is raw fear and desperation in his voice.

The rest of the room melts into a haze, the residents' screams and shouts carried on the air and into the street. I guide him out as more officers enter the pub to control the crowd, and the eyes of the street follow. The bloodied wrench sits above us on the shelf.

25
Patrick

MARIANNE IS WIPING DOWN the windowsill when I put my arms around her, and she smiles at my touch. It doesn't matter that she's cleaning it with a sock. I don't correct her on such things any more, in the way that I would have once. She has settled since our argument, forgetting that it ever happened. Forgetting that dementia is a word with her name now attached to it. She is some glimmer of her other self, the Marianne I met at the dance hall all those years ago. When she danced to the music the other night, it had given me a crippling sense of déjà vu to see her sway like that, a grin on her face, a song in her voice. The radio plays out now and we step along to the song for a moment, our weathered hands enclosed in a knot. She starts laughing hysterically, until I let go.

'What's so funny?' I ask, a smile tugging at the corner of my mouth.

I can't help laughing at the sight of her, slapping her knee with her free hand. Her cackle fills the house. Great howling swoops of laughter rain down on us, at a joke neither of us can remember. It doesn't matter, in the end, what we are laughing at. It just matters that the unapologetic ring of it fills the air of a house that has missed it. It hasn't heard true laughter since the day Henry left. We thought we'd never laugh again.

Collapsing together onto the settee, our legs swing into the air and we let out a collective sigh. Now the laughter has fallen away I heat up some tomato soup, Heinz, the only kind she likes.

I butter bread, great slabs of it, and watch her dip it into the soup eagerly. Her lips are coated with liquid, orange lipstick that I gently wipe away. I wash up while Marianne dries; we watch dusk fall across the garden with silent eyes and full hearts. We have scones with jam and proper cream, watching terrible television and openly enjoying it. Marianne can't answer any of the questions on the quiz show, though she squeals with delight when I answer them all correctly. She applauds me at the end until her hands are red. She makes me stand up and bow, hooting at the creak of my back. It all feels like old times and I drink it up like a man dying of thirst. I know that I should slow down and savour it, that I might never get it again. Though it is impossible to stop or slow down, not when Marianne is Marianne. Halfway through a recorded repeat of *Homes Under the Hammer* she stands and walks towards me, and sits on my lap with her hands laced around my neck. My knees groan under the strain, though the pain is the purest happiness I have felt in longer than I can remember.

* * *

We fall asleep in the sitting room nestled together, and when I wake it is early evening. The last few hours have been so perfect that I could have dreamt it. I get up reluctantly and check the chart on the fridge, confirmation of the bin collection tomorrow. I pull the black bin from the yard with as much quiet as I can muster, leaving the gate swinging open behind me. I line the bin up neatly with the others already out, though I am usually the first. I'm on my way back to the yard when I spot the cat in the alleyway. I lean down and stroke the long line of her tail, too stiff to reach her back. She seems content with the effort, and purrs deeply. It is then I hear the commotion, a voice coming from the street. I roll my eyes instinctively. Family arguments do occasionally spill onto the pavements. The argument, however, sounds one-sided. I leave the gate unlocked, something I'll deal with later, and walk into the living room. I don't notice Marianne's absence at first. It is only as I reach the window that I see her standing in the road. The front door is wide open and I swear at myself for forgetting to double-lock it. By the time I reach her a small crowd has gathered. The family from number twelve are beside her, hands full of carrier bags.

'Hi, mate. We were on our way back from the shops and found her. She's been saying some pretty strange things. Do you need help getting her inside?' the man says gently, as though I am someone to be pitied. He is a relative newcomer to the street, unaware of the history of Marianne's behaviour.

'No, thank you. I can manage,' I say under my breath.

Marianne is crying. Her chin is quivering in the way it does when you're trying to contain something you cannot.

The father nods and holds a hand up in apology. He gathers his children and wife and beckons them away. There are others standing at a distance, concern in their eyes. I see Mrs Montgomery with her walker, mumbling something. Her eyes flash wildly at Marianne, something urgent on her lips. Frank and Margo stand on the edge of their property, their arms folded. They whisper something to each other, edging closer to Marianne as she stands in the road. I give a small smile, both wanting to reassure them and not wanting them to be dragged into the spectacle.

'Everything good over there, Paddy?' Frank calls over.

He is watching Marianne, who is shivering and crying. I nod firmly, placing a hand on Marianne's shoulder. I do my best to avoid their gazes, keeping my head down while I try to steer her inside.

'The man, he's here,' she declares.

I look around to see which man she is referring to. There are none, besides those who live on the street. Our friends and neighbours. Marianne often forgets the residents, calling them by different names or declaring them strangers entirely.

'Which man?' I ask, forcing patience.

'Him!' Her voice has reached a shout, her finger slowly rising to point vaguely ahead. My vision snakes along the path she has drawn. I look at every face, at the people I have called neighbours my whole life, frowns and whispers rippling among them. I hold up a hand in apology.

'Let's talk about this inside,' I say.

'No, no, no. You have to listen to me.'

Her hands are on my shirt, gripping, pulling. Her eyes are wild, spit hanging from her chin.

'He knows where our Henry is.'

She is looking at all the houses now, taking in the scale of them. She could be talking about any of them. Though it is clear she believes our son is in one.

'Marianne, love. Come on inside, you'll catch a cold out here,' I say gently.

I almost coax her, have almost persuaded her to follow me when there is a commotion from the other end of the street. It starts with shouts, caught and lost again on the wind, then crowds running, sirens screaming. I squint, try and make out what the fuss is about. People are shouting, odd words reaching us at the other end.

'What's he saying?' Frank asks, turning to Margo.

She shrugs. Her lips are tightly closed.

I keep hold of Marianne's elbow, firm but gentle. She watches the crowds too, her mouth partially open.

'They found it in the pub!' a woman shouts, tears streaking lines of makeup down her face.

I step an inch closer, tilt my head to hear better, trying to make sense of it.

'I'm so sorry, Patrick,' someone says.

I don't turn to look at them. Don't ask any questions.

'Your poor boy,' someone else says.

I feel a hand on my back keeping me up.

The world is spinning.

Someone takes Marianne into the house, I don't know who, I can't concentrate.

'. . . found a bloodied weapon.'

'Sam's been arrested.'

'Where's the body?'

It all happens at once then, I can see what they are saying in my mind as if I was there myself.

My poor Henry.

* * *

I am already awake when the screaming starts.

The police have been and gone, full of apologies and condolences. They say they will be testing further, but that there was a fridge-freezer, that the initial blood sample was a match, and that they expect this weapon to be the same.

A fridge-freezer?

Left in an alleyway?

None of it makes sense.

I said I'll speak to them tomorrow, though I know what they are going to say.

I vomited. Twice. My stomach hurling at the thought of him stored away like that, the brutality, the lack of dignity. The whole street seeing it, knowing about it before we did.

I can't sleep. I kept Marianne away from the news and she has been asleep ever since.

I'm on my feet the moment I hear it. I'd recognise the sound anywhere. Marianne. There is no light to line the walls; it seems even the streetlamps are asleep. I hurry to the landing, steadying myself with a hand on the wall. I squint to better adjust my eyes to the dark. I am just wondering if perhaps I had drifted off and it had all been a dream when it starts up again. The screaming continues, long and shrill, like a wounded animal. I wrap my dressing gown tight and wobble along to Marianne's room. I switch the landing light on, wincing at its brightness, and fling open her door. It is then I realise the screaming is not coming from her bedroom.

I swing around, my neck aching in protest. I am sweltering-hot, my fingers tingling as I claw my way out and down the stairs. The hallway is plunged in darkness, the ticking of the clock between her screams is haunting. I rush down the first few steps before missing one and stumble into the hallway.

Marianne's screams have stopped abruptly, becoming a jumble of words. I can't work out what she is trying to say. I'm used to her having nightmares – they are a regular occurrence. She often calls out in her sleep, asking for people who have long since died, talking of secrets we have both agreed to bury. She has never, however, screamed in such a way. What has brought her down-stairs? She is usually too scared to leave her room in the dark, and I often find her cowering within the bed sheets. The back door is ajar, a crack of light escaping onto the carpet. A muffled scream makes my decision and I hurtle for the door. I can see Marianne stood still on the doorstep, facing whatever it is outside. I walk towards her slowly, knowing that startling her might prompt her to attack me again. I am just reaching out, slow and careful, when something outside pulls Marianne from me and takes her into the night.

I can't hear anything but the blood pounding heavily in my ears. It takes a moment to convince my legs to move: they are paralysed in fear. I wait until the dizziness has passed before my legs begin to cooperate. The outside light has come on, detecting movement. I look towards the patch of grass and the bird table, seeing nothing but the shadow of moving bushes. The sound of something muffled and contained is coming from behind the bins. I edge forward.

'Patrick.'

Ruth Cavanagh is standing against the fencing, Marianne in her arms. Her face is pale. Eoin is watching us all, something knowing in his expression.

'What the hell is going on here!' My voice cracks. I look frantically around the garden.

'We were walking home. I heard Marianne screaming and came as fast as I could. The back gate is open; she's saying the man ran when he heard us coming. I didn't see him, though.'

I look at Ruth, at the concern in her expression, the firm line of her mouth. I don't know what to believe. Marianne has sunk to the floor by the flower bed. Her arms are bare, her feet are dirtied and splayed out in front of her like a child's. She is shaking and mumbling over and over.

'Patrick, we need to call the police.'

'No.' My tone is more aggressive than I intended.

'No?' She is astonished, appalled. 'You've had an intruder – they've clearly just tried to abduct Marianne or harm her. You need to tell them about this!'

I'm not sure why, but I know this was no burglar. In fact, every fibre of my being tells me that Marianne knows exactly who this was. We can't get the police involved, not now. It will break her.

'This is my house and my decision. The best thing for Marianne is to get her back inside, safe.' I attempt to scoop Marianne up before staggering, falling against the bins. I swear at my grazed elbow, pulling my knees into a position where I can stand on my own. Ruth's arms are around me before I can try.

'I'm so sorry about your son, Patrick. About what they found.'

I swallow. The lump in my throat sticking.

She doesn't wait for a response but takes off her jacket and lays it around Marianne's shoulders. Together, with Eoin's help, we lift her, supporting her underneath her arms. We walk slowly to the kitchen, settling around the table like a mismatched family. We sit and stare silently at one another. Marianne finally stops crying, her eyes red and puffy. She has not spoken a coherent sentence since we found her. She is mumbling about many things now: her mother, schoolwork, Christmas lights. It is all stuck together in a clump I can't pick apart.

I ask her several times to identify the man but she can't. She refuses to drink, to eat, to go back to sleep. Ruth and Eoin don't know it of course, but it feels as though everything that happened in the past is happening again now, as though we are back at that day when everything changed.

* * *

'You'd best be getting home. Thanks for your help,' I finally say to Ruth, genuine in my appreciation. I was suspicious at first, of her and her story, but she seems to care for Marianne in a way that surprises me. This journalist, this mix of stranger and neighbour. She looks at me, her dark eyes blinking slowly. She smiles a little, looks over at Eoin, who is stony-faced. He is holding Marianne's hand.

'You know, don't you?' Marianne asks, looking straight at me. Her eyes are hard and hating. It knocks the air right out of me.

'What's that, love?' I say gently.

She spits out a laugh, pushes the chair back so it scrapes along the floor.

'About the body. You know!' Marianne cries.

I feel my heart sink, feel cruel for wishing she would forget as she always does.

'Marianne,' I whisper.

I eye Ruth carefully, aware she might hear something she shouldn't. She might write about it, tell everyone.

Marianne's voice grows louder, echoing off the walls. 'You know! Our boy. He was our boy.' She crumbles for a moment, overcome by grief.

'Keep your voice down, Marianne,' I beg.

'No! I won't! I'll shout about it.'

She bolts before any of us can grab her. She pulls open the back door with both hands and stumbles onto the step. She throws her head back, face to the sky.

'There's a body there! It's him, it's him, he's there! He killed him! Oh, Henry. My boy. Can anyone hear me? Why don't you believe me? He's in there!' she screams.

I don't even try and stop her. I imagine what they found in the pub will only be the start. I can feel myself caving in. All I've tried to rebuild, everything I've tried to contain to protect us both, is falling around us. I sit and let the debris rain down.

Ruth leans towards me.

'Patrick. She just wants us all to listen, she needs to be heard. I know this is hard, but don't you think it's time? Listen to what she has to say, trust in what she knows. I think it's time she shared her story.'

My head is in my hands, everything is heavy. I feel sick at what I have done to Marianne, at the way I have silenced her. Shutting her off from the outside world as though she was no longer allowed to be a part of it. I did it to protect her, but I fear I have made it all worse. The pressure is too much. I look up at her, slowly.

'All right,' I say. 'But Marianne has been through enough tonight, she's too vulnerable. I'll tell you what I know. I'll tell you so that you can tell them.' I try to swallow the shame before speaking again. 'Our Henry wasn't running from us; he didn't want a new life or a new identity. He liked who he was, he loved us, he just had other people who needed him more.' I pause and she frowns slightly, leaning forward as if willing me on.

'He was a father.' I whisper. 'Henry had a baby.'

DAY FIVE

NEW DISCOVERY IN THE HENRY CARR CASE

Investigators find blood and DNA traces they believe to be linked to fifteen-year disappearance case the day before anniversary, as details of Carr's private life are revealed.

Ruth Cavanagh

14/9/23

The recently reopened investigation into the disappearance of 34-year-old Manchester office worker Henry Carr took a tragic turn yesterday evening. Police confirm that a bloodied weapon was found in the Beehive pub, just off Crow Street, by investigators. Though the blood is yet to be tested, due to the earlier discovery of a bloodied container it is thought to be connected to the Carr case. A 50-year-old man has been arrested on suspicion of murder. Despite no body yet being found, extensive searches of the pub are underway.

The disappearance of Henry Carr has plagued residents of Crow Street and investigators for several years. Carr disappeared from outside his home on Crow Street on the afternoon of Wednesday, 15 September 2008. Henry was reported missing just after midnight by his parents, whom he lived with. A witness reported hearing Henry at about 5 p.m., outside his parents' house.

Despite intensive trawling of local CCTV, attempts to interview each resident of the street, and searches of the local land around the area, no trace of the missing man has ever been found. Following an initial arrest in the months after the disappearance, a man was later released without charge. So the big question remains: how can a man disappear from the street he calls home in broad daylight?

This question has plagued investigators from the outset. It has also piqued the curiosity of a new generation of armchair detectives, thanks to the popular podcast *True Crime Revisited*, which began featuring the case last month.

Theories of what happened to Henry Carr have circulated widely in the years since his disappearance, one being that he simply left the town for a new life. We can now exclusively confirm that before his disappearance, Henry Carr fathered a child with an unknown woman. Carr's father, Patrick, speaking to the media for the first time in fifteen years, explains that he believes this information may have led to his son's disappearance and, what we now suspect, his gruesome death. Carr stated:

'We are completely devastated by the news. The fact that there seems to be evidence of his demise so close to home, to us, is hard to accept. This street has stood by us since Henry disappeared, and we are sure they will stand with us fifteen years later, with this latest development. We found out shortly before he disappeared that Henry had fathered a child, and while he never said who the mother was, this made me sure that he wouldn't have left willingly. That's how we've always known, why we've always said that he hadn't and wouldn't just get up and leave. We've been aware of the theory that Henry may have ran away with his new family, but given he took no items of value with him, we are inclined to believe this to be false. We are a private family and we share this information only to encourage the mother or child to come forward, to give us any information they may have, and to allow us to meet the only piece of Henry we have left. I will not be talking to the press any further.'

If you believe you have any information relating to the Henry Carr case, or indeed are the woman or child mentioned in the article, please get in touch.

26

Patrick

IT IS EIGHT O'CLOCK in the morning when I find Marianne cold on the floor.

I always knew it was possibility. That she might go before I do.

It's the kind of reoccurring fear that creeps up on you in old age; it jumps up on you in the middle of the night. I know it's selfish to want to go first, to avoid the heartbreak that would surely come your way. I know too that she wouldn't cope without me, that she needs me to protect us, to keep the outsiders out. But I have prayed and prayed that goodbye is a long way off. That I will have just a little more time with my love.

I had woken early on account of the fullness of my bladder, yet on my way to the bathroom, I noticed Marianne's door was wide open, cutting a slice of light on the carpet. This was completely out of routine, and after the events of last night I felt my heart drop. I rushed into her room. The bed was empty, the covers thrown back into a tumultuous pile.

'Christ!' I exclaimed. *Had someone come back to take her? Had they finally got to her?* I would never forgive myself if I hadn't kept her safe, as I had promised.

I began to cry, hot tears which only made me angrier. I wiped them off my face and blinked the blur of them away as I took the stairs as quickly as my frail body would allow. It felt as though I was running through water: the faster I tried to go the slower I felt. As I reached the bottom step, I propelled myself in a wild search around the ground floor. I could see from the hallway that the front and back doors were still closed. I whispered a prayer of thanks. The house was deathly quiet. I entered the lounge, suddenly hit by relief and dread all at once. A light was on, artificial against the first rays of morning sunlight. The side table was overturned, pens and newspapers scattered across the carpet. And Marianne lay beside it, her body crumpled beneath a pile of paper and envelopes, some of which she clutched to her chest. Her eyes were closed, her lips tinged blue. I threw myself to the floor, carpet burning my knees as I grabbed at her shoulders.

'Marianne, love.' I tried not to shout, for fear of scaring her. 'Can you hear me?'

Her face was white marble, unmoving. I ran a hand through her hair, the curled white whisps of it. I could smell the talc on her skin, the scent of her perfume. I let the tears fall from my nose, pooling in the fibres of the carpet. My hands were on her hands, the cold stiff slenderness of them, on her shoulders and their frailness.

'Please, don't leave me. Wake up now, love. Come on, I'll get you your breakfast, hey? Marianne. Marianne. Jesus, please. I can't live without you.'

My head was on her chest, lying still and sobbing beside her. I had never felt her so cold.

27
Ruth

'ARE YOU HAPPY WITH the article?'

I kick my boot into the dirt. The ground is hard and cold and I see my breath as I sigh.

'Tom, you cut out a whole section on the treatment of the community by the press, and another section on police failings in the original investigation. So no, not exactly,' I say, picking a wilting leaf from a plant and crushing it between my fingers.

Tom sighs down the line. I can hear him typing on his laptop at the same time.

'I left in what people want to know. I know you care about Crow Street, but the people of Newcastle just want to know the firm facts. Short and sweet, you know?' A pause after hearing himself describe the story as sweet. 'It was good, Ruth. Thank you. I can imagine being back has been difficult for you.'

I scowl down the phone, which feels childish, but I didn't expect him to cut any of it.

'So is there any point going to see the original detective?' I ask.

'Definitely. See if he ever had a hunch about the landlord – Sam, was it? – being involved. You never know what you'll find out, so go.'

'Okay. I'll go. I'm just annoyed because Patrick Carr has never given a statement to the media, Tom. He told me he wanted more about the community in it.' I try to keep the irritation out of my tone.

'Ruth, half of what he told you he wouldn't let you put in the paper. The man was probably so traumatised by the fact his son's potential murder weapon has just been found, we can't know if the stuff he said is even true.' He yawns down the phone and apologises. 'Makes for good reading, though,' he adds.

'He wouldn't lie about it, Tom. He's not that kind of person.' I hear the defensiveness in my voice. 'Patrick was practically red in the face as he told me that Henry had a secret child on the way, he's so ashamed about it, even now. They're Irish Catholics, they knew what people would say. It's not like how it is now – they thought the whole street would shame them. I think he's brave to finally come forward with it.' I say, walking through the long grass.

A gust of wind whistles down the phone.

'How did he find out, then? About the kid?' Tom asks.

'He found a baby scan in Henry's room along with letters to a mystery woman. He completely lost it. He couldn't bear to tell Marianne, but he got into a fight with Henry.'

'The day Henry went missing?' Tom laughs, incredulously.

I know how bad it all sounds.

'Yeah, the day he went missing,' I admit.

Patrick had been defensive with the information. He even settled Marianne in bed before he told the story. There was something he was hiding, something he didn't tell me. I had left feeling dissatisfied, as though I held only half the answers. It didn't feel like the right time to press him on it, though, not with someone trying to attack Marianne as they had. Though it makes sense now that Henry would go to extreme lengths to get cash together quickly. I can see why Robert was the only person left he could go to. Henry *was* preparing to leave the street. He just needed more time before he could get away and raise a family away from the whispers and the disapproval. Though he never got his chance.

'Do you think Patrick was the man heard arguing with Henry that day?' Tom asks.

I hesitate. The thought has crossed my mind. Though surely Mrs Montgomery would have recognised Patrick's voice? They've known each other for decades. I sit down on a worn bench, inching away from the bird faeces and dead leaves.

'I don't know. Something just doesn't add up. Patrick might have wanted Henry to disappear into the shadows if he was going to raise a child out of wedlock, but he had no reason to actually harm him. If Patrick wanted Henry gone, he was achieving it. Henry was clearly trying to gather money together, probably with every intention of leaving anyway.'

'Listen, you're doing a great job. Really. Keep digging. We've already had hundreds of thousands of hits on your article since it went live. The true-crimers must be loving it!'

I smile but feel bad for even talking about it.

The truth is, I feel guilty about writing about any of them. I don't want to expose Patrick and Marianne, I don't want to write about Sam being charged. *Sam.* He won't be. He didn't do it, he couldn't have. He was pretty open about not liking Henry, but not enough to kill him. Why risk your own freedom, your own life, for someone you simply dislike?

'Listen, Ruth, I've got to go to a meeting. I'll call you later. I'm proud of you.'

I smile and hang up. It feels good to have something in print, to put just an ounce of what has happened over the past few days into words.

I was awake all night, thinking about the scene at the pub. Eoin and I had run all the way from the train station, pushing our way through the crowd that had lingered, past the flashing police lights and tape. Oscar refused to talk to me at the scene – he practically snarled at me to get back. It felt like everything had changed. This place. This case.

The Beehive was a sanctuary, where the broken community had healed, where people felt more connected, where I had been raised and loved. Now it was a crime scene, tainted with the image of a bloodied wrench hanging above everyone in the bar. Bile rises from my stomach at the thought of it. I wonder what Robert Knight will think of Sam's arrest. Why would Sam, if he was the killer, make the weapon so obvious, so public, just to say someone else put it there? It doesn't make sense.

I trudge on through the wasteland, watching a bird as it swoops and soars. I think about Marianne, about who would attack her and why.

Is it because of what she knows? That she's the only person who could say truthfully whether Sam is innocent? *If he is.*

The wasteland is alive. There is a mist hanging low like smoke along the treeline, creating patterns with its haze. From higher up you can see Manchester on a clear day, though this morning is far from clear. The destroyed substation and the skeletal remains of its mesh fencing are still a blemish on the landscape, almost overgrown now by the nature around it. It seems symbolic, the raw mess of it. It seems to say more about the street than just about anything else. A sign that the residents are used to brushing things under the carpet, simply carrying on as though everything is fine. I push through the undergrowth back to the street, long strides that kick up the uneven earth below. The police tape has gone from here now and the area is free to walk through.

* * *

The row of houses on the street is yards away, brooding in the mist. I push my way through the back gate of number five and into the house, stomping my boots on the rug. I watch the mud as it falls.

'Late night?'

I jump at the sound of my dad's voice. I put a hand to my chest, feel my heart thundering and laugh.

'Sorry, didn't mean to spook you.' He smiles.

He looks like he hasn't slept – his eyes are bloodshot, his hair wild. He flattens it down, conscious that I'm staring at it. He pulls on his coat, slowly, taking his time.

'It was a late night. Did you hear what happened at the Beehive?'

He grimaces. 'Truthfully? I haven't slept. That's one of my best friends they're talking about, like he's just a character in a movie. He was a person, a good person. So yeah, I did hear about that. I don't know what to make of it.' He pushes his hands into his pockets.

'I don't think Sam would do something like that.' My eyes are pleading with him – I want someone else to agree with me, to know that Sam is someone still worth believing in.

'No one can know what people are really capable of. We like to try and see the best in people.' His eyes glaze over, as though his mind has gone elsewhere.

This must be hard for him, two of his best friends being taken away.

'Well, still. I don't think he'd do that. What type of person harms someone like that and then flaunts it, putting it on display for everyone to see. No, that's not Sam.' I shake my head. *Is it?*

'I don't know. The whole thing's fucked up. I need to get my head straight. I heard about what happened to Marianne. I swear to God, if I get my hands on whoever hurt her . . .' His jaw is clenched. I haven't seen him this angry for a long time. I forget sometimes that these people are like his family.

'She was pretty shaken up,' I say sadly.

He shakes his head as if he can't stand to hear it and picks up his work bag from the hallway. I can smell cigarette smoke as he passes. Suffocating.

I have seen him try and fail to process grief before. I don't like where this is going. He'll be temperamental now. Except, I can't help but ask.

'Do you and Laura Finch speak often?' I ask, watching him closely.

He looks over his shoulder, stern.

'I'll see you later, Ruth.'

* * *

I sigh, hanging up my call and kicking my heels against the brick.

Tom put me in touch with an old friend in the force who was able to get me the name and current address of the original detective. Luckily, I'd managed to grab Oscar for a second among the chaos of Sam's arrest. I asked if the landlord had ever been formally questioned in the original investigation and he hadn't. *Typical.* Of course, the recent podcasts had raised a lot of questions about failings in the original investigation, but I didn't give much consideration to the consequences until now. Scrolling through the comments on social media, the same explanation as to why reared its head again and again.

They had bigger fish to fry.

I hate that expression at the best of times, but it illuminated something I'd always known yet never accepted. Streets like ours, in towns like this, with victims like Henry, just don't matter as much. A working-class man, a criminal record, a dead-end part-time job with parents too weary to breathe down the necks of the officers.

They were left alone.

There are questions that need asking, and if I can be a voice for the Carrs then I want to be.

Pacing the street, I rub at the spot between my neck and shoulder. It's burning again. Feeling my breath begin to quicken

I whip my body round and search the windows of the occupied houses. There is no one around, *is there*? The net curtains of number nine seem to quiver under my stare. It feels as if there is someone just one pace behind, breathing down my neck, ready to strike. I don't know whether to trust my instincts anymore and the clock is ticking.

Sighing, I look back down at the address typed into the note on my phone.

Yorkshire.

I can do it in a day and still be back later to find out any progress on Sam's questioning. I cast a glance over the road to the Carrs, tears pricking at my eyes at the thought of Patrick dealing with last night's news alone. I'm wondering if I have time to check on them when I see Eoin pull up in his beaten VW Golf.

I didn't think he'd want to come, but I'm glad he is.

I wave at Eoin and start to walk to the passenger side when I see a man on the other side of the road, scratching his head, scanning the houses. Is he local press?

They've been hanging around since the news broke, though police have mostly kept them back.

'Hey, you okay over there?' I call to him.

He nods. 'Yeah, I'm the scrap-metal guy. Someone called and asked me to pick up a fridge-freezer they left in the alley but it isn't there. Don't suppose you know whose it was or who called? They didn't leave a name.'

I freeze. Force myself to act normal.

'I don't, sorry. Do you know if it was a man or a woman?'

'No idea but they said it was urgent and, like I say, they didn't leave their name.' He shrugs.

The street isn't closed to traffic but I wonder if the police asked him who he was when he drove in. Oscar will want to know about this.

'Sorry I can't be of more help. If you give me your name and number, I can call you if I find out anything.'

The man waves away my apology and smiles, climbing back into his van. I message the details of the interaction to Oscar, praying it will be of some use in the investigation. Eoin throws open the passenger door for me, grinning like a child.

'Get in, loser.'

I can hear him laughing from across the road.

28
Ruth

THE MOTORWAY LIES BEFORE us like a concrete snake, biting its way through the countryside all the way to the North East. Eoin sits with his forearm slung over the steering wheel, the silver of his watch catching the light. I roll my eyes at his casual front. I can see his left leg jittering. He has too much aftershave on and I can taste it on my tongue as we drive. I run my hands down the edge of the passenger seat, smiling. I remember being 17 and holding on for dear life as Eoin sped around corners in third gear, only having passed his test the week before. He used to pick me up in the middle of the night, when my father was at his worst, and drive me around empty carparks, McDonald's drive-thrus, or country lanes, until the soft glow of morning snuck in and signposted the way back home. I feel a thrill at being near to him, at hearing his laugh, seeing his hand on the radio.

'Are you going to be DJ for me?' He throws a grin in my direction.

'You're still going to hate my taste in music.'

He laughs. 'I can cope.'

The roads are quiet, and we pass only the occasional HGV and family carrier full of children's faces pressed against the windows. I feel guilty about leaving the street, as if we are escaping a burning building and leaving everyone else behind. I think of Patrick sitting at his kitchen table alone, of Sam in his police cell, of Henry, wherever he is. The street is being exposed layer by layer, an open gaping wound. I want to patch it up, make it turn back into what it was before all of this. Eoin senses my thoughts and presses me for music, his tongue in his cheek. There is nothing but the sound of tyres on the road and the engine grinding until I select a song and the first notes begin to play. Eoin stirs as he hears them, clearing his throat to conceal his emotions. I can remember lying in the wasteland to the sound of this. I feel an ache in my chest at the memory.

'Do you still listen to this?' he asks, sneaking a glance at me.

'Sometimes. Not really. Is it okay? I can put something more upbeat on,' I say, hiding behind the curtain of my hair.

'It's okay, leave it on.' He puts a hand on my knee, fleeting.

We both wait until our favourite line blurts out, the one we always used to sing in a half-breath. The one we meant. The one about love being forever.

So I leave it on, and the sound of our song fills the car with something more than memories.

* * *

It is twelve thirty in the afternoon by the time we arrive in North Yorkshire.

I spent most of the journey finding out all I could on the old detective, his famous cases, his progression in the force, his media interviews. He seems stern, sterner than Oscar, and I know I have to play this right. I can't help but feel we are nearing the end; that the secret is waiting, poised, ready to be uncovered. Eoin has been patient on the journey. Enjoying the silences we shared, the music our backdrop. When we did speak it wasn't about Henry, or Crow Street. We filled the gaps that six years had left behind, answering long-wondered questions, and sharing stories of the growing up we had done without each other. We take several roundabouts and winding lanes before we are met with a scattering of villages on the coast. The retired detective supposedly lives in a village five miles from Whitby. Only issue is we don't know exactly which house. Tom's contact had found it difficult to track him down. I get the sense he's a man who doesn't want to be found.

My face is illuminated by my phone, the only light beneath looming rain clouds. Eoin's eyes are on the road, navigating the road signs and narrow one-way streets. The village is stereotypically quaint, old stone cottages and independent shops. We park in the centre of the village. The rain is slanted, lashings of it carried by the wind that soaks us through as we run to a bakery. We stumble inside, laughing like children and wiping our faces with the sleeves of our jackets. The bakery is warm, the windows steaming up with the scent of freshly baked bread, which escapes from the oven doors that are being prised open by the woman behind the counter. She has a friendly face, flushed pink cheeks and a wave of white hair. Her name badge proudly declares her Jane.

'That smells delicious.' I smile and step towards the counter, shivering against the warmth of being inside. Jane beams, removing her oven mitts and limping over to the counter to greet us.

'I should hope so.' She chuckles, a broad accent in her throat.

She watches Eoin with eyes full of humour as he piles boxes of pastries, sandwiches and drinks in his arms until he can barely see us through the stack.

'Hungry, are you?'

'So hungry,' Eoin groans, placing it all down haphazardly on the counter.

The woman begins scanning before continuing.

'Visitors?'

There is curiosity in her voice, the kind I expect in a village of this size. This cosy little town is nothing like the street, and yet the need of people to really know one another lingers here too.

'Yes. We're here to visit someone in particular, actually. I was wondering if you might know where we could find him?' Eoin says, watching her cautiously.

'Of course, I'd be happy to help. Everyone knows everyone round here. Who are you looking for?' She bags up Eoin's items and swings it to him over the counter.

'Sylvia Monroe and her husband, Alan.'

The woman pauses, her hands hovering over the cash register. Something passes over her face.

'Family, are you?' She looks at us fully now, taking in every inch of us. She seems to come to no conclusion when she has finished, still awaiting the answer to her question.

'Family friends, really. We were visiting the North East and wanted to surprise them. My parents lost the address. Typical, really. So we were hoping someone around might be able to point us in the right direction?' I'm talking quickly, the lies falling from my tongue a little too easily. Eoin stays quiet. Jane seems only reasonably satisfied with my response, but she nods curtly with her lips still pursed. The atmosphere has changed at the detective's name. She scribbles the address down on a piece of paper and pushes it to the edge of the counter for me to pick up, her jaw set.

'Give Sylvia my best, won't you?'

* * *

We're lucky. The house is a short walk uphill from the bakery. We leave the car in the village carpark and brave the last of the rain before it stops entirely. Rainwater swirls down the hill towards us as we climb, passing the village shops and the cluster of houses in its centre. We walk over cobblestones and down narrow lanes, past stretches of open fields and farm shops.

'Do you have a plan for when we get there? Do you know what you're going to say to him?' Eoin has hope in his voice. He believes in me so wholeheartedly he has driven the one hundred and twenty miles to get here.

'I was going to improvise.' I laugh at his groan. 'I'm messing. Of course I have a plan.'

Do I? I'm not so sure.

I reach for his arm instinctively and he lets me link it, joining us together. I try to enjoy just being here, being alone in a beautiful spot with him. But it's marred by the rising fear gnawing at my insides that this could all be for nothing. The truth is, I don't know exactly what to say to the detective. I mostly expect him to close the door in our faces. I know how strange it will seem to him that I've tracked him down. But I can't ignore the burning sensation I was left with after what Robert had told me. If Henry really was part of an undercover investigation gone wrong, who is to say it isn't linked to his disappearance?

Every person I have spoken to has only led me to a dead end. Sam, Laura, Robert, even Patrick – they are all hiding something. I can't believe that Sam killed Henry, that he killed him and fifteen years later decided to put the weapon he did it with on display. It makes no sense, it doesn't fit. There has to be something else, something we're all missing. That's why I put the call-out in the paper to the mother and child Henry was hiding. Maybe they can shed light on this overly dark mystery.

I shake away the clouds in my head and tip my chin up to the sky, hoping for clarity. The landscape is getting more remote as we walk: fewer houses and more rolling fields with meandering cattle. We turn around the last bend, just an expanse of lane between us and Alan Monroe. Eoin stops, his jaw clenched. He surveys the scene a little, sweeping his hair back from his face. He reaches down for my hand, laces his fingers through mine.

'You ready?' he asks.

'Not really.'

'Great. Let's walk into the lion's den together.'

* * *

It is an old farm house sitting at the top of a small incline, high enough that on a clear day the fizzing grey of the sea would be visible. It is detached, completely alone and without neighbours for a quarter of a mile. We stand at the front gate, looking up at the top windows. I reassure myself that he could be out, that we might have to call back later. I know that being here is the right thing to do, that if Marianne was able to she would be here herself. I feel like her voice now, hammering on doors and demanding answers where everyone says there are none.

'Shit. Here we are, then.' Eoin shifts from foot to foot.

'You with me?' I ask, stepping forward.

'Always.'

I push through the gate. The path is slate, leading to the enormous wooden door. There is no doorbell, but a brass knocker in the shape of a golden lion. Eoin slams the knocker down with a swoop. It startles us both, and we step back from the door and hover, waiting for footsteps or a voice, or both.

Neither comes.

Eoin clambers over a flowerpot and presses his forehead to a window.

'I can't see anyone. Though there's a dog looking at me like it might start barking any minute.' He stumbles back to join me on the doorstep.

Several minutes pass before we retreat back to the lane. We lean on a stile, facing the lane and the fields beyond. We stay there, lost in our own thoughts until a car drives by.

'Ruth, this lane is a dead end,' Eoin says, excited. 'It might be them.'

We run back up the lane, breathless as the car pulls up beside the house. I can't see a face from where we are standing.

'That must be him,' I whisper, my fingers pressed to my lips.

'Come on, let's get this over with,' Eoin says, leading the way.

We walk with more boldness than we feel, arriving at the gate as the man is unlocking the front door. He must sense our presence and turns, looking nothing like the old photographs I'd found. Mr Monroe is large in stature, his stomach squeezed into a waistcoat. His hair is thick and coarse, ashen grey and combed over to cover the balding spot at the centre of his head. He must only be in his sixties, though his face is creased at every angle. A wild beard covers the lower half of his face, wispy and white like snow. He glares at us suspiciously through watery blue eyes. He stands still, wedged, halfway in and out of his house, his foot in the door.

'Can I help you?' His voice is booming, a deep note across the path.

'Mr Monroe?' I call.

He narrows his eyes, his head cocked to the side. 'Who are you?'

Eoin and I share a look, a second of doubt before I speak again.

'Ruth Cavanagh. I'm a journalist. I was hoping to talk to you about a case you lead a while ago.'

He grumbles under his breath, his bottom lip jutted out. 'I don't speak to anyone about investigative matters, least of all journalists.'

His voice is firm, aggressive even. He turns his back to us.

'We're from Crow Street, Mr Monroe. I'm here to talk to you about Henry Carr.'

He falters. He turns to face us. There is fear in his expression, but something else, too: intrigue. His eyes dart around the lane, and when he is sure that there is no one around, he opens the front door wider.

'You'd better come in.'

He ushers us into the farmhouse, which is filled with flowers in vases and rows of bookcases. The house has cold slate floors and warm broad fireplaces. It is both modest and grand in its furnishing. The dog, a spaniel, circles our legs in delight. It nuzzles the cool wet of its nose into Eoin's hands, as though sensing a kindred spirit. A nervous smile twitches at the corner of Eoin's mouth as he strokes the dog. It follows us into the kitchen where the retired detective drags heavy wooden chairs across the floor, signalling for us to sit. He frets over a pot of tea, the teaspoons clattering against the china as he set cups down on the surface.

'I never thought I'd hear that name again. Crow Street,' he finally says, standing across from us. The detective spits the name of it with disgust, his hands wrapped around his cup. Eoin shifts in his seat awkwardly.

'Have you been retired long, detective?' He hesitates on the last word, his hand instinctively falling to the dog, seeming to find comfort in it.

'Twelve years. Too long. Near impossible to go from a job like that to sitting around.'

His voice is gruff, his face stern. 'I couldn't stick around much longer, not after the Carr case. My career was in tatters, people were out for blood. Everywhere I went that case followed me, people didn't look at me the same. It's why I had to move away. Even my peers, the guys at the station, were seething it was unsolved. Gives us a bad name. The press chewed us up and spat us out.' He looks at me, his eyes alight, haunted. I take a mouthful of tea, choking on its heat and bitterness. Eoin places a hand on my leg to comfort me as if by instinct. He yanks it back just as fast, his cheeks turning pink.

'It's fifteen years since the disappearance,' I say. 'I work for a newspaper in Newcastle, the *Chronicle*.'

'I've heard of it.'

'It's not just that I'm a journalist, I'm from the street.' My words tumble out as I rush to explain. 'So I can see things from both sides. I want to give an insider's perspective. Especially since the anniversary is coming up. Maybe you've heard about the new developments?'

The detective scoffs. 'It's certainly getting attention on social media. Mostly abroad, from what I hear. As for the locals helping? Good luck with that.'

I feel myself deflate. This isn't how I want this conversation to go.

'Mr Monroe, I'm sure you've heard about the recent discovery and the arrest of the landlord of the Beehive pub. The people of the street aren't saying much, but they're not happy. Many believe the landlord to be an innocent man. I've done a lot of research on this case and there are some things I just couldn't uncover.'

'Join the club.' He laughs emptily and rubs a coarse hand over his face. He tugs his waistcoat down and exhales. 'Yes, I did hear about the discovery. Nasty stuff. I always knew this would end that way, that street is a bad omen.'

'I understand that there may be some things you can't tell me, but the family are desperate for answers,' I continue. 'Answers I don't believe they'll get from the recent arrest. Marianne Carr, his mother – she deserves peace. It's all she talks about. We're just trying to find something, anything, which might help.' I clear my throat, aware of how large it sounds in the cool of the kitchen.

The emotional response isn't working on him. He didn't so much as flinch when I mentioned Marianne. Time for a different tack. 'The newspapers mentioned that Mrs Montgomery was the last person to hear Henry alive,' I try.

'Yes. She stated he was arguing with someone on the street.'

'Did you ever find out who that was?'

'We had our suspicions.' He drains the remnants of his tea. 'But no, we couldn't conclusively say who it was.'

'Suspicions?'

He eyes me warily. I sense he is still weighing me up, unconvinced by my intentions. He scrapes his chair back across the floor, planting the empty cup in the sink with a clatter.

'It wasn't all sunshine and roses at home, that's all I can say.'

'You think he was arguing in the street with Patrick Carr?' Eoin asks.

We both turn to look at him, surprised. The dog wags its tail, panting on Eoin's open palm. The detective frowns.

'We know about the child, the one Patrick didn't approve of,' I say. 'I'm speaking as a friend of theirs now, not a journalist. I grew up on that street, and I just can't believe that Patrick would kill his own son. The baby changes things. Patrick has always been the scapegoat. This mystery child could be said to give him motive, I know that. I can understand how a child out of wedlock might be considered shameful for them, that they'd want to hide it . . . but I just don't think it would lead a father to kill his son. Patrick and Marianne have been so devastated.' I pause. 'There must have been other suspects, other lines of enquiry?' I know I sound desperate, and I am, to clear Sam's name and remove suspicion from Patrick. My mind flickers to Robert Knight, surprised by how much I want it to be him rather than the others.

The detective leans over the sink, his sleeves rolled up. He is breathing heavily, his stomach heaving in the tight fabric of his waistcoat.

'I promised my wife I wouldn't speak about this case again,' he finally says. 'It ruined me. It's all I used to think about, dream about. That street, those people, they're the ones with the answers. There's only so much that police work can do if people won't talk.' His voice is booming now, anger swelling in his throat. I sit on my hands to stop their trembling, not from fear but adrenalin. I feel like we're on the edge of something.

'The story is that Henry had no known enemies,' I say, pressing him. 'But I'm not sure that's entirely true. A lot of people on the street weren't happy with him. Is it true that Henry worked for the police?'

The detective freezes.

I continue. 'I heard from . . . a source . . . that Henry was a part of an undercover operation.'

Silence.

'That it was an operation Henry wasn't trained for, that it went wrong in some way. Could that have been connected to his disappearance?' I ask.

The detective spins around to face me. 'Who told you that? Who have you been talking to?'

I inhale, steadying my nerve. I can feel Eoin's eyes on me, willing me to tread more carefully.

'Henry was involved with a dangerous man. I discovered the information by accident, in a book of his. It had an address listed in it, circled several times. I followed up and learnt it was a loan shark. He said that Henry had needed money from him.'

The detective tugs at his collar, his face blooming purple, but says nothing. I feel a rising anger. He knows. He had known back then.

'It doesn't seem that's much of a surprise to you,' Eoin says gently.

'His name was Robert Knight,' I press. 'Was he ever a suspect?' Without realising it, I have stood up, the edge of the table digging into the heels of my hands. The detective charges to the back door and throws it open.

'Get out, both of you,' he snarls.

29
Patrick

THE CORRIDORS OF THE hospital are lit yellow and clinical. The floors have an unnatural sheen that radiates disinfectant. The ward Marianne has been admitted to is a flurry of activity: nurses checking observations and relatives sobbing behind paper-thin curtains. I knead my hands together and try to banish the smell of hospital that sticks to me like a film. Marianne is encased in a tangle of wires, and is wrapped up in a white blanket. I eye the machines anxiously, following the up and down of the lines across the screen. The ambulance got to the house within ten minutes, its blue lights turning the street cold. The paramedics had muttered to one another, unzipping bags and shaking their heads at readings on the various machines they had set up. I had cried just to know she was alive: that after everything we have been through, as long as we are still together, we can get through anything.

But I am anxious and eager for answers. I am furious at myself for not protecting her more, for losing my grip on things in the past few weeks. My own fall had been the catalyst for it all. It has let too many people into our lives. I'd worked so hard to keep Marianne safe. And now it was all for nothing. Now the discovery of the weapon, the blood, Sam being arrested, everything is collapsing around us and we are disintegrating under the weight of it.

We have been in the hospital for six hours. I have moved from waiting room to waiting room, while Marianne has blood tests and scans. Each time a nurse passes by or a doctor appears at the station, I jump to my feet, calling out for answers, reassurance, anything but the dragging misery of not knowing. I have been brushed off at every turn. Marianne has been awake for a while, yet she's entirely vacant. Her eyes are the same: startling clear but unblinking, focused on a spot on the ceiling. I whisper to her softly.

'You're in hospital, love. They're going to get you well enough to get home again.'

She has no reaction at all, just the continuous staring and deep, noisy breaths.

Eventually a nurse pops her head around the curtain.

'Mr Carr, are you sure you won't have a sandwich? It's an awfully long time to go without food.' She is young; she looks barely 25. Her voice is high and floaty, like the start of a song. I wave her away.

'I'm fine, really. Can't say I have much of an appetite.'

'A drink at least? You could do with the sugar – it must have been a tiring day.' She smiles kindly, leaving before I can say no. I close my eyes, pushing the kindness to the back of my mind. People being kind makes my emotions raw, like picking a scab and watching it bleed. I want to remain focused and rational. I can't afford to lose myself, not when Marianne needs me the most. The nurse returns with a cup of tea. It is overly sweet and I scrunch my nose at the taste of it, though I can't deny it is much needed nourishment. It soothes my dizziness and clears the fog that had settled in my mind. The doctor pulls back the curtain sharply, giving a grave smile as he steps through.

'Mr Carr, good to meet you. I'm Dr Jenson, the neurology consultant. I'm here to talk about your wife's condition.'

I stand and extend a hand, pleased with the firm handshake I receive in return. For someone who is usually instinctively mistrustful of white coats and clipboards, I feel immediately reassured at the presence of someone who can help Marianne recover.

'How is she doing? I mean, I know she's not at her best right now. When can she go home? What medication does she need to start taking?' I'm rambling, I know that. I can feel the sweat collecting on my brow. The consultant gives me a look, long and considered. His glasses are on the tip of nose, his eyes gentle over them.

'Mr Carr, take a seat, won't you?' He gestures to the plastic chair next to Marianne's bed. The atmosphere has changed into something dangerous. The consultant flips through the paper on his clipboard, presses some buttons on Marianne's machine, and speaks to her softly. When she doesn't respond he stands back up straight.

'Mr Carr. The scan of Marianne's brain shows that she has suffered a TIA. In layman's terms, she has suffered a clot in her brain which prevented normal blood supply. Luckily, it seems you caught her in time for us to administer a medication which will dissolve the clot before it does any permanent damage.' He smiles as though it is good news he is delivering.

I feel the blood drain from my face.

'A clot?'

'Yes, a stroke.'

I cough, choking on the thought of Marianne suffering alone. I have tried not to guess at what might have caused her collapse. Though I had considered dehydration, exhaustion, at worst a chill from being outside the night before. I put my head in my hands.

'Is it my fault? Is it her diet? Lack of sleep?' My voice cracks. The consultant places his clipboard on the end of the bed.

'No one is at fault, Mr Carr. The stroke could have resulted from a number of things. Your wife's blood pressure is very high.

Hypertension can be caused by a variety of factors, and though diet is among them, so is stress.'

I look up, swallowing hard.

'Well, that's what it'll be. Our son, he . . . well, he went missing. And now . . . now they're saying he's dead, but we still haven't found him. It's not just that, though. She has—' I pause, forcing myself to say the words. 'Dementia. I'm quite sure she has dementia, though she's never been properly checked for it.'

The consultant nods. He doesn't seem alarmed when I mention Henry, nor surprised when I mention dementia.

'Her son, our son, went missing fifteen years ago. The anniversary is tomorrow. They found something yesterday, new evidence they're saying, and they made an arrest. So we know now, for sure, that he's gone. That he's never coming back. I don't know if she overheard the news, if she would have even understood. She forgets and remembers him – it torments her every minute of the day. I try my best, honest to God, I try my best.'

I'm not sure who I'm trying to convince: myself, the consultant, anyone who will listen. I can't shift the guilt that presses on my chest like a weight. I am suffocating beneath it. And then I'm sobbing.

The consultant tries to comfort me. He shares the plan going forward, medicines that will be delivered by a drip, constant monitoring, leaflets on lifestyle changes. Before he leaves, he declares that the nurses will look after us both. It all seems like a ghoulish nightmare, playing on my greatest fear. I blame everyone on the street: Mr Chandra, Laura, Sam, Eoin and Ruth, but most of all, I blame myself. I had let her keep the diary entries in the cabinet, I watched her revisit them day after day. I thought it might help her to remember more than her lost son, to remember me and the person she had once been. Instead, it had cemented a vicious cycle, in which remembering brought only the worst of the visions. The ones about blood and death. Her mental health had been so poor in the years leading to Henry's disappearance that her notes after he was gone didn't seem real. They were nonsensical ramblings, hallucinations, nightmares. Yet, if they were true, they were even more reason to protect her. Of course, it seemed ridiculous. I'm a rational man. I don't dwell on things, I stay clear of exaggeration and hysteria and so it seemed sensible and safe to arrive at the most obvious and logical conclusion. That the ramblings were just that, fabrications of a damaged mind. There was even the diagnosis from the doctor, the mental health issues, the grief, they were all just creating a false reality. There was something niggling of course, a little voice in my head that said, what if? What if it is true?

I don't know what she had been capable of back then, when her mental health was spiralling. Had she done something she couldn't remember? Something awful? The worst thing a mother could do? No, I can't even begin to imagine that. No. Not Marianne. But I don't believe it was Sam either, the man who has stood by us, stood by Marianne when we needed him. He delivered hot meals while I learnt how to cook when Marianne no longer could, carried our washing to the laundrette, would have done anything and everything to keep us going. It can't have been him and it wasn't Marianne. My Marianne.

For the past fifteen years I have tried to protect her, to keep her out of the police's clutches, out of the psychiatric hospital and the system. All my sacrifices have been in vain, all for nothing unless she is safe and happy. I hold her hand until all the other visitors have left, until the nurses try to tug me away from her bedside, but I can't, I won't.

I fall asleep to the sound of her bleeping heartbeat.

30
Oscar

I watch Sam on the camera. He's sitting with his back against the hard, cold brick of the cell and looks like he's going to be sick. He falls to his knees, his hands clenched around the cold steel of the toilet. He throws up into the bowl, strings of what looks like bile dangling from his chin. He wipes it away with the back of his hand and spins around, pulling his knees up to his chest and shoving his face between them. He's crying now, but the real kind that rattles his body and staggers his breaths. He draws in air in great dramatic gasps.

There's something hugely undignified in a man of his size cowering like a child. Still, he's exactly where he deserves to be. I wonder what Sam is thinking as he realises he's locked in like an animal. I think back to the pub. To the brown dried blood clinging to the wrench. I think back to Sam's reaction. Genuine shock, except it couldn't have been. His fingerprints are on the shelves, he was working all day in the pub, and witnesses claim the weapon hadn't been there the night before. The custody officer had said something strange to me on the way in. That Sam had been muttering to himself about how much they had all tried to protect the street, to keep them all together, to keep them free, and it had all lead to this. All the people I've spoken to have said nothing but good things about the man. About how he's spent all his life making the street a home, a community. From what I've found out so far, there's some link between Henry, Sam, Laura Finch, Martin Banks and Peter Cavanagh. They were all close friends and yet everyone says they no longer socialise but refuse to say why. Yet another vow of silence. I've never seen anything like it. They'll only speak if it's to protect one of their own. Even if the person is a murderer. It makes my blood boil. I look back to the monitor, see Sam pull a stiff prison issue blanket down from the bare plastic mattress and cover himself in it.

'Right, let's bring him in.'

I walk down to the cell with the guard. The door is prised open, its groan echoing around the concrete room. Sam wipes his mouth again and stands, his knees almost giving way. He nods at me, a greeting. He knows why we're here. He trudges after us slowly, his feet dragging beneath him. He has already spoken briefly to his solicitor, and I hope he's prepared a statement. She probably advised him to say 'no comment' to everything.

To start answering questions and then change to 'no comment' later looks suspicious on your part. Better to stick with that the whole way through. That's what solicitors will say, and they're right.

I lead him to the interview room. A small, square space with a two-way mirror along one wall. Everyone hates the thought of being watched from the other side, spied on, judged. Sam sits compliantly in the chair and I remove his handcuffs. He rubs his wrists and drinks the cup of water I put down before him.

The room is cold; I'll crank up the heat later. My partner Eleanor sits beside me, turns on the device that records the interview and speaks into it, declaring the time and the people present in the room. Sam's solicitor is standing behind us and walks over to take a seat next to Sam. She opens her file and clicks her pen.

'To start with, Sam, I'd like to ask what your relationship was with Mr Carr,' I begin, my hands knotted together.

Sam looks across at his solicitor who raises her eyebrows, probably encouragement to heed her advice. He ignores it.

'He was a childhood friend.'

'A friend? Interesting. So you stayed friends for all those years?' I ask.

'For some of them, yes. Most people on the street are pretty close, I'd say.'

Eleanor looks down at her case file and then back up. I continue.

'I see. When you say for some of them, could you be a bit more precise?'

'A group of us were friends for a long time. We were all there for one another when we needed it, you know. We had each other's backs. That all changed when Henry got himself into some financial trouble. He was borrowing from a lot of us and couldn't pay it back.' Sam's looking at his hands, focusing on a dry patch. He tries to rub it away.

'Is that what led you to kill Mr Carr in September 2008?'

Sam freezes. Looks up. His eyes wide. He hadn't expected that so soon.

Got him.

He licks his bottom lip, sits upright in the chair.

'No.'

He doesn't elaborate further, doesn't lose it. Shame.

'Where were you on the day in question?'

'I was at work.'

'All day?'

'No, I had the afternoon off.'

'The afternoon Henry disappeared, you weren't at work?'

'No.'

'So how did you spend your afternoon?'

'I can't remember. Nothing much. Watched some TV. Did some laundry. It wasn't very memorable. It was fifteen years ago.'

'So you have no one to confirm that alibi?'

'I suppose not. I live alone.'

I nod, let a small smile curl my lip. 'I see.'

Sam grunts. He looks across at his solicitor. She's making notes but gives him a look. She did warn him. I sit back a little, let Eleanor have a go.

'You see, Sam, the evidence against you is quite significant. The new witness whose memory was jogged by that podcast states they saw you arguing with someone who may have been Mr Carr outside your pub on the afternoon in question. We don't have an alibi for you on that afternoon, you admit yourself to having fallen out with Mr Carr over money, and just last night we found a potential murder weapon with Henry's blood on it. I'd say that's pretty compelling, wouldn't you?'

'I can't tell you how it got there, all right? I'm being framed.' He's anxious now, his hands gripping the table.

'By who, exactly?' Eleanor asks.

He falls silent.

'Let's say someone did plant it in your pub. How exactly would that happen without your knowledge?' I ask.

'I don't work 24/7, you know. I have cleaners, other bar staff.' He sounds annoyed.

'And the eyewitness who names you in a fight outside the pub that afternoon, fifteen years ago? Who were you fighting while apparently off-shift?' Eleanor probes.

Sam picks up the plastic cup and squeezes until it crackles.

'I can't remember.'

'You're going to have to do better than that,' I say.

I know how he'll be feeling. His heart and brain are in conflict, his instinct for self-preservation rushing through his veins. Sweat is beading his forehead, his armpits damp, his back probably stuck to the plastic fabric of the chair. His solicitor leans across, is about to say something when Sam speaks.

'It was Robert Knight. The loan shark who lent Henry money. We were both owed money from Henry. He wanted something done about it and I said to leave it be, he was struggling.'

I look at him blankly. He repeats himself.

'I was fighting with the loan shark.'

'Is that where the money came from? The four grand? The day after Henry vanished?'

He swallows. 'No. That money hasn't been touched. I'm saving it for someone. Someone who needs it. It has nothing to do with this.'

I roll my eyes.

A knock at the door. An officer enters the room. We excuse ourselves from the room and pause the interview. Sam watches us go.

* * *

I close the door behind us and we press ourselves against the far wall.

'So the report is back with fingerprints from the fridge-freezer. Sam's fingerprints were there but there are others too. They came back with a full match of someone on our database. Someone else from the street.'

'So there's other people from that place involved?' Eleanor says. 'Not a huge surprise.'

'Something about this doesn't add up. The wrench, the wallet, it's too coincidental. Why put the weapon up there? Why leave the fridge-freezer in the alleyway for collection? Right there in the open? And why all right now? It feels like it's all been done to throw us off the scent.'

'This fucking street.' Eleanor groans. She pushes her head against the wall.

'I have a feeling this has only just begun.'

31
Ruth

THE GARDEN OF THE farmhouse must be at least an acre. It is sectioned by slabs of stone, which separate the garden into different areas like a patchwork quilt. The dog sprints towards the treeline at the far end, its nose pointed to the sky. It is hunting something, or someone.

The detective smiles affectionately at the dog. We are an odd trio – me, Eoin and him – as we walk in silence. Eoin shoots me a look. Neither of us know how much we can trust the man. After yanking the door open, he'd snarled at us to leave – and then followed us, telling us to come with him. It was confusing, unsettling.

Mr Monroe walks ahead of us, his eyes fixed on a small structure at the bottom of the path. A greenhouse. The clouds have cleared to reveal a blue sky, frosted and gripping the air like a vice. I chew on the inside of my cheek, my mind racing. If the police were somehow linked to Henry's disappearance and death, there is every possibility that this man was involved, and that we could meet the same fate.

'Not much further,' he mumbles.

We reach the greenhouse as the dog emerges from the bushes, a dead bird clamped between its teeth. It wags its tail at its find, grotesquely delighted at the carcass it sets down at our feet. We all stare at it before the detective cuts through the silence.

'Well, here we are.'

He grunts as he fumbles with the door, its lock covered in rust. The greenhouse is in poor condition, its glass cracked, broken and dirty. It appears an abandoned project, though as we step into its humidity there are several live plants climbing towards the roof. All three of us squeeze inside, uncomfortably close. Mr Monroe begins to fuss over the plants, tipping old water into their pots and running wilting leaves through his fingers.

'The greenhouse was a gift from the wife,' he finally says. 'She thought it would keep me busy in retirement.' He scoffs. 'She knew I was scarred by my years in the force, from the piles of bodies that were stacked up outside my door.'

Eoin inches closer to me, his arm brushing mine.

'She thought that if I could grow life, sustain it and keep it safe, then I would feel some sense of healing.' He zones out for a moment, his eyes clouded over by a memory he can't vocalise. He shakes his head and laughs, waving his hand over the few fruits of his labour. 'You can see how that worked out.'

'What is it you want to show us, detective?' Eoin's voice echoes against the glass, threatening to break the balance. The detective looks at him with a blank expression, as though it is all perfectly obvious.

'You see that bag of compost down there?' He signals to the enormous sack slouching against the side of the greenhouse.

We nod in silence.

'It's ironic, isn't it, that when we want things to be born, to grow, to thrive, we have to first pour something rotting, dead, on top of it?'

A shiver carries itself up my spine at the darkness in his voice. I take a step back towards the door – instinct. He steps towards me.

'I can't say much about the undercover operation; those files were destroyed long ago. It was kept from most people in the investigation. Even now I don't know the full story, and I certainly didn't know about it during the first few months of my investigation.' He shakes his head. 'For what it's worth, Sam was someone we looked into. He has a darker past than you probably know about. I think he hated Henry, friendship gone wrong. Part of a strange group of old school friends on the street. Dark stuff.'

Old school friends? I think back to Laura's yearbook pictures, to my dad, to Sam, to Martin. I shiver again.

'Something happened that bound them all together. Couldn't tell you what exactly, but something bad enough that they all stayed tight-lipped from a young age. My guess is they took the same approach with Henry's disappearance.'

'What has this got to do with compost?' Eoin eyes the bag warily.

'You want to know where I think Henry Carr is? Hidden, buried, dead. The weapon was just showboating. A killer getting restless, perhaps? That, or it was kept to throw police off the scent if it was ever needed, and clearly it was. Putting a weapon in your own pub? Nonsense. Where is the body? Where has it been all this time? The only possibility that seems to make sense is that he's buried beneath that sorry excuse for a building the community threw together in the wasteland behind Crow Street after he vanished.'

Eoin sucks in air. My mind somersaults.

'The summer house?' Eoin gasps. 'What? Why? That was built by the whole street, someone would have seen something, reported it. They were all looking for him.'

'Were they?' The detective gives a wry smile. 'I always hated that expression: *it takes a village to raise a child*. I've come to much prefer: *it takes a street to kill a man and keep him hidden*.'

'You honestly think he's buried under the summer house?' My voice is monotone, my mind playing the theory out. The summer house had been erected not long after Henry disappeared. It had brought the whole street together. I remember how exciting it had been, as a child, to watch everyone make something beautiful. Especially beside the carcass of a substation – that thing had felt like a curse for too long. The summer house was all of ours, a shared home. There hadn't been one person who lived on Crow Street not involved in it. How could a body have been hidden there without everyone knowing?

'You want to know why that undercover operation went wrong? It was a sting into Robert Knight's operation. Henry was convinced to take part because he knew Knight, already owed him money; because we felt Knight would trust him. But someone tipped off Knight and his gang, we even feared he got to one of our own. We went to raid his group at some abandoned building they used as a headquarters, but they were gone. All the evidence was gone. And then Henry vanished.

'No one knew Henry was working with us, we made sure of that. There should have been no one in that raid that Henry knew, and there wouldn't have been if someone didn't want him killed. The only people who knew Henry was in trouble with a loan shark were his friends on the street. They admitted as much in later interviews.'

I don't know who or what to believe – Robert had told me it was a corrupt officer who had tipped him off.

Who on the street would have betrayed Henry to Robert Knight?

'Who tipped him off?' I whisper.

'Now that's what we'd like to know,' the detective says, his voice heavy. 'Could have been any of them, Sam the landlord from the local, Laura Finch, Peter Cavanagh. They were reportedly all mates. They went back years. Although, if I remember right, there was also a copper dismissed after the operation. But my bet was always on that bastard friendship group.'

I don't respond, too busy thinking about who could possibly have had a loyalty to Robert so strong that they'd sacrifice Henry for it.

'Of course, the loan shark refused to talk when we questioned him,' the detective continues. 'Robert always refuses to talk. We couldn't charge him with anything. We could never pin anything on any of them. They know how to keep people quiet, know how to keep themselves quiet when it matters.' Monroe spits, the bad taste of it all in his mouth.

Eoin's breathing is shallow, like he's remembered something, like something more is putting him on edge. I want to reassure him but can't. The thought of his mother being involved, my dad, or Sam, or even poor, broken Martin sits heavy in my stomach.

'Even if someone had wanted Henry dead,' I say with desperation, 'and even if they had tipped off the gang about his work with the police, the rest of this doesn't make any sense. No one would have buried him under the summer house. It didn't even go up until months later.' I fall silent, then turn to Eoin. 'Marianne helped build it. She wouldn't . . . no one would have done that to her.'

'But she knows something,' Eoin says quickly, his words tumbling out like falling stones.

The detective snaps his eyes to him.

'What has she been saying? Tell me.' His retirement fades away in that instant. The cop, the detective: he is still there, still in uniform beneath the years and the sorrow. I put a hand on Eoin's arm, an action he reads and understands. He doesn't say another word, none of us do. The dog nudges Monroe's leg, a soft push with its nose.

'You want to know something?' the detective finally says. 'Every newspaper article you read, every police interview we ever conducted, we only ever spoke to Patrick Carr. He wouldn't let us near his wife. Everyone in the press always remarked how

strange it was not to hear from the mother of the missing man.'
He scuffs the ground with his shoe. 'We always thought it was
suspicious, and when we found the blood on Patrick's sweater
we were sure he'd stopped us talking to her because she knew
he was involved in Henry's disappearance. Of course, he claimed
hiding her away and forcing her to say "no comment" was to
protect her. Christ, what I would have done to speak to Marianne
Carr.' He shakes his head, his eyes dark.

'The blood on the sweater you think it was from . . . that
Patrick murdered him?' Eoin asks, his voice small.

'No way to know. The lab results came back but the evidence
just wasn't substantial enough. Only a few spatters and no way
to know how they got there. It just wouldn't hold up in any trial.
But why hide the sweater? As much as everything points to
Patrick Carr, I think that would be too simple an answer. Besides,
how does an old man hide his son's body, then fifteen years later
move a fridge freezer and climb high up in a pub to put the
murder weapon on display all while staying undetected? Unless
someone's helping him, I can't see it myself. The landlord? I don't
buy it. A lot of people on that street hated Henry. He made
trouble for them, mingling with men like Robert Knight, and I
got the sense that they never really forgave him for that.'

'Enough to have him killed?' I ask.

'People have killed for less, my dear. That street will do
anything to protect itself.'

We all fall silent, digesting his words.

'So the only two leads you couldn't follow up were Marianne
and the summer house?' I ask.

Monroe smiles sadly. 'There's three leads left in this case and
if you live on the street like you say you do, then you're the best
hope of getting anywhere with them.'

I feel a tingle in my palms, the answers within snatching distance.

'Marianne, the summer house . . .' I pause. 'What's the third?'

'The woman who saw the killer's face. Mrs Montgomery.'

'I thought she just *heard* the argument?'

'No, I believe she saw it.' He shakes his head. 'She's stood at the window for years watching the comings and goings of the street. She knew everyone there and more. She saw the argument. And she saw who he was arguing with.'

I look across at Eoin. We need to speak to her. She might just be able to help provide a lead that will prove Sam is innocent, that Patrick is too. Eoin tilts his head to the ceiling, then looks at me with the smallest smile, and I know: he's in for the ride.

* * *

The sun is dipping behind the clouds as we leave Yorkshire, the detective's words and the mystery of Henry Carr chasing us no matter how fast we drive. The sky is ablaze in orange, tinging the black clouds with liquid fire. The radio is on loud, the bass vibrating through the car and in our bones. Eoin's eyes are clamped on the motorway ahead, his face illuminated by brake lights and the setting sun.

'Do you think he knew?' he asks.

'What?' I turn towards him and feel my seatbelt cut into my neck.

'Henry. Do you think he knew he was going to die?'

I turn back to watch the hills roll past the window.

'I saw something once,' he says, his brow furrowed. 'It was called *Pictures Moments from Disaster*. It was photos of all these people just before they died. They all had no idea of course, how could they? Except, I've always sort of thought that maybe there's some sense, some part of us that knows. You hear about it, don't you? Family members saying weird stuff just before they die, suddenly creating a will, telling someone they love them. It's as though some small part of them sensed they were leaving soon.

That their story here was being cut short. Sometimes when Henry's name is mentioned or I see his photo, I just wonder whether he ate his breakfast that day like normal, or if he had plans for the next day, or was there a part, just a little part, that sensed something big was about to happen.'

I exhale, pull myself up straighter.

'I don't think so. I mean, in the films there's always the music building or the pace quickening. It kind of makes you think life must be like that too. But it's not. Death is like falling off the edge of a cliff you didn't know was there. At least, that's how it was for Mum. She knew she was sick. Her skin was yellow, paper-thin. She used to be wrapped up under all the blankets Dad could find and yet she would shiver, her collarbone protruding like a blade when it fell down just a little. Her breathing was shallow and she was so weak. She'd tried to finish the story we had started together but she couldn't, so I read and read until she fell asleep. I'm not sure if she could even hear me by then, in the hospice. One minute she was telling me about what we could read tomorrow, the next minute the nurse told me to fetch something for her, and when I got back she was gone. Maybe she said it to make me feel better, to keep my hope alive because she couldn't bear the thought of being honest. But I think what I really believe is that she couldn't quite come to terms with the fact that for her there would be no tomorrow. It isn't wired into us, to accept something that huge. It's beyond what we are capable of understanding.'

Eoin turns the music down, snatches a glance at me.

'I'm really sorry, Ruth. In all the years we've known each other, I never wanted to ask. I just didn't want you to have to talk about something so painful. In a selfish way, I'm not sure I could have brought myself to see you like that.'

'I understand. It isn't your fault. Honestly? I haven't ever been ready to talk about it until now. Seeing Patrick and Marianne's grief scared me at first. I didn't want to face my own and leave myself vulnerable like they are. I just haven't felt brave enough. The truth is, Marianne's bravery, fighting to be heard, she inspires me.'

He smiles, and I know he feels the same.

I squeeze my eyes shut and try to remove that last image of Mum from my mind.

He must sense my turmoil as his hand finds its way on top of mine.

'You're okay.' His voice is soft velvet over the sound of rubber on tarmac.

I look down at his hand encasing mine.

'Yeah. It's just this case, being back. It's hard listening to other people's grief when I guess I'm still carrying some of my own.'

'It can't be easy with your dad going through it all again too. You can stay at my mum's with me. She won't mind. She loves you, she always has.'

'No, it's okay. It's something I've got to deal with. It's just having to think of everyone as a suspect, knowing Patrick's heart is breaking, knowing Sam is rotting away in some cell. It feels like we can't trust anyone.'

He nods, ponders this for a moment.

I look across at him, at the slump of his shoulders. I know what I did to him all those years ago, leaving and never once coming back. Not a visit, not a message.

'I was crushed when you left, Ruth. No real goodbye, no closure. You just left and never came back. I used to keep my phone on loud every night, just in case you needed me, in case you called. You never did. I thought about messaging you, I felt like a part of me had been cut out. Every day I wanted to call you, to come and see you, but it wouldn't have been fair to you. You had a new life.' He shifts in his seat. 'I know the street was somewhere you needed to run from. You wanted to wash it off your skin and start over. I'm not proud saying this, but you leaving, how easy it seemed for you to cut me from your life, made me sour. I focused on every negative thing, every bad feeling, and I guess I sort of hated you for a while – that made it easier. I still missed you, like a deep ache that I couldn't be free of. I tried to move on, tried to think of life without you in it, and then you came back and I guess I realised that actually I loved you. Always did.'

I taste the tear as it settles on my lip. I can't even look at him, can't bear to see the hurt in his face. Every time I thought of him, I imagined him happy. I suppose I built a false narrative in my mind, something that was easier to live with.

'I'm sorry.' It's all I can manage.

'I know. I am too.'

I squeeze his hand, wait to feel him squeeze mine back. We stay like that for a moment, letting the radio and the sound of the outside world filter in. If I say too much, I'm worried I will never stop, that I will empty myself out and never fill back up.

'I left for myself, because I had to.' I pause, letting out a whisper. 'But I still loved you.'

The sky cracks open, pinks and oranges smeared across the skyline. He looks over, I see the corner of his mouth lift, his eyes change.

'Then that's all that will ever matter,' he finally says.

DAY SIX

32

Patrick

I PUSH THE BOWL of porridge across the table. It is still full. My stomach growls but my mind can't connect. The thought of eating anything disgusts me. The house feels cold without Marianne in it, and despite turning up the thermostat on the boiler, I'm still shivering at the emptiness of everything. I've been up since six thirty. I have washed her sheets, dusted her room, and made sure everything is ironed and folded and perfect for her return. I wiped down the layer of grime on the framed photograph of Henry from her bedside table, choking on emotion at the sight of him. I was so proud to have a son, someone to carry our name and look after Marianne in her old age. Now we have no one but each other. I have seen the date on the calendar, tried to ignore it, tried to imagine a life without it looming over us. I have to stay strong for Marianne. We are the scaffolding keeping each other from crumbling. I think I may have failed at that too. We've never spent longer than a day apart in all our years.

Every anniversary that marks another year of Henry being gone has been hard, all fourteen of them. Some of them Marianne spent mourning, wailing, clutching at the things Henry has left behind. The recent years have been milder now that Marianne is unaware of what day it is. We've spent anniversaries walking through the wasteland, down the canal, anywhere that would separate us from the street that swallowed him whole. I don't want to think of which type today will be, especially with what the police have found. Now there is no question mark, no hope, no maybe that he might one day walk through the door. It is definite. He is gone.

It fills me with darkness to wish that Marianne would forget our son, such is the cruelty of life. Though it would be easier, kinder, if she did. My stomach convulses at the thought of what she might say to the nurses in her delirium, drugged up as she is on medication. I pray that today is the day the doctor will discharge her. They said there would be little permanent damage from the stroke, though they noted some concerns about her dementia prognosis. How fast things have all changed, that the word dementia now settles on my tongue without a stir. I hate the thought of her on a ward full of strangers, cementing her confusion and treating her clinically. I'm the only person who can care for her in the way she needs, in the way we both need. I carry the bowl to the sink with trembling hands and get myself ready for the hospital, stuffing newspapers and sandwiches into a plastic bag. I pack her a clean nightdress and her slippers before picking up my cap and stick, counting down the minutes until I see her.

* * *

The sky looks as though it might split open by the time the bus approaches. It has been delayed over half an hour. I point at my watch in an aggressive manner, struggling to control my outrage with the driver, who promptly sticks two fingers up in response and misses my stop. I could cry as I watch him drive past, smoke billowing from the exhaust.

I am still there twenty minutes later when Peter's van pulls up. 'You all right, old fella?'

I could hug him as he opens the door and beckons me in.

He isn't much of a talker, Peter. He never was, but there is no denying that his heart is in the right place. He was a good friend to Henry when they were children, always on our doorstep waiting for him to go out and play. He stuck up for Henry when it mattered and has stuck around ever since. Every gutter that needs clearing, every time the lawnmower needs mending the man is there. Unfaltering in his commitment to being Henry's friend. He gets it, what we have lost. Losing his own wife changed him, just like losing Henry changed us. The whole street has kept us going. It's the same with Laura, was the same with Martin, even Sam, though that name now makes me sick.

I think of all the times I saw tension between them both. Sam barring Henry from the pub after bringing his new friends in, the unpleasant looks on the street, the rants Henry went on about him over dinner. I feel dizzy, like the world has tilted but I know I must try to concentrate on what matters: Marianne.

After I've reassured Peter that I don't need escorting to the ward, I clatter across the courtyard of the hospital's main entrance much later than I had intended, my stick banging and plastic bag swaying as I rush towards the swinging doors. I shake my head at the line of smokers outside, drips attached to their arms, their hospital gowns billowing in the breeze. I find the whole place draining; I can feel the life being sucked from me as I walk beneath the fluorescent lights and breathe in the scent of disinfectant and longing. I am exhausted by the time I burst onto the neurology ward and take a moment to collect myself at the nurses' station. The nurses guide me, hands on my elbows, to Marianne's bedside. I have not quite finished telling them about the need for clearer signposting in the corridors when I spot Frank and Margo at either side of Marianne's hospital bed.

'What on ear—' I gasp.

Margo stops arranging flowers in the vase she has brought and gives me a wary smile. She hugs her cardigan more tightly around herself and turns fully to greet me.

'Patrick, lovely to see you. We thought we'd ease the burden for you and give Marianne some company.'

'It isn't a burden,' I say, hackles raised. 'Who told you Marianne was here?'

Margo gives Frank a fleeting look, as if to convey that she told him this might happen.

'We saw the ambulance the other morning and couldn't get hold of you to check everything was all right. Frank saw Laura in the corner shop and she explained what had happened. We just want to support you. It must be very difficult.' Her voice is a whisper then, as if Marianne might hear. Marianne is, in fact, chatting away to Frank as though nothing at all is the matter. Her eyes are bright, colour in her cheeks. I feel my heartbeat ease at the sight of her, the missing part of myself stitched back together.

'That's very kind of you, Margo. But there really is no need, we can manage just fine. I'll take it from here.'

I give Marianne a kiss on the forehead and begin unloading the plastic bag, placing her items beside her and moving the gifts Frank and Margo must have brought to the side.

'We've not been here long, Patrick. It would be nice to stay a bit longer; it's been some time since we've managed to talk to her like this. We miss her, we miss both of you,' Frank says, his voice as soft as ever. His moustache shifts as he speaks, lifting compassionately into a smile. I can't deny that I have missed their friendship, our Saturday night films, our trips to the Beehive. If only I could tell them why: that I can't afford to let anyone too close to us, that they'd be dragged into something much darker, much more dangerous. I am tired, so tired, of pushing everyone away just to stand alone. I look at Marianne's smile, gazing up at Frank as she speaks.

'She keeps calling him James. I'm sure the medication she's on isn't helping. Though she seems happy enough,' Margo says.

'James was her brother,' I say, placing Marianne's slippers underneath the bed.

'Yes, I remember.' Margo sounds hurt, and my stomach turns with guilt. I give a solemn smile, all I can manage, and look around at our surroundings. The ward is alive with visitors, concerned family members plumping pillows and chasing nurses for answers. It is sickly hot, as hospitals often are. I fold my coat over the back of one of the chairs and perch on the edge of the bed. I look at Margo, her arthritic hands clasped together while Frank, tired and frail, gives a laugh with all the life he has in him just to make Marianne smile. I feel tears building. These people have been my family, my chosen few, and even after years of pushing them away they have still come to support us today. I am lucky; I'm not sure how I have forgotten that. I exhale the worry from my lungs like the dusting away of cobwebs, and give Margo a hug that makes her gasp. It is clumsy and awkward but it is friendship and a love that doesn't need words. Then we sit as old friends, reminiscing and pulling threads from Marianne's memory until all four of us are laughing about the happy days we all remember.

* * *

I spend the time between visiting hours in the hospital café. For someone who declares myself increasingly anti-social, I make several friends. People are strangely transparent in hospitals, sharing information that they never would in any other circumstance. Of course, I never share much myself. I am a much better listener. My favourite visitor to the café is a little girl: she must only be five and has a halo of golden hair swept back into two plaits. She still has the innocence and curiosity that I admire about children. In particular, their ability to be direct. The girl clambers onto the chair beside me and stares up at me, all big brown eyes and long eyelashes.

'Are you sick?' she asks, crumbs dancing on her chin from the cookie in her hand. I look around for her parents.

'No, my wife is. I'm here to visit her.' I take my reading glasses off and meet her eyes, taken aback by her boldness. Are all children like that? Had Henry been like that? I can't remember, and a sadness fills the space in my chest. The girl chomps loudly and drops a chocolate chip onto her skirt. She looks at it nonchalantly before flicking it onto the table beside us.

'Is she going to die?' she bellows, more crumbs falling. It is a fair enough question, though I feel my body jerk in response. I see her parents spot her at my table and they hold a hand up in apology.

'I very much hope not.' I clear my throat. 'She's strong, my wife.'

'That's good,' she notes, taking another large mouthful of cookie. She kicks her legs against the chair. I let myself smile.

'Yes, I think so too.'

The parents rush over, young and flustered. I wave away the apology, the mother pulling the little girl off the chair by an elbow and cleaning her face. It so happens that the apology extends into an hour's conversation, with us sat together at my table like a mismatched family. I learn that the child's name is Grace, and that her older sister is unwell with pneumonia on the children's ward. By the end of the hour, Grace is sitting on my lap as I tell her stories, as I might have done if I had ever had the chance to be a grandfather. I tell her about Marianne, about Henry. I'm not sure how I do it, speaking about my lost son with such freedom. It all feels much easier when the person listening doesn't know how the story really ended. The family goes after that, explaining that their car parking ticket was expiring. Little Grace reaches up and clamps her arms around my neck, planting a ferocious chocolate kiss on my cheek. It makes me wince, not from disgust but surprise and overwhelming emotion.

The past month has stirred a change in me that I can't quite put my finger on – maybe I am too close to understand it fully.

The crowds in the cafeteria disintegrate, scurrying away to relatives and homes. I am left alone.

I'm in the middle of Bernard Cornwell's novel when I spot Ruth and Eoin looking lost. I hold up a hand, confused for a moment as to why they are here at all. Eoin spots me and grins, walking over and slapping me on the back like an old friend. They had driven straight to the hospital as soon as they heard the news about Marianne, they explain. As much as I grumble, I have to admit I quite like Eoin. There is something genuine about him, something real. Ruth, on the other hand, had to prove herself to me, but she has done so beyond measure. She brings a feeling of safety to Marianne that I wasn't sure she could feel again. I see there is a bunch of flowers in her hand, a card in the other. I can just make out Marianne's name scrawled across the envelope.

'Patrick, how are you?' Eoin sits in the seat beside me.

'All right, thank you.' I give a smile and place my glasses on my book, turning to face them more fully.

'We're here to see Marianne, is that okay with you?' Ruth asks nervously.

It has begun to strike a chord with me, just how much everyone wants to help. It makes me feel less like I am drowning. Besides, Henry's anniversary is pressing on me enough, threatening to pull me under. I'm surprised Margo didn't mention it, though I suspect she wanted to avoid upsetting me. They were his godparents. Are still, I suppose.

'Of course, thank you. Your mother not with you, lad?'

'Working, sadly. She sends her best and says she'll be over later. She knows what day it is for you both.'

I tilt my chin. I can't quite muster a nod. I feel myself stiffen, every muscle pulled taut. Eoin looks up at Ruth, something in his expression. I look between them both, sensing something is waiting to rear its head.

'What is it?' I ask, my voice gruff and impatient. I have firmly had enough of secrets, of words hidden in expressions, and the waiting. Always the waiting.

Ruth sits on the other side of me, the flowers across her knee with the card sliding on top.

'I'm really grateful for the statement you gave to the paper. I know it was brief but I also know how hard you find talking to the press. Especially after how they treated you, making you a suspect.' She swallows, shifts in her seat. 'I really think Marianne needs the chance to speak too. You've protected her so fearlessly all these years, more than anyone else could have, but I think she needs this, Patrick. She needs to be listened to, to feel she has a voice. I know her memory is bad and she gets confused, but she seems to have these moments of clarity, where she wants to tell someone, anyone, the truth.' She is speaking so fast the words are tumbling, falling at such a speed I can barely catch them. I feel myself growing hot, a sickly heat pricking every inch of my skin. I open and close my mouth, finding the words before losing them again. Before I can verbalise any kind of response, Eoin leans forward.

'Patrick, we want to help you find your son. To find out what happened to him. We can try and do what that detective didn't.'

'What detective? What are you talking about?' I demand.

'We spoke to Mr Monroe. We asked him some things about the case. Just to see if there was something we could do, anything we could do to help you and Marianne have some closure. We really believe Sam is innocent. He's being set up, he must be. We just wanted to find out something that might help prove his innocence. We – we also heard about you being a suspect, Patrick; he told us more about the blood on the sweater you hid. I don't believe a word of it – I know you wouldn't hurt him.' Eoin is smiling, trying to be reassuring, but the words fall flat, landing awkwardly between us. I stand hurriedly, with no plan of what to do or where to go. I am floundering.

'Is that why you're here? To question us? To exploit my Marianne while she's on her sickbed? I've already given you your quote.' I am shouting now, the table shaking as my fist slams down into its centre. Ruth flinches, her whole body recoiling from the sound of it. Eoin stands, clearly hoping to calm the situation, his voice low.

'We wouldn't dream of doing that, Patrick. We're not here to mention any of this to Marianne. We know she's vulnerable. We just want to help.'

'Well, don't. We don't need your help. We never needed it. I'm just sorry I ever let you two get near her. I can see you for what you really are now. Vultures, like the rest of them.'

The cleaning staff in the cafeteria are staring, whispering among themselves. Ruth places the flowers and cards on the table. I stare at them.

'I'm really sorry, Patrick. I think this has all come across wrong,' Ruth says. 'Any further articles I write will be a way of remembering Henry.'

I steady myself on the chair. 'I don't want to hear about this again. I think you should both leave.'

I pick up my stick and coat. It isn't my job to prove Sam's innocence. As selfish as it sounds, the focus on him keeps the focus from Marianne, and it finally puts this behind us. That must always be my concern. I can't get involved with anything else. Not today. Especially not today. I am suffocating with panic at the thought of people remembering, of people talking, of information that might shine a light on Marianne and what she knows. I know what would happen. Police everywhere, forensics, courtrooms. I shudder. I can't let that happen to her, I won't. I walk without thinking, out into the air and wondering how I can get Marianne out of the hospital and into hiding before that woman gets any closer to her.

33
Ruth

Autumn has begun to crawl onto the street, whispers of cold air and almost-naked branches fill the spaces between houses and people. The inhabitants of Crow Street are walking, hoods up and heads down, as though they're avoiding what is lurking right in front of them. News of Sam's arrest has rippled down the street, and while the whispering is an octave louder than usual, it seems as though everyone is trying to keep secrets concealed. It isn't clear what the consensus is on Sam's arrest, whether he is guilty or not. Though all the passers-by I have tried to interview have seemed defensive of him. Most are also angry that the Beehive will be closed for the foreseeable future. Something has changed in the atmosphere, as though a great reckoning is coming. There are no more greetings in the street, no waves as people pass by, but guarded nods and rushed excuses to scurry back inside.

'I feel awful,' I say, and I do.

I know how hard today must be for Patrick, seeing him earlier at the hospital reminded me just how fragile he is at the minute. His anger towards us, it's just a symptom of everything else he must be feeling. I mean, it's the anniversary of the day that changed his life. I think about Marianne, alone in the hospital, wrestling with her memories. I wipe a stray tear with the cuff of my jumper.

'I know. It isn't your fault.' Eoin's hand encircles mine, the warmth of it melting into my skin. We are sitting in Eoin's childhood bedroom, curled up together in the single bed like teenagers. We stay still for a while, just feeling the rise and fall of our chests merging together. The world feels much safer here.

Eoin exhales. 'They'll have to release Sam soon if they're not going to charge him.'

Everything seems to have gone wrong: Sam arrested, my time here coming to an end, Patrick cutting Marianne off from us. I feel a swell of sadness at the thought of never speaking to her again, or seeing her dance with Eoin and laughing with her chin to the sky. I can't shift Patrick's reaction from my mind. It couldn't be more obvious that he is hiding something. But what? If it really was Sam who killed Henry, then that clears all blame from the Carrs, doesn't it?

I spoke to Tom after the outburst at the hospital, a rushed phone call that I hadn't really wanted to answer. Then he had told me something that I can't shake. Tom had spoken to Oscar, looking for an update, and he'd reported that Sam had confessed to arguing with Henry before he disappeared, that the argument started because of some money Henry wanted Sam to store for him. Given that Henry already owed Sam a decent sum, it all bubbled over into what sounds like a pretty blazing row. It seems that despite it, Sam kept hold of the money but it appears was never paid back what he was owed.

But was that enough to inspire him to *murder* Henry?

It wasn't just that. The blood in the fridge-freezer was confirmed to be that of Henry's, and Sam's fingerprints were found on it. Except they weren't the only ones there. There were more: so far the only other prints they had identified were from another member of the friendship group.

Laura.

I haven't told Eoin, I can't. I don't even know what it means myself.

Oscar said they're running further tests but that they'll want to bring Laura in for questioning too, later on. He's made me promise to say nothing until then.

I put my hand on Eoin's arm, feeling the muscle taut beneath his skin. He turns to face me, and pushes my hair behind my ear.

'We can't be complacent. We have to just focus on what we can do. Talk to Mrs Montgomery, like we agreed. There has to be another answer.'

It's his way of spurring me on, telling me this isn't over yet. That he's with me all the way. I feel guilty for keeping this from him.

I sit up, cross my legs. He's right. We can't be complacent.

'Let's go over what we know so far,' I say, and watch him smile, putting a hand behind his head while he looks at me. 'Henry disappeared fifteen years ago. Though openly no one will criticise him and the press have never dug up anything bad, Sam claims he was a flawed guy who made bad decisions. That he brought bad people to Crow Street.

'The wallet has been planted by someone, maybe to distract attention away from them, we don't know. What we do know for sure is that someone is ringing in and giving tip-offs – someone knows something and wants to talk. Now the potential murder weapon has turned up in Sam's pub, on display for all to see. There was a fridge-freezer found in the alleyway with Henry's blood and Sam's fingerprints on it, though from what Oscar has said they can't be certain that multiple people won't have passed it and touched it. Especially considering it was out in the open. If it was Sam, why would he keep that for fifteen years and then suddenly put it on display?'

Eoin groans. 'That's the thing – there really is no logical answer to that, which is why I think it isn't the right one. If he did keep it with some fucked-up plan to reveal it fifteen years later, he'd know he'd be caught and arrested. To what end?'

'I don't know. The Henry that Sam described isn't the one I remember. He was friends with my dad, he came round all the time. He was a good person who just did what he had to for his unborn baby, by the sounds of it.'

'I know. After you spoke to my mum about the yearbook thing, she opened up a little bit. I think she might have loved him once, but accepted just being his friend. Your dad, my mum, Sam, Martin – they were tight, weren't they.' He smiles sadly.

'Yeah, except from what Martin said when I went in his house, things turned sour between pretty much all of them. All stemmed from Henry borrowing and not repaying money, and maybe some weird love triangle involving your mum by the sound of it.'

Eoin grimaces. He hasn't seen his dad for years, but it seems the thought of his mum being with anyone else doesn't sit right with him.

'They all lived on the street when he disappeared,' Eoin says quietly.

We sit on that statement for a moment, listening to the wind howl outside. I look at the slope of his shoulders, and the hollow at the base of his neck. I clear my throat.

'Let's forget about that for now and start at the beginning.' I wring my hands together. 'In the original investigation the only real lead they had was from Mrs Montgomery saying she heard an argument between Henry and another person, though she didn't recognise the voice. They then searched the Carr home and found a bloodied sweater, but the discovery wasn't substantial enough to be treated as evidence in the disappearance. After questioning Patrick, they let him go.'

Eoin nods. 'Yeah, they did search the surrounding public land but couldn't find anything. Which makes the discovery of the wallet fifteen years later in the wasteland seem like something that was planted.'

'But how did the person who planted it get hold of it? The wallet wasn't found in the original search of the house – the police just assumed the wallet was with Henry wherever he went. Whoever planted that wallet must have got it from Henry after he disappeared.'

Eoin frows. 'Didn't Mr Chandra tell you that the person who phoned in about the wallet said they saw Patrick plant it?'

'Which doesn't really make any sense. The man has spent fifteen years basically hiding himself and his wife from the world. Why would he want to plant something that would reopen the case?'

'I don't know,' Eoin says, rubbing his jaw. 'If the case had interest because of social media, maybe he panicked. He knew the wallet wasn't found in the original search, so the police finding it wouldn't bring them immediately back to him. Maybe he thought he was protecting Marianne by doing it. He has kept her hidden for fifteen years because she knows something, she wants to talk but he won't let her for some reason. Maybe he just wanted to make sure no police got her in an interview room, hoped planting the wallet would make them pursue other lines of enquiry.'

'That would mean he'd have to have hidden the wallet during the original search, or else that he got the wallet from Henry himself after he disappeared. I really don't think he's guilty, Eoin. Someone tried to threaten or kidnap Marianne just the other day, and it wasn't Patrick. Whoever it was knows that Marianne has information.' I think of Marianne's journal. About what she saw.

'I know. I don't think so either, but it might help to look at it all objectively for a minute. Patrick told you he and Henry argued about a child that Henry had with a mystery woman after he found the scan. I wonder what happened to the baby?'

'I thought about checking the hospital records for children born within a few months of Henry's disappearance, but we don't even know how old the scan photos were,' I say, exasperated.

'Yeah, it's all too vague. We do know that Henry went to a loan shark for money and because of that got involved in a sting operation gone wrong. Robert Knight found out about Henry's deal with the police and messed him up pretty good. The police seem to have covered that up, but why? They never told anyone about that information and Robert was never even investigated as a potential suspect. That's the bit I don't get.' I can hear the frustration in Eoin's voice.

'I don't know, but either way, Mrs Montgomery is the only person who might be able to identify the killer. She admits hearing the argument and says she didn't recognise the voice, suggesting she didn't know the person at all.'

'Unless she lied to police and *saw* them but doesn't want to say who it was.' Eoin shrugs.

'So where does all that leaves us?' I ask, looking out of the bedroom window to the street below. 'Patrick is the most obvious, but seeing his grief and his love for Marianne, I just don't think he's capable of it.'

'I know, I don't believe it either. The next most likely suspect is Robert Knight. He said he hated Henry, and revenge is a great motive. It makes sense that he was never caught, if the police are covering up the sting operation.'

I nod in agreement but find myself smiling at him. He isn't a journalist, or a detective, just someone who loves the street so wholeheartedly he would do anything to remove the secret that has blighted it. I lean over to kiss his cheek when I hear shouting from downstairs. Raised voices that waft up through the floorboards and settle uncomfortably between us.

'I thought Mum was on the phone, but I think I can hear someone else.' He pushes himself up onto his elbows, his ear cocked towards the door. Laura's voice is obvious, the rise and fall of it like a song we both know every word to. The other is harder to hear, but as I approach the landing, there is no mistaking who it is.

'It's my dad,' I whisper.

* * *

We spill out of the house together, our feet heavy on the pavement.

'Are you sure that's what he said?' Eoin whispers.

'Yes, I think. I swear I heard him say that as long as Mrs Montgomery keeps quiet then she would be all right.'

He sighs deeply, steadying himself.

'I guess we know where we need to go then?' I ask.

He grimaces in response.

We walk slowly until we are standing side by side, taking in the wilderness that is Mrs Montgomery's house. The path that stretches from the pavement to the door is covered in weeds and broken plant pots. The flagstones are uneven, their jagged edges waiting to snag unwelcome visitors. The net curtains in the window that were once white are yellow with smoke stains. She has simply blocked out the world and lives as she pleases. During my childhood, Mrs Montgomery had been the figure that the children ran from screaming, erupting into laughter when they were a safe distance away. But now I understand: she was just a woman who kept to herself. Why not, when the world outside is so cruel? She seems content with her own existence, with a purpose only she knows. Yet, standing outside the menacing face of her house, the prospect of talking to her feels more daunting than I expected. I hate feeling afraid. I glance down to Patrick's house. The curtains are still not drawn. That isn't like him. Eoin follows my gaze.

'Should I knock on their door and check everything's all right?'

'He's probably still at the hospital. We can call round later and apologise,' I say, focusing on Mrs Montgomery's house. The curtains at the front window twitch, a free corner moving an inch. Eoin steps forward, making himself more visible. The last thing we want to do is scare her. He knocks against the black of the door, the only one on the street that was never painted a bright colour. After two minutes there is still no answer. I step closer to the window, trying to peer through the grime. I work my way from left to right until a gasp escapes my throat. A wild blue eye meets mine, a withered hand reaching up to the glass. I put a hand to my chest, feeling the racing of my heart as it claws at my ribcage. I hold a hand up in apology.

'Mrs Montgomery, it's Ruth and Eoin from across the road. We'd like to speak to you. Is it all right if we come in? We can chat somewhere more public if that would help you feel comfortable?'

I force the tremble out of my voice, pull my face into a smile. The wild eye disappears from the glass, plunging the house into a deathly stillness. I wonder if she remembers me, or if she was in too much shock a few days ago to register I was the one who helped her with her cat.

'I don't think she wants to speak to us,' Eoin says, retreating to the pavement.

'I can't blame her,' I remark sadly, my eyes still lingering on the spot the eye had been. Our backs are turned when the door creaks open. We spin round to wild wisps of white hair and a claw-like finger around the door.

'Mrs Montgomery.' I smile, stepping towards her.

I hover there, waiting for a response or an invitation inside. Neither comes, but the finger and wild hair retreat leaving the door ajar and a question mark in its space.

* * *

The inside of the house is an empty shell. It feels hollowed out and exposed, bare plastered walls and light bulbs left naked. The walls are damp with cold and the floorboards are bare, black with dirt and dust. There is nothing scary about the reality of the place. It is just sad. Tragedy lingers on every surface. It doesn't feel much like a home at all, but something stripped back and left to rot. A black and white cat strolls up to greet us, nudging our legs with its head. It looks almost identical to the one I scooped up out of the road and I have to look twice to confirm it isn't the same one resurrected. Mould crawls up to the ceilings and patterns the walls with black tendrils. We stand rooted in the hallway, listening for a voice or a noise that might indicate where Mrs Montgomery has gone. There is nothing but the sound of our breath dissolving into the moisture in the air. A sadness spreads through me at the thought of Mrs Montgomery living like this for so long. Eoin extends his fingers to skim mine, an action that makes me jump before I realise what it is and hold onto him firmly. I close my eyes and take a step, then another. I enter the kitchen first, taking in the stacked-up dishes and the stench rising from the bin that overflows and scatters itself along chipped floor tiles. I wonder what has happened to Mrs Montgomery in the past, whether something in her life has pushed her to hide and retreat in this mess.

I turn in circles. Mrs Montgomery is not at the kitchen table. The stillness of the house only makes me feel more anxious. The cat has followed us, meowing every now and then with a soft curiosity. Passing by us, it leads us towards the open basement door I had taken no notice of before and disappears into the shadows.

'No way am I going down there,' Eoin whispers, peering into the dark basement. We hear a voice below, footsteps and a rustling. I push past Eoin, the hairs on my neck standing on end. I have to admit, it does seem like the point in a horror film when viewers would be screaming at the TV. The point where the characters meet a grisly end. *Ah well.* It'll make a good story. There is no light hanging over the stairs, just solid and impenetrable darkness as we feel our way down concrete steps. I can feel Eoin's breath on my back, fast and sharp. We take the stairs at a steady pace, our ears honing in on the slightest noise below us. And then Eoin's foot slips, sending him hurtling into me, concrete meeting his back. He yelps in pain, his free hand saving his head from hitting the sharp edge of a step. I'm knocked to the bottom, my arm clinging to the handrail in an effort to bring us to a stop. We both catch our breath, groaning.

I stand, my head spinning. My eyes are not yet adjusted to the darkness, and a rainbow of colours dances in my vision from the fall. Eoin is writhing in pain on the floor. He signals for me to carry on and I kneel beside him for several moments before he convinces me to go to Mrs Montgomery as he collects himself.

I push myself towards the dim light, edging deeper into the room, and find Mrs Montgomery hunched over a sewing machine, her crooked fingers fumbling with a needle and thread.

Mrs Montgomery shows no awareness of my presence, though she must have heard me approaching. The cat leaps down from her lap, meowing at me and circling my ankles. I clear my throat, a false and theatrical noise that makes me cringe. Disturbing the silence feels wrong. Mrs Montgomery ignores me, staring down at the thin line of thread between her fingers. She is engrossed in the task. It is several moments before she gets the thread through the needle, a wild smile pushing the sagging skin of her face upward. She gives a delighted cackle. She turns to face me, the wisps of her hair sending flickering shadows behind her. I run my tongue over my bottom lip, suddenly self-conscious as Mrs Montgomery's piercing blue eyes work their way through my skin.

'Mrs Montgomery, it's lovely to see you,' I say, trying to sound as normal as possible. 'You might not remember me – I'm Ruth from number five. We met earlier in the week when your cat sadly passed. I really am sorry about that. I want you to know – I buried him in the wasteland, near the summer house. If you want to go visit him. I put a little stone on his grave.'

Silence.

Just the blue eyes boring a hole in my centre.

I take a breath, continuing. There is no delicate way to ask the question, no small talk I can summon that might soften the blow.

'I was just wondering if I could ask you some things about a statement you gave to the police about Henry Carr?'

There is no change in expression, the eyes remain unblinking. We are two women simply looking at one another, finding we are more similar than we might have imagined. Both at home on this street but not. I find I can't hold her gaze, and glance around at the room. It is completely empty besides four boxes at one end and the sewing machine in the centre. There is a rusted patio chair in the corner, which I unfold and pull along the floor to face her. It all feels very much like theatre, a play under the spotlight.

'In your statement you said you saw Henry that day in the street – the day he disappeared – and then you heard him arguing with someone. Could you see what he was doing? Who he met?' I say it lightly, my tone unassuming.

Silence.

I nod.

'Mrs Montgomery, I think you didn't just hear the argument. I think you saw it. Can you tell me who it was he was arguing with?'
Silence.

'Do you have any idea where he went after the argument?' I look up a fraction, finding Mrs Montgomery's eyes still on me. Even the cat is watching, mild curiosity on its face.

'I'm not sure if you know this, but today is fifteen years since Henry disappeared. His mother, Marianne from number four, is in bits about it all. I'm not quite sure how she and Patrick both kept themselves going all these years, not knowing where their son is. Not knowing if he will ever come home. They know he's gone now, and Sam has been arrested. But I – and I think all of us on the street – don't believe he's a guilty man. If you could help in any way, I'm sure Patrick and Marianne would both be really grateful.' I'm staring at my notebook as I speak, my words falling like water.

'They do know.'

Her voice sounds strained, unused to being heard. Though strong despite its shaking. I try to guard my expression. I swallow, cross my legs.

'Who knows? What do they know?' I ask.

'The parents know.'

There is something in her voice I can't put my finger on. Is it mockery? Relief at finally talking? I can't tell.

'Patrick and Marianne? Was Patrick the man you heard arguing with Henry that day?'

Mrs Montgomery looks down, shaking her head. She runs her withered fingers down the wool of her jumper, her long nails snagging the loose threads, then continues with her thread and needle, turning her body away from me. When interviewing people for stories, I like to know something of their background, their context. It makes asking questions easier: I know what tone to use, what title, what small talk to frame the questions with. I feel entirely stranded with Mrs Montgomery, stranded on an island with nothing else around.

'I don't know what it's like to have children, Mrs Montgomery, but I can't help imagining what it must be like to bring a life into this world and then lose it. Henry deserves to be found, properly and with dignity. He deserves to be remembered as a person, not as a mystery.'

Mrs Montgomery stands, her thread and needle falling from her hands. Her shadow extends across the wall, meeting mine.

'I do know. A son is a precious thing.' Her voice has risen, booming bigger than the woman herself. I'm caught off guard. I'd never questioned the rumours about her from the street, that she'd always lived alone, despite going by the title 'Mrs'.

I gasp. 'You have a son?'

Eoin reappears, a framed photograph in his hand. He tries to mouth something, shielded from Mrs Montgomery's view. I shake my head, I don't understand. I can't see him well enough to know what he is trying to tell me.

He walks towards me and puts something in my hands, a faded picture in a frame. I can make out two figures, their arms around each other's shoulders, slung in casual friendship. Mrs Montgomery ignores us, trying to thread her needle again.

The light is playing tricks on me, morphing the faces in the photo into anyone my mind can conjure. I shake my head to dispel what I see. It can't be. Can it? But it is.

Henry Carr as a teenager with his arm around the shoulders of a young Robert Knight.

* * *

It suddenly all makes sense. I knew Robert grew up on the street too. If he was involved in Henry's murder, it makes sense that Mrs Montgomery would protect him, that she would rather fall into silence than give her own son up. I shudder at the horror of it, of Robert living in luxury while his mother grows frail in a house that is crumbling around her.

'Robert's your son?'

Mrs Montgomery snaps her head up at the name, her eyes wide and white.

'The man Henry was arguing with that day, was it your son? Did you see them? Is that why you wouldn't tell the police?' I ask, my voice fast and low.

Mrs Montgomery stands, the chair scraping on concrete as she eases her limbs into motion. Her frame is bent, hunched over at a painful angle. She points at the photograph, her eyes narrowed and accusing. Eoin hands it to her, never taking his eyes from her face. She clutches it to her chest like it is a piece of Robert, maybe the only piece she has left.

'I don't just have one son. I have two. Robert and Neil. Neil was a police officer. He's an alcoholic now because of Henry Carr, a shell of a man. So apologies if he doesn't have my utmost sympathy,' she spits. I try to gather my thoughts. Two sons? Why do we not know this?

But the pieces are falling into place. It must have been Neil, Mrs Montgomery's son, who betrayed Henry. He knew Henry was involved in the undercover operation against Robert's organisation, and he must have told Robert. But why didn't anyone ever tell us that Mrs Montgomery had two sons, that they knew Henry? Why would Alan Monroe not know this? Did Laura know? Did Martin?

'We know Robert lent Henry money that Henry never paid back. We've spoken to him,' I say gently.

I expect a reaction, though not the one I get. Mrs Montgomery looks surprised, hurt, sad almost, at the knowledge we have spoken to Robert. I can't imagine how long it has been since Robert has bothered to visit his mother. I wonder what has become of Neil, and if she ever gets to see him. For all these years we have assumed she was lonely by her own choice, a recluse by nature, someone detached from the outside. Really, she was a mother who had lost two sons to the same rot.

'Robert kept his promise. When they were involved in the substation accident. He stayed silent like the rest of them, covered for them all. He just wanted to be their friend, to be let into their circle. I lost my son that day.' Her chin quivers.

I feel my jaw clench, teeth grinding.

'Substation accident? You mean the one in the wasteland where the worker got injured? I read about that when I was looking up news on Henry. What does this have to do with Robert? Or with Henry?' I am talking too fast as my thoughts race to catch up.

It's all becoming clear now. Laura, Dad, Sam, Henry, Martin – all of them bound together by a lie.

'The person who burned the substation down was never caught. The worker almost died in hospital. It was one of them, wasn't it? Is that what this is about?' I demand.

Eoin turns to me, confused.

Mrs Montgomery gives a slight nod but says no more.

I bend over, my hands clutching my knees. My father, Eoin's mother, our friends, all tied up in something that almost killed someone. I remember reading that the worker was found by members of the street – those involved never called it in. Why would they do that?

'What's going on, Ruth?' Eoin asks, anxiety in his face.

'The substation accident. It was before we were born. I think our parents might have been involved. Henry too. They must have been in their teens. They're all protecting each other, even now. Bloody hell. It's what's tied them together. What if that's why Henry's dead? What if he wanted to tell the truth and they all knew they'd finally get in trouble?' My mind is racing; I clasp my hands together behind my head. 'Mrs Montgomery, was it definitely just Robert with Henry that day? Did you see anything else?'

She turns to face me and I fear I'll be met with further silence.

'They argued as grown men do. Robert had told me that Henry owed him some money, that he was playing him for a fool. I could understand his anger – people were always under-estimating my boy. Not me. He always had so much potential. He was going to do great things, until they poisoned his character. I know what he is now, good and bad. I didn't see much more

S. L. McManus

than that, just some tense words. They saw me watching and left. They went towards the wasteland.'

My palms are suddenly clammy. I've seen Robert's violence first-hand. I remember what the detective said about the summer house, about his inkling that Henry is buried beneath it. What if it involves the substation too? It pains me to hear Mrs Montgomery speak so nonchalantly about seeing Henry walk away that day. She doesn't doubt Robert's innocence for a minute.

'The wasteland,' Eoin repeats, his voice hollowed out.

He reaches for his phone. I shake my head, a single movement. I don't know who he wants to call but I don't know who to trust. The police might still be more involved than we know.

'Yes, Robert was always spending time out there. They all did, as children.'

'Who?' I ask, though I think I know the answer.

'My boys, Neil less so because he was older, Henry, Sam, Peter, Laura and Martin. They were always fighting about something – girls, money. They always underestimated my Robert because he was younger than them, weaker they thought.'

The layers of this killing seem to have no end. It confirms what I suspected, that there is something that ties them all together. I need to get away, to re-evaluate, to breathe. I pick up my notebook from the chair, turning to thank Mrs Montgomery and say goodbye when a hand grabs my elbow. Fingers dig into my flesh, bone burrowing its way into my skin. I can smell stale breath, and look up into the sunken face and yellowed teeth of Mrs Montgomery. Her eyes are not full of hatred, but warning.

'My son wasn't the only person to argue with Henry Carr that day.'

I try to ease my arm from her grip, opening my mouth to explain that I already know Patrick had argued with Henry that day when she cuts me off.

269

'I heard them right before he went into your father's house.'

* * *

'Shit.' I am pacing the pavement of Crow Street.

My head is pounding. I bend over to retch but there's nothing. I am empty. 'My dad's involved. He has to be. He was the last person to see him alive.'

'Ruth, calm down. They practically lived opposite one another, and we know they were friends.' Eoin is standing with me in the road, watching me closely. He's holding his arms out as if ready to catch me. The houses feel as though they are closing in around us, pressing us together. We both eye my house, our hearts in our mouths.

'Why doesn't anyone know about this? Think about how many people live on this street, walk by, stare out. Why didn't Mrs Montgomery ever tell anyone? Why didn't Dad ever tell me? He was his best friend.' I'm pacing, stamping out my thoughts with each step. 'What if Henry threatened to go to the police about the substation fire? What if it was all of them and my dad helped kill Henry to keep it quiet? Your mum could be involved too, along with Martin and Sam. It explains Sam's fingerprints on the fridge-freezer.'

'You can't assume your dad is guilty just because of what she said. You've said so yourself – he isn't the best at talking about emotions, especially grief. And as for my mum – Ruth, we don't even know for sure that the substation fire was because of them.' Eoin phrases it delicately, though he's aware of how naïve this sounds.

'I don't know what to think.'

I can feel myself floating. I don't want to ask any more questions. Maybe it is better to accept Sam as the sole killer. The police clearly think they have enough to arrest him. How would anyone else have snuck the wrench into the pub? No. It is better to accept his guilt, write my final article and go back to Newcastle. To get away from this place.

Tom will be happy with that: Sam, the beloved pub owner, who killed Henry Carr and then displayed the weapon in his pub for all the world to see. But it's not *right*. It doesn't fit.

By coming back to the street, I thought that I could set my ghosts to rest, heal some old wounds and break my first crime story. Instead, coming back has stirred up a storm inside me: my relationship with Dad, my love for Eoin, and my need, my desperate urge, to help Marianne find closure. As if it would bring me my own closure. I could cry at how selfish I've been, how stupid. It feels like I've been toying with people's lives, playing at being a detective when there is more at stake than I am capable of understanding. I thought I had the chance to give a voice to someone who had lost it. Instead, I've discovered nothing and helped no one. Or maybe I've discovered too much that doesn't help anyone. I look up to see Frank and Margo, their faces white, their mouths shouting in a jumbled note. Eoin walks towards them, his hands up to calm them.

'What's wrong? Hey, what's wrong?'

Margo falls into his arms, her face wet with tears and crumpled with worry. She can barely speak, her voice lost in the enormity of the moment.

'It's Patrick. He's taken Marianne from the hospital and gone God knows where.'

34

Marianne

TRAFFIC RUSHES ACROSS THE dual carriageway, horns blaring and lights flashing. Marianne doesn't know where she is. She clamps her hands firmly over her ears. The sound of it all works its way into her skull. She spins in circles to find something she can recognise. She reads street signs, their names foreign on her lips.

'Where am I?' she whispers.

'Marianne!' A voice calls her from further down.

She doesn't recognise the old man in front of her, dressed in a cap and a beige coat. He has a small suitcase in one hand. His other hand is outstretched towards her, a slight tremor in it. His voice sounds familiar but she can't place it; it floats around and slips through her fingers like silk whenever she tries to catch it. She is frightened, frightened of the speed and noise and of the stranger trying to make her go with him. She stands glued to the spot, fretting over whether to step forwards or back. She feels groggy from what the doctors at the hospital pumped her with. Tiredness pulls at her like a tide. She looks at the bank of grass to her left and considers lying down and going to sleep. She feels as if she has been walking for hours; her feet are beginning to blister, her legs swollen. She looks down at her feet, the soft velvet and the woven flowers.

'Slippers?'

She feels a drop of water on her scalp and dries it with the tip of her finger, looking up at the clouds. Grey and wet and typical. She can feel the fear building, that familiar and horrid beast that haunts her. A fear of something she has forgotten, something important, something dangerous. She looks for a bus that will take her home but can see none, just lorries blasting by and cars with no intention of stopping. She holds out her hand to stop the traffic, wobbling on the edge of the pavement. An HGV blurts its horn, swerves an inch to miss her outstretched arm.

'Jesus, Marianne! You're going to get yourself killed.'

The man is back. He has put his belongings on the ground and is rushing towards her. He looks exhausted, his eyes are hooded and bruised. He is shivering too, zipping his coat up to his chin. He looks menacing, charging at her like this.

'Who are you, then?' she cries. 'What do you want? I don't have any money.'

She pushes his hand away, grimacing at the coarseness of it. The look in his eyes scares her. She takes a step back, fumbling in the bag that is crossed over her body. She finds a purse with various pictures and instructions inside, names she doesn't recognise, an address she can't place. She ignores it all and finds some change and throws it in his direction.

'There. Take it. That's all I have.'

It lands at his feet and circles before lying flat. He steps over it and reaches further towards her.

'Marianne, please, you'll freeze. We need to get away from here.'

Marianne? She doesn't know her.

35

Patrick

THERE IS DESPERATION IN my voice and I try to quell it out of fear it'll scare her off. I glance over my shoulder, paranoid. I have a strong sense we are being hunted. That the truth has been exposed like the ripping up of a floorboard. I know they'll bring Marianne in for questioning, and that it will probably kill her. I can't lose her, I just can't. She's clearly petrified, quivering, muttering Henry's name now. She knows details the police need, details no one else has. But Marianne seems to think that Henry is still with us, that he will turn the corner and run to us with open arms at any moment. He was warm, affectionate. His love for Marianne had always been obvious, unwavering. Even now her memory is failing her, her body is remembering. It makes me ache, even all these years later. I thought about it once, telling the truth. Admitting exactly what she had been saying, what she still believes she saw. It was a concept I had once romanticised, the truth. I can see it now for what it is: heavy, bleak. The truth has consequences, good and bad. My duty is to protect my wife, even if that means hiding the truth. Even if means never seeing my son buried, saying goodbye.

'Let's get you home,' I say gently, reaching for her again.

She relents, allowing me to take up her arm and link it through mine. We walk together, as we always have, side by side. The traffic rushes past us, impatient. Half a mile down the road a car screeches to a halt and pulls up onto the kerb beside us. A door is flung open and a voice cuts across the space between us.

'Patrick, what are you doing? Are you mad? You can't just take Marianne from the hospital!' Eoin cries.

My heart quickens. Is it anger or fear? It feels like both, knotted together.

Ruth pulls herself from the car, places a hand on Eoin's arm.

'We've been looking for you for an hour. Please let us help you, Patrick,' she says.

I look from one to the other, my muscles tense and ready to run. Fight or flight. I put the suitcase down at my feet. Marianne is grinning at Eoin, some corner of herself probably reliving their dance. She steps towards the car before I can pull her back.

'Well, come on then,' she calls, as Eoin guides her into the back seat. She pats the seat beside her, smiling. She leans forward and whispers to Eoin like a child, her face cracking into a grin. She erupts into a howl of laughter at his response and struggles with her seat belt. My plan is disintegrating. I bury my face in my hands for a moment before exhaling and picking the suitcase up off the ground.

'Christ, I'm tired. I'm so tired of running.' For a moment I think I might cry, the exhaustion pulling and pushing me. My mind relives every moment, every lie, every feeling of guilt that moves me further away from myself. I am at a dead end with nowhere to turn.

Fine.

If they want to know, we will have to do it my way.

The only way.

'God forgive me. Fine. You want the truth? You can have it on one condition.'

'You name it,' Ruth says, her face set.

'We're going to the sea.'

36

Patrick

THE WHITE FROTH OF the sea fizzes beneath us, spraying our feet in kisses as the sky and sea blend together. It feels as if we are standing on the edge of the world, the feeling of oblivion at the base of our feet. There is a call from seagulls overhead, guttural cries that echo and fall before being swallowed by the water below. I inhale sea and salt, cleansing my soul.

'This is it?' Eoin asks.

'This is it.'

I slap a hand onto Eoin's shoulder as we stand at the head of the pier. We are an odd pair, with years stacked between us. Still, we have forged a sort of friendship that sidesteps barriers. It isn't just that we are both from the street, or that we are men, but we understand one another on a level I can't explain. Like we are two people who know what it means to love even in the most difficult of moments.

I'm tired of running, tired of lying, of hiding. I know what could happen, but it has to be said, has to be done. Today of all days. It has taken me fifteen years to accept the facts, that when Marianne and I are both dead and in the ground, there will be no one left to tell anyone what has happened. It is the only thing we can do for Henry now. I'm worn down. There are too many people asking questions, too many who need answers. I'm tired of the sleepless nights, of worrying about what Marianne might say or do. The only way to protect Marianne now is to come clean. I'm torn between knowing what is right and doing what is best. I have never been quite sure which way round it all is.

I stare down at the swelling sea, churning itself below us. This is the place it has to be; it is only right that the truth is told in this place. I know that Marianne will remember best here, in a place she feels most like herself. The place where our journey began. It has to be Marianne who tells her truth, to finally have people listen to what she has to say. She has had her voice stolen for too long. It doesn't matter how long it takes for her to remember. I had insisted on driving by Crow Street first, on going to the house. I put all of Marianne's unsent letters and scrawlings into a plastic bag. They are her prompts, her internal monologue. She needs them to remember every detail.

I breathe in slowly, tasting the whole sea in my mouth. It has been a long time since I've been back, though now I am it seems like no time at all. I can still remember kissing Marianne at the end of the pier when we first met, dancing to the music of the carousel. What I would do to have those moments back, to see Marianne dance and laugh and sing. That is the cruel reality of loving someone, that it means losing them too.

Southport stretches out around us. It was her favourite place in the world. I was worried that she wouldn't recognise it, it has been so long. Yet as soon as we turned onto the main strip, Marianne pressed her face up to the window. She was saying something none of us could understand, though it was undeniably joyful.

'I proposed here, you know,' I reminisce, watching Ruth and Marianne walk arm in arm down the pier. I think back to the song that was playing somewhere distant, the wood digging into my knee, the butterflies in my stomach. Back then the world felt like something to be conquered. How young I had been.

'It's beautiful.' Eoin smiles. 'How did you know she was the one?'

I lean on the railing. I chuckle and take off my tweed cap, flattening down the hair that stands on end.

'When you know, you know,' I say simply.

We both look out at the swell before us, churning up long-buried debris. I wonder what will happen, what will be said. One thing is for certain: whatever happens next, Crow Street will never be the same.

37
Ruth

PATRICK HAD BEEN THE first to suggest ice creams. Being here made him seem lighter. The seaside has that effect on people, it brings out some long-lost part of us. After we had our ice cream, Patrick and Eoin wandered off, leaving Marianne and I together. We sit on the pier, our ankles crossed. In sync. The rain has stopped, and far out at sea the first rays of sun are shining through the clouds. I haven't been here since Mum died. It is somewhere we always went together, running along the beach with sand between our toes. The feeling of being near the sea again means being near to her.

Marianne is tapping her feet in a rhythm on the planks of the pier, to a tune that only she can hear. She laughs when she puts a foot wrong, dropping the length of her skirt and admitting defeat. She is a different person out here, away from the street. I feel guilty about ruining it by asking dangerous questions.

Patrick gave me the bag full of Marianne's letters and writings on the ride here. I spent the journey sifting through them all as Marianne watched the world go by. There was something I hadn't noticed that day in number four. Most of the writings were marked with numbers in what seemed like a random order; some had sentences scribbled out and words in capital letters. I had to splay them across my knee and the back seat to see them in their fullness. However hard I tried, I just couldn't make sense of it. It was a maze that only Marianne could escape from, the numbers only made sense to her. The horror in some of the words jumped from the pages:

murdered

bloodied

screams

Marianne had begun to pay attention, her fingers sifting through the papers. Sometimes she would become distracted or confused and it would take several moments for her to come back to it. Eventually, she read more intently, before handing several extracts to me, a look of fierce determination on her face. She put the papers in an order that I didn't understand, though it must have made sense to her. Slowly, carefully, they began to take shape, the scraps of fifty or so pieces of paper lying like shrapnel over the both of us. By the end, Marianne had her story from start to finish. The disappearance of Henry Carr.

* * *

I wait until the wind drops before holding the pages out, Marianne's hands clutching at the scarf around her neck.

'When are these from, Marianne?' I ask.

She looks over at me briefly. 'I can't remember.' Her voice is lost to the wind as she turns and stares out at the sea.

'Were these from the day your son disappeared?'

'Can you see that?' she asks, pointing into the distance.

I follow the direction of her finger but can't see anything but mist and grey. She can see something I can't, something that none of us can. I leave her for a moment, letting the wind fill the silence. Then I try again.

'Marianne, did you write these?'

She looks down, reads a portion.

'I wrote those after I saw it all.' Her voice is carried away by the wind. I contemplate suddenly whether I want to know after all. I have a sense of great foreboding. Now that Eoin and I have settled what was between us, the street, for the first time in my life, has begun to feel like home. There is still fear and confusion and unease, but amid it there is an outline of home that wasn't there before. I don't want to lose that now, to have it tainted and pulled from beneath me. But I have to, for Marianne.

'Would you be able to tell me what you saw?' I ask tentatively.

Marianne looks down at my hands, at the papers fluttering. She takes the papers from me, reading through them slowly before nodding firmly.

'I always kept a diary,' she whispers. 'I just can't remember it all. Even with this, I get confused.' A tear balances on her eyelashes, drying in the strength of the wind.

'It's all right, really. We can do this at your pace, Marianne. Just tell me what you do remember. Tell me what you've always wanted to say but no one was listening.'

Marianne considers this for a moment, her head tilted to the side. The white wisps of her hair balance in the breeze, like static electricity around her. I lose her again for a moment; she retreats to some far-off corner of her mind. She tilts her chin eventually, her eyes distant.

'I know who killed my Henry.'

38

Patrick

I WANT TO WALK and walk but eventually my legs give in, and Eoin finally talks me into sitting on a bench. I just want to see everything here, remember everything. We have managed to walk along half of the promenade and I'm happy with that.

'I can't tell you how long it's been since we've left the street,' I tell him, gazing out at the sea. 'We used to go out in the car every weekend. Had to give that up eventually, couldn't afford the insurance.' I take a sip of lukewarm tea from the polystyrene cup in my hands and press my back against the bench.

'I'm glad we're here then.' Eoin smiles.

'You've become a friend of ours, lad; I'm glad.' I say it while avoiding eye contact. We dangle the unspoken out of sight for the moment, just enjoying the sea air. It's me in the end who brings it closer, choosing to get the conversation over with.

'Come on then, lad. What do you need to know?' I ask, trying to keep the anxiety out of my voice.

Eoin shifts in his seat, his hands a ball in his lap.

'We know that Henry was having a difficult time before he disappeared. He was trying to claw some money together. He even visited a loan shark.'

I close my eyes. I don't even want to think about it.

'We spoke to Mrs Montgomery,' Eoin continues. 'We know that there were three people who spoke with Henry on the day he disappeared. Two of them never spoke to the police. We think one of those is the guilty party.'

'Three?' I ask, confused.

'You, Mrs Montgomery's son Robert, and Peter Cavanagh.'

I balance my cup next to him and push my hands underneath myself, sitting on them to stop the shaking. I feel old suddenly, older than I have ever felt. I try to ignore the burning in my chest and let Eoin continue.

'The disappearance of Henry Carr seems to be this big secret the street is hiding,' Eoin says. 'The thing that everybody knows the truth of, but no one will say. I know that you're trying to protect Marianne from what she's seen, from what will happen next. But you need to do this, she deserves to be listened to. If it really wasn't Sam, then he deserves his freedom. We all deserve answers. Your son deserves to have a dignified burial, for this whole thing to have some closure.' Eoin rubs the back of his neck anxiously. 'It's not just that. I'm worried, Patrick. Who knows what the killer could go on to do to someone else? What he might have done already.'

I sigh, my shoulders hunched. 'And me? What if it was me? That's what you want to say next, isn't it?'

Eoin doesn't respond.

I glance back at Marianne, at the only person in the world I have left. I have done all I can to protect her, whether for right or for wrong.

'Look, lad,' I begin softly, 'it might not mean anything now, especially after hiding and lying all these years. The truth is, I think Marianne *does* know what happened to Henry. She tried to tell me, though her mind wouldn't let her see it clearly. It blocked out any real clarity, but she saw him. She ran back that day and told me. I just – I didn't believe her. I thought it was the medication, her illness. I started to wonder if the theory of him running off with a woman, whoever she was, to start a new life was true and I was ashamed of it. The shame stopped me even thinking about searching for the woman and child, though part of me longed to. To have a piece of Henry.' I look down at my cracked palms, feel the guilt seep through every pore in my body. 'I couldn't believe what she said. None of us could. Every time she pointed the finger towards another person I would go over and there would be nothing, no body, no blood. Nothing. Nothing at all. Jesus, the whole street must have let me in to search at one point or another. We fought about it so much she began to doubt herself. It sent her mad, I think. Her mental health got worse, she hallucinated, heard voices. Henry never came home, and she accused everyone on the street of killing him. She thought they were all playing tricks on her.'

Eoin leans forward, his head bowed. I carry on, too afraid to stop in case I can't muster the courage to tell him.

'In the beginning, just after he'd gone missing, there were so many names she whispered. I'll admit, some came up more than the others. One in particular, but I stopped hearing it. And then it became a "he" or a "they" and even Marianne didn't know any more. I couldn't cope with knowing it was one of our own. Call it weakness, call it cowardly. She tried to tell me day after day, for years, and I didn't listen, I shut it out. She had been unwell for so long, you know. I wanted to believe there was no truth to what she was saying. What she said didn't make any sense, anyway – she even blamed me at points. So if it wasn't true . . . it meant that Henry could still be out there somewhere, living, laughing. He'd just left because he was mad at me. It meant he could still come home one day. So for years that's what I chose to believe: he was angry at me, punishing me. That he'd be back.'

'But you believe her now?' Eoin asks, his eyes sad.

'There's part of me that still tries to fight it, but after what happened at the Beehive there's no other answer. I suppose I do believe that Marianne really did see it that day. The very first name she gave, not the ones that came after. It's just taken me this long to accept it. She thinks about it every day, talks about it every day. It's not a hallucination, or an illness. It's the nightmare of the truth.' I bring the cold tea to my lips, trying to force my throat to open.

Eoin stirs. 'Why try to keep it a secret, now that you believe her?'

'I'm still afraid. They knew she was ill, vulnerable. But that kept us safe – they didn't see her as a threat any more since no one on the street believed anything she said.' *Not even her own husband.* 'So I decided to keep the secret. I thought I was doing what was right. Hiding ourselves away. Protecting her from everything outside.'

I am ashamed. Ashamed of what I have done. Silencing Marianne, leaving Henry to rot, avoiding the whole street just to keep her away from one person, just to make sure he didn't come after her. If we both stayed silent then we stayed alive, that was always the unwritten rule.

'Why would you not tell the police? She could have told them everything; it all would have been over,' Eoin asks, confused.

'No lad, it wouldn't. It will never be over. You don't know what it would be like for her, to be questioned and interrogated, to have to relive it over and over. To remember it all, not just snippets she'll forget in the next heartbeat. It would have destroyed her. Her illness was already eating away at her. I know how it works – she'd have been referred on and on and passed around like an object. Undignified, impersonal. I couldn't keep my son safe. I failed him as a father. I couldn't fail my wife too. Do you not think I'd rather see him buried? To be able to visit him, speak to him, apologise? Christ, hiding it all has destroyed me too.

But it's the last and only thing I can do for her, to keep her with me.'

'So what's changed?' Eoin asks gently.

'After her stroke, I began to think. I don't believe I can protect her any more. I don't know how much longer she'll be with us. Once she's gone, there's no one left to remember.'

39

Ruth

THE AIR AROUND US is growing cold, the threat of winter pressing in. Marianne giggles every time the wind licks at her hair, or wraps around her ankles. She must feel entirely free. She is starting to remember things slowly; she becomes agitated, starts speaking. But in the next breath she forgets, and then she's laughing, smiling. It is exhausting, constantly clambering back five paces and starting again. But I don't care how long it takes. I encourage Marianne slowly. This has to be done Marianne's way.

'I was in the kitchen when he came home,' Marianne said. 'He was in a foul mood, very agitated. Course, he wouldn't tell me what it was all about, just shouted something about his father and slammed his door.'

'Henry was angry at Patrick?' I ask.

Marianne ignores me, staring down at her feet, her brow furrowed. I smile at a family passing by and turn to face Marianne.

'Did you speak to Henry when he came home, Marianne? The day he disappeared – did you speak to him?'

'I would have once called Margo for advice; she always knew what to say. Except everyone thought I was mad. The street called me "mental Marianne". I heard them. Whispering.' She looks down at her nails, inspecting them closely. Her face has gone blank, she begins fidgeting, turning around and staring down the length of the pier.

'Had he been acting differently before he disappeared?' I ask, trying to keep my voice calm and steady. There is so much I want to ask, and I have to restrain myself. I don't want to agitate Marianne.

'Who?' Marianne stands, spinning around and looking back at the blurred figures of Patrick and Eoin. She eyes the run-down shops and deserted beach, confusion settling on her face. It takes several minutes to get her back on track, calming her, stroking her hair. She is murmuring about her mother waiting at home, of Henry lost in the wasteland. A couple walk by us on the pier, hands joined and laughs thrown into the cold air. We watch them until they are a distance away. Marianne can't seem to remember if she spoke to Henry, or why he was angry at Patrick, though I can only assume it stemmed from the argument about the child he fathered. I try a different tack.

'Someone said they heard Henry arguing on the street the day he disappeared. Is that the same argument? Did you see who they were?' I whisper gently, my head on Marianne's shoulder. Her smell comforts me and she takes my hand, her fingers cold.

'Oh yes, he was arguing with lots of people then. He seemed so angry all the time. I didn't know what to do. I was painting in the garden when I heard them, shouting at one another. I went around to the front to see what was happening. He hated that, me getting involved in things. I just wanted to help.'

I stay still, listening, waiting.

'He was arguing with someone. Well not just arguing, fighting. It was becoming physical. Then they started to calm down. The man invited him into the house, which seemed odd after all that went on. Though he was quite a secretive person, Henry. I suppose he didn't want the whole street hearing his business. I tried to leave it alone then, when things had calmed down. But time passed and I never saw him leave. It was getting late. I had his dinner on the table.'

Her voice has grown smaller, shrinking into nothing. She pulls at a loose thread on her sleeve, watching as it unfurls into her hand.

'Did you recognise them? The person Henry was arguing with?'

'Yes. Oh, yes. But his name. I can't remember his name.'

I don't want to keep pushing; I can see Marianne's mind turning. She is engrossed in the thread of her sleeve, though her mind must be spinning and unlocking memories she has long since forgotten.

'Did they mention a fire, Marianne? A fire at the substation on the wasteland? When they were arguing?'

She shakes her head.

'I went to the door and knocked but no one answered.'

I have to bite my tongue to stop myself asking which door. I have to remember for this story I'm not a journalist interviewing her, but someone who cares, someone who just needs to listen.

'I needed to find him,' she continues. 'So I tried the alleyway. The gates were always open. I got in through the back door.'

A shiver passes through me. Marianne strokes my face, smiles.

'Are you all right, Mother?' she asks, her eyes tearing.

I swallow. I don't move. Just let her trace her fingers along my cheekbone. She does it so tenderly. She doesn't know it's me. I don't tell her I'm not her mum, I don't say anything, I just let her exist in whatever world she is in at this moment.

'I went in,' she says. I jump as her voice disturbs the peace. Her eyes have turned glassy, as though she is no longer here but there. Remembering something she is holding in the palm of her hands, something she could drop at any moment. 'The door under the stairs was ajar. Just like our house, everyone has a cellar for storage. But it seemed a strange place for them to talk. Even if they are old friends.' She laughs at the thought, then sobers again. 'I couldn't hear anything, but that's where they had to be. All the hairs on my arms were standing on their ends.' Marianne shows me her arms, smiling. Her smile falls away slowly.

'I could sense something. I took those steps slowly: they were steep, you see. I could hear something then, muffled, a struggle, a fight. Then there was a scream, a blood-curdling scream, and I froze. I waited what felt like a lifetime. I couldn't move until the screaming stopped. I waited until there was no more sound, but then I kept going down the stairs.' She shivers, taking the bottle of water I offer. I say nothing but my mind is in overdrive. It has to be Robert Knight in Mrs Montgomery's house. That horrible empty cellar Eoin and I had seen: that was where the violence, the argument, happened.

I think back to when I met Robert, how I was alone with him, and I feel ill. I wait for Marianne to settle before asking if she wants to continue. It takes a few moments of reminding her what we are talking about and where she was up to in her story before she can go on. Drizzle has started to fall and the fine silvery beads of the rain settle like pearls on Marianne's silk scarf.

'I still hear it in my sleep,' Marianne says softly. 'The scream. I spoke about it with the doctor, after it had all happened. He couldn't understand why I was so fixated on that one thing, the noise of it. He didn't believe me, of course. Thought I was mad, just like everyone else did. He thought it was my way of coping with the trauma of a lost son, making up a story of where he was. I wish I'd stopped on the stairs. I wish I'd never seen it.' She starts to cry. Guttural sobs. I take her hand.

'I don't think you're mad, Marianne,' I say gently. 'I believe you.'

Marianne sniffs, wipes her nose with the back of her hand. I wonder if anyone has ever told her that before. Three simple words: *I believe you.*

'I wish I had left,' she says finally. 'But I didn't. I kept going, and I saw it. I heard it.' She closes her eyes. Her lip trembles. Her entire body is shaking.

'What is it, Marianne? What was the noise? What did you see?' I ask, searching her face.

'The sound of metal on bone. The sound of him killing Henry.'

40

Patrick

EOIN LEANS OVER THE railing to look at the swirling sea beneath.

'Sit down, lad,' I say firmly, patting the empty seat beside me. Eoin looks over at the pier, at Ruth and Marianne. They both look fragile, like dolls. There is something about the way they are sitting, leaning against one another, moulded into one. It makes me happy and desperately sad. I think about what it might have been like, to have a family and keep it. To build memories together that didn't fade away or resurface like a nightmare. I don't mean to be self-pitying. Not at all. This isn't about me. It's about her, it's always been about her.

'Just please tell me. I need to know the name Marianne gave,' Eoin pleads, turning to face me.

'I feel sick to my stomach just saying it,' I say through gritted teeth.

It's true, my stomach is churning. 'I didn't believe her. How could I? I've chosen to ignore it for so long, convince myself she wasn't thinking straight. Yes, she said his name, but she also said others too. I'd convinced myself his name didn't stand out, that I couldn't hear the way she spoke it, haunted. But I could. And then she stopped saying the names altogether. She blocked it all out to cope; she couldn't remember a face or a voice. Not really. It was the only way for her to survive. Christ, she even accused me at times. I just couldn't get my head around it. They were friends. I didn't understand. I still don't,' I say sadly.

Eoin sits beside me, his leg juddering. He looks as nervous as I feel.

'Patrick, please tell me,' he says.

I nod. Close my eyes. 'I'm sorry, lad. Marianne was like a ghost when she came back to the house, her hands covered in blood. She couldn't even speak. She had fallen and cut her head and scratched her hands so I thought the blood was her own. I got her in the bath, helped her wash it all off. I didn't give a thought to myself, to the red stains transferring. She just lay there – she couldn't even talk, couldn't tell me where she'd fallen or how she got hurt. I didn't realise until it was too late that most of the blood couldn't have been hers.'

Eoin puts a hand over mine to stop the shaking. I smile gratefully. Wipe a stray tear with my free hand, sit on it to keep it contained.

'I see that now as the beginning of the end of Marianne; she was never the same again,' I finally say. My voice is barely holding out. 'No one would be. Not when you've seen your own son dead. I still don't understand how someone can do that – anyone – but especially a childhood friend.'

41
Ruth

I FEEL FAINT, CONVINCED for a second that I might collapse
to the ground. My face burns while my limbs remain cold. I grip
Marianne's hand to steady myself. Marianne seems unfazed by
what she has described, seems relieved just to have the weight
of it off her chest. Her eyes seem brighter. I can't help but wonder
if she understands the magnitude of what she has said, if it
resonates with her in the way it once did.

I let go of Marianne and bury my head in my hands. The
image in my mind, the violence of the crime, sickens me. This
isn't a film or a podcast or an article, this is a person I knew, a
man who sat at my kitchen table with my family and me. Someone's
friend and son and lover. This is a person who dreamt of living,
of raising his child, of growing old with the person he loved. He
probably woke up that morning thinking of the rest of his life,
and in an instant, in a moment of violence, he was gone. Now all
that is left behind are the survivors, his family, his friends. I cross
my arms hugging my body in an attempt to hold myself together.
Marianne is smiling. Her grin looks gruesome. Painted on. The
very idea – that dank cellar under Mrs Montgomery's house;
Robert Knight, hacking a man to death – and his mother watching
her beloved son be murdered. I want to cry.

'What happened next, Marianne?' I ask, trying to keep my
feelings out of my voice. Marianne might respond badly if she
knows I am upset, so I force myself to act normal, keep my voice
level. Keep my hands from shaking.

'When, dear?' she asks, her eyebrows pushed together. She looks at me earnestly, wanting to please. I can see that she's tired, that I won't be able to keep her here much longer.

'On the day Henry disappeared, you followed him and the person he was arguing with into a house. You saw him attacked? What happened then?' I speak slowly, to give her a chance to think back.

'Henry?' She repeats the name, her lips overexaggerating the word. 'Henry.' She says again, heavier this time. 'Henry.' She repeats, higher this time, her voice cracking down the middle.

'Marianne, are you okay?' I'm on my feet, I look across to Eoin and Patrick in the distance. They're too far away for me to see their faces properly. I want them to be here, to help me.

'HENRY!' She screams this time, falling down onto her knees, scraping her skin on the wooden planks. I kneel beside her, hold her up. She collapses into me, buries her head in my neck. Her tears melt into my skin, her breaths hot and staggered. I let her calm down, let her take small inhales until she comes back to herself.

'I screamed. I couldn't help it,' she says eventually, almost matter-of-factly. 'And he saw me. I turned for the stairs. There was nothing I could do. I could see that my boy was gone. I ran as fast as I could, but he was faster. He was so quick. He had my ankle in an instant, he pulled me down those stairs. I hit my head. I waited for him to kill me. But he didn't, though he said he would if I ever told anybody.'

She pulls herself onto the bench, wipes her mouth with her sleeve.

'When nothing happened, I looked at him. He was crying, frightened. He started saying that he never meant to kill him, he was just trying to warn him off. I kept hoping it was all a dream, that I would just wake up and Henry would still be there.'

She ran a tongue over her lip, frowning. 'And then, and then I . . .' Her voice trails off, she is struggling to remember. I'm on the edge of my seat, willing her to continue. It is the only thing I need to help her now, the identity of the man.

'What then, Marianne? Think about what you felt, what you saw,' I whisper urgently. Marianne looks at her hands, crunching the plastic water bottle between them.

'Where's Patrick?' she asks, worry in her voice.

I feel better that she remembers him. That she wants him. 'He's gone for a walk with Eoin. He'll be back in a minute. Please, Marianne. I know this must be a horrible thing to remember, but it's so important. Please tell me who he was.' All Marianne has to do is say it was Robert Knight, and then we can go to the police and it will all be over.

'The man? Well, you know him, don't you?' Marianne asks, almost conversationally.

My breath catches in my throat, my clothes clinging to my skin. How would Marianne know I've met Robert Knight? Maybe she's confused.

'What do you mean?' I ask slowly.

Marianne takes my hand. It is her turn to comfort me now.

'I saw you going in that house, dear. Do you live there?' she says.

'Where? Number nine?'

A laugh. 'No dear, number five.'

I shiver, goosebumps trailing down my arms. I lean forward.

'Is he your father?' Marianne asks. 'Peter?' She says it gently.

'My dad?' I feel like I'm choking. I want it to be a mistake. 'Peter Cavanagh?'

I am standing before I realise. The ground is moving beneath me. That can't be right. She's confused again. She's accusing anyone she can remember. It wasn't my dad; it has to be Robert Knight.

Yet Marianne winces at my father's name and nods slowly, the creases of her mouth sloping downwards. The wind tugs at my clothes, pulls me out to sea. I feel as though I'm drowning, I wish I could. How I wish I could. The truth is too huge, too much. My father. With his violent temper, his drinking . . . All these years I thought he had been punishing himself for Mum's death, maybe even for the suffering he'd inflicted on me. All these years drinking himself into a stupor, living in a house that was falling down around him.

But a murderer? Why? Could it really be about the fire at the substation? Does this mean that there are more of the street involved? I can't believe he'd kill for that, to cover a stupid teenage mistake.

'But why?' I whisper.

It seems a question Marianne can't answer. I've lost her again. She is glancing around in agitation, searching for something. She stands on shaking legs and begins turning in circles. It isn't something, it is someone. She must be looking for Patrick. I pull out my phone, calm myself down until I can press call.

'Ruth?' Eoin's voice anchors me for a moment. Then I'm on the verge of tears, the heaviness of the day suffocating me.

'Eoin, can you bring Patrick? I think Marianne needs him.'

Eoin says nothing, the line goes dead. I watch their distant figures move towards us, small dots that grow into the men we love.

They look like soldiers returning from war; they have battled something together. I wonder if Eoin has learnt what I have. Bedside me, Marianne is fretting. She doesn't settle until Patrick reaches over and pulls her into his arms, cradling her. Marianne sobs in slow wails.

Patrick is still someone Marianne remembers. She remembers his love. In sickness and in health has never seemed more poignant. I watch Patrick and Marianne fuse together, and then look away, giving them their time, their privacy.

Eventually they part. Patrick takes the bag of scrap paper from the bench where we left it. All of Marianne's memories, the torment, the scraps she cried over night after night. He takes Marianne by the hand and walks her to the end of the pier. He gives Marianne one of the handles and they stand together, leant over the railing, emptying the bag into the sea. The slips of paper flutter like snow and fall noiselessly into the swirling depths.

They keep the bag between them as it billows and fills with air, floating like a balloon. They stand still for a long time, the backdrop of Southport behind them. The rain falls heavy now and forms a curtain around them, shielding them from whatever will come next. It isn't over – it has really just begun.

But I know that they can face it, so long as they are together.

* * *

You can think you know what family means, what home is. That despite the chaos and darkness of the outside world, the four walls you call home are different. Mine had always been a source of chaos, something fractured beyond healing. Still, it was home, and it had always been entwined with my identity. Something I couldn't separate from myself, no matter how hard I tried. It was something I was beginning to accept. This fractured part of myself. It was what made me, me. I carried that wound gently, began to love it with the compassion I think it deserved. I believed that despite everything, family are those that we know inside out, like looking at the palm of our own hand. We can follow them, trace them, understand them. While there is no doubt that secrets linger, family is the unit that contains them.

Since coming back here, I even believed that Dad was changing, that part of him recognised where he had gone wrong, and that we could find a way back to one another.

These expectations were false. Perhaps it's family we know the least, and it is those closest to you who hide the darkest secrets. I had long ago accepted that my father was a mystery, that he was tortured and conflicted in ways I would never understand. He'd taken it out on my mother, and on me, and then on himself. It was a brutal reality, but one I could accept. But not this.

He is violent, yes, but a murderer? Has a part of me always known what he was capable of? I feel like I am teetering on the edge of a dark lake, my reflection staring back at me. If Peter Cavanagh is a murderer, then who or what am I?

I could laugh at the cruel irony of it all, the story I wanted to investigate, thinking my knowledge of the street would give me some special insight into Henry's disappearance, maybe even figure out what had happened to him. Instead, it has blinded me to what everyone who lived here knew – the secrets they've all kept for fifteen years. The secrets that concealed the hard truth. That my father, Peter Cavanagh, killed Henry Carr.

Why had no one talked in all that time? Did they know they were protecting him? Were they just trying to protect themselves? Maybe they thought they were protecting Marianne and Patrick? Or . . . maybe they were trying to protect *me*? Henry vanished when I was 10 years old, just after my mother's death. I had to live on the street with my father for eight more years, until I could finally escape.

If my father had been arrested and convicted, where would I have gone? I have no other relatives, no one who could have taken me in. I'd have been lost to the system. What little I had, gone. Was that a worse alternative to living with him? I don't know. I don't know anything. All I know is that this street raised me, they lifted me up on shop counters, ushered me into dry hallways, fed me hot pub lunches, squeezed pocket money into my palm; they all played some part in my survival. Now that I think of it, after Henry died, there was nearly always a resident around me. They all kept me safe in the only way they knew how – they kept me on the street, brought me up like their own.

I shake my head, overwhelmed. I've spent so long hating the street, blaming it for the secrets, the silence, the hiding. I was wrong. I thought the street was trying to protect the killer. Perhaps all this time, the street was protecting its own. Perhaps it was protecting not just Marianne, but *me*.

42

Ruth

THE SCREECH OF TYRES cuts through the air. I fling myself out of the passenger seat before the car has come to a complete stop. It is raining heavily, droplets like bullets stinging my face and hands. I can hear Eoin getting out of the car. I can feel the street watching. I help Marianne out of the car carefully and usher her into the house, shielding her from the weather. Since telling her story on the pier, Marianne looks exhausted, wrung out. I don't know what comes next, but I know that it has to be here. This story has to end on the street, where it all began.

Once in the house, I settle Marianne onto the sofa. Patrick stands white-faced in the doorway. After Marianne is seated, he takes my hand and squeezes it. An apology? I don't know if it will be enough. I feel betrayed by everyone. My tears are hot on my cheeks. I know for the first time in fifteen years he'll be the one to ring the police. I move to Eoin. I know what I have to do next, I can see him read it in my eyes. He looks pained. There's nothing he can do to stop me.

My boots make waves in the puddles as I march up the path of number five. I feel my phone vibrate in my pocket and I ignore it. Tom will have to wait. This is about more than him now, about more than an article. I falter at the door, the key cold and heavy in my palm. I'm unlocking something else, something more. Dad should still be at work now, so my fear is overtaken by anger.

After stepping inside, I stop to take in the shell of a house. I want to tear it down, brick by brick. I look around the house, where my mother died, where Henry died. It has always been haunted. Mail litters the hallway. Rubbish is heaped in the kitchen. The living room is filled with cracked and sagging furniture, old beer cans, and more rubbish.

I look at it all with disgust. Seeing it for what it really is. I hear Eoin come in behind me, his breath heavy. The rain drips from us to the floor, a mirror.

'Ruth, please, Patrick is about to ring the police.' His voice is pleading.

'No,' I say, firm. I have to do this.

Throughout my childhood, after Henry had vanished, I heard rumours. That his disappearance drove his already mental mother over the edge – crazy. That she screamed of death, a murderer among us and a body in the walls. I joined everyone else in the eye rolls, the grimaces, the jokes that she was a woman gone mad. That a woman grieving can't be believed.

I stand in front of the door to the cellar, the space under the stairs I have been in and out of a hundred thousand times. I used to come down here as a child when my father stumbled home drunk and angry. I'd hide in the dark, curled into a ball to make myself smaller until he passed out on the couch and I could go to bed. My hands are shaking.

'Here, let me.' Eoin opens the door and steps inside, flicking on the light illuminating the stairs and the basement below. It is filled with more than I remember from my childhood. Eoin moves cautiously down the stairs, and I follow. It smells dank. It always has; I thought all cellars smelt this way. The thought makes me shudder.

'There,' I say, pointing at the wall at the end of the space smothered by boxes, tools and more rubbish piled haphazardly in the small space.

I don't remember ever seeing the wall before. When had it been put up? What is it trying to hide? I swallow back a cry.

We move through the cellar, shifting boxes and bags out of the way until we reach it. It's a fragile structure, a boarded-up back wall that has been thrown together. It looks rushed, like it was put up in a hurry.

'Tear it down.' My voice sounds detached, alien.

Eoin looks at me like he's about to argue when I push past him. I tear at the thin plaster and board with my hands, trying to find any snag to pull on or break. I don't realise I am screaming until the echoes fall back on me, piercing screams as my nails bleed. I could collapse with exhaustion. More layers of secrets and lies. This must be how he kept Henry hidden. Eoin helps me rummage through Dad's toolboxes, finding a large hammer. He hands it to me, his expression tortured. I take the cold hammer into my hands. It is heavier than I expected and it takes all of my strength to swing it, but I do. Over and over until the lies come down.

43

Oscar

I PRACTICALLY FALL OUT of the car, the paperwork on the full fingerprint match from the fridge-freezer in my hands. It was a tough print to lift but they did it.

'Careful, Eleanor. Even if this isn't our guy, he was arrested for domestic violence about sixteen years ago.'

Eleanor nods and we run to the house, my fists pummelling the door.

Eventually the young man, Eoin Finch, opens the door. His face is haggard, exhausted. I can hear something coming from within the house – distant thudding and angry screams. I force myself past him and run inside. The cellar door hangs open; the thudding is coming from there. I run down the steps without a second thought.

When I see the scene in front of me, I have to bite down on my lip. Even after years in the force. Even then. I have to stop myself from shouting out.

44

Ruth

IT IS ONLY AFTER the entire police unit arrives that the scene begins to feel real. Men and women in hazmat suits rustle through the house, their words muffled.

We so very rarely had visitors in number five. Only really Henry. The cruelty of it makes me cry. I never even let Eoin come over. Now the house is crawling with people. Strangers. I can barely speak to make a statement, desperate to find my father, desperate to see him locked away. I try to control the shaking in my hands, the shaking in my legs, the shaking in every part of my body. Oscar leans forward, coffee on his breath as he whispers.

'I know this must be hard, but we really do need to know. Anything you can tell us to help us find your father.'

I look blankly back at him, thinking of all the crimes he must have dealt with, the sobbing loved ones. And I wonder how I should be feeling. They haven't removed Henry's body yet. Multiple black bin bags line the floor, duct tape around shapes I don't dare look at for too long. I have overheard the whispers, their theories. They say that Dad must have kept the fridge-freezer down here to store the body in at first. Maybe he stored it so that he could plant it elsewhere later on, to keep it from decomposing and smelling. On a street where everyone is always watching he must have struggled to move and dispose of it. Maybe he knew freezing it would buy him time, and if he ever did plant it, that it might confuse the police over when exactly he died. Maybe he thought it would give him enough time to have a solid alibi. They think that maybe when the wallet was found, he panicked, thinking someone was onto him and decided to finally get rid of the fridge-freezer Henry had been shoved into during his panicked cover up. Except, the men he ordered to collect it were delayed and, just maybe, in the meantime, Laura and Sam noticed Dad's erratic behaviour, with the sudden appearance of the fridge-freezer, maybe they even challenged him and found out more than they ever imagined. Too scared to call it in and share their discovery, too scared of whatever it is he has over them, they tried to frame him in whatever way they could. Did they plant the wallet? Deep down that's the theory that makes the most sense to me, though of course both are denying it wholeheartedly. There's still so many unanswered questions but it seems that sensing the impending betrayal, Dad must have put the murder weapon in the pub to point the finger at Sam. Except, these are all just theories. No one but Dad knows what really happened.

All I want to focus on is that Marianne's son is found at last. It is viciously cruel that, for fifteen years, he has lain across the street from them, hidden in someone else's home. In my home. I screamed when we found him, deep in the cavity of the false wall. All this time I had been chasing a killer, chasing Henry, and both had been in the house with me from the start. It is what Marianne had known all along, what she had thought of every day as she looked out of her bedroom window at number five.

I tell the detective everything with slow breaths, pauses in the middle of sentences, drinking glasses of water to quell my nausea. Already it feels unreal.

When the interview is over, I'm told to head down to the station to file a formal statement. It is hard to leave the house, to leave Henry alone again. The whole thing is undignified. My heart bleeds for him, a man I thought I had known. The house feels alien now, a foreign place that I inhabited once. I can never live here again, never set foot in the haunted space that has taken two lives.

I knew that the street had secrets, I just didn't know they were my own.

I pray that there are no more to be uncovered.

45

The Killer

PETER CAVANAGH'S LEGS ARE aching. He has been crouched low in the wasteland, watching the scurry of officers on the street, running in and out of his house, for what feels like hours. He grabs fistfuls of wild grass and yanks, grateful for something to take his seething anger out on. Finally, he crawls towards the summer house, something that can provide shelter from the rain until he gets his thoughts straight.

He saw the police vans, the flashing lights, outside his house before he took the full turning into the street. He had nearly crashed trying to swerve back round, his mind in overdrive.

How had any of it led back to him? Someone wants him locked up for what he did. Someone who knew. Since that day, he had tried to cover every angle to send the police knocking elsewhere. He knows no one had seen him plant the weapon. There was no CCTV, nothing. The fridge-freezer had been unfortunate. The scrap man had come late, and it was out there too long. Someone found it first. When news of the ridiculous podcast reached him, he was furious, furious that it was being dragged to the surface. He had made a mistake and paid for it ever since. He had hated himself every day, punished himself every day. Pushed his daughter away over it.

He wanted to get rid of the body once and for all, give Ruth a chance at a normal family life. He had intended to scatter it up and down the Bridgewater canal. It all would have been too decomposed by the time anyone found it to say who it was. But he hadn't managed to get that far. None of it – the framing, the planning – was enough. Ironic for it to be his own daughter to hunt for the answers, to be the only one to listen to a woman everyone had ignored. He is strangely proud of the woman he raised, though he knows he can't take any credit for who she has turned into. Not really. He was never a good enough father for her, never worthy of being in her life. He knows that. He has always known but it hasn't stopped him hoping. He wipes a stray tear with the back of his hand and swears. Showing emotion, even now, is difficult.

There is a lot he regrets as he sits there in the darkest corner mulling it all over. He had to take matters into his own hands the other day, after Marianne stumbled out in the road, practically pointing him out as the killer in the middle of the street. He had only wanted to scare her by breaking into the garden that night, trying to grab her from the house. He hadn't expected Ruth and the lad to be there, or to see Patrick moving so quickly.

He has to talk to Ruth, to explain. It wasn't for him, it was for *Ruth*. Even sending someone to the street to try and warn her off reporting on the case. Everything has always been to keep their family together. She wouldn't have understood back then; he's not even sure she'd understand today, but he needed to keep her now she was back; she is all that he has left. Everything he has done has been for Ruth, to protect her. He's never been a good man, a gentle man, but he loves her. She has to understand. Everything he's done, he's done for love.

He lays low until the sky grows dark and the first scatterings of frost begin to grow on the grass. He slips out of the summer house and clambers through the undergrowth, cutting across to the canal bank. The barges are tethered and bobbing haphazardly in the rain. He stops to catch his breath, looking down at the cuts and grazes on his hands. They want to strip him down, make him out to be a monster. He won't let them. He hadn't meant to kill him that day, but Henry was stronger than he thought. When the argument escalated it was Henry on top of him, Henry's hands around his neck in resistance. The wrench was just the first thing his hand found; this wasn't some premeditated slaying. He'd been drinking, he'd just found out about the affair, he wasn't thinking straight.

Peter's eyes flash with anger. First Henry had stolen Laura from him. Laura was *his* first, Henry was his friend. Who does that to a friend? He had been happy enough when they hadn't worked out, though he had moved on himself by then.

Katie was everything he needed, everything he wanted. She could set him straight. She could fix him, and they'd be a family. At least for a while. When the cancer came, the cracks started to really show. To lose Katie to cancer was one thing, but it was at her funeral he had learnt the truth. He lost her all over again.

Robert had been the one to tell him, the only one of all his so-called friends who had the guts to be honest with him. It didn't matter that Robert had his own motives, that he was blackmailing Henry for his own gain. What mattered was the truth.

Learning of Katie's betrayal didn't just take Katie from him all over again. It took the last member of his family from him; it snatched his daughter right out of his hands.

He isn't Ruth's biological father.

Henry was.

46

Patrick

MARIANNE STARTS SOBBING BEFORE the detective asks the first question.

She is worn down to the bone. There are things she simply can't remember: if Peter had made her help hide the body, how she had escaped, what happened next. It is all pushed together in her mind, jumbled up and impossible for her to separate. Eoin has been brewing tea all evening, and Ruth sits beside Marianne to calm her, though nothing can any more. I slip away when no one is looking. I have become invisible in the chaos and I use this to my advantage. I snatch my cap and coat, a flashlight from the drawer. The rain has started to pelt down, grey bullets that disintegrate as they hit the ground. It makes everything harder; I can barely see, barely walk. I am scared of falling. What use will I be to anyone then? There is still a flurry of officers in and around number five. They eye me cautiously, their hats tipped low. I find my way to the wasteland before anyone can stop me. It looks haunted in the dark, branches like clawed hands and shapes that look like gaping mouths. Is he out there? It's hard to tell. I feel like I've been running from him, hiding from him, for fifteen years. Every time we glanced at each other in the street, each time I saw him in the shop. It was like a punch to the gut. Now I'm the one hunting him. He's got away with it for long enough. He has taken the only two people I had. The loves of my life. I'll never get them back. But I can try and get some sliver of justice. I shine the torch into the vast black, barely making a dint in its bulk. I walk slowly, shaking against the rain. It's almost an hour until I hear something. A snapped branch. Heavy breath. I freeze. I turn the torchlight to the noise.

'Patrick, you can't be out here,' Eoin says gently. He steps forward. 'Not alone, not with Peter still around. They found his van abandoned by the Beehive a little while ago.'

'Who do you think I'm looking for?' I shout, tears building.

There's a police helicopter overhead, the cutting sound of its engine making us sink a little lower, our hands over our ears. Its blinding spotlight flashes over us briefly, then moves on.

'He's out here somewhere, lad, I can sense him,' I yell against the noise.

'Patrick, leave it to the police. They'll find Peter. I'm sure of it. You're going to get yourself killed out here; you can barely walk.'

I lean on my stick, feel myself crumple.

'This is all my fault,' I say, the sound of the rain drowning me out. 'Can't you see? Marianne tried to tell me, tried to tell everyone, and I was too weak to see it as the truth. I just couldn't believe her. The blood on her hands that day, I was sure it was her own. She had banged her head somehow, fallen. It was bleeding as she walked up the garden path. I just washed it all away, I was cruel, I was awful. If he's out there now, it's because of me. I'm not having him going after Marianne again. What about Ruth? I'm going to finish this.'

'Then I'm coming with you,' Eoin says.

The sound of the helicopter fades away, leaving only the stirring of the undergrowth against the wind. We carry on, searching and finding nothing. I almost give up, almost throw myself to the ground when I hear it. The snap of twigs up ahead, under the arch of the bridge that stretches across the canal. A fox screams in the distance and Eoin moves ahead, shielding me from whatever is in the dark. We approach the noise slowly, our feet catching in the long grass. The torch sweeps in front of us, a small circle of light. The grass is too long, the night too dark for us to make anything out. We seem to both hold our breath as we wait. There's a muffled cough. A rustle. I'm not sure if I want it to be Peter or not. Eoin slips ahead through the gap in the vegetation. I can hear the branches snagging on his clothing, clawing at his skin. He battles his way through with his elbows, making a space for himself in a hollowed-out place between two thickets. He pauses. I walk further ahead and try to see what he is looking at.

Peter Cavanagh stands at the edge of the water. Eoin holds a hand up to me as if to try and stop me, but once I have started nothing can slow me down. I push forward, stick-first, and face Peter Cavanagh with square shoulders and a pounding heart. Peter spins, his face cast in shadow by the bridge. I am wheezing. Something makes a soft splash in the water. The emptiness of the tunnel causes everything to echo. Everything is amplified, even our fear.

'Patrick.' Peter nods, his voice cracks. It is clear he has been crying.

He doesn't sound surprised to see us, though his fingers twitch with nervous energy.

'You son of a bitch,' I spit.

We glare at each other like two men prepared for battle. As though we are standing before a great abyss. I wonder if we will both return.

Eoin pushes his way through and joins me, facing Peter in the darkness. 'Peter, the police are looking for you,' he says quietly. 'You've run long enough, it's time to hand yourself in.'

I have never seen Eoin so enraged, so quietly full of hatred. I can see that he loves that girl; I remember them even years before, inseparable. He's seen what Peter did to her, is still doing. Stealing Ruth's happiness, her home. Eoin is one of those rare people who loves in both the noise and the silence. Now here he is, doing what he couldn't do for her all those years ago. Peter stands like a man waiting to be hanged. And then his eyes flick towards something behind us, fear filling his face.

The figure is shadowed against the black silk of the water. She walks forward, step by step, until she is a stone's throw away.

'Is it true?' She is shouting, her eyes black.

Peter stands still. He could bolt, but he looks as though he is struggling with himself. Something inside him must want to stay – even now. He loves her, that much is plain to see, but too much has gone wrong. She is the last piece of goodness in him, the thing he must have hung onto so desperately for so many years.

'Ruth.' His voice cracks, his hair dripping with rain. 'Whatever they've said, whatever lies they've told. You're mine, you're still my daughter in every way that matters. He wanted to take you away from me, you have to understand. I couldn't let that happen.'

She frowns, caught off guard by what he says.

'What do you mean –' She stops, the colour draining from her cheeks. 'If you're not my Dad then who is?'

The silence extends between them, heavy.

Peter's mouth opens and closes silently, his chest rising and falling in great swoops as he looks erratically between Ruth and Peter. Something unspoken is confirmed for her then and her eyes are alight.

'Is Henry Carr my father?'

Eoin spins to face me.

The words don't land at first. They float like mist. I can't quite make out the meaning. I stare, dumbfounded, the cogs in my brain whirring. My Henry? Ruth's father? Then I see.

The last pieces of the puzzle fall into place. The sonogram I had found, the one that caused us to argue that fateful day. Henry hadn't *just* got someone pregnant. He wasn't waiting to be a father. He already was one.

He'd kept the scan all that time because it was precious to him.

He'd been a father for years.

Ten years.

My hand flies to my mouth, keeps everything in that threatens to spill out.

'It's loyalty that matters, it's love,' Peter shouts back.

He sounds different to how I remember. Like something in him has frayed and snapped.

'I may not have been the best husband and I certainly haven't been the best father, but I loved her. I love you. *I'm* your father. I raised you. Not *him*.' He spits the last word.

This isn't a man who fell out with an old friend, this is a man who was betrayed, still feels betrayed. I don't feel any sympathy; it doesn't justify what he did. Nothing does.

'Is that what you call it? *Raising me*? You practically dragged me up! I don't know where I'd be if it hadn't have been for the people on this street.'

Ruth stands stock-still now. The truth is still swirling around her. 'So it wasn't about the substation? Is that true too? Did you start a fire? Did you almost kill someone else?' she shouts.

He frowns at this, thrown off guard. 'Who told you that?'

She doesn't respond.

'We all kept our promise that day. We were kids, stupid kids. Martin was messing around with a cigarette. It was an accident but we all stood by. We were all as guilty. We tried to help the man. Robert dragged him away from the worst of it but he was badly injured. We agreed to never utter a word about it. We were ashamed of what happened, but it was an accident. We vowed to protect Martin, to protect one another. We all kept that vow until the end. I promise you, Ruth. That's the truth.' He looks emotional now, his eyes glazed over with tears.

She shakes her head. 'When did you find out about the affair?' She keeps her tone measured, sad.

'I never knew,' he says, tormented. 'He was my friend. He came over all the time. I invited him into my home. Our home.

I had no idea. Stupid me. Stupid, stupid me. Too blinded by love to see. And then Robert told me. At her *funeral*. They'd all known. They'd all been laughing behind my back the whole time. I guess that was his way of getting back at me for roping him into the accident all those years ago.'

There is venom in his voice, but it doesn't mask all of the sadness. He looks broken. The alcohol, the hate, the violence – it has consumed him.

'But when he died, no one talked. So I had to try and hold onto you. We only had each other. Those who knew kept their mouths shut to protect you. They knew it was better for you to stay here, to be raised on this street. He couldn't take you away from me. No one could.'

'Then the case started making the news again, and people started calling, stopping me in the street, asking me if I knew what happened to Henry Carr. The wallet also turned up in the wasteland. I can have a guess at which bastard betrayed me there.' He sneers. 'That got the police involved. I knew he had a picture of you in it that your mother had given him. He showed me that before he died. His wallet must have fallen out of his pocket when we were arguing on the street. I prayed that it was gone. That no one ever found it. Someone wanted the case reopened. Wanted me nailed for it. Suddenly it was being spoken about again. And then you came home. That was all I wanted, Ruth. I just wanted to keep you safe, with me forever. He took my Katie but he couldn't take you.'

He laughs at himself. I have to force myself to not lunge for him, to not grab him by the neck. Peter stands with his hands curled into fists. His eyes dart to me, something silver in his hands.

'I'm sorry, Patrick,' he says, his voice slithering, dangerous. 'I warned Marianne. I warned your son. I tried to be a good man, I promise you I did.'

I say nothing. I look back to Ruth.

There are a million things I want to say. Despite the moment, I smile. I actually smile. All this time I thought I had lost my family, and now I know I haven't.

I only see a glimpse of Eoin as he lunges forward.

The suddenness of it catches Peter off guard.

He tries to sidestep, tries to be quick, but he loses his balance. His arms are windmilling, trying to hold onto something that isn't there. There's nothing left. His eyes are haunted as he falls – it all happens in slow motion.

His head hits the rock with a crack.

It echoes beneath the bridge. As we stand in silence.

The blood seeps out and blends into the rainwater running through the grass. His eyes lose focus, stare at all and none of us. Reaching out to Ruth one final time, he rolls into the canal.

The man who made Henry Carr disappear, vanishing himself.

SIX MONTHS LATER

Epilogue
Ruth

WINTER HAS MELTED INTO the first signs of spring. The dead is coming back to life, colour sprouting from places of darkness. It is as though the world is waking, stirring from a bad dream. It stretches out its arms and yawns, a golden sun for a mouth.

The street stands gathered together around the perimeter of the wasteland, their arms linked, their eyes forward. It makes sense for it to end where it had all begun, together on the outskirts of the street. There is a warm breeze blowing between us, and the thickets curve in a dance. It seems fitting that nature should reclaim him, after everything he has been through. Ashes to ashes, I think, as I search for Eoin's hand and find it. He squeezes it gently like a pulse, keeping me going, keeping me alive.

I scan the crowd and find Oscar. We smile at each other, just enough.

I think he's glad to rid himself of Crow Street. I understand that.

It is easy to see the flaws in it, the darkness, the secrets. Yet just underneath, squinting out between the cracks, is the truth. This isn't a community of poverty or wickedness, but one with a firm sense of family and belonging that transcends all else. It is a street that has been harmed by the outside world, forced inwards, and in turn they had held onto each other. It seems ironic now but I finally feel like this is the place I have always belonged. Peter Cavanagh had tainted that, hidden it, but he hadn't counted on one thing – the sense of family in this street pervading all else.

I feel desperately happy knowing that Mum had found a sense of love and safety in Henry, even if it was short-lived. There is a sadness gnawing deep inside me at never having known him properly, at never looking into her eyes and acknowledging exactly who he was. He died for me, for both of us, in his desperation to give us a proper life together.

I continue scanning the circle and notice Mrs Montgomery hovering at the periphery, as she always is. Standing just in the shadows, watching. Perhaps she is the greatest mystery of all. I scan the circle and grin: at Mr Chandra; at Martin, who has ventured out for the first time in so long; at Laura beside them; at Sam. Always at Sam. My heart aches for how he suffered. For what many thought he had done. For what he did for me. Keeping that money safe, just as he promised Henry he would. He sat down with me once the police let him go and explained everything. He wanted to hand the money over at the right time, when I returned home and settled my demons. When I knew who I really was and what the money meant. I'm still working out what to do with it, but using it to find somewhere that feels just as much home as the street does seem like a good place to start. The plaque is unveiled by Patrick and the circle erupts into a respectful applause. The respect for Patrick and Marianne generates this kind of response, it is a kind of communal closure to the grief they have all watched them suffer. It seems only fitting to put it in the wasteland. I was sure to write about it in my final story for the paper. I hit my deadline, and the story I had written about Henry in the *Chronicle* was a success. The issue sold record-breaking copies and was our most viewed online story ever written. I had the inside scoop. *I was the inside scoop*.

Even that is an understatement. It doesn't feel like a betrayal to tell the story, I am not a Cavanagh any more. My article has led to some pretty serious job offers: London is calling. Though I haven't answered, not just yet. I look at Patrick and see family, and it puts a lump in my throat I find hard to remove. He has wanted to spend every day with me since, as though if he misses one more day of my life, he won't be able to forgive himself. I am the last piece of Henry he and Marianne have, and I know he doesn't want to lose that.

Marianne isn't in the wasteland to see it all. Since that day on the pier, her health has declined. The doctors have admitted she doesn't have long left. And so I am sticking around to be here while I can. Patrick is going to need us, Eoin and me. Eoin has become something of a son to them.

Patrick even has a picture of the four of us framed in his hallway, back at the pier Marianne is so fond of. The four of us stood smiling, Patrick and Marianne, Eoin and me. I had smiled through tears when he'd shown it to me for the first time, my mismatched family. I'm still not sure where home is at the end of all this, and for now it doesn't matter. My home is in people, and I have finally found mine.

I look across at Laura, who looks about as broken as a person can be. Her knuckles are white from gripping Eoin. There're still some mysteries the street has kept. Still secrets that live behind its doors. The police never did find out who planted the wallet. Though my guess remains firmly with Sam and Laura, a form of redemption for whatever happened in the past. What Peter had over Laura, Sam and Martin isn't for me to judge. We have all done things we would rather forget, it's just we're often lucky enough that the consequences aren't quite as serious. It's time to give them all some peace. This street suits a mystery, and the identity of the person who planted the wallet is one I am happy will remain unsolved.

As the sun filters through the crowd and kisses our skin, I look up at Eoin. He has made it clear he wants to be with me, that for him it was only ever me. I think too much has happened between us to carry on as before, too much trauma, too many memories in each touch. It is enough to be friends in love, to be careful, and gentle and kind. I tell myself maybe. There is always maybe for us.

We are opening up a new chapter in our lives, all of us. Our stories will carry on, separately and together. That is the one thing Peter Cavanagh hasn't been able to take from me, from the street, from any of us: stories. The story of Henry Carr's disappearance was told and retold until finally we came together and discovered the truth.

I thought I had lost everything, but I was wrong. I have gained family, and for the first time in my life I know what true happiness feels like.

After the ceremony is over, and the street begins to drift away, Eoin takes my face in his hands, curving his palms around the horizon of my cheeks. I melt into the warmth of them, the home of them, and know: we still have a story left to write.

Mrs. Montgomery

I STAND AND WATCH the circle grow closer, shoulder to shoulder.

Something in the air has shifted, as though we all stand on new ground now.

This is no longer the same street we have inhabited for the past fifteen years, exposing the truth has made the land feel different somehow.

I catch eyes with the reporter, Ruth, her dark hair like tendrils as the breeze blows.

She tilts her head. There is a question in her expression, something niggling.

I suppress a smile at that. That she hasn't quite found all of the answers like she had hoped. Sometimes you don't find them in what people say, but in the things left unsaid.

I crane my neck to see a plane cross overheard, its jet stream like an arrow.

I wonder if my Robert is on it, off to a place that no one can ever find him. I hope so.

It makes my heart a little lighter, eases the sense of guilt that has gnawed at me.

It hasn't been easy, planting things at just the right time, calling the police incident room in just the right way.

I am both everywhere and nowhere, invisible to others and yet they are all so visible to me. There is nothing I do not see. I am a watcher. Easy to be discounted when you are both old and a woman, such a wicked combination. Yet, I must admit, it has worked to my advantage.

I didn't just hear the argument that day, I saw it.

I saw Henry drop the wallet, I saw Peter half drag him into the house. I scurried out, collected the wallet as insurance. Don't misunderstand me, I wasn't to know what was about to happen. Though when Henry was reported missing, when he never came home, I knew. I knew from then on what must have happened to him.

Peter was always the worst of them but Henry was no angel either. Both of them, plus Laura and Sam too, led my Robert astray. That substation fire, that mess they dragged him in to. That poor man that was injured. The guilt Robert felt and what he became. He was never the same boy after that, he never smiled the same, could never quite feel happy. He was always looking for another risk, something that might help him to feel alive. His life spiralled after that, you see. The only way was down. He could have been anything he wanted, would have been anything he wanted, had he not met them. My poor Neil, he was too loyal for his own good and was dragged into Robert's world. I blame them for that too.

Waiting was the hardest bit, choosing the right time for revenge takes a lot of strength. I had to be sure Robert had enough money saved up to finally help his brother's recovery and also the means to get out of the country, just in case when Peter was caught he sang like a canary about the substation. About the drugs, the crime. I shudder to think where Robert would be now.

With the anniversary looming and Robert's business ventures blossoming, I knew now was the time. Taking the wallet from underneath the stone in the yard, I crept out into the wasteland and dropped it, delayed the collection of that fridge-freezer, and called tips in whenever I could.

I'm not proud, don't mistake me. I don't agree with the life Robert has fallen into, but I cannot blame him. The blame falls on me, for not doing more. The blame falls on those so-called 'friends', that led him straight into a moment that altered the course of his life.

There is part of me that feels some sympathy for the other victims in this, that poor girl thinking that man was her father. We can't always choose our family, but I'm glad hers wasn't him.

I turn my back on them, the people of the street, the community that thinks we are all known to each other. It couldn't be further from the truth.

Peter is just the first to fall.

The things I know, the secrets this place still harbours.

One by one, I will bring them to light.

It might take a street to keep a secret but it takes just one woman to set it free.

ACKNOWLEDGEMENTS

The inspiration for this book came from an interaction I had back in 2019. After moving to a new street, I bumped into two elderly women in the alleyway behind the houses. Their whisperings and outrageous stories of that street lit a match and *The Secret at No.4* was born.

Writing has always been one of my greatest passions. In particular, sharing the voices and experiences of communities that are not often heard. *The Secret at No.4* places a lens on a small portion of the working class North, the elderly, the vulnerable. In the end, the story comes down to the power of listening. The Marianne's of the world certainly deserve our compassionate attention.

I feel very lucky to be able to share this story and have the support of so many amazing individuals.

Firstly, thank you to you- the reader for picking this book up and giving it a chance. Thank you to Ki Agency and in particular, my amazing agent Anne Perry who loved the street of characters in this book almost as much as I do. Her passion and commitment to the story made all the difference.

Thank you to my wonderful editor, Meg Jones at HarperNorth for her attention to detail, her enthusiasm and most of all her unwavering patience. Thank you, Meg, for loving this story in the way you have and believing in it from the very beginning. Thank you to the whole team at HarperNorth for their support and time. I'm so grateful it was you that championed this with me.

This story reflects the age old saying, 'it takes a village to raise a child.' This book is for the village that raised me. The teachers and mentors that took me under their wing changed my life. In particular, thank you to the strong, independent women who inspired me and continue to inspire me. You know who you are. You helped me to get here, I can't thank you enough for that.

Thank you to all of my family, particularly Mum, Dad and Siobhan for their love, wicked sense of humour, and their unwavering belief in me. Particularly to Mum, who provided me with endless books that inspired my love of stories. Making you all proud is always my best motivation.

Thank you to all of the early readers of this story. Your patience and kind words meant the world.

Thank you to my wonderful colleagues and friends for their support and listening ears, in particular to Charlotte whose passion and limitless energy for this book kept me going when things got tough.

To Nell, for always brightening my days. Even when that meant wagging your tail at me as I worked.

Lastly, thank you to Alex for being my rock. All of those difficult moments were made easier with you by my side. Your support and boundless love are the reason I have been able to do this. I am so grateful to call you my partner.

Harper North

would like to thank the following staff and contributors for their involvement in making this book a reality:

Fionnuala Barrett

Samuel Birkett

Peter Borcsok

Ciara Briggs

Sarah Burke

Alan Cracknell

Jonathan De Peyer

Anna Derkacz

Morgan Dun-Campbell

Tom Dunstan

Kate Elton

Sarah Emsley

Dom Forbes

Simon Gerratt

Monica Green

Natassa Hadjinicolaou

Megan Jones

Jean-Marie Kelly

Taslima Khatun

Sammy Luton

Rachel Mccarron

Molly Mcnevin

Alice Murphy-Pyle

Adam Murray

Genevieve Pegg

Agnes Rigou

Florence Shepherd

Eleanor Slater

Angela Snowden

Emma Sullivan

Katrina Troy

Daisy Watt

For more unmissable reads,
sign up to the HarperNorth newsletter at
www.harpernorth.co.uk

or find us on Twitter at
@HarperNorthUK

Harper
North